THE MARRIAGE BUNDLE

First Book of The Sacred Bundle Series

By:

Earlene Gleisner, RN/Reiki Master

www.standinginbalance.com

Magic Valley Publishers
Long Beach, CA 90815

White Feather Press
Laytonville, CA 95454

THE MARRIAGE BUNDLE
First Edition
By: Earlene Gleisner, RN/Reiki Master

Published by:  **Magic Valley Publishers**

6390 E Willow St, Long Beach, CA 90815

in conjunction with

White Feather Press
POB 667, Laytonville, CA 95454

The characters, events, and locations in this book are fictitious. Any similarity to real persons, living or dead, is coincidental and not intended by the author.

Copyright c 2010 by Earlene F. Gleisner
ISBN: 978-0-9845275-1-9
First Edition   First Printing – January, 2011
Printed in the United States of America

Publishers Cataloging in Publication Data
Gleisner, Earlene

The Marriage Bundle: a novel / Earlene Gleisner. - 1st ed.

To Yuwach:

the man

who walked beside me

for 32 years

and shared his life

with me.

Acknowledgments:

I always wondered about the names an author lists on this page. Now I know the value of being able to have a format to thank those stalwart first readers who gave comment, corrected typos, suggested changes, and wrote smurky faces on post-its when they really liked a phrase or a scene. My first group consisted of my husband, Yuwach, Sharon Parker, Melanie Sinclair, Jane Buckley, and Anne Botnick (who read the work twice). Hannah Kusterer, Krissa Kyle, Deb Fry, Robert Waters, and Paula Mulligan were the second group. Margaret Fetty did editing duty and Maria Hall and JaneAnne Narrin offered first reviews. All suggestions and comments were more than valuable; they were downright inspired.

It was hard for me to hear my first agent, Nancy Ellis, tell me this book needed deep editing, but she was right. Thanks for your guidance. My second agent, Victoria Lea, gave me validation by taking up my project, and though unable to place the manuscript with a publisher, her enthusiasm kept me going.

I had no idea how obsessed I would become with telling this story. Nor did I know there would be additional books on the horizon to complete the tale. My husband, Yuwach, was been a worthy supporter through all this, as well as the person I relied on everyday to keep my feet on the ground and my body on schedule with such things as eating and sleeping.

L. R. deserves more than applause; she deserves a crown of gold for providing me with the wherewithal to finally publish this first book of a long-held dream. A grand thank you for Susan Amari Gold's skill at developing a website (www.standinginbalance.com) to bring me all together in one place, a daunting task. See her other passion at www.essential-wisdom.com

Last, but not least, I thank you, the reader, for joining me on the beginning of this journey to find your point of balance in all our relationships.

The Marriage Bundle
A story of relationships across time

By Earlene Gleisner,RN/Reiki Master

Contents

Chapter I – April, 2004
The End of the Beginning

Hands, not my own, shimmer in the air before me and are outlined in thin, flashing, neon lights, clamoring for attention. 'Ghost hands,' I think, watching vaporous fingers as they thicken and thin, like ground fog slithering across an early morning meadow.

I struggle to focus on my driving and the highway ahead through the hologram of fingers, their chipped nails and swollen knuckles embedded with dirt, but am forced to watch while both thumbs twist spindly brown grasses against forefingers. My heartbeat quickens, scattering across my chest. 'Be calm,' I tell myself. 'It's just another vision.' But, quieting my nerves is always hard, when, for a moment or two, my mind straddles two worlds.

My anxiety heightens as I attempt to shift my fingers on the leather-covered steering wheel. The message I send for my right hand to lift is blocked.

Warm buzzing builds at the back of my neck as I watch grasses twined into rope and formed into a loop. Tension vibrates my ears and lower jaw then rises to the top of my head. I can no longer see the highway. My hands disappear. I am left only with the vision of time-worn hands fashioning a rabbit snare.

"Sellie, SLOW DOWN!" Flyn shouted.

I gasped. Ghost hands shimmered gone as red lights flashed in front of our car. I pulled the wheel to the right, narrowly missing a Black Ford SUV turning left onto a gravel road. The brakes jerked us forward in our seats. We stalled and perched on a slim shoulder of California Highway 101

North. As I blew out a breath, my heart raced on without me.
Tears formed.

"Where were you?"

"I . . . don't . . . know," I said.

I could feel the spring sun filling our Chevy Tracker,
but all I saw was a glowing beam in darkening shadows. I tried
to clear this tunnel vision, but it was as if I wore transitional
lenses which darken in daylight and lighten indoors, only it
wasn't getting lighter, except through a pin prick in the center
of the lens. Screaming tones whined outside my ears. I
blinked and jumped when the passenger door slammed.

Flyn strode around the front of the car to pull at the
driver's door, his angular face blank. A jerk of his chin told
me I was being replaced; he didn't need to holler. Whenever a
tension or a crisis arose, Flyn could charge the air with silent
commands, taking control without words. He became a
warrior, his every movement purposeful. There was no use
arguing.

I lurched from the driver's seat and stepped in front of
the hood, struggling with feelings of guilt, unease, and dread.
Guilt because, until recently, I'd been in control of these
moments when I tranced into an altered state of consciousness.
My unease swelled because I wanted to control them, but
couldn't. Dread warned me that something was developing.
These visions were demanding my attention, and, as yet, I
hadn't deciphered why.

Crawling into the passenger seat, I reviewed my inner
hallway and checked all its doors. Carefully examining the
special locks I'd imagined into place on each entry, I made sure
I was protected from intrusion by spirits from the other side; I
kept tight control on their entry into my life. Only if I wanted
to confer with them in psychic space about the meaning of
energy fields I saw around individuals who came to me for
help, would they be allowed entry. *Why am I having trouble
funneling these spontaneous visions into a regular schedule?* I

wondered.

A quick breath and my imagination grounded me, as I traveled with my mind's eye through my body and my feet, then through the floor of the Tracker. I propelled my inside eyes past the crust of our planet beneath us, through layers of rocks, silt, granite and all strata that comprise our Earth, until I came to Her center. After I slowly released my breath, I sucked in another one to keep my channel opened wide. Dancing light streamed back to me from Her source which filled me, starting at my feet, then up through my legs, pelvis, abdomen, chest, and throat, until the light streamed out of the top of my head. My senses stilled as I became a beacon, shining into the Universe.

I didn't want to open my eyes. I breathed softly, listening. I heard the motor purring under Flyn's steady acceleration and sensed the road under our car. Traffic was lessening as we traveled into the hills of Northern California, so I released a sigh and tried to relax while Flyn drove the familiar curves past Cloverdale then Hopland. I steadied myself and opened my eyes.

The scenery was awesome, after months of rain and snow. Blooms sprouted pure white and pink on pear and apple trees. Fine yellow pine pollen floated on soft air. Bright green grasses overlaid every inch of Mother Earth, growing like baby's hair after a sweaty nap in the sun. Oaks sported red-tipped leaves while dogwoods sprayed petals over the road.

Now that I'd time to detach from my near-accident, I realized I owed Flyn some kind of explanation. "It had to be because the air got so warm in the car," I said, "and the sunlight flashed in my eyes when we drove past that long stand of poplars."

"What had to be?" Flyn asked as he shifted gears.

"The reason the veil split," I whispered, watching for his reaction. If there had been any way to disappear right then, to trans-locate to another universe, I would've pushed the 'bye-

bye' button. Flyn was still so new to me after two years of being together. I'd hoped to keep my secrets a little longer.

At first I thought he hadn't heard me, then he turned and pinned his deep brown eyes onto my hazel ones, trying to see beyond my words. Flyn's eyes softened as they scanned my face and body. "You're pale and shivering."

I nodded. Spatters of light blurred my sight as I tried to fight a chill starting at the base of my spine. "I saw hands that weren't my own," I said, closing my eyes.

"What were the hands doing?" Flyn asked softly.

"Making a rabbit snare," I answered, wondering how I could know that as a fact, then knowing there was another, more important question. "I'm wondering what it means; this was so different from my usual visions."

He nodded. "Well," dividing his attention between the highway and reaching to finger short strands of hair at my neck, "Can't help much . . . don't know about your visions or . . . even what's usual or . . . unusual." He traced the outline of my ear with his thumb as he watched the road and quietly said, "Wish you'd tell me."

I hung my head, hesitating to share this part of my life with him. *'We haven't been together long enough,'* I'd been telling myself, but I had to admit: I'd never told David for the same reason, and he and I were married twenty-five years before he died. If I hadn't thought I could trust David in all that time, how was I ever going to trust Flyn to understand? I was afraid I couldn't. That's why I'd used silences to sidestep his questions or redirected conversations to keep him, as well as everyone else in my life, off track. But my tactics weren't working with him. And to make matters worse, the doors and locks I'd erected to protect me from spirit intrusion were opening from the other side. I wasn't in control anymore.

He sighed and said with finality, "Well, whatever's going on, these things you're calling visions are happening more often." His hand stayed warm on my neck. My anxiety eased. I rested my eyes on Flyn with his gray-streaked, raven hair, bristly eyebrows, and a nose that showed, with two distinctive knobs, that it had been broken twice. Years of working construction in the sun had weathered his face. Squint lines and laugh lines collected around his eyes. A single, deep crevice between his brows took center stage when he concentrated or was troubled.

He continued to drive with one hand resting on the steering wheel, instead of gripping it white-knuckled like we did when we drove in city traffic. He whistled a mindless tune between calling out names of birds he recognized in the air. "Hawk" he shouted when he saw one sitting atop a telephone post. "Vulture," he said pointing to four of them swooping across fields in search of left-overs. "Slow down! Life's too short to race through it," he yelled after passing cars rushing ahead of us.

This four hour trip to the hill house with Flyn had eased the pain of my visiting the two-story, log cabin my second husband had lovingly built. After David died in '95, I'd tried living in these mountains alone. The twenty miles from Willits, where my friends lived, might as well have been a trillion miles to the left of the Big Dipper. All but a few of those women with whom I'd worked and socialized had remained close, while the rest became distant memories during David's terminal illness. With soggy brain from being housebound during the last years of his life, the isolation of widowhood nearly killed me. Two solitary and rainy winters at the end of a dirt road was enough. After Sam, my son, married Angela in the May garden of 1997, I left. His sister, Shawna, had married Michael under the same rose trellis six years earlier. I had done my motherly duty, seen them into their new lives with equal fanfare; I was free to be me.

By July, I'd packed the house, moth-balled the closets, and high-tailed myself to the bright lights of Oakland. Now I had a massage therapy practice there and in San Francisco, as well as a flourishing psychic phone counseling service. And, I had Flyn, who was sharing my covers, so to speak, since he'd moved in with me over a year ago. Life was just fine.

Living as one half of a 'couple' again had been a challenge for me. I'd lived as a wife, twice, and had survived both an early divorce and seven years of widowhood. I'd been hard to convince that I needed another man in my life. Until Flyn. I smiled. Flyn had curled my toes the first time he'd crossed my path. A Monday, I think it was.

We'd bumped into each other in the entry way of the San Francisco office building where I shared space with two others, Haley, a counselor, and Roxanne, another massage therapist. I was hurrying to meet a client, and he was late to the studio where he taught Yoga. I was told this fact later, after having badgered everyone in the building with questions about his identity.

Haley was the last one I'd pumped for details about the dark, handsome man in gray sweats. She'd snickered, "He's the guy who just called to find out who the good-looking woman was with the spiked hair in the white cotton, harem outfit."

"You're kidding! He noticed me?" I squealed like a teenager, fighting for control over fluttering butterflies in my stomach. During the next 30 days, we bumped into each other so many times, we both admitted it must be fate, because neither of us had tried to be in the same place at the same time. The attraction had intensified with every chance meeting, to the point where I could tell an hour or so before our paths were going to cross. Flyn admitted he'd had his own premonitions about me. His first trip to my studio apartment had been highlighted by the deep wrinkle of his forehead.

"Are you alright?" I'd asked him.

He had nodded as he scanned the room

Hairs stood at attention on my arms. "You're looking as if you can't believe what you see."

"I can't," he said, as he removed his leather jacket. He shook his head. "I thought . . . "

I waited. I shifted from my toes to my heels, and then I couldn't stand the suspense, especially in my own home, wondering if I'd done the wrong thing inviting him to my house for supper. "You thought what?"

"Sorry," he said, running his left hand through his thick black hair. He shrugged. "I thought I'd just been imagining things . . . I never . . . believed . . . I was actually 'seeing' you."

"What?" My hand raised to my chest in protection.

His hand reached for my arm but something stopped him. He shoved his fists deep into his jean pockets. "I've seen your place before . . . many times . . . almost every time I've thought of you and wondered what you were doing."

"That's not . . . possible."

He shrugged again. "It's true." His eyes rested on my face. "I don't know what kind of connection we have. It's pretty . . . strange . . . but . . . there's something here I can't explain."

When he reached for me this time, he stroked my arm with his fingertips. "I've seen you sitting on that circular, braided rug, reading a book or cooking food in a room that looks like a bathroom." He turned his head and nodded in the direction of where I did exactly that.

Moving closer to me, he said, "I've watched you at the table when you talk on the phone or toss and turn as you lay in your bed in the middle of the night or . . ."

"Or what?"

His breath on my cheek made my skin erupt in chills.

". . . brush your teeth."

I snorted.

He grinned then laid his cheek against my temple.

"Anything else?" My breathing was definitely becoming constricted. I could barely choke out the words.

"Never saw you naked," he whispered.

"Good," I rasped, self-conscious about the direction gravity was taking my stomach and breasts. I'd vowed that if a man was to join me for an intimate evening, he'd do it in pitch darkness. I wasn't comfortable with Flyn having a peep show without my staging it.

Besides, I was supposed to be the psychic here, and I hadn't been privy to a preview of him. I'd only been flooded with emotional charges and a heightened awareness of his presence anywhere within 10 miles of my body.

What he was doing to my skin and innards now by standing so close was past bearable. I decided I had no idea how I was going to swallow dinner, let alone complete the finishing touches on the pot roast in the crock pot.

"Turn it off," he suggested, leaving me wondering how he knew what I was thinking.

I'd dutifully walked in a daze into the over-large bathroom where one wall was converted into a small kitchen and turned the switch to 'off', then had returned to his arms.

I smiled at my memories, letting my eyes gradually adjust from looking into the past to seeing the present. Green grasses were knee high, and rose-colored tips were enlivening the stark winter branches of the gnarled oaks that had stood along this country highway for decades, if not centuries.

As Flyn turned the car onto Covelo Road and headed through Dos Rios, I wondered how many times I'd made this drive either alone, or with or without David, the kids, or Flyn. I could calculate the number of trips by the number of years I'd been coming here. David had begun wooing me in 1978 with promises of a home 'off the beaten track'. Now it was April of 2004, and that meant twenty-six years of aiming the car up and down these hills. Unpaved auxiliary roads meandered off this two lane highway that led to the Round Valley Indian Reservation. The deep-rutted ones reminded me of a favorite painting hanging on my mother's wall, of a muddy road disappearing into the distance and lined on both sides with fall-decorated trees. As a child, I'd dreamed about living at the end of that road. As an adult, the reality had been more than I'd expected.

Our driveway climbed steeply to the east, then north, winding through arched oak branches and past shiny madrone trunks, until it leveled onto a flat mountain top.

Flyn parked near the back porch, then took our suitcases and pillows into the house. He was lifting the cooler as I grabbed for my briefcase and computer. "Could be our schedule," Flyn said as we juggled our arm loads. He had to be thinking about my near-miss and my explanation.

"Too much?" I asked, as I followed him into the house, appreciating the look of his torso as he walked in front of me. I loved the sight of his sturdy body, the way he moved with a confident gait, and, of course, I loved the way his butt looked in his blue jeans. He was fit from daily weight lifting and yoga, and it dawned on me this was the first time I'd seen him wear jeans during our drive. He usually dressed more casually, in sweats, when we traveled for a weekend; his jeans were for working in the garden and mending fences. I had thought we were only here to air the house, check the watering system and relax, before going to McKinleyville for our friends' wedding on Sunday. *'What's he doing in work clothes?'* I thought.

When we returned to the car, he answered my spoken question, "Too much and too varied." He stopped lifting food bags out of the back of the car, and turned to me. His deep brown eyes penetrated through to my soul. "You've got too many irons in the fire, Sellie."

"Now where've I heard that before?" I contrived a laugh, feeling air fill my belly. This had been a routine conversation with David years ago, and the topic had been coming up more frequently with Flyn over the past year. I side-stepped the subject by breaking eye contact and busied myself by loading plastic handles on my arms.

He stopped me with his left hand and pulled me close to

his chest with his right. "I've been telling you this the whole time we've been together," he said softly. "It's hard for me to get any attention when you've two offices in two different cities and do phone counseling every evening." He stroked the back of my shoulders and neck, leaving goose bumps to spread to the top of my head.

"Ah. And I'm thinking you need a little attention," I said softly. Still not wanting to look at him, I dropped my head to his shoulder, and let him draw circles on my back.

"Could use a little, all the time," he said in my ear.

I forced a giggle and felt like a foolish, school girl, self-conscious of the false sound in my twitter. I wasn't feeling coy and sexy. I was feeling . . . *'What?'* I asked myself. *'Trapped? Out of sync?'* No matter. I knew by the look in his eyes that the food wouldn't get put away, nor would the house get aired before nightfall.

I sighed very, very slowly to prevent him from perceiving my deep breath as a sign of distress. I didn't want to explain my hesitancy, because I didn't understand it. *'Am I losing interest in sex? Or am I getting too old for spontaneity?'* Rubbing my head on his shoulder, I worried. With every ounce of focused concentration I could muster, I released the indescribable tension in my body. *'I love this man. He's filled my life with so many moments of magic. There's just no excuse for this except . . . what?'*

I kissed his chin, working to relax and go with the flow. "Let's at least get the food inside."

"Uh, huh," he answered, making a Herculean effort to empty the entire car in one last trip.

With sunshine spotlighting us from the kitchen skylight, he gently caressed every nook and cranny of my face with his nose and lips. *'Why do I keep myself so busy?'* I thought, and acknowledged my habit of ignoring personal body signs that announced my desire to make love. When was I going to realize the more I looked into people's diseases or emotional messes, the more I needed to surrender to my own needs, and to Flyn's? I had no reason to distance myself from him.

"You're thinking again," he whispered.

"How can you tell?" I asked my question from behind closed eyes.

"You aren't kissing me back."

"Oh . . . well . . . you're right," I admitted. "I've trouble turning off my mind."

"I noticed."

"Yeah, I guess you do," I said. "I just . . ." I groaned as he rubbed his hands deeply up and down my spine. He slipped his hands underneath the elastic waistband of my old-lady jeans and edged my panties with his fingertips, claiming even more of my attention as they slipped under the cotton and settled softly on my hips. His light touch brought the familiar tightening to my pelvis, and I loved his hands on my skin, the way his touch lingered at each hidden place on my body without hurrying, the way he moved his hands with such calmness and lost himself to the sensations at the ends of his fingers. I gasped as he pushed underneath my layers of sweaters, up my sides, to loosen my bra, then cup my breasts. His thumbs awoke my nipples, and I responded with the sudden desire to feel the smoothness of his skin.

I unbuttoned his flannel shirt, but my fingertips touched his T-shirt. "I hope the bed has a blanket on it," I said, as he propelled my shirts over my head. The house was downright cold from spring nighttime temperatures having hovered at only 35 degrees. We hadn't started the wood stove, and I shivered at the thought of cold sheets against naked skin on a freezing mattress.

"I've checked. The sun's on the pillows," he grinned, "and if we're really quick, we can dive under the comforter to get warm together."

"Deal," I squealed, my pants dropping around my ankles and my bare butt hitting cold air. I helped him pull off his pants and shirts. In our socks, we raced down the hall to the bed, diving and huddling between paisley-printed flannel sheets under a musty, down comforter.

We quivered, wrapping arms and legs around each other, gasping at the cold and trying to take deep, calming breaths. His body warmed faster than mine. I pillowed my head on his shoulder and nestled my body under his left arm as I huddled against his torso and legs. Layer by layer, my skin thawed until my inner organs simmered and basked in his caresses. Across my cheek and chin. Around my neck and ear. Over my breasts to my belly then around my hip and fanny. With his age at fifty-five and mine holding tenaciously to fifty-nine, I had to wonder what he felt as his hand cruised over my lumps and bumps. I marveled at the way he loved to touch me. He seemed in constant wonder at the changes in texture around my nipples whenever his fingers or lips brushed lightly across their tops, and how my breasts molded under his hand. He never failed to make me feel young and lithe and winsome. The way his fingers explored every inch of my body made me realize that, for him, each time we made love, it was as if it were the first time.

Rising above me, he entered slowly, prolonging that first, special moment of connection. He moved with a slow and penetrating rhythm. Then he stopped.

"Sellie," he sighed with a touch of exasperation. "You're going in and out."

"So are you," I giggled.

"Yeah," he smiled, balancing with his arms on either side of my head. "But you're thinking again. What can I do so you'll let the world go away?"

I ran my hands up and down his sides, stroking the scar along a lower rib where his body'd met the road during a motorcycle accident. "I don't know of anything you can do . . . but sometimes it helps for me to concentrate on my hands as I touch you."

"Ah . . . well . . ." He said as he slowly pulled away and lay on his back. "Then, touch me," he invited.

Spreading my fingers in the middle of his chest, I marveled at the firmness of his muscles, the lack of hair on his chest. I'd thought he'd shaved until he'd told me his heritage. With a Welsh father and a Lakota mother, his skin was pale gold in the sun, and he had no hair on his torso or face. I nibbled one nipple with my lips and tongue, as I dipped my hand to the edge of his rib cage to stroke his stomach. I teased him by touching everything but his manhood. His muscles grew taut, until he placed my hand where he wanted it.

He held me close, then with one deft move, settled me on top of him. We stilled until my wanting became too urgent. In rhythm, we reached that crest of sensation that left us breathing hard and grinning at each other.

Together we sang, "Oh, OH, Oklahoma!" and I sank onto the bed beside him. Sometimes we sang the first words of other appropriate or inappropriate show tunes, but this one was a favorite. Snuggling in the warm sunlight, I felt as if I never wanted to move again, so we dozed, and I relaxed deeper and deeper into sleep.

I don't know when he got up, but I missed his warmth. From my place under the sunlit comforter, I heard him in the kitchen, banging the stove pipe to prepare for a fire and some heat in the house for the night.

Unable to budge, I drifted between oblivion and a space that was not quite sleep, not quite awake. Then I passed from one cloud to another, then from one door to another, down a long hall. Squares of gray linoleum embedded with strings of red and blue, like the dormitory floor where I'd tried unsuccessfully to have a college career, tiled its length. I became lost in the patterns. Then the floor stopped being a floor.

It is a piece of ground standing on top of a pedestal which teeters in a wind I hear speeding past my ears. I lift my arms. I float. Flying high above a landscape of trees and roads, houses, trailers, and barns. I dip to see if I can recognize features of the land. It's unfamiliar. I glide higher in the sky on an updraft, circling until I'm soaring above clouds in an atmosphere I've never reached before.

Funny, I think, 'I remember flying before. But . . . how can I be so fully aware of what's happening?' As easily, I suppose, as my ability to control my flight pattern first with one wing tip then the other. Prickles rush over my body when I perceive that I have feathers and wings, not arms. I am a bird and am in awe at the transformation.

I hover over a clearing in a forest area, then descend for a closer look. A woman dressed in a hide tunic is standing near a campfire. I soar again, uneasy. I swoop and return to the valley nearby; the houses and trailers, the barns and the roads, are no longer there. I see only grasses and a stream glistening along the western edge of the landscape.

I lose air current, and flap with my wings to gain the next layer, then float and regard the land below me. Smoke trails a thin line into the sky from that same, small campfire. She is still there, her gray head now bending over her lap. The nearby bushes wave in the breeze. A bare foot breaks from the tree line. A man in a breech cloth of skins walks to stand beside her, and I see his hand pull a knife from its sheath at his side. I am afraid.

I call out but the only sound I utter is the high-pitched, piercing scream of an eagle.

They turn toward the sky. The woman stands, pointing at me. I feel drawn to her, as if some kind of energy links us, and I fall toward her finger. I scream again. My shoulder shakes with the vibration of the air. I feel squeezed as I lose control.

Flyn's arms were gentle and warm around me as he lifted my shoulders off the bed.

"Shhh," he said as he rocked me. "You were dreaming.

It's over. If I'd known you were going to have a bad dream, I wouldn't have left you." His shirt smelled of pine pitch from the wood he'd carried from the shed.

I smiled into his chest. "So you're not saying we wouldn't have made love, you just wouldn't have left me?"

"I'll never apologize for making love to you." His answer was muffled in the nape of my neck.

"Good," I said, admitting to myself that I'd no idea what I'd do without his stabilizing love.

"What was it?" he asked as he lowered me onto the pillow and stretched full-length beside me.

"I saw her."

"Which her?"

"I think it was Amach," I said with a sigh.

"You've seen her before?" He asked with the crease deepening between his eyebrows.

I hesitated. So unsure of revealing myself, but needing him to stay beside me until the fear of this last, spontaneous trance faded. I hedged, "I've not seen or heard from her for years . . . and . . . but . . . I have to tell you, what's happening is different from what happened twenty or so years ago." I stopped to think. *What was different?*

"In the beginning and like now, she came to me without my bidding." The familiar sense of dread covered my skin. "After the first few connections, we made some agreements and then, it was as if she whispered in my ear, telling me things I needed to hear to do my work. Now, she's appearing in a moving picture that I can't stop . . . and . . . there's other people in it. Like it's her life and there's some reason I need to see it." I shuddered and huddled into his smell. "This time, I was flying over her. It looked as if this guy in a breech cloth was going to kill her, but now. . . I'm not sure." He covered my naked shoulder with the comforter.

"And, Flyn"" I gasped, suddenly remembering. "I was an eagle, with wings and feathers. It was so real . . . so much more than a dream."

"Doesn't sound like any kind of dream I've ever had . . . more like this vision thing you said you had in the car."

I stared at the knotty pine ceiling, testing the flavor of his suggestion. "Perhaps," I shivered and closed my eyes. On the backdrop of my eyelids, I saw her finger pointing at me, felt myself falling toward her as if submitting to her command. I opened my eyes to prevent the room twirling around me.

"What else?" He watched me intently.

"I, well . . . it was as if . . . but I'm not sure," I stumbled with my explanation. With a deep breath I tried again. "I think she was summoning me."

He tightened his arms around me, and I wanted to believe that he could prevent that from happening. I considered telling him more about Amach and her contribution to my life, but the words stalled in my throat.

"I know you've got an idea about what's happening. You can't tell me you don't." He squinted his eyes and pouted his lips in thought. "Are you keeping me in the dark about something?"

His question made me take a sharp intake of breath. He pulled his head back to regard my face. His chin lifted. "I suppose I could take a guess. Let's see . . . Maybe you're like my grand-dad who gets messages about the future of this out-of-control world, or . . . maybe this has to do with the weird stuff at home?"

I silently repeated his words to myself *'This out-of-control world?'* A kaleidoscope of pictures gathered on a movie screen behind my eyes, like those theater news clips I'd seen as a kid in the 50's. At that time, they'd shown pictures of new technology, like telephones and televisions and how to build a bomb shelter. Now they showed threats of overpopulation, droughts, genocide, and rebellions. Tragedies of every kind were occurring on every continent of our Earth. Global warming and corporate pollution flitted through my mind, concerning me as much as 9/11, the Patriot Act, and the war on terrorism. Our world was being altered while we slept and ate and showered and made love.

'Weird stuff at home?' Well, our home life wasn't as much of a mess, but mysteries occurred daily. My apartment's lease agreement was lost, then found in one of Flyn's tennis shoes. Turquoise rings we'd exchanged when we'd celebrated our second anniversary had disappeared, until we'd found them in the sugar bowl. For three nights in a row, the sound of invisible rattles had awakened us at odd hours as they danced across our bedroom ceiling. The eerie beat of his grandfather's elk hand drum had sounded the night Pop Pop had fallen and broken his hip, yet the drum was locked in Flyn's mother's storage room.

Neither of us had explanations. Flyn pestered himself with questions, and I tried to make light of them. I didn't want to admit to Flyn these occurrences were only a set of recent, unexplained events in my life. Odd 'stuff' had been happening to me since I'd been born, and more, since I'd realized I could see things most others couldn't. Once I'd found my niche as a complementary therapist, 'stuff' always occurred when I facilitated energy and spirit helpers to expedite the healing of my clients.

I was grateful when a fly buzzed our bed, droning slowly in a clockwise circle. I watched until it settled on the dresser. "That's huge! It's too cool in the house to have been awakened by the heat of the fire. How'd it get in?"

"Must've left the door open with that last load of wood. Sorry." He unwrapped himself to close the front door then returned with the fly swatter.

"Ahhh . . . wait a minute. Let's invite him out rather than kill him," I suggested.

He looked at me strangely. "A friend of yours?" he asked.

"Could be," I answered as I stepped naked from the

covers into the chill. "He came for a visit, not annihilation."

"Sometimes you DO sound like Pop Pop." He sounded exasperated. As he left the room, he hollered, "What's for dinner?"

"Hamburgers, and you're cooking!" Feeling smug that the distraction had saved me from revealing any more about my secret, I waited in the cold to watch the black fly. It ambled across items on my dresser top, things I'd forgotten to tuck away into drawers after our last visit. It strolled across my favorite turquoise earrings that my friend, Haley, had given me long ago, and then briefly sat in the circle of my garnet ring, an heirloom from my mother. On a gift from Estelle, a silver pendant of a hand holding a blue-stoned heart in its palm, the fly lingered; it seemed to be kissing the heart. Estelle's face took shape, and I remembered she'd called before we'd left the city to ask if she and I could spend some time together on Saturday.

Even though I craved some space to be alone here on my mountain, I'd agreed to meet with her tomorrow. Estelle wasn't just a friend, she was a comrade, a partner in experiments with other worlds. I had no idea what she wanted because she'd been evasive when I'd asked her why she sounded so serious. I hadn't heard that tone in her voice for over twenty years. That was when we'd tapped into information from the Universe while working her grandmother's Ouija Board. Those times had led us to a doorway that had peered into the possibilities of the future, as well as into the secrets of the past.

Chapter II - 1984
Seeing beyond ourselves

"I can't believe we're actually doing this," Estelle called from her living room.

"I can't either," I shouted from her back porch, a postage-stamp sized slab of uneven cement built outside her kitchen. Gazing at her horse barn and newly-planted apple orchard, I watched Clarabelle, her mule, and Oliver, her thoroughbred stallion, emerge then disappear, as a misty fog thinned then thickened in the morning breeze. Oak branches, bare of leaves, poked through the liquid haze like arms of eerie aliens lurking in a gloomy lagoon from some Steven King movie. I sucked my cigarette and wondered if I was getting in over my head.

Since I was a kid, I'd loved ideas and books investigating that side of our world described as unseen. I thrilled when I could create experiences with my imagination, while others plodded through their daily lives, that is until the visions and the voices didn't go away. If I'd been more reckless, I'm sure I would have dropped LSD or eaten hallucinogenic mushrooms. As it was, I'd done time addicted to wine and hard liquor instead. There was no other way I could make the crazy visions I thought I was imagining, go away. Booze had helped me numb the edgy experiences of my multi-dimensional youth.

I hadn't been off the 'spirits' very long, or had much experience keeping the creepies at bay, yet here I was getting ready to call to the universe and invite 'whatever' to talk to me.

When Estelle and I'd first talked about working the Ouija Board, I'd felt no qualms about sitting with the inscribed board between us. It seemed such a tame idea, and I'd worked it with friends in high school. It had been no big deal then. We'd had some laughs, gotten confusing messages, and had come away with what we thought were predictions, which in my case seemed to have come true. *'Then why am I so nervous?'* I asked myself.

Smoke ascended from the smoldering ash of my Marlboro. I missed the menthol-flavored Salems I'd smoked since high school, but David, who was pushing me to quit, told me that menthol was as addictive as nicotine. I agreed to break my mint-flavored craving as a first step. *'Quitting is a good idea,'* I told myself, every time I lit one of these awful-tasting sticks. Better for my health and better for my image as a role model for my kids. As a substitute, I sucked peppermints with every cigarette to make them taste better. *'Guess that's a good sign,'* I consoled myself, wishing I hadn't agreed to stop my favorite stress-relief method for keeping my mouth shut. I also wished I hadn't agreed to this experience with Estelle. Something was going to happen that was out of my hands, and I knew it in the pit of my stomach.

"Want to meditate first?" I asked, hoping to buy some time before we positioned ourselves at the Ouija Board.

"Don't think so. Let's just do prayers and protective light . . . and . . . oh . . . we need to be sure to ground ourselves." Estelle had scrubbed dishes and silverware with a sudsy sponge then rinsed them through cold water in a plastic pan in her sink. Breakfast cups and plates were dripping on a towel, and she was digging into her apartment-sized propane refrigerator. *'Too organized,'* I shuddered, thinking how much she reminded me of my mother. *'Well, maybe not.'* My mother stood tall at five-foot-seven and weighed one hundred and forty-five pounds, thin and lithe. Estelle and I looked each other in the eye at five-foot-five. Where I was pudgy around the middle, she had a waist line. Estelle also held a different view of life and how to live it, than my mom did. That was one of the reasons I was drawn to her when we'd met in a massage class at Heartwood College for the Healing Arts, outside Garberville.

I crushed my cigarette on the cat's saucer. "Ever done the Ouija Board before?" I asked as she closed the refrigerator door.

"Just by myself," she answered.

"And so now . . . just how did we get to this place where we've decided to do this?"

Estelle turned and looked at me with her devil eye; that was the left one that got all squinty when she eye-balled me with all of her attention. "Don't you get nervous and back out on me, Selena."

I tried to create a smile. "I know I said I'd done this before with girl friends but it's just. . . well . . . it's different this time."

"OK, but didn't you tell me the board foretold the man you were going to marry?"

"It did," I admitted, "the first one." I entered the back door and hung my flannel-lined rain coat on a dragon-headed hook. Suddenly I felt exposed like I'd just undressed and was standing in the hall, naked. I shivered, then wrapped my arms around myself. "Now that I think about it, we messed around for a long time before we got the hang of it. We constantly accused each other of pushing the pointer. Once, my best friend swore I'd dashed the . . . what's it called . . . the planchette, across the board when we'd spelled out a sentence that was kinda weird."

"What sentence?"

"Something about standing between the worlds."

"But what . . . did that mean?" she asked as she spread mayonnaise on three pairs of rye bread slices before flopping first cheese then squares of pressed ham onto every other slice.

"I don't remember now," I said as I stood picking crumbs of freshly cut bread with a damp fingertip. I shrugged,

"I swore I hadn't 'pushed' the wooden pointer. And the message seemed . . . so . . . other-wordly." Grunting at my memory of five girls squealing in the dark every time we heard something strange outside, I wondered again what Estelle and I were doing today. I brushed my hands together; we didn't have any idea what we were doing either.

"What was it about the board foretelling your futures?"

"Let's see . . . I remember we'd asked the board who each of us was going to marry, and my answer was RED. I can't remember the other answers, and I've no idea how it worked out for them, but I married a man with red hair who was nicknamed Red."

"So that proves the information was correct." She returned jars and plastic bags to the fridge, then covered the sandwiches with a damp towel.

I scrunched up my face. "It could also mean I'm highly suggestible, and married someone who fit the description."

Estelle turned to me, hands on her hips. "Now wait just one minute! How long before you met him?"

While I counted dates and years, I admired her festooned ceiling. I loved the tie-dyed bedspreads nailed there to cover the water stains in her sheet rock. Her flamboyant ceiling made me smile. Counting on my fingers, I answered. "It was about two years before I met Harry, or rather Red, as he liked to be called."

"Well that proves it, then." Rubbing lavender oil into her hands, she crossed the red and beige Persian rug in the living room portion of her cabin.

"Proves what?" For the first time, I noticed she'd hennaed her medium-length hair. The gentle, reddish auburn made her skin paler than usual, and I watched as she shoved the couch and coffee table together to make a space for a small table and two chairs. Estelle was always in motion, whether working with her clients or at home. I felt like a slow poke behind her with my sturdy legs and torso. She was a bundle of energy; I was a plodder.

"That you're connected to the spirit world."

"Don't say things like that!" I whispered, instantly breathless. "I just hope we're not opening a door into something we shouldn't." *'There!'* I said to myself. *'I've finally admitted it.'* My chest tightened as I watched Estelle remove the Ouija Board and its heart-shaped pointer from its box.

"There's no such thing as shouldn't!" Estelle said as we tugged the mahogany end table nearer to the window. "There's just the need for caution and to be very, very clear we don't want wayward or negative spirits messing with us. I've read this book that says explicitly that those who get misguided answers didn't set up correctly. They probably had no idea they needed to put up protection when they started, or that they had to keep their questions simple. I've read all about it. I know what we're doing! That's what we're about today, and if you really want to back out on me, I can understand." Hands on her hips, she turned to me, "But, Selena, I would be *very* disappointed." Her voice pitched into that soft whine she created when she was trying to talk me into doing something I wasn't sure I wanted to do.

She'd already badgered me into taking more classes about body work and holistic healing, than any other practitioners we knew. It wasn't that I hadn't wanted to study reflexology, aura reading, Jin Shin Do, as well as two advanced massage therapy courses; I'd enjoyed every one of those classes, in the end. It was just that I didn't think I needed to research working with different essential oils and toning sounds, and I had no idea when I'd use past life regression or self-hypnosis, energy healing or chakra balancing. I smiled at my friend and rolled my eyes. "Oh, alright! After all, you *did* read a whole book on the subject, right? We just have to follow the instructions and see what happens, right? What can it hurt anyway? It's not like we're trying to manipulate anything or anybody, right?"

"Right! We just want to reach the other side and find help to improve our healing practices." We each brought a chair from the kitchen, and she handed me a pillow to sit on.

"Uh, oh! I'll be right back!" I squeezed my thighs together to prevent a gush of blood from trickling past my Kotex. I doubled over with pain from the cramping, then, as I sat on the toilet, I contemplated my relationship with my uterus. '*How can one little organ dictate what I wear, where I go, and how I feel most days?*' A gynecologist and my clinic doctor predicted I could outlast the fibroids if I could endure the long periods and heavy bleeding until menopause, but I was 39 and holding, and not sure I was going to make it to the age of 50 when the rest of the females in my family had started the last leg of their reproductive years.

"Are you coming out soon?" Estelle mewed. When she saw me readjusting my wad of double pads, she probed, "Are you alright?"

I sighed. "I'm fine, just my usual two-week period at its predictable beginning." I wished there was a way I could deal with these fibroids without having surgery, or waiting them out.

Estelle plugged in my tape recorder. It was beside us on the wine-colored, overstuffed couch. A spare tape sat nearby. Candles beamed from the blue-tiled window sill, and we stood facing each other in the middle of the room. She offered me the abalone shell with smoldering Southern Californian sage she'd used to clear the energies of the room, and I took a deep breath of the smudge to clear my head. The edges of my body shivered, oh so delicately, and a weight lifted from my heavy shoulders like a cool wind had puffed it away.

She stoked the fire in the wood stove. We settled onto our chairs on either side of the table and grinned at each other. "I'm glad we're together on this," I said.

We held hands across the table and breathed our grounding breaths into the center of the Earth and out to the Universe. We used our out-breaths simultaneously to create a protective bubble of light around us, top and bottom, then sent out good intent from our hearts to all beings.

Estelle closed her eyes and began. "Here we are, doing some work with the Ouija Board for the purpose of our education. We're serious. We're not playing any games, although this is reported to be a game board. We don't want any spirits to play with us, or misuse us in any way. We desire to speak to a spirit who will come through and give us advice from a universal level about healing and healing practices."

We opened our eyes at the same time. "That should take care of it, shouldn't it?" she asked.

I nodded, and we positioned our finger tips on either side of the planchette in the middle of the board. With suspended breaths, we tried to relax our shoulders and arms.

Estelle announced, "We're calling out to Infinity to talk to a spirit who might want to come through this board and give us information about the healing work we do, or about our personal lives."

The planchette stirred. We stared wide-eyed at each other and Estelle mouthed the question, "Are you?"

When I shook my head to mean I wasn't pushing or pulling it, we both released our breaths and tried again to relax. My heart raced as I became aware of a change in the air around me, a vibration that hummed. I signaled Estelle with my eyebrows, but her eyes were closed.

"Who's here? Please give us your name," Estelle asked.

The planchette awakened, this time skimming across the board, then centering itself. I nearly fell off my chair trying to keep my hands in place. To stabilize myself, I widened the span between my feet and rolled my shoulders to ease the tension building there.

The planchette traveled to the letters, N A N.

"Is your name Nan?" Estelle asked. We had decided, when we were organizing ourselves for this, that only one person would ask questions at a time.

The planchette moved to the word NO on the board, then drifted over the letters again.

N A N P O O K A, it spelled.

We both giggled. "Is your name Nanpooka?" Estelle asked.

The planchette moved to YES on the board.

"Well," Estelle said. "Thank you for coming. Have you ever been on this earth plane?"

Y E S

"Have you ever been a part of our lives?"

I called out the letters, and Estelle tried to make them into a phrase or sentence:

A T A N O T H E R T I M E   O R S P A C E

The planchette hesitated then pulled our hands to spell another block of letters.

N O W   O N L Y   F R O M   T H I S   S I D E

"Wow," Estelle said, regarding me with startled eyes. We were both at a loss for words and questions. She nodded her head at me to take over. I asked the first thing that entered my mind.

"Well, I wonder what it is you want to tell us?"

H E A L   A L O N G   N E C K   W I T H   M A S S A G E

"Do you mean to use massage to heal our client's necks?"

The answer was NO. I was confused for a second, then thought to ask, "Do you mean we need healing along our necks with massage?"

O N L Y   O N E

"Does Estelle need healing along her neck?" I asked because I knew I wasn't in any pain.

Y E S

"Yikes," Estelle interrupted. "How did you know I slept wrong last night and have a crick in my neck?" She was staring at the board. "I didn't even tell Selena."

The planchette remained still; the air quieted. The faint buzzing I'd noticed earlier was gone. Then, it blossomed with edges of light.

"I'm feeling a really strong energy here," Estelle said with wonder in her voice. "I'm asking if the personality named Nanpooka has returned to talk to us?"

The planchette moved to NO.

"This is a new personality? Would you like to give us your name or how you are called? We will watch."

A M Y

"Do you have any connection with either of us?"

Y E S

Estelle asked, "Are you connected with me?"

N O

"Are you more connected with Selena?"

Y E S

"Has she known you in this lifetime?"

The planchette didn't move.

I took over. "I see no answer. Have I known you in this lifetime? Are you an entity like a spirit guide who's been with me in this lifetime?"

The energy around us began to shimmer, but there was no answer.

"Was your name Amy in this lifetime?"

N O

"That was clear," Estelle said. She took over. "Does this mean you did not take human form in this lifetime?"

The pressure of the air pushed against me to the point where I couldn't expand my chest to breathe.

The planchette hesitated and inched to the YES.

I signaled for Estelle to continue asking questions.

"We appreciate your coming through so strongly at this time.

We would like to know if you are connected in some way to Selena's personal development?"

Y E S

"Could you spell out something for us so we can understand what it is you want to teach Selena?"

M A S S

"There is something about a mass that you want to tell Selena?"

Y E S

Our hands were drawn all over the board, passing back and forth across the letters and numbers printed on it. The planchette hovered over different letters but didn't stop long enough to let us begin spelling anything.

Estelle asked, "Are you having difficulty communicating in our terms? Maybe . . . here's a better question. Can you tell us why you've come through today?"

I W A N T T O M O M

"Mom, is that correct? Does this mean you want to be a mother?"

N O

"Does this mean you want to talk to your Mom?"

Y E S

"Is Selena your mom, Amy?"

Y E S

"Can you tell us in our Earth years, when Selena was your Mom? Can you give us a date?"

M A Y

"Can you give us a year?"

1 9 6 4

I felt as if my heart had plunged from the 32nd floor of a high rise to its basement. I didn't know where I was. I was shaking so hard, I pulled my hands from the planchette to hold onto myself. "I can't believe this! It's too much." Vomit rose in the back of my throat; I couldn't breath. I pushed myself away from the table and tried to stand, but my legs were too rubbery.

"What're you doing?" Estelle screamed. "Don't lose contact," she pleaded. "Please! Put your hands back on the planchette! This spirit's here for a reason. The way you're reacting tells me there's some kind of truth here."

I tried again to rise from my seat, but now I felt heavy, as if my body had morphed into a slug. I didn't have any muscles to stand up and tried to beg Estelle with my eyes to stop, but she glared at me and ordered, "Tell me what this is all about!"

All I could do was replace my finger tips on the wooden pointer. '*So much distance and time between then and now,*' I thought. So many years without my having told a soul. Slowly, I did as she asked and told the story. As I began, I felt as if I were talking about someone else, some other young person, woman . . . really, who was from another world. "There was a time in my life . . . just after high school . . . before I tried college, when . . . when I thought, " I had to take a deep breath. "When I thought I was pregnant."

A rush of shame made me dizzy. "It was never confirmed but . . . I just knew. Oh, God, Estelle, I was so scared. If my folks had found out I'd have been disowned, especially by my Dad. I just knew I'd be out in the cold. I didn't know what to do. I tried going to a doctor for help, but I met one of my mom's friends in the reception room, so I pretended I was waiting for someone." A burst of tears made me unable to continue.

"Was it like in the spring of '64?" Estelle asked.

I nodded. "The spring semester," I cried. I gulped and continued. "I was two months late . . . I was . . . worried. I fell on the steps leading to Cowell Hall Library at Berkeley one rainy day when Denise and I were visiting our friend Kate at the university. That night, I started a very heavy period. Denise was a nursing student and thought I might be having a miscarriage." Every hair on my head felt as if it was standing.

Looking at our fingers on the planchette, I asked, "Are you the baby that was trying to come through me at that time?"

Y E S

I sobbed so hard I could hardly sit straight. Estelle asked for me. "Do you have something to say to Selena?"

The planchette moved to YES then spelled: M A S S T R Y I N G T O A B O R T

"Does this have something to do with what is going on in Selena's female organs right now?"

Y E S

"Are you saying that she'll abort the fibroids?"

N O

"OK, then . . . does it mean if she stops the aborting process she'll have less bleeding?"

Y E S

"What can she do?"

F O R G I V E

I jumped from the table. "I can't do this anymore! I don't know where this is coming from! It's too much!"

Estelle didn't budge. "Selena's really upset. I hope you'll stay with me, Amy. Tell me what she has to forgive so she can be healed of this bleeding. Can you tell me who she has to forgive?"

H E R S E L F

Estelle looked at me. "Don't leave this. You've come too far. Tell me how this happened. What do you have to forgive yourself for? Please Selena. This is just too important. Whatever it is, you've got to face it."

I blew my nose. I could barely talk through the lump in my throat. "I can't remember the details now." I waved my arms helplessly. "I mean . . . this all happened . . . twenty years ago." I tried to stifle another sob. "I do know I felt guilty. I'd been at a party, drunk again, and had gone off with some guy afterwards. I didn't even know who he was." I twisted the Kleenex around my fingers while I paced the room. "I wasn't really popular, and I thought this might lead to something. I didn't think; I was too drunk. When I let him get on top of me, I knew it was wrong, but, hell, it was the 60's, and I just . . . well . . . crap, I just let him do me."

I sat down, wishing I could disappear into the chair cushion. "In a strange way, after I'd realized I might be pregnant, I was excited. I'd always wanted to be a mom."

The planchette hovered in the center of the board under Estelle's fingertips.

"I . . . I guess I've . . . well, I think now that . . . I've always felt guilty about how I got pregnant in the first place. I mean I didn't even know the guy. And then I felt like a failure because of losing the baby." I swiped a tear from my cheek. "For a long time, I celebrated her birthday on the date I thought she would've been born."

Estelle asked, "You thought it was a girl?"

I nodded.

The planchette swung wider across the board under Estelle's hands.

"Put your fingertips back," Estelle ordered. "You have to finish this, Selena."

"I guess," I said, sniffling.

Estelle asked, "Is the process Selena is going through today part of her healing?"

Y E S

"Will the mass go away on its own?"

N O

"Will she have to have surgery?"

Y E S

We both gasped at the quickness of the answer. "Will she have to have surgery soon?"

N O   1 9 8 7

"Well that's definitive," Estelle added

I   L O V E   Y O U   M O M

There was a pause. I   F   O   R   G   I   V   E

Y O U   F O R   N O T   W A N T I N G   M E

As soon as we'd deciphered the letters into a sentence, I whispered, "Oh, Amy, I did want you, but it was the wrong time. And then, when I met Red and got pregnant, I was so happy I was going to be a Mom. I didn't even mind marrying him until later. Why didn't you come through then and be my daughter, Shawna?"

S H E   W A N T E D   Y O U   M O R E

Estelle said to me, "Well, that's interesting, since you two are having such a hard time getting along these days."

My 17 year-old daughter, Shawna, was nothing but a problem, but thinking of her now helped me to center. I said with a shrug, "Could be the way it works. Maybe Shawna needed me more as a mom so she could finish some kind of karma. Is that right, Amy?"

The planchette hovered between our fingers, levitated off the board, then crashed onto the wood, dashing from letter to letter.

I   A M   S T U C K

Estelle and I stared at our hands, then at each other. I asked, "Are you stuck in me? Is that why these fibroids are growing so large?"

The planchette moved very slowly to YES, then spelled out: S A D

I started to cry again. "I'm sad too, Amy. I had no idea that I was keeping you stuck by not forgiving myself and not letting you go. I can do that now, Amy. Will that help you?"

B R E A K   T H E   B O N D

I wiped my dripping nose on the back of my sleeve so that I wouldn't lift my hands from their perch on the planchette. "I will. I promise. I'll burn the little notebook I kept of my writings. Will that help?"

Y E S

"I promise I'll do that when I get home tonight. I'll kiss the notebook and burn it in the wood stove, and let you go."

I AM FLYING

The planchette shifted under our hands then strayed between a few letters but never stopped long enough for us to put them into a sequence.

"Goodbye, Amy," Estelle said softly. "Thanks for coming today."

The air around us dulled in a crazy way, as if the sun was hiding behind a cloud, or the quality of the air had shifted from light to shadow. I realized that the consistency of the day was more like it had been when we'd started. The room had been brighter while the entity or energy or the 'whatever' of Amy had been present.

Estelle and I sat in shocked silence. I was exhausted. She had circles under her eyes. My shoulders and hips ached. All I wanted was to withdraw my hands from the planchette, assume the fetal position, and sleep.

We removed our hands from the wooden pointer at the same time. My mind was unable to comprehend the mechanism that spelled the words across the board.

"Look," Estelle pointed through the window. In the eastern meadow near her house and through the thinning fog, a rainbow arched. It ended hidden in the trees. "If I were a betting woman, I'd bet Amy sent that as she left."

I nodded. My throat tightened with a mixture of relief and sadness. My mind was swirling. *'How had we brought that spirit energy to us? How had we pointed to those words, made those sentences? How did it work?'*

I wanted nothing more than to discuss today's experience without any reference to what had been revealed about my youth because I'd always felt so guilty about this secret. Along with the uncontrolled drinking, it was the worst thing I'd done as a young woman. I wasn't buying the idea that talking about it would make me feel better, although I wasn't feeling as heavy under the weight of the shame of it. "Can you believe what just happened here?" I said. We examined the quiet board.

Estelle said, "Not just what happened but what might happen next?"

I lifted the planchette, turning it over and over in my hands. It was lifeless. I shrugged my shoulders, "Now, if I were the betting woman in the room, I would lay odds we ain't seen nothin' yet."

Estelle grinned. "*And,* we *are* going to find out, aren't we?"

I rolled my eyes, "I guess."

We packed the board and its pointer into its case before returning our chairs and the table to their places. I tried to sort through my feelings while we had a cup of licorice tea and a ham-and-cheese sandwich on home-made rye bread. Her mismatched plates and cups cheered me with their kaleidoscope of colors and textures and patterns.

Estelle was the epitome of the "Hippie" culture. Having come from my conservative family where I was the only child, I admired her freedom and her large, boisterous family of five half-, step-sisters and brothers. Where I'd rarely, if ever, been left alone in my family's home while my parents took off for a weekend, she and her tribe had been left on their own for weeks at a time, which had resulted in many adventures. Listening to her talk about her memories was one of my favorite past-times when we were together. Today, though, it seemed as if neither of us wanted to stray from our first Ouija Board experience.

"I'll transcribe today's taping," I offered.

"That'd be great! I'll do it next week." Estelle chewed her sandwich. "Ya know, that was a powerful session."

"I guess! Who would've thought a little wooden pointer . . . I mean . . . I could have sworn you were pushing it half of the time, but, Estelle . . . you'd no idea of my past."

She pursed her lips together. "To tell the truth, I never

would've guessed you were *that* free back then."

I flushed. "I really wasn't . . . that free, Estelle." The homemade bread hardened into a stone in my stomach. "To say it plainly, I was a drunk . . . even before the age of nineteen. I was drinking before I'd entered high school."

"Didn't your family suspect?" She shook her head. "I mean, coming home drunk from parties?"

I finished the last bite of my sandwich. "My drinking wasn't a big deal in my family. I was five or six years old the first time I got drunk, because my dad had me retrieving every unfinished champagne cocktail I could find at some wedding. I'd find one, drink some, then take him the rest. I've heard the story forever: 'Oh, you should have seen her! She was the cutest little thing, stumbling along, trying to walk straight to get the half-filled glass to her daddy."

I said with disgust. "It wasn't until they found me passed out under the piano that my mother got furious."

"I don't get it. How did that make you an alcoholic?" Estelle peeled a banana.

I took a breath. "It didn't, but I think because everybody laughed and the story's told to this day as something cute, I got the idea that there was nothing wrong with drinking, even to excess. My mom's family made their own booze during prohibition, my parents had happy hour every night, and I regularly got sloshed with them. There were other things happening too that I wanted to keep under the dull wraps of being drunk; I thought nothing of drinking while I was pregnant with both kids." I shrugged.

"It wasn't until I couldn't get through the day without having bourbon in my milk at noon, or through a conversation with Red without a glass of wine in my hand, that I began to think I had a problem. And then I nearly killed my family."

Estelle's eyes widened, but I stopped her questions with my hand raised between us. "I don't want to talk about any of this anymore! I'm done for now!"

I gulped the cup of warm tea. I hated Estelle's interrogations about my childhood or my years with Red. I wanted to hear her stories, not mine. Her life was more dramatic, filled with family fun and sibling rivalry. I'd rather hear about her current boy friend, Roger, than share what was happening with David and my kids in our 8' x 40' decrepit trailer. It seemed we were never going to break ground for our dream house. Plus, there were far too many memories and feelings unsorted in my mind.

Now, after that session with Amy, I wanted to separate myself from this event, after I'd burned the notebook, of course. I only wanted to sit in a little patch of sun and not think about the baby that died inside me, or how the experience might have affected me, or how I got into that situation in the first place. I was terrified to look at my family and childhood. Suddenly I wanted a cigarette.

Estelle snickered. "You're getting agitated."

"Yeah . . . I am." I sighed at her. When I found my cigarettes and lighter, I dragged my body to the back door.

"Wish you wouldn't smoke. If you've got to smoke, have a toke with me. You'd be calmer." Estelle offered.

"Estelle," I said. "I can't start on marijuana. I've already battled my way out of a bottle."

"But it's not addictive. I can take it or leave it."

"Famous last words," I retorted.

"Hey! Be nice! Just because we uncovered a piece of your past that's affecting the present, doesn't mean you get to be all weird about it. For Pete's sake, if there was anyone on the planet who has compassion for you and what you went through, it's me."

I pulled deeply on my Marlboro and gagged at the harsh taste. "I know," I choked. My eyes watered from the smoke, or maybe it was memories. In one of our weekend Chakra and Massage classes where we'd spent the night together, Estelle had confessed to two abortions, which explained the blockages and shielding I'd discovered in her Second Chakra. She'd discovered a hole in mine which we'd related to the deadening fibroid. I'd never correlated my miscarriage, which I'd shoved into a deep recess of my mind, to the empty space she'd envisioned. Maybe the exploding size of my fibroids was my body's way of filling in the space.

I closed my eyes and pictured the rainy day when I'd slipped on the library steps. The indignity of the fall had hurt my ego more than the scrapes on my hands and knees, and when I'd started bleeding later in the motel room, Denise had wanted to take me to the emergency room. I'd refused. Being a nursing student, she'd shown me how to massage my uterus to speed the process and express all the tissue to help stop the bleeding. Alone in the shower, I watched clots and red tissue collect on the floor of the green-tiled stall. It didn't feel right to leave the debris in the metal grate across the drain for Denise or the motel maid to clean. I didn't want the remnants of my baby in the sewer. I remembered sobbing and feeling like such a failure, wishing things had been different so I could've borne a baby of my own. Carefully, I collected every bit of the tissue and clotted blood. I wrapped them in three layers of toilet paper and then in a paper towel so I could hide the packet deep in an inside pocket of my Samsonite travel case. As soon as I was home alone, I dug a hole under a red rose bush and buried the small package, asking the Earth to accept my offering, and for help to make this life count for something. I prayed to the God or Goddess of the Universe to help me turn my mistake into something good.

"Selena, where are you?"

My cigarette had burned so low, it had scorched my fingers. Estelle's arms came around my waist, and she pillowed her head on my shoulder. Her body radiated against mine; her steady breathing against my back soothed me. I dropped the cigarette stub and let her guide me onto her bed in the far corner of her cabin. She laid me down, crawled next to me, and held me like I'd always wanted my mother to hold me. We dozed until I gradually awoke to her even breathing next to my ear. I sensed when she came awake.

"I haven't thought about that time for forever," I said slowly. "When I look at it now, my desire to be liked, the drinking, the loss of the baby that never should have been . . . It's all a part of me, my sexuality, my consequences. I don't know how it all fits, but it could be a reason for this growth in the walls of my uterus. I mean, stranger things have happened to people, right?"

Estelle nodded. "Oh, yeah. Stranger things have happened and will continue to happen." She stretched her neck back and forth. "Can't get over the clarity of Amy's transmission and how she was so sure you were going to need surgery. Gave us a specific date too."

"But now I've got the problem of being cynical. It's like my marriage to Red. Were the words from the Ouija Board a prediction or a suggestion? Am I going to hold on for another couple of years to have surgery because she said so? Or is it a matter that what we did today will alleviate enough of the urgency so I'll be able to wait that long?"

"I think . . . if you let her go . . . you'll be able to wait for a couple of years. It's like she brought the past forward, connected it to the present, and made a little prediction of the future. Whew! Sellie! I mean, what kind of entity is it who can tie it all together like that?"

"Puzzle to me," I answered.

"Just think, Sellie! Amy gave you an opportunity to change your life." Estelle's enthusiasm was growing. "This stuff's fantastic."

I inwardly groaned.

"I bet we can get more information the next time we do the board. I bet there's a teacher out there who can tell us more about disease and tumors and healing and stuff like that. I sure can't find anyone in this town. We can ask these questions of whatever or whomever becomes available for us from out there in the Universe."

I shrugged. Even now that we'd started this process, I wasn't sure about it. Estelle had gotten off easy with receiving instructions about healing her neck; I felt I'd been given a personal whammy! *'What other kinds of intimate stuff would surface?'* I didn't want to think about that. In the long run, I knew I wanted more knowledge about the healing of minds, bodies, and spirits. Having been a lab technician for years, I'd seen my share of diseases and their accompanying pain and suffering. Surely there was something more than bright lights and cold steel to bring a person into a place of balance and promote total body healing. I wanted to know more, but I wasn't eager to be told more about myself.

"My God, Estelle, what're you going to get me into next?"

"Well . . ."

"Well, what?" I leaned onto an elbow and tried to give her my most scathing look.

"Well, I did have this other idea."

"Uh-oh, I already feel like it's a 'no'!" I flopped back.

She sat cross-legged next to me on the bed. "Don't say that. It's just that I've been thinking if the two of us can bring in such entities, think of what four people with like-minds could do." She fluffed her hair and stretched her neck, not looking at me.

"What four? And when did you start thinking about this?" I asked.

"Well now, it was when I was talking with Gunthar the other day and told him what we were doing, and he . . . "

"Estelle! I thought we'd agreed this was between us."

"I couldn't help myself. I was so excited; it just popped out of my mouth. Besides, he and I've been working on similar things."

"You can't tell him what happened today!"

She touched my shoulder, "Selena, I wouldn't do that to you."

"I hope not!" I rolled my head back and forth on the pillows. "Do I dare ask what you have in mind?"

"Well, we could have you and Gunthar and Crystal and I meditate together and see what happens."

I grimaced. "I don't want to wait and see what happens. I would rather have us pick a topic and meditate on it. I don't want to go into a kind of alternative awareness without a plan."

"So, you'll do it then?"

I was caught. An uneasy shiver had flashed across my shoulders as she'd described her plan, but it had a tingling edge to it. *'Curiosity?'* Then I shook myself, *'Why am I even thinking about agreeing to this?'* After today's experience, I didn't want to get involved with another of Estelle's schemes. I floundered. I didn't want to hurt her feelings, and I had a kind of repugnance toward any more of her new age ideas, but I had to admit to an inflating wonder and curiosity about what this could bring into our lives. An edge of urgency to step into this next experiment nudged at me. There were feelings swirling inside me that were beyond myself. Beyond where I was standing. Poised in my heart.

"I haven't said I would," I said weakly, wondering what in the world was happening. I thought of an ultimatum that might shift her plan. "I'll think on it *if* you promise none of you smoke dope before we do it."

Estelle hesitated. "Well . . . I'll have to ask them."

Suddenly angry, I lifted myself on one elbow to face her. "*That* means you've already talked to both of them, haven't you?"

"Oh, Sellie!" Estelle pushed her lips forward in a pout. "Don't be mad."

"Haven't you?" I pushed her back on the queen-sized bed picturing all manner of tortures to get her to tell the truth. I began tickling her. "Don't lie to me. I know you."

"OK . . . Well . . . OK! Stop! I can't . . . stand it. I have . . . but . . . stop it!" She was screaming and trying to tickle me back. Then she hit me with a pillow.

I found another and toppled back on the bed as I tried to swing it in her direction.

She scrambled onto her knees as I pulled myself into the same position. We faced off, each with pillows in our hands, laughing and shrieking.

"What's going on?" a deep male voice overrode our squeals from the kitchen.

We fell to the bed, laughing. She took me in her arms and hugged me. I hugged her back. "What would I do without you?" I whispered.

"I think your life would be very dull," she whispered back and kissed my lips.

Roger, her current partner, was home for lunch and stood next to the bed. "Can I join you two?"

Estelle smiled a "I-double-dog-dare-you" smile and challenged me with a glint in her eye.

I withdrew from her arms, "No, thank you."

"Chicken," Estelle taunted.

"Perhaps," I said a bit sadly. "More than anything else, I'm committed to one person." It was always like this. Estelle would never stop pushing me to cross certain personal boundaries. "Gotta go," I announced as brightly as I could and turned away from her teasing smile.

"See you next week?"

"Oops, no. It will have to be in two weeks. Shawna has a field trip, and I'm an adult advisor."

"You'll think about the other experiment?" She and Roger followed me, walking arm and arm through the kitchen.

As I donned my coat, my heart fluttered oddly. "I'll think about it. But you've got to get the others to promise. I need to feel safe."

"Oh, alright," she said as she left Roger and held out her arms to me. "Take care of yourself. See you in two weeks."

After hugs, I walked through fading fog to sink behind the wheel of my 1970 yellow VW bug. The gray upholstery had absorbed comforting warmth from the clouded sun, and I basked in its hospitality, feeling my body sag from the morning's rush of adrenaline and crying. A battery clock stuck to the dashboard with super glue revealed I was on the verge of being late to retrieve Shawna and Sam from school, a junior and a freshman, respectively. If I lived through the next few years with two teenagers, while juggling shift work at the hospital, a massage practice in town, doing the books for two businesses, helping David on the house and keeping our marriage alive, I was going to get a medal. These times with Estelle kept me going. Whether once a week or once a month, I had to pursue my own interests.

I checked myself in the mirror, fluffed my newly-cut bangs and realized I hadn't thought to ask Estelle if they made me look younger. My silver brown hair hung to my waist when it wasn't pulled into a bun or ponytail. When I was trying to be professional, I twirled it high into a circle on the top of my head. My thick hair dragged me down sometimes, the bangs an attempt to lighten the load. I wished I could just cut my hair to within an inch all over my head. My features were even enough. I didn't need hair styling tricks to make my face look longer or slimmer. With naturally arching eyebrows, a well-formed mouth, and a firm chin, I thought I could almost pull off bald, with big hooped earrings to add flamboyance. I slumped in my seat; they needed me to stay the same. At least David did. He loved my long hair. He didn't like me to rock the boat, so to speak.

"Yeah, but what do *I* need?" I asked myself. A blank gaze returned the stare of my hazel green eyes in the mirror. Caught in my own look, I stared deeper, focusing past my lids and eye lashes. Deep wells of glassy water tugged at me, dragging me in. I couldn't pull my attention from the dark-centered swirling green whirlpools, and watched in horror as wrinkles formed on my smooth cheeks. My hair turned the color of wood ash, and my face changed. I was no longer me, but an old woman who suddenly smiled, tilted her head, then vanished.

Chapter III - April, 2004
Home is Where?

Following the fly out of the bedroom and down the hall, I stumbled on the rag rug and slid naked into the kitchen.

"Now aren't you a sight," Flyn teased from his crouched position in front of the wood stove. After closing the damper, he watched me lose my balance while struggling into my pants.

I turned away from him, feeling a flush of embarrassment color my face. "How you can find pleasure in my sagging breasts and stomach, I'll never know. I can hardly look at myself in the mirror."

"It's not the sight as much as the fact you're the woman I love and who loves me," he said coming close and tackling me around the waist.

"No more, not right now," I pleaded.

"No? Is that a promise of more?"

"Flyn, act your age!"

He surrendered and backed away. "And how old's that?"

"Fifty-five going on sixteen, for sure!"

He chuckled while forming hamburger meat into patties on the counter and watched me scramble into the rest of my clothes out of the corner of his eye.

My clothes had chilled while on the floor so I butted against the heating firebox of the cook stove. Here was my favorite perch on a winter morning with a cup of hot coffee or tea in my hands for 'butt warming' time. At the apartment, I substituted the routine with standing over the hot air grate in the floor, my robe fanning around me to capture extra heat before I dressed for work.

I eyed my other favorite warming spot on the window seat in the dinette area which faced the garden and the southeast corner of my property. Even if clouds thinly hid the sun, with my back to the window, I got my morning jolt of warmth and my caffeine fix at the same time. Now, the window was in shadow as the sun hung lower in the western sky, so I wiggled my butt against the warm metal and sighed with pleasure.

In the kitchen, the cook stove backed against the used-brick fireplace that faced into the living room. David had planned these two heating devices to share the chimney. *'Clever man,'* I thought.

I'd salvaged the cast iron and sheet metal pieces for this Waterford stove from my mom's storage shack, assuming it was an heirloom from my Scotch-Irish heritage. I'd heard many stories about Meoma, my great, great . . . or was it great to the fourth power, grandmother? One of the stories being she had cooked on this stove for the entire MacLiesh clan when they'd first settled in California's Gold Country, as well as an alleged herd of miners. No one could remember how many husbands she'd outlived by the time she died, but she'd had only one cook stove.

I had thought this was it, when I'd brought it to David for our home. After some research, David had declared it was too modern for the time in which Meoma had lived. I'd been disappointed and always wondered what kind of stove she'd used. What had she looked like? What was the real story of her life? No matter, I supposed, as I wiggled my butt next to the welcomed warmth of the wood box. Refurbished and repainted black, it not only warmed the house but boiled water, cooked soup and stews, baked bread and pies, and kept dinner at an edible heat for a latecomer in the warming ovens across the top. I loved it.

My microwave oven was used for heating summer

meals, and my propane stove for fast cooking, or canning and making jam. If I had an overage of vegetables and fruit to can, I used to set up an outside kitchen in the shade with a portable stove near the green house. It was cooler under the oak trees than inside the house; we called it natural air conditioning.

Feeling warm and cozy, I dared to walk the familiar circle around the used-brick hearth David had fashioned in front of the open fireplace, another wonderful place to stand or sit so crackling warmth could seep into one's spine.

The living room was chilly, and I gave it only a quick survey. Even though the maple furniture was recovered to match new drapes, and I'd changed the rugs on the parquet floor, David's hospital bed still appeared as a hazy hologram in my mind. My chest tightened. I breathed carefully, testing to see how my body would react to the memories in this room of his last days. When the guilt-ridden questions hovered too near, I pushed my memories with my breath until they retreated behind a thick door in my mind. Thankfully, as the span of time broadened between his death and now, those questions and pictures receded faster each time I returned to walk the circle around the fireplace and wood stove, from kitchen to living room and back again.

Today his presence seemed more like a warm image in my heart, and this cabin was no longer a prison of despair. My mind and emotions were healing. In fact, these walls felt like they were welcoming me home. *'This is a good thing,'* I thought, sidestepping a fallen piece of oak from the wood stack. By the time I'd moved to San Francisco, I'd been frantic in my need to escape.

Now, I could return for visits with growing enthusiasm, even unpack for a two-week stay without the crawly feelings of guilt and soul-shattering loneliness. I could embrace a vacation of solitude with no television, no fax, no street noise, no sirens at all hours of the night, and no clients . . . unless I wanted them. I could return to the city refreshed, ready to do what I loved to do: help people.

"I surely love this place," I said as I roamed the kitchen, touching my blue Delft plates, the knotty-pine cabinets, the wine-colored counter tiles.

"Good," Flyn said. "Then, we can . . . I think . . . let's talk about living here full time, and letting go of your offices in the Bay area." He kept his back to me as he spoke and finished cleaning the counter.

My heart lurched. "And just how long have you been thinking about this?" I flushed hot, his words spiking into my stomach as if they were flaming pokers.

He peeled an onion.

"What would we do for money?" I asked, peeved that he hadn't answered the first question.

"I bet you could phase out your work in the city and in Oakland. Have people travel to a Ukiah office. You could . . . do your psychic counseling work . . . here . . . over the cell phone." He stalled, then added quietly. "I've got other possibilities too."

"What?" I screeched. "You can't go back into construction with your back! Or maybe you think the local hunters and loggers are going to want to stretch and hold poses to Buddhist chants or soft music?" The sound of my voice hurt my ears.

Flyn had fallen from a roof fifteen years earlier and suffered a broken back that had taken years of surgery and therapy to repair. He'd developed his yoga practice to help others, and to keep himself in shape. His were traditional classes, and I knew they weren't filling as fast this year as in previous years. Even though Flyn was a good teacher, there were fewer people who wanted to practice his classic style. Competition for students had increased with many new age Yoga classes focusing on special populations, and others which incorporated personalized techniques. I realized he was tired. Since he'd moved in, he'd added my crazy schedule and commitments to his, and we hadn't had a break in our routine for over a year.

He continued to face the counter with his shoulders raised toward his ears.

"I'm sorry, Flyn. I really am." I wanted to go to him, but I was paralyzed with shock from his suggestion. "You've taken me by surprise."

He shrugged. When he didn't answer, I tried another question. "How many students did you have this week?"

"Two," he answered.

"That doesn't pay the rent for the studio, does it?" I said quietly.

"And that's due by the 30th." He turned. "I've been paying it out of my savings for the last couple months. It feels like I'm draining my reserves just to keep busy. I'd be better off developing my web design business. Maybe finish my training as a Drug and Alcohol Counselor. I know we could make it work here, Sellie."

I forced myself to stay calm, to listen to his reasoning. All I wanted to do was plaster my hands over my ears and run around the room screaming. What he was suggesting was far beyond anything I wanted to consider. I liked the way my life was scheduled. I liked living near Piedmont Avenue in downtown Oakland, sitting in a different coffee shop every Sunday, watching people stroll the street. I'd already lived in isolation. I had no desire to quit my life in the city and return to life in the back hills. A long weekend to spring clean the house and gardens was enough for me.

I wandered the circle again, talking to myself, trying to deal with Flyn's sudden suggestion. I knew that I loved this house. I was lucky to have been able to hang onto it after David had died, because he'd been lucky to find the property some thirty years ago, lucky to have dug a well that artesianed water. Adding an attic to his plans when he was designing this log house, so my children, Shawna and Sam, could have separate rooms, had made it more than suitable for our family, even though the added cost had delayed construction while we saved the money.

These forty acres with his dream house were worth a fortune, well over a half a million dollars, as it stood, with porches, a deck, and out buildings. I'd never really thought how much it was worth until a local logging company had offered to remove the old growth pine and oak for $25,000. Real estate agents had started badgering me to sell the week after David had died. In no uncertain terms, I'd refused their offers. Even when I'd put my life in storage, I knew I wanted to return eventually, but coming back was truly the farthest thing from my mind.

When I reached the kitchen for the third time in my disturbed state, Flyn suggested, "I could transfer the two students to Mark's group and only have to pay a partial month."

I stalled in front of him. "You're serious about this," I said, feeling another hot flash burn across my scalp.

He faced me and crossed his arms over his chest. "I'm not making it down there any more, in more ways than one."

"What do you mean 'not making it'?"

"The noise, the pressure, the constant people." Flyn grew so quiet, I had the feeling he'd entered a room where I wasn't welcome. When he looked at me, his eyes begged me to understand. "I'm close to some kind of edge, Sellie. It's an edge I've crossed before; it wasn't pretty. I could say I'm losing myself, I guess. I'm not proud of what . . . I . . ." He shuffled his feet. I could tell he'd been giving this a lot of thought. His body shifted again. "I could stay up here for part of the time while you did your thing in the city."

My heart sank as I realized this was his compromise. I didn't know how I would cope. I'd no idea how I could do what I did without him. Fire lapped the insides of my stomach. "Is this your way of having me do it on my own until I'm sick of it so I'll do what you want?"

He scowled. "I'm not trying to manipulate you into anything. I'm not like your first husband or even your second. I'm being straight with you. I don't want to drain our resources, and I'm done with the rat race down there." He raised his hands. "We agree that life's changing in the cities. I think it's time to consolidate. Look at what's happening in this world. Every thing's shifted since 9/11. My staying here and setting this place up for full-time living is a way to cope." He began to search through cupboards.

I opened my inner windows to read his energy and thought, *'What's making you so pushy?'* Blue light tightened around his upper torso then expanded into the kitchen. My mechanism for reading people didn't always work with my partners because my aura was intrinsically bound to theirs; I had to guess. *'Maybe he's just frustrated because his student base is gone, or, maybe, he's just venting.'*

I tried to remember if he'd ever described 'this edge' he was referring to. All I could remember were descriptions of his dealings with a step-daughter and ex-wife and the trauma of losing his son. We were both recovering alcoholics. *'Was this the kind of edge he was talking about?'*

If that were true, I knew we could deal with it. We'd dealt with so much in the two years we'd been together. *'But this was different.'* He'd never suggested such a specific plan out of the blue. Our life together usually evolved as we talked and shared, not like my first husband, Red, or David, my second, who made decisions, then expected me to go with the program. Those two had been like my father who would announce he wanted to move to a new town and expected my mother to deal with all the details and make it happen. She had never had a choice. I had never had one in either of my first two marriages. Now, I wasn't sure what my choices were. I began to sink into the quagmire of confusion about what I wanted and crushed my urge to curl up under a quilt of dull, gray batting, letting the deadening covers bring relief to my anxiety.

Through my mental dialog, I heard a sound. A cabinet door opened and banged shut. A shiver ran the length of my body, and I pushed through the haze covering my eyes to see Flyn turn toward me. His surrounding energy shifted to a clear gold. There was no hidden agenda. He was telling me his truths, I realized. My chilling wrap of fear melted, and I opened to him and listened.

"I don't want to continue to do work in the world that has no value to anyone else. I just need some time to myself. What's wrong with me being up here, doing the fix-it things we've talked about? I'm capable and self-sufficient." He continued his search through the cupboards.

I walked to the propane stove and opened the storage drawer. Five different-sized cast iron pans lived there.

"And . . ." he grinned at me, "if I hang out here long enough on my own, I might even be able to find things."

My alarm bells had stopped ringing. I stood on tippy-toes and kissed his chin, then to give myself time to think, left kitchen to wander into the garden.

The sun was just above the western horizon. Lengthening shadows from the trees edged this section of open meadow and formed hound's tooth patterns on the earth. Opening the wire gate to the garden, I was greeted by old and new weeds. Grateful I'd planted bulbs last fall, I meandered from one pot of sprouting daffodils to the barrels of blossom-laden strawberries. I thought of my two offices and the studio apartment we rented in Oakland. I thought of how lonely I would be without him, but then, I reflected, I could read during the evening rather than watch television. I felt a pang of loneliness imagining myself walking along Piedmont Avenue by myself on Sunday mornings, but I relished the thought of how I could sleep in for as long as I wanted on the mornings I didn't have clients. '*Some things need to be fully considered,*'

I thought.

From the vantage point of the garden, I could see the south-eastern corner of the house where there were no porches. Some shingles were loose on the roof. Incredibly, the logs, stacked on top of each other to form the walls, still shone with their protective coating. David had built a lovely log home. Huge pines had been felled from the land and treated to retard fungus and mold. The living room was two stories high and an slim overlooking balcony holding a small bathroom that separated the two upstairs bedrooms. I faced the outside of our downstairs bedroom where, during winter months, sun streamed onto the bed. I loved to read or nap there during an early winter afternoon.

So many memories here! I smiled when I remembered how the kids, even as teenagers, would chase each other around the freestanding fireplace and wood stove between the living room and the kitchen. Now the grandkids did it. Could I live here again with a different man, a very different human being? Would old memories take me over and interfere? How could I ever erase the memory of David dying in the living room? I hugged myself.

In the garden, the hardiest of weeds, the dandelions, were already producing brilliant yellow flowers. Too bad they turned into such prolific seeds. I remembered mindlessly blowing their feathered heads all over the grass as a kid. I never understood my parent's anger until I'd had to wage my own battle against them. It was always the case between my childhood dreams and adult realities. Even my adult dreams had met with complications. Like the dandelion whimsy of floating seeds, I'd found my ideas, when planted in my everyday life, would blossom into challenges far beyond my original flight of fancy.

Is that what could happen to Flyn's idea? It seemed simple now. What difficulties would he be creating for himself, for us? And what was really my problem about his dream of living here? "The only way I can come back is if it's my dream too," I said to myself.

There was a chance we could make it financially. I knew Flyn had other ways of making money, especially if he finished his counselor courses through Mendocino Junior College. I could let go of my San Francisco office and concentrate on my Oakland clients. That office was closer to Kaiser hospital, from where I received more referrals than I ever did from UC San Francisco Medical Center. I could find an office and begin building a practice in Ukiah.

The cell phone must've rung, because Flyn yelled from the back door and stood with it in his hand. "For you," he hollered. I wished he'd just let it ring over to voice mail. Wiping muddy fingers on clumps of wet grass, I arrived at the back steps. Flyn mouthed the words, "I love you," as he handed it to me. I smiled.

"Hello, this is Selena." I said then heard a raspy breath at the other end of the line. Ice chips prickled around my navel.

"I've been . . . reach you," the voice said. I couldn't tell if it was a man or a woman. When the voice stopped, I heard shallow breathing.

"This is a weak connection," I said as charmingly as possible. The sense of being in a dank swamp permeated my nose. "You may have to repeat yourself." I heard a sound that might have been a laugh, but was more like a groan.

The breathless voice said, "I hope . . . . you can come . . . see me?" and ended on a high note, as if it were more a question than a statement.

"Well, that depends," I said sincerely. "Can you tell me your name and where you are?"

"In Eureka," it said.

"California, I hope,"

"Yeah."

"What can I do for you?" I asked, the swampy feeling

making me sick to my stomach.

"I can't . . . talk much."

"I can hear that you're having trouble breathing. I'm wondering if you can write me to say what you think I can do for you, or is there someone there who can talk for you?" I had a flashing insight that another person might be nearby and that I was talking to an impervious membrane behind which many things were hidden.

"No one here. Can you . . . come?"

Sighing deeply, I looked at the beauty of my garden in the fading light of the spring sun. A back-drop of peach-flavored clouds silhouetted the trees that edged our land. I didn't want to leave my home, so soon after arriving. I'd been hoping for a lazy morning in bed over coffee, more time to ponder Flyn's proposal and my various reactions to it.

I also knew that when the gifts of second sight and healing hands had come to me, I'd promised to go wherever I was needed. This was one of those cases that arrived every few years to make me feel I'd made a mistake with that promise. I reminded my heart that it always worked out for the best. Challenges like this came at a time when I needed to learn something or when I needed to consider change. That was one of the many things I'd learned with Estelle in the four years we'd worked the Ouija Board. Nothing occurred without a reason. To participate in events and to open ourselves to new people brought us gifts of insight and healing and an understanding of ourselves, far and above what we could have dreamed.

'Here's a new challenge,' I told myself, trying to put this person's request into perspective. I took a deep breath and hoped whatever this was about would fit into the scheme of my life.

"I can come, but not until Sunday. We'll be through Eureka on our way to an afternoon wedding in McKinleyville, so I could see you in the late morning. Would that be alright?"

The voice softened. "When you . . . get . . . to the Mall . . . call. I'm . . . not too far."

"Can I know your name?" I asked, hoping to get an idea of gender.

"Potty."

'*Well, that certainly didn't help,*' I thought.

"I'm . . . nicknamed . . . Potty." The voice gave me a phone number. All I could tell was that I was talking to someone who was very, very ill.

Chapter IV - April, 2004
Estelle's Passion

"I need a favor," Estelle stated as we stood on the rim of the Medicine Wheel she'd permanently created in the meadow behind her home. Each quarter of this twenty-four-foot-wide circle was colored with different painted stones. One section was red, the next black, the third yellow, and the last white. I couldn't help but feel it was ostentatious, too much like a declaration of Estelle's own involvement in a learned set of teachings, rather than a tribute to the Sacred Hoop of Native American peoples. It was the same with her recent blackening of her silver blond hair and her wearing it in braids down her chest. Too much. But Estelle was Estelle. During our twenty-plus year relationship, I'd come to realize she needed big gestures to help her feel the essence of whatever she was currently studying.

"Sure," I responded.

Estelle hesitated.

'*Uh, oh!*' I worried. '*Did I answer too fast?*' I thought I heard Estelle talking, but I couldn't hear her over the roar of the air that was charged with glistening particles; a jet stream of bright dust rotated around me. I became its core, stranded and isolated in its swirling center of debris. Surrounded by a tempest of sound and wind, time warped. Seconds stretched like rubber until it seemed as if I'd been staring at the colored medicine wheel for half the day. I was afraid to move as particles passed higher and higher over my head. I grew dizzy. I knew my feet were firmly planted, yet I stumbled and fell sideways to the ground. The spell broke.

"Well, I didn't think my request was that

overpowering," Estelle said, sounding annoyed.

"I can't say whether it was or not, Estelle," I sat on the earth. "I feel sick; I didn't hear a word you said."

"I can't believe this!!" Estelle said, apparently more than just a little irritated as she hauled me onto my feet. I settled on a nearby oak stump, one of a cluster grouped outside the Sacred Wheel. Small talking groups could be accommodated here during experiential seminars on the Medicine Wheel, which Estelle offered. Students would stay for a weekend or an overnight, camping in the meadow.

I collected my thoughts to explain what had happened. "It was like I was standing in the middle of a tornado. I mean . . . the wind . . . was so loud . . . it drowned your voice."

Estelle gave me her squinty look that said she wasn't sure she believed me. She shrugged and sat beside me, rubbing her hand across my shoulder blades while she stared into the distance. I had to wonder, with her attention someplace other than me, whether she was looking into what had happened, or into a place I couldn't see?

Where ever she was, I was having a hard time returning to my body; I wasn't feeling secure in my mind either. A shiver stalked the nerve endings of my spine, and I tried deep breathing to put myself back together, to bring my attention into the present, but I couldn't catch my breath. Needle points of pain stung my skin.

"Did you hear *anything*?" Estelle dropped her hand from my back. There was pleading in her voice.

I focused on my concern for my friend. "What is it, Estelle? I've never seen you so disturbed."

"It's just . . . it took me . . . a long time to figure how to explain everything, and now I've got to do it all over again."

"Practice makes perfect?" I offered as a joke to break our tension. Touching her arm helped me clear my head and stop the prickles of pain dancing along my skin. "I'm sorry," I offered, when I saw a tear roll down her cheek. "Please . . . go on."

"I've met a man," she said simply.

"O . . . K . . . ," I said slowly, wondering why this was such an important piece of news. Estelle was always meeting men. Each one held her attention until the fascination wore off, but each remained in a special place of her heart, during and after her time with them.

"Now, don't be a prude," she said matter-of-factly.

"I . . ."

"Yes, you are. I can tell by your face. I know I'm in a relationship with Dwayne, and Eduardo is in relationship to his work. This is beyond anything I've ever felt before."

"O . . . K . . . ," I saw more tears pooling. Surrendering my judgment, I wrapped my arm around her shoulders. "I'm listening."

"You know when I went to that retreat outside of Sedona last month?" She dropped her gaze to her hands which were fumbling with something in her lap. "That was the 'Stalking Your Past' with that woman follower of Don Miguel Ruiz, the guy who wrote 'The Four Agreements'?"

I nodded.

"Well, I never attended any of the sessions," she admitted. "I met Eduardo when I checked in. He never left my side. It was as if we were meant to meet, and I've never really felt like this before. Oh, Sellie, it's the most wondrous thing. We never even made love."

"Well, that's a first," slipped out before I could stop myself. I leaned into her and chuckled to make sure she knew I was teasing her.

"I know. I'm shocked too." Her tears gave way to a slight smile.

"We talked and talked . . . and walked and . . . rode horses all through the canyons. I met his mother and sister at the old ranch where they were staying. I cooked for him and washed his clothes, by hand."

Alarm bells rang. I knew Estelle hated washing clothes, even in the washing machine. I tried another jab at humor: "Did you iron his shirts too?"

With an almost a dreamlike quality to her voice, she admitted, "You bet I did!"

"Uh, what's the deal here? Estelle? Who's this guy? Did he hypnotize you? Or what?"

"I felt such peace, until . . . ," she took a quick, deep breath, " . . . until I had to come home."

The silence deepened. Her tears overflowed their banks, descending along her cheeks into her lap. All I could do was hold her as she gathered her breath.

"He begged me to stay. I changed my ticket home twice, but I couldn't do it a third time. I'd run out of excuses to Dwayne, and Heather was ready to pop with my first grand baby." She finished with a sob, "I've never felt so torn."

'Oh, shit,' I thought. *'Now she's going to tell me Eduardo's her soul-mate.'*

"It's deeper than being soul-mates."

I groaned. She gave me a darting look. "It's more like we were the same person. What I did for him was like I was doing it for myself in the most loving way I've ever experienced."

My shoulders sagged under the weight of my cynicism about new age terms. Yet, I didn't have a whole lot I could say. After all, I was living with Flyn, who was five years my junior, because we'd had this uncontrollable urge to be next to each other. Was it destiny? Karma? Being 'soul mates'? Or just hormones? I'd no idea if there was something to any of it, or all of it. I wasn't qualified to cast doubt on her experience, nor was I in a position to believe her interpretation either. All I could say was that because of my work with people from all walks of life over the past twenty years, I was beginning to understand there were different kinds of connections that occurred between individuals. Whether it was some kind of past life connection, I couldn't say. Something intertwined our existence with those who walk with us as our parents, our children, our partners, or even brief walk-ins. All I could do was hear her story, acknowledge her feelings, and encourage her to get to the point.

"We made agreements." She brushed at her cheeks trying to stop escaping tears from trickling to her chin. "And that's the part I need you for."

Shaking my head, I sighed and wondered what on earth she was getting me into this time. "Wait," I begged. "Before you tell me . . . I have to know . . . who is this guy? What's he do?"

Estelle turned on her stump so we could be face to face. She focused deeply into my eyes. "He's a Shaman, Selena, a healer, a visionary. He sees the coming world events, and he teaches about things we need to learn so human kind can survive. He's committed to his work and his family, and he's vowed never to have children of his own. That's why he doesn't cross the line into sexual activity, but, oh, my God, he oozes sensuality. He's so full of life, not of himself but of the Earth, the Moon, and the Stars. It's no wonder he has to keep the location of his home a secret. If I was so smitten that I wanted to do anything for him without question, think of the thousands of other women he must have touched in the same way, just by walking across the street!" She stopped to catch her breath.

"And it's not just women. Men follow him too. He has people trying to get at him all the time who are happy just to sit at his feet." Her hand swept the air at ground level to punctuate her words. "That's why he's having to return with his family to Mexico. He can't stay in Sedona or in the States. People are like eating him alive here, so . . . I . . . I won't . . . be able to see him unless . . . I go to Mexico." A ragged sigh punctuated her words. "I am the only one, besides his mother, he's ever allowed to touch his clothes since he became a

visionary man. I mean . . . I bathed him, Selena. And . . . then
. . . he bathed me. It was better than any sex I've ever had, but
. . . the time we spent together . . . may be all we'll ever have."

I waited and watched as her tears increased.

"I had to leave him, and he," her voice caught on a sob,
"was as crushed as I was."

I held her close. Her sorrow shook my heart. After a
time, I released her and she washed her face with her hands and
her tears.

I was in a total quandary. "I'm afraid . . . I don't
understand what part you want me to play in your agreements."

She answered in a rushed voice, "You're a Shaman
yourself. You do ceremony."

I was startled. I rephrased her statement. "I create
personal growth rituals to assist people in their healing. I'm
not a Shaman."

"You make ritualistic bundles," she said breathlessly.

I shook my head again and closed my eyes to the
intensity in hers. "I help people create meaningful tools for
releasing or bringing in energy."

"Damn it, Selena. You have to help me."

"Damn it, Estelle," I opened my eyes, my entire being
frozen with quick anger. "I don't have to do anything . . .
especially when you don't tell me what you want me to do! I
feel you're boxing me into a corner, so I'll feel destined to do
something before I know what it is."

Estelle grabbed my wrists. "I want you to put together
the personal objects I've gathered, to make a kind of ritualistic
object that will bind Eduardo and me together for always."

I tried to twist out of her grip. "I don't know anything
about what you're asking."

She held on tight "You've helped people create
personal objects that they've used in ritual." She parroted my
words back at me.

"I told you. I help clients do it for themselves." I flung her hands away.

"Then help me bind our spirits so Eduardo and I can be together for all eternity." She dropped her head, fingering items in her lap.

"Estelle, why do this? It's going against the natural world. And he isn't here to participate. It's like binding yourself to him without his consent."

"But I do have his consent." She lifted a hand to reach for me but stopped before she touched me. "Or rather, I have things from his person."

I was shocked. "Does he know you have these things?" I watched her face as she lifted her chin in typical, stubborn Estelle fashion, which let me know she was on the verge of truth.

"He gave some of them to me."

"Some? What'd he give you?" Now I tried to see into her eyes, but she eluded me.

"Hair from the mane of his favorite horse, pebbles he received from his spirit guide which he's kept in his medicine pouch. He even gave me one half of the dried butterfly wing he uses on his altar." By the way she stared over my shoulder, I knew there were more items. "He and I prayed together that last evening, and he gave me these things from his bundle."

"Go on."

"He told me . . . that I would . . . I was to share in his destiny if I kept them with me."

I wanted to shake Estelle until her teeth rattled, but I kept my hands to myself. "There's a hell of a lot of difference between sharing a destiny and being bonded for eternity."

"I'm serious, Sellie."

"And I'm serious when I say I don't know anything about this kind of thing. I carry a medicine bundle holding special tokens I've received when something important has happened to me. I'm aware of the ceremony around carrying and releasing a Spirit Bundle when someone dies. I've been taught some lessons around creating and protecting a woman's bundle, and I've started to become aware of predictions around the need to collect items to create an Earth Bundle. These are all for personal or universal purposes, but I've never really heard of a . . . what can I call it . . . a marriage bundle."

"But it could be done?" Estelle asked hopefully. I scanned my memory for any references to something like this, but all I could remember were marriage ceremonies where a couple pledged their love and made life-long commitments to live honorably with each other. I'd witnessed one Native American wedding where the families stood behind the bride and groom and participated in the tying, exchanging, and retying of eagle feathers. The couple and their relatives had been blessed with the smoke of a sacred peace pipe. The wedding pair had shown their intent to step forward in their lives together by walking under one blanket.

I shook my head. "I wouldn't know where to begin," I admitted. "It would be like you were bringing together your essences or spirits into one." I stood abruptly as a strange dizziness attacked me. I turned to her, "And I don't think it's a good idea in the first place. You've a partner and a life here. He has family and commitments there. Why would you want to do this?"

"So we could be together for all eternity," she repeated.

"Or until the next man comes along, you mean."

"That's cruel," she said, her eyes blazing.

"That's the real truth," I said, defending myself from her glare.

She softened her face. "How can I convince you?" She lifted two leather pouches hanging from one thong from her lap.

"What are those?" I asked, suddenly feeling hairs raising on my neck.

"Items from our bodies and our lives to go into the bundle."

"What did you collect from him, Estelle, that he doesn't know you have?"

"It's not your business."

"You would have me do this blindly, with no idea what you've collected for this bundle of yours?" I snorted. "That's bullshit, Estelle! "

She stood, ready to stomp toward her house. I grabbed her arm, spinning her to face me so I could give her an ultimatum. "Then tell Dwayne to move out. Pack your bags, move to Mexico, and go take care of Eduardo for the rest of your natural life. Devote yourself to him."

"I can't, Sellie," she pleaded in a whisper. "I can't take him my debts; I can't leave my mother, my daughter, and grandchild. Even Eduardo's mother told me my place was here. She gave me her blessing and said I was the only woman her son had ever loved. She saw it. Why can't you?"

I released her. I waited for my pounding heart to grow still and my breathing to quiet. "I hear what you think your intent is, Estelle. I just don't think you've considered the ramifications of this act. I don't know that much about it, but I can guess the making of this kind of bundle creates an energetic bonding. It sounds so simple, but it's not. For the positive commitment it makes, there's an unknown dark side. You can create a focus for yourself, but I've no idea what happens when you create a focus for someone who doesn't know it's happening."

"This whole thing has to be done consciously so you can be sure no other elements are bonded with the ones you've brought together. You have to do more than pass each item through purifying smoke. You have to look at the energy around each piece so you're sure there's no spirit attachment or other negativity brought into the bond. Please! Think this through, Estelle."

She plopped onto the stump. With the leather pouches in her palms, she brought her hands and face together with a kind of reverence I never imagined Estelle could hold. It was as if she were paying homage to this man, something I'd never seen her offer to anyone before this moment. I watched as she rocked. Her shoulders shook with silent sobs.

A crushing energy pressed against my heart and my lungs. My eyesight darkened and blurred until I saw a light surrounding her, more than her own aura, more than the layers of her energy fields. As I separated from my body . . .

I am entranced . . .

An overlay of light enfolds her then coalesces into a sword of pale green light with a fire ball on its point. It strikes toward me. A warning clangs in my head, too late for me to shield myself from being penetrated through the protective veil around me. I am punched in the face and fall backwards, landing on my butt. In slow motion, my head hits solid earth.

A flood of warm water moves through me, investigates every crack and crevice of my body, and I feel heavy enough to sink into the ground that transforms into a consistency that is both soft and moist. Mud inches over my arms and legs, around my neck, licks my mouth, then closes around my nose.

Suddenly the glowering face of Amach materializes in front of me. Her gray hair is in disarray, her mouth forming words I can't hear. She shakes her fist at me but I grin, pleased to see her after all these years. She points her finger at me and a heaviness sits on my chest; I can't breathe. Pain sears the middle of my forehead. I get it. This isn't a friendly visit. She is warning me.

I force myself to close my mind and lock my energy centers, as a black oozing presence surrounds me. I fight against the malaise seeping into my muscles and bones, to lift my head so I can open my mouth . . .

I screamed myself awake.

Estelle was at my side. "What happened?" Her eyes were wide as she wiped blood from my nose.

I could only tremble, then turn aside to vomit.

Chapter V - 1985
Amach's First Contact

I stood unsettled in a corner of Estelle's kitchen as we waited for the others. We'd been working her Ouija Board for over a year now. At first, we'd been true to our original commitment, but we soon found we couldn't keep to our schedule of weekly meetings. Between family and work responsibilities, we'd fallen behind in transcribing the lengthy recordings of our sittings; seven days between sessions hadn't been long enough. We tried every other week as a first compromise, until Estelle had become involved with another man, named Infinity, or maybe it was Eternity.

Estelle straightened her sleeves and pushed her streaked hair behind her ears. She'd been frosting it every other week with different tones of blond or brown, since she'd experimented with a permanent that left her with what had resembled a frizzled mop on her head. The supposedly mild solution had singed irregular clumps of hair so badly, they'd looked thin enough to disintegrate in a mild breeze; other strands had remained straight as steel rods. Because she was always changing hair, I thought it was about time she had a hair failure. I realized my attitude was due to an extreme case of sour grapes, because, well . . . I wished I had her nerve, but since I didn't, it followed that, if I couldn't try something different, she could experience a wee bit of a disaster every once in a while.

At least I didn't want to change my male relationships as often as she did. I'd stick with the one I had, thank you. Her men rotated through her bed and her life as often as her hair color changed, or so it seemed to me. If she met one she thought suited her better, the one in her arms was shown the door. Most went willingly, grateful for their time with her. Others, like Roger, created nothing but drama and trauma during their removal from her life and home. Changing from Roger to "blankety-blank", whose name I never intended to remember since I hadn't liked him, had pre-empted our time together, and it almost ruined our friendship. I couldn't imagine why she'd adored 'what's his name', so I'd tried to make her see reason. I'd liked Roger, so had listed his virtues. She hadn't wanted anything to do with my list. She'd thrown a fit and locked herself in her bathroom until I'd left.

In the face of losing her in my life, I'd decided to remove my nose from her business. Then, within three months, she'd discovered the new guy was a liar and a cheat. So we'd postponed our sessions until she was free of him, and I'd worked hard to keep myself from telling her, "I told you so."

As we set out cups for tea and cookies, I tried to remember if there had been one or two others between that jerk and her current partner, Bobby. We were both grateful this one was at least employed and responsible, if not a little dull, and with just a tinge of a red-neck.

The break from the intensity of our sessions had suited me. I was trying to make changes in my own life: from my full-time, rotating shifts at the local hospital to employment that was part-time and on-call, while building my massage practice in Willits. David and I were finishing the plans and preliminary county building applications for our log house, as fast as two people could attend all the mandatory meetings. I wanted to start sawing and hammering and painting. I wanted out of the twenty-five-year-old, un-insulated trailer we'd been living in since we'd married in 1979; our blended family was bursting at its seams. I'd brought the two teenagers. David had brought two dogs, four cats, and a garden.

For the past two months, I'd been feeling the lack of

our weekly connection with spirits through the Ouija board; Estelle and I'd become an awesome team. We'd gained personal and professional insights with the help of Amaman, our main spirit teacher. I was, however, relieved that our erratic lives had postponed her psychic group experiment. In fact, I'd been hoping she'd forgotten it. But, Estelle never forgot anything. Unlike me, she never procrastinated. She pursued her plans with full force. Nothing could resist her determination when she wanted something. And, today was the day.

As the others slowly arrived, I wondered if they'd been hounded as doggedly as I had. I'd arrived for this event mentally kicking and screaming. Acid bit the lining of my stomach as it churned, and my skin felt bruised from Estelle's badgering.

I found myself shy, unsuccessfully keeping busy so I wouldn't gawk at the other members of our foursome. I was dressed in elastic-waisted, polyester pants and a print shirt. The outfit could only be considered 'straight' when compared to what the others were wearing. I would have blended perfectly at Mervin's or Penney's; I stood out like a sore thumb here in Estelle's tie-dyed living room.

That wasn't the only problem. Estelle had dropped a bombshell with the announcement she and I were going to work the Ouija Board before we began our group work. Without asking if I thought it was a good idea, she'd decided she wanted assistance from Amaman, our primary spirit helper. While Crystal and Gunthar were getting comfortable on pillows on the floor, I stood rigidly in the middle of the room. I was suspicious of Estelle's intentions. I wouldn't put it past her to want to create some kind of drama, and I was in no hurry to sit at the table and be a spectacle. I had come to be part of a circle, not part of a performance.

Estelle pleaded with me under her breath. "I'm sorry I didn't call to tell you. This just came over me this morning. I kept getting this urgent feeling all day yesterday that we're supposed to ask for help before we start doing any group experimenting."

My brain picked up her words: "I didn't tell you" rather than "ask you." She'd done it again. My heart sank. She'd maneuvered me into a position where I'd be a goon if I refused to work the board with her. I didn't like being put on the spot. Besides, we'd never worked the board with others present; I didn't know what would happen.

Estelle nodded toward the pillow next to her, directing me to settle there. All I could do was make a face and comply.

"Let's introduce ourselves," Estelle suggested so brightly I wanted to crown her. "I know all of you, but you don't know each other. A little shared information will help us bond." Estelle beamed. "Names and goals would be good, I think."

I had no desire to start the introductions. Thank God, the young woman across from me volunteered. Dressed in filmy harem pants and a gauze shirt, she was slight of build and seemed to be hiding under golden brown curls that cascaded around her face, down her chest and back to her waist. If my hair had been that thick and curly, I think I might have wanted to live inside it too.

"I'm Crystal," she announced as her nose pointed outside her waterfall of hair. "I want to earn my living as a song writer/performer, but I'm presently waiting tables at Tsunami. I believe our highest purpose is to heal our planet and all who dwell here. I pray my songs can make a difference somehow." Her voice drifted inward, then returned. "I use my hands and voice to do massage and toning, to heal vibrational imbalances."

I shifted on my pillow, ready to speak, when the angular man to my left lifted his palms, highlighting his words with fingers that floated in the air. "I'm known as Gunthar," he said through thick gray-blond hair and a beard that hid his chest. His piercing blue eyes twinkled with mischief as he saw my eyes take in his bleached hemp clothes and get caught on the details of his thickened penis, outlined through the thin material of his crotch. I blushed. His eyes grew merrier. He wasn't wearing underwear, and I planted my attention firmly on his mustache.

"I'm an environmental activist and artist." He breathed deeply. "I'm trying my best to help others through use of my psychic abilities." Another deep breath. "I do personal readings to facilitate perceptual changes in people's awareness of their relationship to the world around them." His gaunt arms settled into his lap as he rested his hands, palms up, on his knees.

'*Shit!*' I thought, '*I don't want him reading my mind right now!*' before I introduced myself. "I'm Selena. I've been working as a massage therapist for the past five years, learning all I can about healing myself and others. Estelle and I've been searching for help through classes and personal work. The Ouija Board has been an experiment to receive an overview of information. I'm not sure what she's got in mind for us today, but it will be interesting." I grimaced as I passed the introduction torch.

"Now Sellie, don't be a spoiled sport," she chided, patting her skirt on her lap. "I'm Estelle. I do a personal style of bodywork that works to effect a balance between my clients and their world." She thought for a moment. "I think that says what I'm about." Then she cocked her head and added, "I also believe we're meant to do be doing some kind of work together."

An uncomfortable silence stretched between us.

"Let's all hold hands and take deep breaths," Estelle suggested. "I know we've had experience in building energy and creating sacred space as a working environment, and that's what I think we should do now. Let's start by aligning our breaths. Agreed?"

I watched as Estelle closed her eyes and an edge of a smile lifted her lips. She seemed to be zipping us along toward some kind of picture she was holding in her mind, and I quickly inserted a prayer for protection, wondering if the others were offering theirs. A growing lump of exasperation sat in my gut, and all I could do was hope we shared comparable intentions.

I shook my head and closed my eyes. I pushed out a breath with the realization, I was in it now, whether I wanted to be or not! I offered my sweaty palms to Estelle and Gunthar as we moved closer and waited for Crystal to join our hands and complete the circle. Hearing them start their deep breathing, I couldn't help but feel I was a pretender in the circle, an outsider with no business trying to be psychic. As they continued inhaling and exhaling together, I concentrated on the air as it passed the edges of my nostrils. Seconds must've turned into minutes, while I lost track of time and settled into the rhythm of our breaths. My strangeness departed. Time held itself without borders until I felt I could no longer float within it.

I opened my eyes to discover others were coming awake at the same time. A tingle climbed from my neck to my scalp.

As if on cue, Estelle and I lifted from our pillows and took our seats at the Ouija Board table. She began with her usual sing-song declarations and request. "Is there any message needing to come through?" The planchette seemed frozen in place underneath our fingers. "Is there a teacher who wishes to offer messages to us either personally or around the work we're going to do here today?" The room was silent until Estelle whispered, "I just felt someone give me a shove."

She continued louder. "If you're here, please come through now."

The back door banged open then shut. We jumped. A great wind gusted through the house then disappeared. The planchette began to wander across the board.

"Please identify yourself!" Estelle commanded.

The planchette hesitated, then spelled A T A B

I asked, feeling quite shaken with the events, "Is Atab your name?"

Y E S

"Are you connected to anyone here?"

Y E S

"Who are you connected to?"

A L L O F Y O U

Estelle interrupted my train of questions, "Did you open and close the back door?"

Y E S

She continued, "I'm curious, was it you who gave me the constant message to work the board today?"

Y E S

"What would you like to say to us today?"

B E W I T H M E A N D W E W I L L E X P L O R E T H E R E A L M S O F P O S S I B I L I T I E S

I interrupted and asked, "Who are you to us?"

I A M T H A T P A R T I C L E O F Y O U T H A T S P A R K S A L I V E W H E N Y O U U N I T E

The planchette arched between the edges of the letters printed on the board, and Estelle attempted to put them into words as I called out each letter.

A R E Y O U R E A D Y T O E X P E R I E N C E T H E U N I O N O F Y O U R S E L V E S F O R T H E H I G H E S T G O O D

"Are we ready?" Estelle asked us.

We answered with a unanimous "YES".

T H E N I T I S T I M E F O R Y O U T O L E A R N T O F O C U S Y O U R M I N D S H E A R T S A N D S P I R I T S

O N O N E T H O U G H T I T W I L L
M O V E M O U N T A I N S O R R E M O V E
M O L E S.

We laughed at the unexpected phraseology after I'd composed the letters into words. I had to be sure I understood and asked, "You mean the kind of moles that grow on the skin?"

Y E S

Crystal giggled, "Oh, come on! This can't be happening! You two are making this up. It's more like we're getting messages from a comedian, not a spirit entity."

We looked at each other and shook our heads. "Crystal, we aren't doing anything but letting our hands follow the movement of this wooden pointer. We've had all kinds of exchanges with entities on the other side," Estelle said as she shifted in her chair. "Don't put spirits into just a 'serious' category." Then she closed her eyes and continued to interview Atab. "Are you a male energy?"

Y E S

"A female energy?"

Y E S

"What is it that our group should do in this moment?"

S I T I N M E D I T A T I O N T O
G A T H E R Y O U R F O C U S T H E N
O P E N Y O U R T H I R D E Y E S O Y O U
C A N S E E T H E S I G H T S

Gunthar asked, lounging on the floor pillows, "You mean we'll see something together?"

Y E S

"I wonder . . . " Estelle began, then continued, "Will it be part of our healing work?"

N O

The planchette wavered between letters as if this spirit was gathering its thoughts.

B E G I N B Y A L L O W I N G

COMMUNITY TO BUILD
BETWEEN YOU

"But I thought we already did that," Estelle said as an aside to the group.

YOU HAVE CIRCLED THE
ENERGY

THERE IS MORE TO SEE
BEFORE YOU PRACTICE FOCUS
ING THE SAME COLOR TO A
POINT IN THE CENTER OF YOUR
CIRCLE

THIS IS A HEALING TOOL
WHEN DIRECTED ON CENTERS
OF THE BODY

"Are we to concentrate on someone special?" Gunthar's voice was so close to my knee. I jumped. I glared at him to move away, but he was too enraptured with the conversation to pay attention to my scowl. Then I was drawn to the movement of our hands.

NOT YET

Estelle took the next set of questions out of my mouth. "So you want us to make a circle, open our third eye, and focus on a particular color together. We are to do this all at the same time. How are we to pick a color? Do you mean for us to focus on our own centers?"

The planchette went straight to NO then . . .

PLACE A PIECE OF PAPER
IN THE CENTER OF THE CIRCLE
AT FIRST IN EACH OF YOUR
MINDS CHANGE THE WHITE TO
A SELECTED COLOR THEN
REMOVE THE PAPER TO FOCUS
A COLOR THERE

I was confused, so I said, "Please clarify."

THERE WILL COME A TIME

W H E N   T H I S   C A N   B E   D O N E   I N
A   C R O W D   Y O U   W I L L   B E   A B L E
T O   D O   I T   A T   T H E   S A M E   T I M E   I T
C A N   B E   D O N E   I N   A N   I N S T A N T
A F T E R   Y O U   H A V E   P R A C T I C E D

Crystal asked, "This is part of our preparations, isn't it Atab? All this is to prepare us for what's to happen on our earth?"

The planchette immediately swung to YES.

T H E R E   A R E   O T H E R   G R O U P S
F O R M I N G

Estelle asked, "Will there come a time when we can contact these other groups?"

A F T E R   Y O U   H A V E
L E A R N E D   T H E   D I S C I P L I N E

A L S O   T H E R E   A R E   P E O P L E
W H O   W O U L D   C O M E   T O   H U R T
Y O U R   I N T E N T

B E   A W A R E   T H E R E   I S   N E E D
F O R   S E C R E C Y

Estelle was startled and turned to me with a question in her eyes. "Wasn't there some earlier work we did with our spirit guides where we were told certain negative entities would try and manipulate us and gain power for themselves on our earth?" When I shrugged my shoulders in confusion, she asked the board, "Do you refer to these?"

I N   A   W A Y   B U T   I   S P E A K   O F
T H O S E   W H O   W O U L D   L I K E   T O
I N V E S T I G A T E   T H I S   P R A C T I C E
F O R   T H E I R   O W N   P U R P O S E S

"So we've got to be careful who we tell about all this?" Crystal asked.

A T   N O   P R I C E   S H O U L D   Y O U
A L L O W   Y O U R S E L V E S   T O   B E   E X
P L O I T E D

I couldn't help ask, "Is there any specific way we need to protect ourselves?"

NO YOU MUST MAINTAIN PROTECTION ESPECIALLY IN THIS ENDEAVOR

Gunthar asked from my knee, "What is the motivating energy behind this exploitation?"

The planchette remained unmoved for what seemed like many minutes.

"It feels like we're done," Estelle announced quietly.

"NO!" Gunthar stood beside the table glaring at the board. "What is the motivating energy behind these exploiting entities?" The planchette shivered awake.

MANIPULATION OF YOUR POWER FOR THE WRONG CONCERNS

I asked, "And we can trust each other here?"

YES

The planchette swung away then returned to the YES

YOU ARE CLEANSING AND MAKING READY FOR THE GOOD OF MORE THAN YOURSELVES THERE IS ONE MORE

"What do you mean, 'there is one more'?" I asked.

SOMEONE HERE STANDS AS TWO

"What does that mean?" Estelle demanded..

ONE OF YOU HAS LINKED SELF WITH GREATER SOURCE

"Who has?"

YOU WILL KNOW WHEN ALL IS READY

Estelle and I stared at each other. I'd no idea what to ask next. A strange mixture of anxiety and excitement filled me, and with no desire to experience more, I removed my fingers. Estelle's sharp shake of her head made me return them to the edge of the wood.

"Do you have any more to say to us at this time?" she asked.

A L L   O F   Y O U   A R E   C H O S E N B Y   Y O U R   I N T E N T   A N D   Y O U R H O N O R   A N D   Y O U R   W I L L I N G N E S S   T O   P U R G E   Y O U R S E L V E S   O F Y O U R   N E G A T I V I T I E S

A shock wave of chills crawled up my spine as I finished interpreting the letters. I wanted nothing more to do with this connection and pulled my hands from the table, trying not to bolt from the room. I didn't just want to run to the bathroom, I wanted to escape out the back door and into my car. But my body would not respond. Instead I found myself in the kitchen, getting a glass for a drink of water. I placed my hands under the flowing faucet, first palms up then palms down. My agitation lessened. I took a deep breath, turned off the faucet, and returned to the circle.

All four of us had retreated; no one was in the room. Gunthar reappeared from the bathroom, air-drying his hands. Crystal was staring at herself in the mirror, her hair now framing her face rather than covering it. Estelle stood like a statue on her front porch, her cat in her arms. She returned when Gunthar invited, "Guess we'd better practice. Someone get a piece of paper."

"But wasn't there something we were supposed to do before we focused on the center of our circle?" I asked.

"Something about building community and seeing the sights," Crystal offered.

Estelle plopped onto her pillow with a sigh. "Guess we'd better follow instructions."

On our pillows, we decided to breathe at the same tempo. Gunthar began counting, "In . . . one, two, three, four. Out . . . one, two, three, four." When we were breathing together in rhythm, he quieted.

My muscles became limp to the point of melted butter, and I felt as if I was falling. I brought my attention into my third eye and enjoyed the swirling colors until they cleared. I saw myself sitting in a similar fashion with three other women. We were dressed in black habits that billowed around us on a black and white tiled floor. To my left was a woman with a wizened face, encircled by a dirt-spattered wimple. Her cheeks sagged with wrinkles, and her chin folded several times under her neck. Across from me sat a younger woman, her black hair in disarray; her eyes glassy. To my right, a middle-aged woman held herself with a straight spine and was forcing deep breaths into her abdomen. We were in a small room with whitewashed walls that rose toward an angled ceiling above us. Distant sounds of clashing steel crept closer. Pounding feet ran from the end of a long hall toward us. Other feet followed. I held my focus for as long as I could until pain seared through the back of my head. I gasped and released my hands from Gunthar and Estelle with a shake, then held my head.

Groaning erupted around me.

"That was frightening!" Crystal said.

"What happened to us?" Estelle cried.

"I don't know what happened to you," I reported, "but I think I was hit in the back of the head while I was sitting in a circle with three other women."

Gunthar shook his hair and beard, bringing himself into the present, but keeping his eyes closed. "I could see a clay floor where I saw the four of us, formed in a circle. We were . . . wearing brown robes with hoods. A young boy in a long tunic charged into the room to . . . to warn us, I think. We scattered." Gunthar's face took on an expression akin to rapture. "Before we moved, though, I smashed some kind of statue that had been in the center of our sitting circle. The statue fell into four parts, and we each collected a piece before we ran."

He opened his eyes. "The last I remember was a man with a scythe-like sword running at me from around a corner as we fled."

Estelle was rocking herself with her eyes closed. I hugged myself watching a movie of emotions play across Crystal's face.

"I can't say if I was a man or a woman," Crystal spoke as if she was still in a trance, "but I was with three others too." She sighed and raised her eyebrows, then lowered them. "We were wearing skins and had long hair in braids. We weren't Native American; more like we were from Sweden or Norway." Crystal squinted her eyelids as if trying to remember every detail of her vision. "We were in a hut made of straw and mud. It was burning around us. The roof was falling in. I could feel the heat!" She returned to us with a shiver.

In unison, we turned our attention on Estelle who was pale and holding herself tightly. "I don't know what tribe it was, but I was praying with three others too. I believe we were women. We were perhaps in a tepee . . . or a hut . . . or whatever . . ." She flipped her right hand in the air. "It was some kind of structure that was circular. We were sitting around a bowl of some kind. I couldn't tell if it was made of clay or wood, but all of a sudden the structure was rocking. It fell as if someone had pulled it over. We were exposed to soldiers and guns. I felt a pain in my chest which must have been a gunshot. I didn't see anything after that."

We sat, each in our own thoughts. Four videos played on four screens in my head. I was viewing the scenes the others had described. I could have told them their visions in as much detail as my own. As I watched each of the simultaneous movies, I saw one of the participants stuff something into a bag and hide it under our clothes. In every movie, one of us escaped while the other perished. Again I heard shouting as pain seared into the back of my head. I gasped. "If that's what this spirit means about seeing the sights, I don't like it."

As much as I wanted to return to the vision to see its end, I also wanted to leave. My body wanted to pace the room at the same time it wanted to sit as still as possible. *'What just happened to us?'* I wondered. We hadn't experienced a shared vision. Finally I voiced my wonder. "Isn't it uncanny how each of us saw a similar theme but in different cultures and maybe even in different time frames?"

Estelle was thoughtful. "I wonder if that's what he meant when he said other circles were forming. Maybe he meant they had been formed."

Gunthar cleared his throat, "I've a feeling it was more about our having been together in another time where we were doing this same kind of work. And a reminder about our need for secrecy."

We shifted in our seats. *"Were we in danger?'*

"Ah . . . so . . . do we continue?" Estelle asked.

"You mean, practice with focusing a color in the center of our circle?" I asked.

Crystal opened her arms to us all. "We've come this far, why not?" she invited.

I had to admit I wasn't feeling all that adventuresome. My skin itched and hurt at the same time as if I was having the worst reaction to poison oak I'd ever experienced. I traced my hesitancy to continue and found a lingering fear around whoever in my vision had hit me on the back of the head. I wanted to know more about the situation. Who was I? What had happened? Would it happen again if I fell into another trance? I wanted to find meaning in what we all had seen or thought we saw. Scanning the others in the room, though, I saw Gunthar and Crystal nod their heads in assent to Estelle.

I wanted to say no. I wanted to leave, until a wind blew through my belly and filtered through my muscles, filling me with calm. My mind became lost in wonder about this technique of focusing. Without further thought, I surprised myself by agreeing to go on. We settled to focus through our third eye.

"What color?" Gunthar asked.

Estelle answered, "I don't know . . . we could . . . I . . . well, what do you all think?"

"What would be easiest?" I asked.

"Blue," Crystal offered.

"I think green," Gunthar said.

"I don't quite know how to do the shade," Estelle said.

Impatience gripped my chest, "This is silly!"

"I agree," said Estelle. "I don't quite understand it, but after all that's happened, I suddenly feel self-conscious, like someone's watching who's going to grade me on how I do."

After a moment of silence, Gunthar spoke, "I'm wondering how we'll know if we succeed or fail? How can we know we've all the same shade?"

"I've a thought," I said. When no one interrupted, I continued, "See that blue ball over there? Let's bring it in the middle and soak in the color, then remove it and see if we can visualize it together."

"Good idea!" Gunthar retrieved the ball and set it in the middle.

We were quiet for about five minutes, until Gunthar took the ball out of our center.

"I can't do this," Estelle complained.

"Maybe if we had a piece of paper to focus on now," Crystal suggested.

"Wouldn't work for me," said Gunthar. "It would change my focus."

We stopped talking and starting breathing deeper.

"Please breathe quieter," Estelle complained.

Crystal raised her hand to her mouth and coughed. Gunthar switched his legs into lotus position. I felt as if I were beginning to melt again until Estelle scratched her arm.

Inside myself, I laughed, thinking that this experiment wasn't working very well. It was going to be another experience I could retell to David for a laugh; another one of those crazy situations Estelle had talked me into. This one was going to be worth at least two chuckles and a guffaw.

Then I became uncomfortable. Maybe I shouldn't divulge the details of this group's activities. Even if we failed to produce any kind of discernible effect, I should respect the privacy of our efforts. I reflected on the strange synchronicities of our individual visions.

One moment, I was sitting on my pillow. In the next, I splintered from my body. With no more than a breath, I was watching our circle from the corner of the room. I had the unique experience of observing our experiment from an outsider's point of view and started to laugh out loud, but my breath was strangled.

The 'I' of me melted within my skin, while my consciousness traveled as 'no one' to a place that was 'no where'. It was surfing atop a dark wave, then diving deeper and deeper into a trance, until I felt sucked into a black hole. My brain filled with pressure, as if something had joined my cells. Pain reverberated against the bones of my skull.

Estelle interrupted our group effort again, "I can't . . . "

"STOP THIS AND FOCUS!" a guttural voice shouted from my mouth.

"FEEL THE LIGHT POURING FROM BEHIND THE BACK OF YOUR HEAD. BREATHE IN, NOW HOLD, THEN BLOW YOUR BREATH TO THE CENTER OF THE CIRCLE. AS YOU DO THIS, LET YOUR BREATH CARRY THE COLOR YOU HAVE BEEN HOLDING BEHIND YOUR EYES. STOP LOLLYGAGGING AROUND! THIS IS TOO IMPORTANT!"

Chapter VI - April, 2004
Time to Trust

I didn't want to be in our Chevy on Highway 101 this early. I wanted to be on the land, checking for trillium along the creek, watching for animal tracks in the mud, and listening to the calls of whatever migratory birds had stayed the night.

I huddled in my thermal parka, struggling with my attitude. Opening my passenger window an inch, I could smell the spring green of the day. Fresh fog nipped at my nose, and I could detect a whiff of ocean air, that distinctive tang captured in the uppermost branches of the remaining redwoods towering along 101; they had been beckoning salty breezes for centuries. I sniffed again, then took a deep breath. My nose reorganized the scent of wood smoke outside the car, and inside, a hint of fried bacon from our breakfast.

My eyes caught on tiny yellow flowers of scotch broom, the light green, fuzzy tips of firs, the reddish-green sprouts of oaks. I tried to surround myself with the magic of spring, the mystery of nature coming alive. Despite the lush beauty streaming past our car, I frowned and sighed.

I'd been looking forward to attending the wedding of our friends in McKinleyville this afternoon, ever since we'd gotten the invitation. I tried to believe I was fulfilling some kind of destiny by squeezing my promised meeting with Potty between our two hour drive and the wedding at 3 PM. Having wrestled all night with Flyn's proposal of yesterday, I was in no mood to take care of some unknown person or watch someone else's happiness.

'*What in the world is this Potty about?*' I wondered. I stole a glance at Flyn and sighed. '*Why does this man want to change our lives?'*

I worried about his admission of about being at some kind of edge. *'What does that mean?'* trying not to shudder while I worked through my thoughts. If I had secrets about my life, then I had to accept the fact he might have kept a few himself. I just hoped it was less than what I was holding. I mentally shrugged, trying to stop myself from wondering about him and our future, as well as Potty and our meeting. I consoled myself with memories.

As we cruised north through the puddles of last night's surprise rain, I sought the landmarks of hidden paths forged through the underbrush to the Eel River from the highway where only the locals knew the way. A few led to no more than shallow pools. One, across from the old Mad Creek Inn, was a favorite hangout where nude bathing was the 'thing to do' every summer. A steep cliff provided ledges at different heights for teen males to show their diving courage. One season, Sam had proudly sported his bruised butt from a cannon-ball dive gone awry to anyone who asked him. The Inn had been a romantic treat for David and I until the roof of the restaurant collapsed. The cabins standing in seclusion in the surrounding woods had reportedly been hideaways for Hollywood stars and crime lords during the 30's and 40's. One unconfirmed legend told of Clark Gable and Carol Lombard spending their honeymoon here before she was killed in a plane crash.

We continued past Leggett and its Drive-Thru-Tree park to where the highway narrowed into a picturesque two-lane road through stands of redwoods. Another memory arose as we passed apartments that had been fashioned from a motel called Howling Wolf Ranch. Years ago this land had been a training ground for lions and tigers and bears as circus or movie performers, with the public welcome to spend time helping and living in the crew's accommodations. One of its rustic suites had sheltered David and I during a runaway weekend. Unfortunately, the resident bear had a cold and had sneezed all night making the lion 'growly'. We'd slept poorly, for that and other reasons.

"Where are you?'

I flushed, oddly embarrassed. "I was keeping my mind off this thing with Potty," I said, feeling his eyes on me. I couldn't help but wonder if he'd been reading my thoughts so I quickly changed them to something that was truly bothering me. "I'm also mad at myself," I exhaled in a spurt. "I always ask who referred a new client to me. I always check out new ones, especially when I go to their houses, and I never go without having a clear idea of what they want. I've broken all my rules."

"You must have some idea," he chided me. "I've seen you pick up on things just by hearing a person's voice."

I shrugged, "Yeah . . . sometimes . . . but . . . not this time." I stretched my neck tiredly. Not being able to read Potty had nagged at me too, and I'd grappled with that problem during the other moments I wasn't consumed with Flyn's request. Every time I'd turned over, I'd faced either dilemma. *'Why am I not receiving any kind of psychic clues?'* Every time I reached my mind toward her, I'd only sensed dampness. *'Have my antennae gone on strike for some reason?'* I sighed. *'Maybe I'm tired of seeking the true meaning behind someone's request or illness.'* I sniffed. *'Maybe I want a break too.'* I scratched my head. *'Maybe Flyn has the right idea.'* I regarded the landscape. Sun slipped through the thinning fog and danced off ripples in the spring-swollen river. Pictures of our living off the land flitted through my mind much like fish darting through water.

"What's up?"

"Damn it! Stop reading me!" I was becoming unnerved by his sensitivity to every shift in my thoughts.

He puckered his lips, something I saw him do whenever he considered his words. "You're not that hard to read when your face changes with every thought." He quieted for a moment. "I watched you with a blank face as if you'd moved far away from me. You tightened it into a frown, then your forehead cleared, like a light went on."

I shook my head. "This thing between us gets eerie." I'd never had a partner this 'in tune' with my moods, let alone my thoughts. "You and I are so connected . . . all I've got to do is picture a project and . . . well . . . you go do it."

"I do?"

"I told you this was eerie."

He grinned as he took his eyes off the road for a quick glance. "Well, now that's handy . . . or . . . annoying. Do I go to the bathroom for you too?"

"Not yet," I grinned at him. "No, it's more like I think about taking the roast out of the freezer for dinner, and you get up and do it. Or, I think about opening the windows, and you're doing it before I get out of the chair. Or, I'll think some kind of philosophical thought, and you're telling it to me like you just got this big revelation. It's amazing and . . . spooky."

"Does it work in reverse?" he asked after he'd shifted for a hill.

I thought about his question as I watched a seasonal waterfall crash into a gully by the side of the road. "I don't think so," I answered. "You've never mentioned it. I mean, . . . you'd have to say if I'd just done something that you'd thought about."

"Guess not then." A smile twitched his lips. "I do keep trying to put thoughts into your mind all the time, but never get to first base."

"Depends on the thoughts," I said.

Flyn looked at me sideways and wiggled his bushy eyebrows. "What am I thinking?"

"That you want to pull over to the side of the road and finish making love, which you started this morning, but we were running too late to finish."

"Not too bad," he said to the windshield. "If I didn't know any better, I'd say this woman's a psychic."

I laughed, wondering if he knew just how close to the truth he'd called it. "I just know you and your enhanced libido."

His voice softened. "Can I help it if I love you and love being close to you?"

I hesitated, then spoke carefully. "Actually, you can't help being who you are, and I can't help being who I am, and, somewhere in the middle there, you get these crazy sexual fantasies."

I grinned, but he was silent. I worried I'd hurt his feelings. Sometimes I felt so old when I compared myself to his 55-year-old energy. Were we really meant to be together? Then, other times, it seemed I had quite enough energy for the both of us. Being almost 60 was not a turn-on for me, but it never seemed to faze him.

He was still quiet when I offered, "Did I say something to annoy you?"

"Huh?" he lifted his eyes from the road and looked at me. I sensed no particular hidden feelings around the edges of his body; it was more like he'd been day-dreaming, and I'd pulled him back into the car.

His eyes smiled, then his mouth. Facing the road, he said, "I was submerged in a lovely scene about you and me and a bed."

"Get off it!" I hit him on the shoulder.

"Nope, I liked it right where I was."

"Do you do that often?"

"What?"

"Think about us . . . I mean . . . about us our making love?" A quick glance from him gave me little to read of his face, except from the side.

"Well, can't say I think about it all the time, like every minute of every day. But your skin's so soft, and I like being next to you. It takes very little for me to create images of us making love. What about you?"

I gave it some thought and realized that sex and lust and such things didn't hang around the corners of my mind. It was hard for me to admit I thought of it at all. "I think it's more spontaneous for me. Like, there's some way you look in a certain shirt or in a pair of jeans that makes me aware of your body and seems to bring a response in me. Though more often it's after we've shared thoughts or part of our history with each other or when I can feel close to your feelings about something. That's when I seem to want to be under your skin, or at least next to it. I don't seem to need to fantasize about it."

"Just means I'm a man and you're a woman."

I laughed. "That's true. Men and women are definitely different, although I've not compared reasons for sexual arousal with too many."

"There's an idea. We could create a questionnaire. Do our own study of the differences in arousal themes between men and woman and write a book about our results. Make a million dollars. Then we could both stay home."

"And do what?"

"Make love, eat, and watch TV."

"No, thank you. I want to do a little more with my life."

In the silence reigning after my flip remark, I realized I'd shot him down, as well as terminated our discussion about him giving up his yoga practice and me closing one of my offices. "I mean . . . oh, Flyn . . . I meant . . . maybe . . . We could find another topic for a book and work on that together." I felt the hole I'd dug for myself deepening. "With both of us thinking about it, I know we can develop other ideas to help us make a living so we can spend more time up here than down there."

Flyn offered his hand to me, comfortably bigger than mine. They were usually smooth. Today it was pocked with water blisters from chopping wood. I could feel where some were bulging with fluid and where others were ruptured and crusty.

"You worked too hard yesterday," I said.

He shook his head, and, with his thumb, stroked along my wrist, then pulled my hand to kiss my knuckles. "I never work too hard, just hard enough." He placed my hand next to his chest. "You don't trust me yet, do you?"

I wanted to withdraw my hand. "What makes you say that?"

"I mean, you don't trust that I really love you, just you, not what you can do for me, or the value of your land, or the connection to the people you know." He said this quietly.

I mentally counted the broken center lines of the freeway.

"Sellie, we've been together for more than two years, but . I don't think you believe me when I say I love being with you, that I love who you are and that there's no other reason."

I wanted to stop him, but I didn't know how. I didn't know why I felt fear curl in my belly. He cradled my hand between his thigh and his palm and . I strained to hear his words over the hum of the motor. "I love watching you in the firelight reading one of your books, or at the apartment wrestling with a problem client. It amazes me how much you care about people; I'm bewitched." He checked me sideways, and I felt the intensity of his focus. I turned to meet his eyes. The love I saw was overwhelming. It made my eyes water and spill over.

"I want us to hang out together." He divided his eyes between looking at me and watching the road. "I worry about you. Like today. Whatever this is . . . that you've gotten yourself into . . . I don't want you to go alone. But you'll do it. Without me. And, I'll worry until I see you again."

He released my hand to shift for a slow truck in front of

us. "I don't have a history with you or your children. I've never met anyone in your family except your mother one brief afternoon. Is everyone a renegade like you?" He focused on the road ahead. "I want to know more about you, and I'm more than a little tired of your hedging about what you do when you work with people. Are you afraid I won't approve or that I won't understand? What's that all about? And I wish you'd start remembering things we've done together rather than trying to bring me up to date about all the things you and David did."

He ran his fingers through his hair. "Sorry," he said softly. "That came out . . . that . . . wasn't how I wanted to say that."

I stared at the pavement of the now-divided freeway, my feelings circling through fear, to frustration, to anger and back. I watched the Eel River as it ran alongside the road, or was the road running alongside the river? Each meandered to their own purpose. Could two people have that kind of relationship? One of being as close to each other as when the highway bridges the flowing water,the other of running parallel and abreast for a time? A relationship where one person sticks to the straight and narrow, while the other wanders afar, until they're ready to return and continue their 'side-by-side' lives? Could a couple survive being less-than-dependent on one another, but inter-related? Was this possible with Flyn? If we lived in two different places most of the week and came together on the weekends, would we be able to hold on to the silent communication we shared? Would it change us, the 'we' of us?

As he shifted gears for a curve, I was faced with the rush of the last part of his statement. He'd dumped a whole lot of his truths in my lap. Had I been frustrating him with my reveries of how my life had been before him? I must've, or he wouldn't have had to say what he'd just revealed. Was I really unable to handle being loved for myself, not for what I could

do for him? Did I really want to flood his senses with the
bizarreness of my other-worldly contacts? Was he in my life
for a reason? Why was I in his?

I said the easiest thing I could. "You're the biggest
surprise in my life, Flyn. I didn't think there'd be another love
in my life. I didn't ask for it . . . for you. I just accepted my
life-after-David as the life I'd been handed and tried to survive.
When I buried him, I buried all thoughts of loving another
person fir five years until you and I started crossing paths, first
in San Francisco, then in Oakland. I had to wonder what was
going on."

"After divorcing my first husband because we weren't
suited then losing the second one after I thought I'd met my
life's mate, I'm floundering with fear that you'll leave me, just
as suddenly as you found me." I couldn't look at him as I
tasted the truth of my words. I flipped my hands in the air in
exasperation. "And, you're right, I don't share everything with
you. And it's not because I don't trust you. I don't share
everything with anybody!! Ever!! I learned to keep pieces of
my life to myself, hidden from everybody I know. I've had
to." I was talking so fast I had take a recess from talking with a
deep breath and give myself a hug before I could resume.

"I don't tell 'everything' as a kind of protection,
although I'm not sure what I might be protecting anyone from.
Many times . . . I do it . . . to protect myself." I seized another
breath, so much pouring from my soul I felt like a steam engine
that had finally reached the top of the hill and was now
speeding down the other side. "I'm afraid if any one person
has all the information about what goes on in my head and
what happens
around me, they're going to think I'm 'nutso'. I don't want
that to be you, Flyn."

Panic gripped my chest. "My life can be so bizarre,
that sometimes I don't believe it myself." I fought tears as one
incident in an elementary schoolyard loomed. "Ever since I

was a kid, I've stood alone with my intuitions and premonitions. I remember one time in grammar school, trying to warn one of the girls that I saw her brother get hit by an automobile while he was on his bike. She'd laughed at me and told the others I was a 'kook', until her brother had been taken to the hospital." I choked. "Then they feared me because they believed I'd caused the accident, instead of understanding that I'd been trying to prevent it."

"I think . . . no . . . I know . . . that's one of the reasons why I drank until about 20 years ago." I felt Flyn stiffen as he drove. "Being under the influence of the booze was a way to block a lot of the visions." The embarrassment of my years of drinking receded as I settled into memories of when my current life began. "I don't remember the exact moment that it happened, but I finally embraced what I was seeing and feeling, and began to help others. Now, most often, I experience a sensation of being connected to everything and everyone. Except for the weird picture I had yesterday while I was driving, and the vision I had after we made love, I feel blessed to be able to see beyond the now."

I turned toward him in my seat, trying to gauge his state of mind. "So . . . if you don't know all about me, please don't get your shorts in a twist. I'm only a little bit of a renegade. And I'm not an ax murderer in my spare time." I ran both hands through my spiky hair and scratched my scalp. "If you're patient, I'll clue you in on as much as I feel comfortable about. But it'll have to be at my pace." I scratched my scalp again. "I have to be sure that you aren't overloaded, and I'll have to keep checking to make sure that you still love me." All my breath left me. "I can't risk losing you," I whispered.

Flyn was silent for so long I felt a hum of despair begin to vibrate in my chest. I fought against its isolating pain with logical thoughts. *'He asked, didn't he?'* I argued in my head. *'Yeah, but you didn't have to tell him so much. No one has ever accepted you.'* I felt him glance at me and held myself rigid in my seat.

"You can breathe now," he said.

I tried, but my chest was too tight. I sniffed and nibbled at my right thumbnail, then reached my hand onto his thigh as he let up on the gas to shift on the tightly-curving road. I softened my shoulders, letting myself feel the warm car, recognizing it as a safe haven from the storm of the world. Is that why we often shared bits and pieces of our past while we drove? I suspected the cushioning in this metal cocoon during long road trips, without the distractions of cell phones, clients, and family was what brought us closer together.

"I'll never think you're crazy, or 'nutso', as you put it," he said after a few miles. "I think there's more to this connection between us than either of us realize." He hesitated. "I . . . sense things too. Like . . . when you were on the bed with that vision about this Amach. I got a weird feeling in my head, dizzy-like, but more like I was bobbing in space; I don't understand it. And I got some kind of hit in the chest yesterday while you were with Estelle. Maybe, just maybe, I'm supposed to know stuff so I can be your anchor, or help you in some way, or bring you back if you go too far. Or maybe I'm supposed to protect you somehow or add to your skills.."

I felt him turn his head. "Look at me, Sellie." I was met by his deep brown eyes. "Believe me when I say this. There's some reason we're together . . . why . . . we fit the way we do. Coming to trust each other might be the first step in figuring out what it's all about."

I squeezed his thigh then released it to bring my arms around myself. He'd given me lots to think about. The comforting rhythm of the whirring tires created a space in my brain where his words could settle. I had to admit that if I had to rely on someone, it might as well be Flyn. No one else was volunteering, and he was so very willing.

"It'll take time," I said.

"Most things that are worthwhile do," he answered

softly.

I rolled my eyes to distract myself from the tension in my chest, and I turned on the radio, punching the seek button to find the public-supported station originating in the Eureka area that played classical music on late Saturday mornings.

News blared from the door speakers instead. The final report from the second 9/11 commission was done. My quiet bliss was shattered. I moved to change the station but Flyn stopped my hand. "Let's listen," he said.

I humphed and tried to concentrate on the scenery. *'We'll never know the truth around that tragedy,'* I thought. I didn't want to believe it was the result of some kind of conspiracy, nor did I want to think it was the beginning of America's last fight for survival against a Muslim world. I especially didn't want to consider the new Homeland Security laws that felt more like an excuse for big brother to scrutinize our lives and monitor our movements.

"We've got to see this new movie by Michael Moore," Flyn said.

"Why?" I answered. "I read 'Dude, Where's My Country?' That was enough for me."

"But the movie shows the actual footage."

"Maybe," I said. My heart wasn't in this conversation. "No matter how much or how little of it's true, it's scary."

"Maybe, I'll go alone," he offered.

I nodded, feeling less anxious, trying to float in my seat as Claire de Lune drifted through the car and noted when we passed the high water mark showing where the '64 flood line had been well over the roof of the car.

At the Ferndale turnoff, we decided to take a quick tour and promised ourselves another trip to the play tourist there. Many original Victorian homes had been restored, and I knew Flyn would enjoy the different architectural styles. I also wanted a chance to connect with the people who'd lived in the houses. Sometimes, when I placed my hands on the inner wall of a once-occupied room, I could envision stories and dramas that had unfolded there. Faint movements and sounds swished at the edge of my consciousness, and, if I had enough time, I knew I could step into a moment and share their existence. This kind of visioning was controllable and was the bonus I enjoyed when I exercised my gift, even when I tapped into an emotional tragedy.

"We're here," Flyn announced. I surfaced from my thoughts to see us struggling through the heavy traffic of south Eureka. He found a place to park at the Mall. We stretched our stiff muscles as we walked to find a phone.

'OK, Potty,' I thought. *'What's your story?'*

Chapter VII - 1985
Amach comes again

Estelle made our introduction to the spirit world of the Ouija Board with a singsong cadence that lulled my body into a space near sleep and left my mind drifting and expanding. I secretly hoped to pop out of my body and hover in a corner of the room like I'd done briefly with the psychic group. I imagined it was much the same way a spirit might view us. I also wanted to be free from the confines of my skin. What I didn't want was to be pushed around again and squeezed aside by whatever had taken residence inside of me during that first time of channeling.

"Selena . . . where are you?" Estelle brought me back.

"Uh, well . . . here, I guess," I answered, feeling guilty for not paying attention.

She pursed her lips. Ever since I'd arrived at her cabin today, she'd been in a rush to get to the Board.

"Estelle, have a little compassion, will you? I'm still unsettled by what happened." If I'd wanted to be honest with her, I would have admitted I was flat out scared. The hairs on my arms felt like they would never lay flat against my arms, especially when I remembered how some kind of power had surged through me. "To tell the truth, I'm not sure *what* happened."

She relented. "I'm sorry." She fussed with the planchette, moving it back and forth between letters and numbers between her fingers. "I have to admit . . . I've no idea what it was like for you. I can't imagine being pushed aside in my own body and not remembering what I said. If we'd known anything like that was going to happen, we would've had the tape recorder on. But we didn't, so I can't play back your . . . um . . . the words." Her eyes softened. "Would it help any if I told you that you made sense . . . or that the voice coming through your mouth sounded commanding?"

I slumped in my chair. She stood to step behind me and pulled my shoulders toward her. My head rested on her stomach. She stroked my hair. "We tried to write it all down for you afterwards, but, for me, it was like I lost consciousness after you gave your . . . I mean . . . the directions. When we compared notes, we found we'd all dropped into a deeper awareness of light and color. That's when we were finally able to do the assignment. I frankly can't remember your exact words, just the timbre of your . . . er . . . the voice."

Her hands massaged my forehead and temples, and her touch soothed the ripples of a headache that had been throbbing in shallow waves above my eyes all morning.

"I appreciate that you all were able to reconstruct the sentences you heard my mouth say. That's not the whole problem for me, though. I want to know how in the hell it happened in the first place."

"It's hard to know," Estelle admitted. "Look, maybe it had to do with how we worked the board. Remember how that first spirit being, Atab, said something about one being two? Maybe that's what he meant? That you and someone or something else were connected."

I nodded. "Could be his words set up some kind of suggestibility."

"You cynic!" She pushed herself away from me and returned to her seat across the table. "I don't think his words set up any kind of a suggestion for you to suddenly talk in a different voice. I was there. You weren't '*you*'."

"Well, then, so what or who was I? A spirit? A being from another world?" I had to voice all my doubts. The only way I knew was to badger Estelle with questions. "What if it was just a group hallucination? What if all our experiments

here are figments of our imaginations? What if the little
pointer just spells what we think we need to hear?"

"Then how come neither one of us can tell if the other
one is pushing or pulling it along? I know I'm not. Are you?"

"Of course not."

"Then it has to be something bigger than the both of us,
or we'd sit here for hours staring at each other."

That stumped me. I laughed. "That'd be weird, sitting
and waiting and nothing happening."

She grinned in agreement then grew serious. "Maybe
we have to accept the existence of a spirit world, a place on the
other side of where we sit that contains beings who watch us,
as well as watch over us."

"OK, so now . . ." I shuddered. "Are we talking about
the board being some kind of doorway?"

She nodded.

"And maybe prayer is a doorway too?" I offered.

"Maybe, and perhaps meditation and drumming and
chanting."

"And group focusing?" I added.

"Could explain how something took over your body."
She scooted deeper into the pillow on her chair, then tilted her
head. "The visions we each had, when we came together,
could've had something to do with what happened to you.
Who knows? Maybe all four of us can channel a spirit being.
You were the most open and receptive and ready." She
beamed at me. "Hearing your, I mean, that voice made my
skin explode with electricity!"

"I'm glad you enjoyed it."

"Didn't you?"

"Not particularly," I muttered.

"Oh, come on, Sellie! So much happened that day . . .
It was far out and exciting! What about the fact we each had a
vision in different lifetimes and cultures?"

I felt stubborn. "I don't think I can trust those visions,

and I don't want . . . "

She interrupted, "But it was about the four of us being together before."

I made my voice quiet. "Couldn't our personal interests have constructed the origin and culture of our visions? Gunthar says he saw a Muslim lifetime, and he admits he studied comparative religions before he became an agnostic. I had an early Irish or Scottish vision, and that's my heritage. Yours was Native American, and you seem to resonate with that culture. Crystal's vision had a Nordic flavor, and she admits her grandmother is of Swedish descent."

"Who knows?" She lifted her hands in exasperation as if to say: 'who cares?'.

"I think it's important, Estelle!"

"Why? The best part's that you were opened as a channel."

"I don't think there was any 'best' about it."

Estelle grunted and rolled her eyes.

I crossed mine at her and directed my gaze to our table with its new arrangement of tape recorder, pen and paper, and spare tapes. I sighed, "I guess if we're going to get anywhere today we need to get started."

"I've already started," she reminded me.

"I know, and I really was listening . . . while I was thinking."

She gave me her 'Yeah, sure' look and pursed her lips, took a deep breath, and closed her eyes. "We are looking for someone from the other side who can explain how Selena spontaneously channeled an entity during our group meditation."

As she described to the entities in the spirit world what had happened, as if none of them had been there, I couldn't help but continue to review the details of my chilling experience. It hadn't lasted long, and I'd no memory of it. While words had spilled from my mouth, I'd been focused on my stomach being squeezed so tight, I thought my waist was cinched to a one inch diameter. My breath was so shallow, I'd panicked, fearing I would never get enough oxygen to survive.

After we'd all returned to some kind of sanity, they'd told me of their shock at the tone of my words. Each admitted they'd opened their eyes to see me pale, with my own eyes closed, pointing in a clumsy manner to the center of our circle. Estelle thought she'd seen a mantle of grayish-purple around me, a color she trusted, so she'd closed her eyes and followed the instructions they thought I'd given.

This had happened 10 days ago, and its intensity remained with me. Something had taken over my body and spoken through my mouth. I'd had no choice in the matter, either in the coming of the entity or my speaking for it, if that's what I did. I don't believe I became so agitated with the group that I pretended to speak in a different voice to get them to focus. In fact, what I do remember before the voice took over was me viewing the entire experiment with a level of humor. Whatever happened then, I sure as hell didn't like the phenomena, nor did I plan on repeating it. I never again wanted to feel pushed aside within my own body while screaming silently for help. I didn't want to experience the agitation or the sudden release when I'd regained access to the holes in my head where my eyes lived. That was the point when I knew I was alone in my body. Now I hoped I could get some clarification regarding the 'event'.

When Estelle finished her remarks, I completed the words to the rest of our customary ceremony. "Estelle and I are here in our usual positions, the base of the planchette toward her and the point toward me. We're ready to communicate with . . ." I shrugged as I opened my eyes, and Estelle shrugged with a question in her eyes. I thought to myself, *'Who do I want to talk to today?'* After a brief hesitation, I said, "I call on Amaman, directly. Please, come in. I have questions."

Estelle interrupted, "Can we try something?"

I was hesitant but answered, "Sure."

"We've been taking turns calling out the letters and figuring out the words. Could I just call out the letters and you form the messages as they come?"

"Sure."

"I've a hard a time keeping up, and sometimes I lose track. Maybe I'm spacing out, but you seem to have an easier time figuring out the words from the letters so . . ."

"OK."

We changed the direction of the planchette and notified the spirits. A long empty pause enveloped us.

I started again, "I'm calling Amaman from the universe."

Estelle giggled, "Maybe he's busy."

"Maybe . . . but, I was just thinking about . . . well . . . ok . . . here goes. I'm calling anybody who might want to come through. I need a grand teacher, like a great grandfather of them all . . . OR . . . one of my spirit guides. "

Our hands moved with the planchette toward NO and stayed there.

I said, "I don't know what you're saying 'no' to. Who is this, please?"

T H A D D E U S

"Thaddeus, you're one of my guides? I think you stand to my left side. Is that correct?"

YES

"Was it you who just answered, 'no'?"

NO

The planchette was drawn to NO then YES then NO, as if in some kind of conflict. Then it stopped.

"Do I need to concern myself with who just answered with a 'no'?"

NO

I suddenly felt shy, but persevered, "Thaddeus, you've

been with me in my experiences lately. I need to ask you . . . I want to ask you . . . Can you answer some questions regarding our psychic group last Friday?"

The planchette moved slowly to YES.

Estelle interrupted again, "Kinda of a weak 'yes'."

I nodded and asked, "Is there a reason for this?"

NO

"OK! Well then . . . So I felt my body being taken over by a spirit who spoke through me. Could you help me identify her, because I feel it was a female energy?"

NO

"Can you give me any information concerning this situation that will help me?"

ALL THIS SHE WILL EXPLAIN

Estelle interrupted, full of ideas and questions. "I just wondered . . . before he said 'no' . . . maybe she could come through? Why not?"

I took a deep breath, "Can she come through the board and talk for herself?"

GO TO HER IN YOUR OWN WAY

I shuddered. "Do you mean for me to sit here and allow her to come into my body again?"

YES

Sparkles of pain thundered up my spine and across the back of my head. "NO . . . that's out of the question!"

LET HER TALK

"And tape it?" Estelle asked.

YES

Estelle asked me quietly, "How do you feel about that?"

"How do you think I feel?" I pursed my lips as I brooded, then gave a deep sigh. "I *feel* like I'm being put off. Besides, if this entity takes over my body like it did the last time, I won't be able to ask my own questions."

Suddenly the planchette, with our fingertips perched on

either side, flew across the board, hesitating briefly as it touched each letter that created a word. I had to think fast to put the letters into words then into a sentence.

ALL THINGS WILL COME TO PASS AS THEY NEED TO

I asked, "So you're saying to let go of the planchette and invite this entity in? That Estelle will ask appropriate questions, and it'll be documented on tape?"

YES

I didn't want to give myself over to this entity again. I wanted to ask the questions. I wanted to be in control, but it looked as though I wasn't going to get the chance. Estelle's eyes glistened with excitement. I sagged. "Is there any other advice you can give me Thaddeus?"

The planchette stopped.

"Thaddeus?

I procrastinated by going to the bathroom then getting a drink of water. Relinquishing my body was scary. Being shoved to one side was just plain rude. I didn't like the feeling of peeking around the corners of my eye sockets while someone else stood in the center of my irises.

I returned to the table and placed my fingertips on the planchette. "Isn't there anyone else who'd like to help me?" When the wooden pointer wouldn't move, I gave up and dropped my hands into my lap.

The wind chimes hanging from the eaves of her house sounded their songs, some tinny, some deep. Their music clanged louder and louder until they produced a cacophony of tones. Abruptly they stopped, and I was gone.

*　　*　　*　　*　　*

Hairs rose on Estelle's arms as she lifted her gaze from the board toward her friend across the table. Selena's eyes were closed, and her shoulders were tense. Estelle saw Selena take a deep breath, and witnessed as her friend accepted the inevitable, allowing her shoulders to sink. Selena removed her hands from the planchette and dropped them into her lap.

Estelle could feel her heart pounding, causing her to struggle to catch her breath. It persisted despite deep breathing. She was panicked and frozen in her seat.

The wind chimes clanged wildly, then stopped.

Selena's eyelids opened to show blank eyes, as if no life force existed within them. Estelle blinked, trying to remove a kind of haze interfering with her ability to see clearly. Or was it from focusing too long on Selena's face? She rubbed her eyes, but realized there was nothing wrong with her vision. What she was seeing was a blurring of Selena's features. Wrinkles appeared. Selena's skin tone muddied and reformed itself, as if her cheeks and chin were modeling clay. Soon a different face was superimposed over Selena's very familiar one. Hazel eyes darkened and penetrated into the middle of Estelle's forehead with an intensity so focused, they riveted Estelle to into her seat.

Estelle heard no words but saw lips move. Chilling waves of pin-point pain crashed over her skin. She leaned closer.

ALL THERE IS . . . IS NOW.

Another wave of icicles spread along her spine.

"Hello," Estelle said carefully, noting the voice she'd heard was deeper than Selena's and softer than the one she'd heard at their psychic group.

WE ARE HERE; YOU AND I.

Estelle nodded her head, unable to answer.

THIS IS GOOD. THERE ARE MANY THINGS TO KNOW. IT IS TIME TO LEARN SOME NOW. SOME WILL COME LATER.

The body sitting before Estelle took a deep breath and dropped her chin toward her chest, as if to test the feeling of this strange neck.

SHE WILL KNOW THEM AS I SPEAK THEM. ALL WILL COME INTO HER AWARENESS AS SHE HEARS ME SAY THESE WORDS WITH HER MOUTH

Penetrating eyes again cornered Estelle's gaze and held it as if drilling through her skull.

YOU ARE A GOOD FRIEND TO HER. SHE TRUSTS YOU, BUT SHE DOES NOT TRUST HERSELF.

Estelle watched as another breath lifted Selena's or whoever's chest and ended with a ragged sigh.

SHE'S CRYING INSIDE NOW BECAUSE SHE IS SCARED.

The piercing gaze turned almost sad.

YOU CAN TELL HER THAT I NEED HER TO LET ME COME THROUGH HER. I WILL NOT TAKE OVER HER MIND. IT'S GOOD THAT SHE HAS BEGUN TO ACKNOWLEDGE ME.

A hand moved awkwardly from Selena's lap into the air with the palm open to the sky, then settled on the table.

I HAVE BEEN HER HELPER. I HAVE BEEN BY HER SIDE SINCE SHE OFFERED HERSELF. I HAVE GUIDED HER. SHE HAS BEEN CHOSEN JUST AS YOU HAVE IN YOUR OWN WORK. SHE MUST NOW WALK A PATH THAT'S BEEN HARD TO ACCEPT. SHE'S FOUGHT ME. THAT WAS FINE, BUT IT'S TIME FOR HER TO LIVE HER COMMITMENT. SHE RECOMMITTED HERSELF TO HER PROMISES ON THE MOUNTAIN. YOU MUST HELP HER. TELL HER I WILL BE WITH HER.

TELL HER THAT I CAN TAKE OVER IF SHE IS TOO STUBBORN. BUT I DO NOT WISH OUR TIME TOGETHER TO BE FILLED WITH THAT KIND OF DISTRESS. SHE REMAINS WITH FREE WILL.

Silence entered the room. Estelle dared to whisper, "Do you have a name?"

AMACH

Estelle suffered another wave of chills and watched in awe as a frown grew across Selena/Amach's forehead.

She dared another question. "What is your heritage?"

I AM FROM THE PAST AND THE FUTURE, AS WELL AS PART OF THIS NOW.

Just as Estelle was forming another question, she saw Selena/Amach shrug. WE WALK IN A CIRCLE WITH ALL THE UNIVERSE. TIME AND SPACE ARE COMING TOGETHER. ALL PEOPLES NEED TO UNITE FOR STRENGTH. THERE CANNOT BE ANY DIVISION.

Estelle watched her friend's head move as if in contemplation of these words.

WE MUST COME TOGETHER AT LAST.

The right hand had lifted and affirmed each word then returned to the table. Estelle shivered with the realization she was seeing worn ridges around the bony knuckles of this hand. Selena's entire body had aged.

I COME AS AN OLD WOMAN TODAY, OLD IN MY HEART. I COULD HAVE COME AS AN OLD MAN, BUT I WANT HER TO KNOW ME AS WHEN WE FIRST CAME TOGETHER. THE REASONS ARE IMPORTANT TO HER WORK. SHE MUST KNOW I HAVE ALSO BORN CHILDREN. I HAVE ALSO LOVED MEN AND WOMEN. I HAVE LAUGHED, CRIED, AND HAVE SAT WITH THE MYSTERIES. I HAVE SEEN MUCH, AND IT'S COMING. IT'S COMING THAT THOSE WHO WILL BE STRONG WILL BE NEEDED AND CAN NO LONGER SIT HIDDEN.

Another silence. Estelle wanted to ask so many questions, but held her tongue in hopes more information would come.

I CAN TEACH HER TO CONNECT WITH THE UNIVERSE AND WITH THE MUNDANE.

Estelle waited, hesitated, then struck up her courage. "Amach, how will you be able to teach us?"

HER MOUTH WILL FORM THE WORDS.

A short space of time drifted between them. Estelle watched as the old woman's brow wrinkled in thought.

SHE IS FIGHTING ME NOW. I NEED NOT STAY. I FEEL HER STOMACH GRIPPING. IT'S ENOUGH. I'LL ONLY COME WHEN SHE IS SERENE, WHEN SHE ASKS AND WHEN SHE IS ATTUNED. SHE MUST PREPARE SO THAT I WON'T HAVE TO TAKE OVER.

Estelle watched Selena become herself, as if she'd been hiding behind a mask made of diaphanous veiling and had leaned forward to break through the disguising facade.

*   *   *   *   *

A hot wind had flashed across my body, fading quickly. Slowly I felt whoever had taken residence in my body begin to leave. I was no longer shoved to the side of my brain and the borders of my skin. I was inflating my form with my own essence, and I felt tired. My foot was asleep. Tears hung around the edges of my eyes as I tried to focus on Estelle who was sitting pale and staring.

"She wants to take me over?" I asked.

Estelle nodded, "That's the gist of what she said, but only if you're too stubborn to let her come through when she wants to or when you need her."

I drew in as much air as I could and cried, "YOU CAN'T HAVE MY BODY!" I raised my fist to the ceiling. "Do you hear me? FIND SOMEONE ELSE. I will NEVER do your bidding, not if it means being shoved aside and having to listen to a tape recorder to hear what I or you said! No deal! No way! I won't let you control me too."

I sprang from the table and dug deep into my purse for my cigarettes, then realized I'd quit. "Damnation!"

Estelle moved to my side and tried to hug me, "But just look at all the possibilities?"

"*What* possibilities?" I faced her.

"I'd love to be able to channel a spirit," she said quietly.

"Go ahead. Be my guest . . . I don't want it. You can do it. In fact, I bequeath this spirit being to you. You'll love each other." I went to the kitchen for a drink of water. Estelle followed and leaned against the door jamb.

"If I could, I would." She looked as if she were going to cry. "But this is for you, Sellie," she said. "I have to accept that I was chosen for the work I'm already doing."

I popped a peppermint into my mouth and sucked, trying to get the nicotine craving out of my system with some kind of oral satisfaction. I started cleaning my fingernails with my eye teeth, a childhood habit I'd started when I was stressed and which always led to my biting all ten of them past their quick. I tried more water in my face, anything to feel the skin on my body.

A hug! That's what could help. I needed a hug. I went to Estelle with my arms open. "I can't do it. I can't let go of who I am. I'm only just figuring out what I'm about," I wailed. I stood in the comfort of her arms, my nose buried in the angle of her neck and shoulder. "That's the part I asked to understand when I went on that Vision Quest. I was given insight into who I am and who I'm not, what I want or what I can be.   But, not this!"

Estelle held me close and let me cry into her shoulder.

"I don't even know all the things she said," I mumbled.

"Well, you have the tape," Estelle reminded me.

I nodded. "I guess it would help if I transcribed it, so I can see what I, or this personage, said."

"She's Amach, and it's probably a good idea for you to do the documenting." As she gently pulled away from me, she continued, "I thought I'd never stop feeling the chills all over my arms when you changed into this completely different person. I mean, you looked old, and your hands . . . " She lifted my right hand and turned it over and over, back and forth. "They had wrinkles on them. Your knuckles were enlarged like you had arthritis or like my Grams who worked so hard all her life. And your hands aren't like that now. If I hadn't seen it with my own eyes, Sellie, I wouldn't have believed that you turned into an entirely different person. I mean, how does that happen?"

I shook my head. "I've no idea." Looking at my hands, palms up then palms down, I wondered what they would look like if they weren't mine. "I can tell you, from the inside, I was unattached from my skin and shoved to the side. I could hardly breathe in the beginning, until I learned to take my breath in between her sentences. I've no idea what she said to you."

Estelle saw the tape recorder was still running, so pushed the stop button. "All in all, I think she's benevolent. She doesn't mean you any harm, and she's been with you all along. For some reason, she wants to talk now."

I knew Estelle was trying to reassure me, to help me accept what she thought was a gift. I didn't want to accept the idea. She trailed after me as I went into the bathroom. "Did you make some kind of promise when you did that Vision Quest last year? What did you ask for when you spent that night on the Lookout Rock?"

I stared into the wash bowl, hesitating to lift my eyes and see my face in the mirror. I was afraid of what I might see. I hoped I would recognize myself, my naturally arching eye brows, my high cheek bones and pointed chin. My hazel eyes. My own wrinkles and laugh lines. I didn't want to be anyone else. I gathered my resolve.

"Sellie, do you remember what you asked for?"

I couldn't answer her for the second it took me to gather my courage and lift my head. I scanned each feature until I was sure each one belonged to me. With a sigh of relief, I turned my attention to her question, reciting words as familiar to me as my face because I included them in my prayers every morning. "Help me go where I am needed to help heal myself and others." I continued the litany. "Help me do whatever you will have me do, say what you will have me say."

I opened my eyes to the mirror. "If this is some kind of answer, I don't understand it." I turned to her. "Tell me Estelle, what in the hell do I do now?"

Estelle answered slowly. "Sellie, I don't know what you're supposed to do now. What I do know is you've been asking yourself that question ever since I met you."

I sputtered, "Yeah! So?"

Estelle sniffed and shuffled her feet, as if hesitating to answer. As she lifted her eyes to mine, I could tell she'd decided to spit out her thoughts. "If you'd just sit down and list all the things that *have* happened in your life since the first time you asked that question, you'd probably be amazed. In fact, you'd probably be shocked at how much you've done."

"I guess. But I'd be a lot happier if my purpose or my path or whatever I was supposed to do with my life would announce itself to me in bright neon flashing lights so I wouldn't miss the message."

"Don't we all?" Estelle grumped at me, then softened and offered, "Well, do you want to see if there's anyone who can give you more tangible information?"

"I guess so."

We settled into our places and brought our fingertips onto the planchette, beginning again. "We're asking for anyone who has a message for Selena or Estelle about their life paths to come through at this time."

The planchette shifted under our fingers and pointed.
M A T T H E W

I recognized the name, "Matthew, you're the spirit guide who stands on my right side. Right?"
YES

Estelle asked, "Is there something you want to say?"
B E E V E R F A I T H F U L T O T H E

I N T E N T O F Y O U R P U R P O S E T O
H E A L Y O U R S E L F A N D O T H E R S
I was impatient with this because I thought I was already doing that. I asked, "What else?"
T H A T W I L L B E Y O U R
G U I D E F O R A L L O W I N G A M A C H
T O C O M E T H R O U G H
My mind grappled with the idea of further connections with Amach. Could she help me know what I was supposed to do with my life? I shrugged with impatience, trying to endure. "So the commitments I made on that rock are part of all this?"
A N D H O W Y O U C A L L H E R
A thought came to me. "So when I need help with this commitment, I can call on her?"
YES
"But that doesn't answer my question as to what I'm supposed to do with my life. What in the hell does this Amach have to do with what I'm supposed to be doing?"
S H E H A S B E E N W I T H Y O U
F O R A T I M E
I didn't understand this, but I let it pass and tried to find reassurance about my other concern. "If I do this, then she won't jump in on me again?"

The planchette didn't move.

"That's not very encouraging," I said to Estelle.

"Maybe you can negotiate," she suggested.

"I'm going to have to do something," I admitted. "I don't like being taken over, but I don't think I have anything more to say about it."

Estelle agreed with me over our hands.

I shook my head with a kind of dread filling my chest. "I don't think I had THIS in mind when I made my prayers on that Vision Quest!

Chapter VIII – April, 2004
Meeting Potty

I faced Potty's first floor apartment and eyed the drapes covering the front window. Repeated water stains wavered across the lining and had left rusty imprints resembling a dirty pond with enlarging and receding banks. The faded, pink fabric had vertical blotches, reminding me of a superimposed pattern of Rorschach ink blot designs and leaving me with the bizarre urge to identify as many forms as I could in the irregular creation. My eye detected a dragon, then a mountain, a winged bird, a mask. The mental exercise reduced my feelings of foreboding.

Under the window, I spied a neglected garden where gray grasses from previous seasons were matted and deteriorating. Bright green oxalis with its fluorescent yellow blooms struggled to sprout through the blighted network of tangled weeds. Discarded clay pots were heaped in the corner where rotting wood stepped toward a worn threshold. Chipped clay saucers held black water. "Mosquito nests," I said, and the thought I should turn the saucers over seemed natural. Here I was, looking at these signs of neglect and deterioration, normally unnerving to me, and I had the strangest feeling I belonged right where I was standing, as if what was happening, or going to happen, were both timely and appropriate.

Swiftly, my feelings of rightness and balance were replaced with a sense of sorrow. Tears formed, and, because they rose from a source I could not name, I knew they weren't mine. I came to immediate attention. Without my permission, I'd been drawn into feelings not belonging to me. I could only guess I'd crossed an invisible boundary into the auric influence of a very strong psyche who was suffering from a deep sadness. Quickly I grounded and layered my protective barriers as I had no intention of losing myself to an unknown personage.

I focused on the brown door, crusted with bubbles and flakes of peeling paint. Since the doorbell button was an empty hole, I rapped my knuckles with as much intention of announcing my arrival as I did of affirming my solidarity within my own being. My resolve didn't quite work; my legs quaked with anxiety. If I had to admit to any single truth, at this exact moment, it would be that I wanted to turn tail and run. I couldn't believe I was going to enter this apartment without knowing more about the person inside and with little more than breathless instructions.

Flyn had argued the entire drive between the Mall and Potty's apartment complex, numbering on his fingers every reason why he wasn't happy I was doing this alone.

"One, you don't know her. Two, you don't know the house or the circumstances. Three, you don't have a sixth sense of what this person is like." He'd fumed in silence then blurted. "And four, you haven't had lunch."

I smiled. His final statement had warmed my heart and helped me realize how concerned he was, grasping at any reason to keep me from something he didn't understand. *'Heck,'* I thought as I stood, hammering on the door a second time, I couldn't list *any* reason I *should* be here. *'Well, maybe one,'* I admitted.

I needed to follow through on my commitments, even though I was wary of these signs of decay. I shook myself. *'Creating a negative perception is not a good beginning, Selena!'* I thought. Passing judgment on external evidence was never helpful to my work or someone's healing process.

My stomach growled and brought me into focus, which was exactly the reason I'd delayed lunch. I needed the edge of hunger to keep me alert and give me an excuse to leave after an hour. That was more than enough time, I figured, for a first visit.

I breathed deeply to clear any and all thoughts before pounding on the door for a third time.

Something stumped on the floor inside. I tried the door knob. It turned. I pushed. The door opened without creaking. For that, I was grateful.

A fetid odor hit me in the face. Like the smell of warm fat turning sour. I shook myself and concentrated on detecting other scents: rancid hair, sickly sweat, an underlying scent of strong urine. All this was interspersed with a tinge of kitty litter that needed changing and left-over food which had no relationship to anything I remembered eating. My stomach stopped growling.

"Potty?" I called.

Sounds rustled in the room edging the small linoleum-floored hall where I stood. I stepped into what must be the living room. The first thing I saw was a color TV, flashing muted scenes from the opposite corner. I brushed against a side table that wobbled near a recliner where someone gasped and struggled to sit straighter in the chair. A machine purred nearby, and I guessed it was some kind of oxygen-making unit. A thud sounded on the floor.

"Damn," came the wheezy voice from the phone.

I turned to face the person in the chair and managed to block the only available light source in the room, the TV, thus darkening the person, the chair, and this corner into oblivion. Struggling to adjust my vision so I could gain a better impression. I felt scrutinized by eyes well-accustomed to this dimness.

"Hi," came another wheeze.

"Hello to you," I answered as softly as I could, hoping my face was arranged in its most bland expression. I gave my nose some time to get used to the odor by breathing shallowly through my mouth. *What in the world could this person want from me?'* I smelled the edges of death, and, strangely, the odor of rose blossoms.

"Glad to see you," the voice whispered, "again."

Startled, I asked. "Have we met before?"

A floor lamp clicked on, and I saw a nod. Stringy black hair sported a shock of white hair hanging over a forehead and a left eye. Light green eyes glittered between swollen eyelids, and cheeks puddled toward a chin creating a neck that looked as broad as a bull dog's. Hiding in the skin folds, I detected a pinched mouth on a small head completely out of proportion with the immense body filling the chair.

. "We . . . went . . . to school . . . together."

I searched my brain. What school? High school? College? Massage school? Deciding in that instant, Potty must be a female, I drew a blank,

She grunted. "We've only . . . seen . . . each other . . . once! And that . . . was . . . like . . . virtual . . . reality. "

I must have really looked confused.

"Open . . . your . . . other . . . eyes." This was more than a suggestion; it was a command.

A sudden warmth covered my skin and then a chill. I shivered and stepped away. "Who are you and what do you want?" I tried to demand in a shaky voice.

Again she shook her head. "Look at me . . . with your . . . other eyes." She was winded, but her instructions were firm, the contours of her body rigid. I detected a faint, blue light around her that drew my curiosity.

I quickly grounded, beginning the breathing technique I used to transport myself into another space of reality. I opened and closed my eyes rapidly and sank farther into my body.

When I reviewed her edges through these other eyes, charged light eclipsed her shape. I watched her massive frame reduce to the size of a small girl. I had to close my logical mind and regard the energy before me: its texture, its intensity, how it was forming, and where. I connected my heart chakra with the area of her heart chakra and the center point of my higher guidance with hers. I waited. This level of connection helped me interpret what I was seeing through filters of a source beyond my ego.

As I hit the bottom of my trance, a cacophony of voices, words, images, sounds, and a screaming boomeranged me to my surface so rapidly I was sick to my stomach. I bent over to breathe and to settle my stomach.

"Slow down," I called out. "I can't take it all in."

The woman in the chair struggled to sit forward, reaching her hand as if to touch me. "You . . . offered . . . too wide . . . an opening," she croaked. "Close to a smaller portal."

I stood and regained some balance then grounded myself again before I went further. "Why are you doing this?"

"It's not . . . me. I have . . . something . . . you need . . . to see, but . . . " her voice choked so hard, she couldn't catch her breath. She waved her hand at me then at the water glass on the floor. I reached it and found the pitcher for a refill. After she sipped, she tried again. "I'm dying. You can't help . . . but I . . . can help you . . . you . . . You're in danger . . . somehow." Falling back into her chair, her face and arms shone with sweat. There was a long pause as she settled her breathing. I could see sadness in her eyes but then they became as shiny as steel. "You must . . . make contact. Here . . . read the last page . . . it . . . tells you."

Potty lost her energy for speaking and sucked oxygen through her nasal cannula as deeply as her broken lungs could manage. She waved at an inch thick, yellow, three-ring binder laying on the mobile table in front of her. I opened it to see pockets on the inside of the covers stuffed with small pieces of paper. Dividers separated pages of handwritten scrawl.

"The last . . . page," Potty croaked.

I turned to the last page of the binder and read: *Clear your chakras of all chording. Surround yourself in luminous light and open your heart and your third eye.*

Let me come to you, Selena.

Shock waves hit. "This is bizarre," I said. "How can it be written directly to me?"

"Automatic . . . I thought it was for me . . . until I saw your name."

I looked at the writing before and after this passage; this writing was different from the rest of her journal. And there was more. The following words sent a cold stream of chills dancing along my spine: *Selena, you must make contact with me. I have so much to show you, and you are to help me as you are bonded to me across time and space. An era is closing. You need help with the dangers coming to you.*

Darkness seeped into my being, my vision.

"STOP!" Potty called from her chair, again sitting forward as if she could reach me. "Fill . . . with light . . . Clear . . . your chakras . . . NOW!"

I did as she commanded. When I felt clearer, I opened my eyes and read the remainder of the instructions on the last page: *To see my experiences, go to the Akashic records and enter the door to my lives. Look at it as if it were a movie screen and watch the players from the outside as well as their insides. You are in full command to see and learn all you need. You will know what to do. I will keep you from harm in my world.*

This is very urgent for you to see. There is little time for me, for you, and for saving your dearest friend.

I stopped reading when I realized the writing had changed to the script resembling the section before these instructions. Some entity, and I could only think it had to be Amach, had appropriated Potty's mind and hand to insert this message to me in the middle of an automatic writing session. My eyes stung with emotions that encompassed the entire gamut of fear, awe, wonder, anxiety, anger, and gratitude.

"What the hell?" I let my eyes scan above Potty's head, hoping that some kind of reassurance was hiding there to help me. I felt frustrated when I saw nothing but a blank wall and a smudged ceiling.

With new resolve, I stood at attention. "OK'" I said to Potty and the room. If Amach had information, then I wanted to know what Amach had to show me, and I wanted it now. Since I'd already cleared my chakras and filled myself with light, I could transport myself to the Akashic records. But, what if these instructions were a wild goose chase? What if they weren't? I had to know what kind of danger was stalking me or my friend, whichever dearest one that might be. I decided to test these directions to see if they worked the way they were written.

I looked to Potty. She nodded at me with something I assumed was a smile. For all her inability to move or breathe, I felt safe in her presence.

As I evened my breathing, a cloud formed around me. I saw myself standing in a darkened theater, watching a screen where shadows wavered as if a fire was burning nearby and its light was dancing on a wall.

The smell of rich earth fills my nostrils. I must be in a cave as I can see the sharp jutting rocks of a wall lighten and darken, while a small fire struggles to burn. I investigate what is over my head to see filigree roots and understand I am below a tree grove where these interlacing supports are so thick and braided they can hold the earth together and form a ceiling. Moisture shimmers on the surfaces of the stone and earth. Into the surrounding four walls are carved four inset shelves which each contain a skull facing another across the packed floor. They appear to greet themselves, and I know these bony faces are seated in the four directions.

The cave must be only under a hillock, not deep into a mountainside, because I smell earth on a draft of air from behind me, as if an opening is just around the corner.

Did I enter through that opening, or have I just appeared here? Maybe I came down a warren hole, like the March Hare of Alice in Wonderland? I laugh as movement catches my eye.

Three figures huddle around a willowy fire quivering in the drafty ebb and flow. Smoke tapers and disappears at a short distance above the spindly flame. I identify two young people and a short older woman with gray hair. I have no doubt the latter is Amach, and I will myself to hover near her stooped form as I think to enter her the same way she has entered me.

Instead I float behind the younger woman who is sitting straight with bent head across from a young man dressed in skins. His long black hair is in multiple braids and tied at his neck with a thong. Her dark hair falls loosely across her shoulders and down her back. I am pulled into her body and hold myself small, not willing to inflate against the edges of her being. I am determined to not take her over. Instead, I become aware of her lack of movement and of her sense of what is happening. I sit in her perspective. When I lift my eyes, I caress the form of the man she loves and feel the tightening of her womb as if it were my own. 'It has to be hers,' I think, 'I no longer have one.' I turn to view Amach and squint to see what's in this old woman's hands, then sigh and lose myself into this young woman as she thinks.

'My name is Dacona, of the Deep Valley People. I wonder at the wispy strands of gray hair loosened from the neat coil I twisted atop of my auntie's head. She must be working hard to have become so ruffled. I dare not move, even though I want to see what makes her concentrate so hard. I watch my auntie draw a circle on the earthen floor with the antler of a young stag. One point sits in the center while the outer tip revolves around it, creating a ridge in the mud. She then divides the circle into four parts. From the many little bags and packets in her carrying pouch, she drifts crushed

leaves onto a live coal she has now placed in its center to release a pungent scent into the air around us. When I breathe it in, I feel dizzy, and I wonder at the criss-crossing of sensations in my body. I try to sort them as my mother taught me. Somewhere behind my eyes there is pressure, as if a time of tears is gathering like the clouds forming before a rain. My chest is like a cave of winds. I can only take small gasps of air, and my middle place feels empty. The place between my legs, where Amach worked with a sharpened stone, feels at once hot with an unaccustomed fire as well as raw with pain. I bite back a whimper as I feel this soreness, as well as the edge of pain from a skinless area where she worked the sharp stone over my heart. I feel sick in my stomach, but I have to see. I force myself to breathe more deeply and to keep my eyes open. I want to see what she does, how she makes Marweth and I come together. I know her magic will work. I know once she puts the pieces in place, he will be mine. He will stay with me after the lying in. He won't worry about his parents or his tribe across the mountains. He will stay with me every night and protect me from the stares of Tobar and his son Radin and his skin brothers. I feel a fearful sickness when I see them. I have refused them all. Please, Amach, make Marweth stay with me. Let this binding keep him next to me forever.'

Suddenly, I popped from Dacona's body, soaring backwards through darkness. Faces sped past as Amach hung upside down in front of me. Dacona's sickness stayed inside my stomach even though I tried to deep breathe it away.

The intensity of the young woman's desire made me uncomfortable. Her genitals and breasts had been swollen with want, and mine remained stretched with more desire than I'd ever experienced. This was the discomfort that had made me escape her body, not the sickness. I'd never felt that much passion or lust for another human being. It unnerved me. I couldn't sit in the darkened theater any longer. I needed to be out and away from here and back into my own reality, my own body and thoughts.

My heart beat faster as I fought to surface from this space of visioning. Deep inhales and quick exhales jolted me awake.

I opened my eyes to Potty watching intently from her chair. She nodded slowly. "You were good . . . in that class . . . you've come . . . even . . . farther." She nodded again as if she was pleased to have witnessed whatever she saw me accomplish and whatever was around me while I was doing it.

I said, "I don't understand what you think you saw."

"I saw . . . enough." She said quietly. Her cheeks tightened, and I had to assume she was smiling at me.

"So, now what about you?" I asked. Her penetrating stare made me uncomfortable. I wanted to shift her focus.

She raised her hand. "You're . . . not . . . done."

"I've gone as far as I want to," I said flatly.

"Perhaps . . . but you . . . need . . . the whole . . . picture."

"How do you mean?" I bristled, anxiety beginning to heighten. I'd just been transported into someone's body in a vision from the past and now this morbidly obese woman was telling me there was more? I thought not! My stomach growled, and I wanted to leave.

Potty raised her hand. "I just . . ." After a brief second, she tried again. "Look . . . at me . . . What . . . do you . . . see?"

I shrugged. "Do you mean for me to read you or just take stock of your face value?"

She tightened her cheeks into another smile. "No . . . Not me . . . You'll . . . see . . . My human overcoat . . . is dying . . . anyway. Just . . . read . . . me."

I resisted, then, I relented. She'd told me in the beginning I couldn't do anything for her. *'Why read her then?'* I asked myself, then shrugged and set to the task.

Whenever I'd dipped into my trance state, it was easier

to dip into it again. Somehow after the first unlocking of protective doors, they were would remain that way until I consciously closed them with a purposeful set of actions.

This held true for me again. One breath and my body melted, the familiar tingling rose from my buttocks and enveloped my lower back, shoulders and neck, to the top of my head. I was under.

I fluttered my eyes, superimposing the outer and inner visions until I could rest my eyelids gently closed and see both the seen and the unseen. Potty's aura filled the room. The usual tight-knit ray that edged all bodies was loose around hers, as if she were gradually creating spaces between her body and her ephemeral being. And there were spaces enlarging between her cells as well. She was loosening the web of life that kept her spirit encased within her body.

Over her left shoulder, a separate orb of light pulsated and drew my attention. There, a face formed. It was Amach's. I recognized the wrinkles, the graying wisps of hair loosened from the bun on top of her head, her steady stare. As Potty's mouth moved, words formed in my mind, not in the air that filled the space between us.

"DO NOT FORGET ME. WORK WITH ME. YOU COULD BE IN GREAT DANGER, AND YOU COULD BE ON THE VERGE OF GREAT UNDERSTANDING. BE AWARE OF ALL INFLUENCES. PROTECT YOURSELF."

Suddenly, I smelled burning. I was instantly awake.

Smoke filled the room. Potty gasped for breath. I searched for the cause and saw a wire snaking across the rug from the back of her room heater. It was frayed at the point where her portable table rolled back and forth across it. As I watched, it sparked. The rug was charred from the heat and was now smoldering. Who knows how long before it would rise into flame?

I pulled the plug from the wall and worried about what to do next. Potty, gasping through her nasal cannula, waved at me to remove the heater. I picked it up and took it into the kitchen, surprised at the difference. Where the living room resembled a dismal den, this room was spotless and full of light. Someone was caring for this woman, and that fact eased my heart.

After checking the blackened spot on the rug to make sure it wasn't burning, I fanned the front door to freshen the air in the living room. With the day too cold to open windows, I tucked an extra blanket across her knees and pulled her shawl across her shivering shoulders.

"Is there someone I can call to help you?" I asked, wishing I could do more for this woman who was trying to help me.

She patted my cheek. "My worker . . . be here soon. Glad . . . you came." Her hidden eyes sparkled as she challenged me. "Do . . . what you . . . are . . . meant . . . to do!" She hesitated. "Keep . . . protected!" she added so harshly she started coughing.

"Is that what happened to you?" I asked softly.

Tears escaped the folds around her eyes. "I took on . . . more . . . than I . . . could . . . handle."

I nodded in understanding. Some of us who believe we are chosen to be healers try to relieve our clients of all that ails them. We sometimes fall into the disaster of making choices for them without consulting them, consciously or energetically. The karma initializing someone else's disease can enter our sphere of experience when we take on the battle against it, instead of our client. As healers, we have to know where we end and where our clients begin. In fact, because we are so sensitive, we have to do this in all our relationships. I'd learned this the hard way with my parents, my children, and husbands.

Flyn came to mind. Were my protective boundaries the reason I wasn't 'doing' his thoughts as he did mine? I hoped so. Perhaps I needed to show him how to protect himself from

me? *'Oh, my God! Flyn! How long have I been in here?'*
I'd promised only an hour. I'd no idea what time it was.

"You've . . . got . . . to go," she said.

"Yeah, will you be alright?"

"As . . . right . . . as . . . rain!" she answered.

In that instant, I remembered her. We'd shared an
adventure at the end of a psychic reading class we'd taken.
Our group had experienced shared trances, had performed
simple psychic tasks together, and had taken a very unusual
field trip. For weeks after our adventure, and even now, I'd
had a hard time wrapping my mind around the details of our
experience.

"You traveled . . . on an eagle!" She said. Chills crept
across my chest when I realized she was reading my thoughts.

I answered, "And you started out in a caboose and came
back on a duck with an umbrella."

She laughed out loud, which started her coughing again.
I placed my hand on her chest and felt a heavy draw of energy
through my palm.

When she settled, she patted me, "Best . . . you . . . go."
She pointed to the three ring binder on the floor. "Take that."

I hesitated. "I don't understand. That's your journal."

"Some things . . . might . . . be . . . of interest."

Bending, I brought the yellow binder to my chest and
hugged it. Giving me this collection of her thoughts and
automatic writings might be part of her letting go, and I
couldn't refuse. Sadness clogged my throat.

"I'll be sending you energy and good thoughts," I
offered.

With a nod, she answered "I'll be . . . checking . . . up
on you . . . too."

I found my purse and let myself out into the day. Flyn
waited at the end of the walkway with a bag of sandwiches
from Hole in the Wall, our favorite sandwich shop.

Chapter IX - April, 2004
Coming together

Flyn eyed the yellow binder. I could see him wanting to ask me about it, but, instead he lifted his eyes to my face to focus on me. "Want to eat here?"

I looked over my shoulder at the desolate apartment window and shook my head. "No."

Smells of warm pastrami and spicy Italian meatballs oozed from the white bag in my lap and made me gasp with hunger. I entertained myself with thoughts of the soap opera I'd envisioned around Amach, to keep myself from devouring our lunch, paper bag and all, while he relocated the car. He took forever to maneuver through Old Town Eureka toward Humboldt Bay and arrive at what appeared to be a defunct development project. Nautical flags waved from a standard planted in the middle of a circular deck announcing itself as the center of the deteriorating boardwalk. Weeds grew knee high in empty lots along the town side of the walkway; smelly brown water slapped against the pilings. Enormous signs advertised architectural drawings for shops, businesses, and two-story condominiums, but were overwhelmed with graffiti decorations of such unique word combinations, I blushed.

By the time we settled on a graying wooden bench to eat our sandwiches, food was our only concern. I couldn't swallow my pastrami and Muenster cheese sandwich fast enough and was glad the French roll was soggy, or else I'd have choked on it from lack of chewing. Neither of us spoke until we'd finished the last bit, then we noticed the cool, steady wind gusting across the bay. I shivered, and we huddled closer.

"Hope it's an indoor wedding," he said.

"I'm thinking it's a garden one."

"Then, I hope it's in the middle of four tall buildings with a bonfire."

A struggling fire where three figures sat in mute relationship to each other overwhelmed my thoughts. I disappeared into vision.

I watch, above Dacona. Her head shifts from gazing at the fire to peek at the man across from her. His bare torso gleams in the firelight as if covered in sweat. I hover above him. Smell his body and detect he is lathered in some kind of oil. Without my will, I'm drawn into him and perceive an array of pictures as they flit across his mind. Our heart thuds in our chest, tight with fear.

He is silent with his lips, but busy with his thoughts. 'I am Marweth, Son of Nadu, Brother of Zena. When will this old woman be done? How long must I wait for Dacona? My want gathers in my loins. No more delay, old woman!'

'PHAW! I would have entered her the first moment I saw her if I had not been caught!' We shift, he and I, to ease the tension in our groin. 'She is looking at me. I can feel her eyes. Good! Let her quicken so she will have no fear. I need her in many ways. I am too alone in this strange tribe without my comrades, Kaitm and Marjag. Why did they leave me? Or were they killed? Captured? I have seen no signs of their skin or skulls. Surely a tribesman would have brought trophies of their death into the tribal circle where I was displayed.'

'Who are these empty skulls in the walls who stare at me? Are they from men this woman has killed? Are they part of her power? They mean nothing to me. I worship no thing that is dead. Power is in the living!'

Pain stabs the sheath of his manhood and a point on his chest over his heart where Amach scratched for a piece of skin.

'This rite! What can it mean? Will it make the men trust me? Perhaps if I show them how well I can hunt?

FPAW! Enough! I will do what I must before I give Dacona my seed. She will never have to be with another.'

I raise my eyes with him to meet Dacona's and become locked in the power of their stare. We feel more desire than we can contain; more than when Marweth first saw her in the waters where droplets caught the sun as they slid over her shoulders and breasts and pooled to wash over her hips, buttocks and legs. Our manhood stretches. We must shift to relieve the pressure. All we can think of is exploding inside this woman before us. To subdue her, lay atop her, and fill her with all that we are.

I feel him try to pull our eyes away, his chill of fear. We are caught between our lust and our duty. We want to die for her, and yet we have a mother, a father, and a young sister at home to feed. We never meant to have these feelings. We only wanted to see what was on the other side of the mountains. Perhaps, later, after our joining, we can leave together. We feel lost.

Amach hisses, and we unlock our eyes.

A chill wind wrapped around me. I huddled closer to Flyn and entertained the thought of inviting him for a quickie in the cramped back seat of the Tracker; we didn't have time for a motel room. All I wanted was him to be inside me. '*My,*' I thought. I'd never dreamed a swollen penis was packed with such urgency. I felt as if I continued to carry Marweth's manhood between my legs.

"You left me," Flyn said. "These trances are happening more and more." He showed his concern by draping his arm across my shoulders. "Can I help?"

'*If you only knew!*' I thought, and tried to keep a straight face while squirming to find a more comfortable way to sit.

"What?" he asked.

I gulped. "I don't know what's happening, Flyn. I wish I did, but Potty . . . God, I really don't like that name." I shrugged then continued. "She opened me to Amach on a different level, and I can't seem to turn off the connection." '*Nor do I want to,*' I admitted.

"Was she calling to you this time?"

"Not like before. I dropped into her life again . . . and some of the people around her."

He looked at me strangely. "How . . . I'm . . ."

I knew he was confused. So was I.

"All I know is watching you struggle is making me lonely on this end." He took my hand and studied my knuckles. "I'm here for you, Sellie." When I couldn't talk, he changed the subject. "Where's the map to the wedding? We're just about on time."

I was thankful that he was organized, thankful he was with me. I leaned into him and gave him a long, lingering kiss, tasting Marinara Sauce on his lips, meatballs on his tongue. He groaned in the back of his throat.

"We'd better go," he said.

I was so charged with sexual urgency, I was dizzy. "Where?" I asked.

"Don't know what happened in that apartment, but you're steaming," he observed.

I snorted and felt the silliest grin on my face. "Um, well, it had something to do with the pictures around Amach."

"Whatever happened, I sure approve, but . . . we'd better hit the road." He gathered me in his arms and helped me stand.

I contained my thoughts and tried to stay present in the hopes of being able to follow the directions. I navigated us to McKinleyville, made sure our gift and our food-offering for the potluck, as well as the wedding bouquet, were transferred to the house, then I handed Flyn his wedding clothes. I carried mine over my shoulder while I searched for the bride-to-be.

Magenta was hiding in the guest bedroom while trying to keep tabs on all the preparations in the garden, the kitchen, and the dining room. "I don't think I can do this," she said.

I hugged her. "After five years of living together, why the cold feet?"

"Because I want to know that this is going to be forever, and I don't know of any couple around us where that's even looked like a possibility. In the last five years, all but one couple we've known has gotten a divorce."

I had to think quickly. Magenta was a woman of absolutes, waiting a very long time to make a marriage commitment. She hadn't married the father of her two grown children, waffling back and forth but had been positive two months ago after Talon had threatened to walk out if she didn't marry him. Now she looked uncertain despite the fact her rich auburn hair was curled in ringlets on top of her head, her make-up perfectly toned and blushed for a new bride, and her cocktail length, white lace dress hung from the door frame of the bathroom.

"Look," I offered. "Nothing's absolutely for forever, but, in this very moment, do you believe Talon will do everything in his power to care for you and keep you safe?"

I watched my words come out my mouth and wondered how much that question applied to Estelle, to the couple in the vision I'd been seeing, even to myself. Sometimes my personal truths, when spoken in conversations with other people, were highlighted for my viewing pleasure like the stylized clouds emitted by cartoon characters. Sometimes the words shimmered like neon signs blinking to get my attention. "Alert! Alert!" They would announce, "These words are for you too, Selena!" The last set out of my mouth made me tremble. *Would Flyn do everything in his power to care for me and keep me safe?'* I wasn't sure of my answer to that, but Magenta nodded, "Yes."

I asked and watched my words glimmer. "And can you picture anybody else you'd rather crawl between the sheets with?"

"No," she grinned, "except Robert Redford."

I laughed. Our answers were the same. "You're showing your age. lady. Girls today pick Brad Pitt or Ben Affleck or . . ."

She interrupted. "I want a more experienced male. One who sees me for who I am, not just as a sex object." She checked her nails until she couldn't hide her smile or the twinkle in her eyes.

I could see the teasing. We both knew that being someone's sex object was pretty OK, part of the time, maybe even most of it. "Well, sounds like Talon to me."

She faltered in her gaze. "What if, . . . oh Sellie, what if I'm not good enough?"

"Good enough for what? For God's sake!! You're 47 years old, have been with this man for over five years!!! Has he ever complained?"

Her face cleared again, and her eyes glittered like she had a special secret. "You're right! I'm ready now."

"Thank God," I groaned.

"Listen, every bride gets to have a case of the willies. I'm going to remind you of that fact when you and Flyn tie the knot."

I shivered. The thought of being with Flyn held such delight. The thought of standing in front of my children and my mother and marry yet another male made my head spin.

"I'd rather have a private affair," I said as the bedroom door opened and whooping women descended on Magenta with 'ooohs' and 'ahhs' over her dress and hair and whatever else they could see to gush over. I wasn't an 'ooher' nor an 'ahher', so I retreated to the bathroom to change clothes and comb my hair.

Magenta must have burned sage while preparing herself. Remnants of the scent hung in the towels and took me back to the smudge Amach had created with her herbs. I was once again in the darkened cave, firelight shadowing the walls.

Gray fumes rise from a glowing coal still in the center of the circle Amach had drawn in the clay floor. The flavor of the smoke is at once pleasant and harsh. Dacona and Marweth focus on Amach and her hands and the two pieces of soft hide made from smoke-tanned rabbit skin. The edges of their bodies blur as their eyes grow dull, and I wonder if they have gone into a time beyond this now.

I am pulled into Amach's sensations, her thoughts, feel her body and know her memories. I can see through her eyes this plume of smoke, the flames of the fire, the earth of the cave. With her I watch until these two young people have reached a place of calm. The scent of the Chorca root settles around us.

Items from Marweth's and Dacona's persons, placed into two small bundles, are surrounded by a golden glow of dawn and the rose of eventide. Amach and I exchange the chest skins of each onto the separate centers of their bundles; intertwining hairs from both are wound around a finger nail from each then added to the pile. Auric light reddens when we add the flesh from their most private parts. Amach and I share thoughts as she keeps track of their navel stones. These will stay with their owners, I discover. A mixture of spit, sweat, and blood from each has hardened with the virgin clay figures Marweth and Dacona fashioned into rough sculptures of themselves. These now are exchanged between the two bundles: his into hers and hers into his.

A clap of thunder rumbles outside the cave.

Pounding on the bathroom door brought me to my senses.

'I've got to stop this!' Anger at myself for not closing the portal between my world and theirs made me holler above the pounding, "Just wait a minute!" I struggled to stop myself from dipping into Amach's world again. I knew I had my own life to do, but I was intrigued by the story that was unfolding. I was too curious about these two young people whose bodies

I'd inhabited. I wanted to know about this secret ceremony, this binding, as they called it.

I pinched my cheeks while I stared into the mirror. Ripples of anxiety spread in my stomach. I'd never slipped this easily out of my life into an altered state. I had to close the door between our worlds and bring myself fully into my present life. More banging on the door prevented me. Despite a tinge of guilt, like a flash of pink heat, I smiled, knowing I would have to delay initiating the sequence of actions to separate my life from Amach's.

Besides, the circumstances I'd been viewing and Estelle's request, made me want to observe the making of these bundles. In fact, I convinced myself, I <u>needed</u> to know the particulars. "WOW," I said to my reflection. *'Maybe that's why Amach's showing me the details.'* She was showing me how I could help my friend. I'd be able to do the same for Estelle when I got . . . .

Darkness filled my vision and made me stagger. I knew I was still hiding in the bathroom, but I could no longer see my reflection. Blackened air swirled around me, brushed the top of my hair, then I was hit in the face. My heart skipped. My mouth tasted metallic, and I recognized a feeling of dread. Confusion made me weak in the knees. Something more was coming. This story wasn't going to be finished with the making of the bundles. There was much more to the events than I'd been shown. I felt chastised, and I burned with such shame that, if I could've, I would've climbed into the nearest bed and pulled the covers over my head. That slap had brought me back to being fully in the present. *'Thanks'* I mentally said to Amach. *'I guess I don't have a handle, yet, on why you're showing me these things. Sorry, I got ahead of you.'*

I unlocked and opened the door. Squealing women and heavy perfumes clamored into the bathroom. Their noise and artificial scents chased me through the bedroom, out that door, and past an octagonal shaped dining room dressed in rainbow colors. A traditional white-tiered cake stood amid a blinding cacophony of brightly-tinted, iced flowers. I wondered if they were different flavors instead of that tasteless sticky, white sugar paste.

In my search for the outdoors I ran into Magenta's mother. Her gray hair was bobbed in a Dutch-boy cut so that the edge of her thick bangs dissected her forehead. She reminded me of an aging Little Orphan Annie. I expected Mona's eyes to grow round and her hands to dance, palms out, while she spoke in a high pitched, girly voice. Instead, deep-toned words, gravely from years of smoking, croaked through her pencil-thin mouth.

"Thanks for traveling so far," Mona said with a frail hug. Mona was so thin that her elbow and knee joints were larger around than her arms and legs.

"Ah . . . our pleasure. We both like Magenta and Talon so well." I attempted to pass her stale cigarette presence into the fresh air but decided I'd be rude if I bolted for the door.

"You look flushed," she said.

I grabbed my chance. "Well, I am feeling warm. I was just going to step outside."

"Soon enough." She grabbed my arm. "I need help moving chairs and tables."

What could I do? As long as I could remember no one had ever disobeyed or disagreed with Mona. So I dutifully opened tables and chairs and set them in the pattern Mona wanted then helped to spread rainbow tablecloths. My stress level soared. With my psychic doors opened, I was growing more and more sensitive. My eyes watered from the blinding crush of color of the room. I heard internal dialogue from anyone who came near me, and their tones swelled my brain.

Flyn appeared beside me. "Are you alright?"

When I couldn't answer him, he captured my elbow and ushered me through the sliding glass door off the kitchenette. My head cleared quickly, but I remained separated from my body.

"You look haunted." Flyn attempted to hug me, but I waved him off.

"I'll be . . . ."

"THERE you are!!" Mona called. "Magenta needs you! Hurry! It's time!"

As she stepped aside for me to enter, the door was blocked by a man and woman leaving the house to stand on the deck which overlooked a small patch of grass surrounded by rose bushes in various stages of bloom. They were dressed in buckskins. Her yoke was decorated with shells and both had long leather fringes cascading from the hem of their sleeves to the ground.

Down the man's chest to his waist, tight braids hung over each of his ears. Her ebony hair was combed to below her buttocks. With even steps, they floated into the garden. I was mesmerized by their presence and wanted to follow in their wake feeling their sheer presence could part the waters of the world so I could pass more easily through my life.

"Selena! Magenta needs you NOW!" Mona commanded.

I turned toward the door and smacked into Flyn who was standing as if in a trance. His face was pale. His eyes so wide, I swear, it looked as if his eyelids had disappeared. He didn't know I was there, so I walked around him, wondering if Magenta was getting cold feet again.

When I found my friend, she handed me an abalone shell filled with desert sage and matches. "I forgot to have someone smudge the garden."

"I'll try but I think it's too late." When she looked at me horrified, I said, "There's two Indians out there. They're gorgeous."

"Now, now. They're Lakota. Don't objectify them." Then she smiled. "We're so lucky to have found them. The woman has one of those Universal Life Church minister's licenses. So she'll sign the marriage certificate, and he's a sacred pipe carrier."

"WOW," was all I could think of to say. I stumbled through the house and into the garden where I offered the smudge bowl to the woman.

"Oh, yes! If you don't mind helping?" she asked. "Walk with the burning sage clockwise and offer it to everyone." Her brown eyes were kind and fluttered across my face. "My name is Standing Feather. My partner is Red Buffalo. We call him RB."

"I'm Selena," I said. "I'm happy to help."

As I walked around the garden area, I offered the smoking herb to all in my path. The scent filled my head. The tension I'd been feeling ebbed. Before I'd finished the circle, I felt as if I were a helium balloon floating about the small garden. I had to make a conscious effort to place one foot in front of the other so I could feel the Earth beneath them.

I passed Flyn who was standing beside the man named Red Buffalo. Flyn was speaking quietly but with a level of intensity I'd not seen in him before. The Native American man was listening just as intently. From out of the blue, I received this psychic 'hit' they were brothers. When I looked closely, I saw they had the same flat forehead, high cheek bones, and matching skin tones, although Flyn's skin was lighter. *'What could they be discussing?'* I wondered. They both looked so serious. As if they'd heard me, they separated and turned toward me. Flyn beckoned to me, but I signaled with the burning sage that I wanted to finish. They nodded together.

Standing Feather smiled when I returned the shell. "You've someone following you."

When I looked over my shoulder, she laughed. "Not of this earth or of this time."

I flushed hotly. "Oh, well, yes, I know." I was flustered then pulled myself together. With a breath, I set my feet firmly and connected myself to the Earth's core, then wrapped myself in white light.

"Good," she observed, then eyed me keenly. "That's better."

I nodded, turning to stand by Flyn who was gazing at something outside the garden. My touch on his arm brought him back from wherever he'd gone. He took my hand.

Red Buffalo began a slow beat on his hand drum and continued softly until I could feel a shift in the air around us. He increased the tempo and volume by striking the stretched hide faster and harder, then he began to chant. At regular intervals, Standing Feather sang the same words in a higher, sweeter voice. Suddenly, Flyn's voice joined them. Chills danced up and down my spine. I dared to look at him as he threw his head back as if to howl. His piercing tones added another dimension to the singing.

All fell silent. Magenta and Talon stood at the edge of the circle. In the quiet, Standing Feather motioned for me to pass a bucket of fresh flowers around the circle. Each person then laid their flowers in the center of the gathering of family and friends to create a ring of bright blossoms. She handed me a soft bundle wrapped in what looked like a large pillow case. Magenta and Talon stepped into the inner, flowered circle. They stood stiffly, making every effort not to touch or to look at anything but the buck-skinned couple in front of them.

Standing Feather raised her voice. "Marriage is more than the housekeeping tasks of living together. It's more than a piece of paper . . . more than a contract."

I tried not to gasp. The intent of her words sat hard on my chest and raised the hairs on my arms. I tried to push away from how her words were affecting me, and, as she continued, my sight blurred. I saw four people standing together in the garden, while another picture of three people standing in the darkened cave overlaid the view. Dacona and Marweth were facing each other across the fire. I saw Amach touch each one of their shoulders to attract their attention to her. With quick movements and a sharpened feather quill, she cut a small piece of skin from the center of Dacona's forehead then made her hold it in her palm. She did the same with Marweth.

I heard Standing Feather speaking: "Marriage is a commitment to a spiritual journey, to a life of becoming more truly who each of you are and to more fully become a loving family unit."

Amach combines this bit of skin with the items in Dacona's bag. Marweth's flesh goes into his. She wraps each packet tightly then seals each with what smells like melted pine pitch as she says, "I bind you in body and spirit as you have asked of me. The place of your will is still within your grasp. No matter whether you lay together once or for the remainder of your time on earth, no matter what path you step upon separately or together, you are bound as one, forever."

I see her hands shake as she places the small pouches into each of their hands. A cold wind blows at my back. I am inside her. We shiver from the base of our spine to the top of our head with anxiety. Sickness catches in our throats. Pressure expands our heads while I hear her question herself, 'Is this something I should have done? I have not bound their souls. To all that is above and below, if I have harmed anyone, let it be me.'

Through the dread in my head and heart, I heard the deep voice of Red Buffalo. I came back into myself, knowing it was past time to close the doors between these worlds. I began by bringing in a golden light on my breath, while, with an outward push of air, I expelled any nugget of darkness residing within my body. As each area of my spine cleared, I mentally fashioned a shielded container to mark the boundaries around my being. I struggled with this picture in the area around my navel and around my heart. To bring myself into the present moment, I forced open my ears so I could hear Red Buffalo's words as he stood behind Magenta and Talon, turn them with him to face in each of the four directions.

"From the West, bring this couple the knowledge of their sacred darkness so they may know their fears and turn them into their greatest strengths."

"From the North, bring them healing from within and the knowledge of how to work with the power of all that is. Help them learn to work with each other."

"From the East, bring them the opportunity to begin anew with each moment of their lives."

"From the South, bring them the strength to know new life as it crosses from the spirit world and to release those lives needing to return to the ethers beyond."

"From all that is above, bring them the gift of the overview so they may see the possibilities of each step they take together on their paths."

"From our Mother, bless their footsteps so they may know your energy and offer theirs to you."

I felt Flyn move near to take my hand. His was warm while mine was cold. He held mine gently as we heard Standing Feather say the final words,

"As you stand together in this circle, may the presence of the Great God-Great Spirit who resides in the hearts of each one of us and in the winds of the four directions, these trees that stand so tall, the earth beneath our feet, and all that is around, bless you and keep you."

"May this day be the beginning of a grace-filled walk through life together."

She motioned for me to bring the package to her. I helped unfurl what appeared to be a quilt. Standing Feather and Red Buffalo wrapped Magenta and Talon in the most gorgeous, rainbow star quilt I'd ever seen. They were instructed to walk around the circle in the garden and shake each of our hands. We laughed as they stumbled to get in step with each other and tripped over each other's feet.

"That's your first lesson as a married couple. Learning to walk together, with each other," RB chuckled.

Chapter X - April, 2004
Time to Talk

Morning crested the Eastern hills as rays of sunlight caught the tips of fir and pine trees sleeping in the shadows around the meadow near my mountain home. For seconds only, these tops were in full sun, and the trees resembled lit candles aflame with morning splendor. If I looked away, then returned my gaze, this border between day and night would have descended a foot. In no time, the light would speed along the length of the trees until everything was bathed in slanted and shining rays. As long as I stared at this premiere sun line, it seemed as if I could make the brilliant edge delay its journey down the trees to the earth.

I liked to begin my day holding onto this first instant, this initial moment, when everything (nature, my mind, the day, my family, The Universe) was brand new. Yesterday was done with cheers or jeers; tomorrow wasn't a consideration. This precious second held the potential of opportunity. It was without blemish or problem. If I didn't look away, I believed I could keep it safe. Of course, I learned the more I tried to keep this single moment in limbo, the less likely I was to experience laughter or hugs or accomplishments. Now I held this glorious instant of time with excitement. *'What would the next moment hold? What could the next second become?'*

Lack of sun made my anticipation for the day's events harder to build. I discovered very early on how a person needed particular qualities to survive rainy winters in the Northern California mountains. One had to know how to light one's own internal spark, how to treat the rain like liquid sunshine, and live a life full of self-made opportunities and rewards.

I often wondered how the local Native people had survived. They must have been better attuned to seasonal rhythms, with fewer expectations than we have in this modern world. Had they been practical by saving their handwork for the long, rainy days inside their huts? Was the winter a welcome relief from a summer of hunting, trapping, skinning and drying meats, and the fall's gathering and preparing roots, bulbs, and acorns? Did they hibernate? Or go about their lives without a thought to the pounding water on their heads?

I wondered if Flyn realized what living here full-time would mean. Standing to watch the sunlight descend to the bottom of the trees, I didn't have a clue about his knowledge of living in the woods. I only knew he'd worked construction until he'd fallen off a roof. He'd been forced, then, into years of surgery and rehabilitation for a broken back and left femur and had struggled against an addiction to prescription medication that included morphine. Yoga had been his salvation, and, if he didn't stretch and loosen his muscles every morning and evening, he was crippled with pain. I knew he was fit enough but was he experienced enough? I guess we'd find out.

One phone call had canceled his classes and his monthly contribution to the rent of the yoga studio. I was now the main breadwinner, yet again. All I could do was hope he'd be entertained by hauling trees and firewood or digging mud from the ditches to keep our road clear. I'd have to tell him about cleaning rain gutters regularly and sweeping the stove pipe and chimney to keep the creosote from building since we'd be having regular fires come winter. How would he take to reading by kerosene light if and when the electricity failed? Would he now consider it important to read David's lengthy notes about the complicated water and sewage systems?

David had built an amazing home, first in his head, then with his hands. When I'd lost him, I'd no idea how anything worked. I had to take myself by my own hand and shake myself out of my stupor of grief. I'd needed his notes and drawings, as much of my common sense as I could muster, and to remember snatches of things he'd done or said, to deal with any problem.

If life were like it had been in the 50's, when there seemed to be less crime in city, I might've sold out and moved permanently to San Francisco, but I hadn't been sure I could survive there, so I'd kept the land and house as my ace in the hole. I'd no idea if living in the city would be easier or scarier than living with bears and skunks. I'd just wanted something livelier than isolation. Now in 2004, after the changes since Y2K and 9/11, I had to agree with Flyn. No one knew how Bush Jr's war on terrorism was going to finish. Even November's election between him and Kerry was unsure, although I knew I wanted someone in there who was more committed to peace than oil profit. After a lot of thought and a lot of talking in the car as we returned from the wedding, I'd agreed it seemed the time to move to the mountains and be more self-sufficient.

As I repacked our car to drive south and alone, I thought about all my choices in the past few years and compared them to this one. *'So, OK, Sellie. How do you really feel about this situation where suddenly you're supporting two people, again? I don't remember when you voted for this particular part of the equation of moving to the mountains!'*

I stuffed and restuffed a rebellious bag of trash that wouldn't stay inside the Tracker's back door and asked myself a cold hard question. *'How'm I gonna manage this transition?'* The trash bag fell again. I kicked it before I picked it up and punched it into a different corner of the car. Now, I had to reconstruct my entire schedule so I could live part-time in the woods with someone who seemed like a stranger. Since Magenta's wedding, Flyn'd become a puzzle. Tears stuck in my eyes and throat. I felt as if I was standing in a quagmire of sucking sand.

"Almost ready?" Flyn called from the door.

I tried to redirect my thoughts, to shake off my mood as best I could. "Almost!"

He must have sensed the strangling feeling I had all over my body, because he came down the porch steps. "Hey, now! You're not going to be gone for weeks, just four days." He started to take me in his arms, but I pushed free. I stood with my back to him.

From Friday evening to Monday night was less than three days. The time between his proposal and his execution of it had been so rapid, I felt as if I'd been bulldozed, boondoggled, and bamboozled. Anger spread across my chest making me struggle for each breath. I crossed my arms around myself and hung on.

"What's wrong?" he asked quietly, turning me to face him, his brown eyes dark with the question.

Searching for my reasons for this current mood, I flapped my arms helplessly at my sides then wound them around myself again and turned away from him. I searched the fenced garden as if my answer might be found in the blossoming roses or the berry bushes or the blooming dandelions.

I felt his hands on my arms. I wanted to scream. So I did. I screamed so loud it echoed against the trees surrounding the house. I hurt my throat. He didn't flinch. His hands remained on my arms, without a tremble. With his steady presence in the face of my emotions, I realized I could say words which had been stuck in my throat for almost 40 years.

"I feel used!" I shouted to the garden, then turned quickly to catch a glimpse of his face. He brought his hands to rest again on my biceps and gave them a slight squeeze before removing them and hugging himself. We were like two closed vessels facing each other. I saw his eyes begin to search for something unseen in every inch of my face. His eyebrows scrunched together, and wrinkles waffled his forehead. The deep crevice between his eyes became a bottomless cavern. I had expected shock or a indulgent smile, but it was as if his computer system was sorting through every file and folder of his memory of me and reclassifying information into new categories. He was lost in his own process, so I closed my eyes and sought the source of my words.

What arose on the back of my eyelids were pictures. I saw myself struggling to stay whole and solvent after David had died. Granted, I'd decided to be alone. I'd refused to live with Shawna or Sam, or give way to my terror of being alone. I'd been on my own with no one to support us but me, since David had begun to falter with his prostate cancer. Alone, I'd watched him slip from me, deteriorating before my eyes while I held our lives together with whatever strength I could muster. For five years he'd withered before turning to dust. I looked at our lives before his illness and saw me working to support my children's needs while he supported our home and the land. And prior to our marriage, when I'd been a divorcee with two children, I'd more than two full-time jobs to make ends meet. Red had left me with so much credit card debt, I'd barely been able to reach up to touch bottom.

And here I jumping in to support another man without my full consent or conscious approval. I held on to my anger and opened my eyes. Flyn had tears in his.

"Sellie, God help me! I never . . . I just thought about me, my world, how I needed to escape. I never thought about you; how you'd meet all your appointments, clear my stuff out of the yoga studio, buy food, lug it to the apartment, then come here with provisions for us."

He opened his arms and pulled me to him. "I'm so sorry."

I still hugged myself while his arms wrapped around me, wondering at what I was hearing.

"I . . . never . . . considered your life these past years,

what you had to do," he continued, stroking my back, careful not to crush me. "You've carried your own load for a long time."

I was startled. He'd read my mind. He took my shoulders and pushed me away so he could look me in the eye. "And these visions or whatever . . . you shouldn't drive when you're pulled out of yourself so often. I just didn't think." He ended with a tight hug around me.

As he talked, I melted. When he finished, I opened my arms to him, craving the warmth of his body, his caring. I felt humbled at the depth of this understanding that occurred without me having said anything to him. *'How do I merit this guy?'* I asked myself, and a little voice answered from somewhere inside my head with the words: 'IT'S TIME.'

I didn't recognize the voice. It wasn't from the front of my head so it wasn't my own thoughts. *'Time for what?'* I thought to myself.

'TIME TO TELL SOMEONE EVERYTHING,' it said.

I shuddered, and he held on tighter before loosening his hold. "What is it?" he asked.

I searched his eyes, then whispered, "I think I'd like to let you know what's going on with me. But, I'm nervous about it."

"I'll pack my things." He left me with a kiss on my brow, and I wondered where on earth I'd begin.

Perhaps me coming clean about what happened at Potty's would be a good place to start. I'd told him she was dying and how I'd done what I could. He'd asked about the binder, but I'd explained she'd wanted me to read her journal. I held on to myself. I needed to tell him about my vision during the wedding ceremony of our friends. And then there was Estelle. I thought, *'If I tell him about me, maybe he'll tell me about what happened between him and Red Buffalo.'* I had to admit a growing curiosity there.

I paced the driveway, waiting for him and thinking.

'Detailing my life might help me create an overview so I can figure out what in the hell's going on and what to do next!' I shrugged. *'Maybe?'*

He drove, and I was grateful. "So what would you like to hear about first? Potty, Estelle, or the wedding?"

He side-glanced at me. "Who's Amach?"

"Oh . . . well . . . now that's the $64,000 question." I hesitated and wondered how to begin that saga. I took a deep breath and plunged in. "So here's the facts as I know them at this moment. Amach came into my life over 20 years ago as a spirit who used my body and mind as a channel. We'd finally struck a deal because I hated being pushed aside, especially since I didn't know what she said through me unless a tape recorder was on or someone was writing it down. After we'd negotiated, she didn't come spontaneously any more, except for a few times. She'd hang out like a guide for me when I worked with clients. She'd put thoughts in my head I could choose to say or not to say, when I was with Estelle or this psychic group we developed."

"How'd she find you?" Flyn asked.

I paused, searching my mind for an answer. I looked at him and admitted, "I'm not sure, Flyn. I was alone, then, she was there. I asked her one time: 'Why me?' I don't believe I've ever gotten an answer. Although, she mentioned how I asked for her."

"And did you?"

I shook my head. "I don't remember asking specifically for a spirit-being to enter my body and start talking through my mouth. No, it was more like I asked for a way I could help people. She said I'd done that a few times, though I don't remember except during a vision quest on the mountain in Estelle's back forty. I have to admit she's been true to her promises about not taking me over anymore. She would just give me messages about people when I worked on them or first met them."

"What'd she say about me?"

"Ah . . ." I was embarrassed. "We've not been speaking since before David died."

"May take more than one trip up and down this highway for me to hear all the stories," he said.

"Could be," I answered, working diligently to sidestep painful memories from the past.

Chapter XI - 1982
Selena, Go to the Mountain!

Stones slid under my feet as I struggled to climb the steep incline behind Estelle's house. I tried to keep my mind off the promise I'd made not to eat food or drink water during my time on the mountain.

'*OK Sellie, that was an exaggeration.*' What I was climbing was really a hill. No need for me to make more out of this experience that it was. This was a vision quest and a chance to be alone and think about my life. *'Good, Sellie, that was more to the point.'*

My arms ached from carrying my sleeping bag, back pack, two leather pouches, and the pole I'd crafted as my 'Light Gatherer.' I looked at the smoothed length of madrone and at its combination of feathers and beads, red string, crystals, and bells. Why in the world had I constructed this thing? *'Because Estelle had read about one in a book and thought I should,'* I answered myself. I'd no idea what it was supposed to do for me, and, quite frankly, I wished I didn't have it, so I left it under a bush.

After reaching the top of the first forested hill, I followed a deer path until it disappeared. My plan for this quest was to continue to the top of the ridge to find the look-out rock she'd shown me last year. Another animal path meandered in the direction I wanted to go, so I meandered with it. After a few paces, I lost my footing and slid several yards down the side of the hill. I managed to keep my feet under me, but scraped one hand as I grabbed for anything I could reach. Finally my right tennis shoe found a purchase on a rock outcropping. Adrenaline roared through my head; I sucked air and leaned close to the side of the hill, pebbles rattling past me to the bottom of the slope, while a stellar jay chattered at me. I felt lectured about my folly, being here on my own.

"God damn it! What in the hell do I think I'm doing?" My blasphemy quieted the scolding bird. *'Oops, no cussing! OK, reframe!'*

"Oh, Great Spirit, help me. This path is hard, and I've no idea why I decided to do this."

'To be alone,' came my first thought as I dusted my hands. "Well, I certainly am that," I said to no one in particular. Leaning closer to the side of the hill to keep my balance, I scanned the area above me, looking for a better route. "Looks like it's straight up," I said, trying to clear my mind with a forced sigh, then another.

A thought flashed through me that took a moment to process: *'Perhaps the way one gets to the top is part of the experience.'* I stood still as I wondered if my preparations for a personal vision quest were just as important as standing on the flat rock all night? Maybe just as important as fasting from food or water? Just as important as this morning's shower? As my first night's sleep after I came down? What if it's all important: from the time I got the idea to do this, to a moment next year when I don't remember the details of this experience and decide to do it again? Perhaps slipping was telling me to slow down and watch how I approach this quest?

My attention caught on tufts of dried grass poking from an assembly of stones on the steep hill that whispered 'caution'. I could slip on these stones and the grasses underneath, so I avoided them. Bigger rocks, spaced at intervals beneath the loose soil, resembled a natural staircase. I balanced one toe on the first one and found it sturdy, so clambered to the next plateau. Alert for a path, my eye snagged on a large depression of earth filled with drying oak leaves.

Walking around its edge, I measured it to be over eight

feet in diameter. Could I be so lucky? When Tara, our friend studying local Native American culture, had told us about ancient ceremonial fire pits, I'd listened with half an ear. I didn't believe something as important as she was describing could have gone undiscovered on this side of the ridge. But, Estelle had said, with only one logging operation of these hills in the mid-1980s, every inch of land had not been scoured. In fact, her family had made the effort to preserve the forest and land from wanton destruction.

I adjusted my pack and bags but had to surrender to the cramp growing in my right arm. My sleeping bag and pouches hit the earth, and I unbelted my back pack, sighing with relief as it slipped from my shoulders. My mouth registered its first sensation of dryness, though I pushed the wish for water to the back of my mind by focusing on the depression in the Earth.

I wished I'd listened better to Tara's description. I think she'd said the local natives had used these pits for quests and for something called 'watching'. I poked a broken branch into the pit before I dug my hands beneath the crinkly layer of leaves and found clumps of decaying matter, then strata of soggy slime. I waded into the center and sank to my knees, disappointed I hadn't sunk further. The one thing I remembered Tara saying was these watcher pits were deep enough for a quester to stand and not see over the edge of the pit. I pulled my legs up and kneeled so I could lift decomposed materials to the surface. As I laid each layer aside, I reached into a hole up to my arm pit, still not hitting solid earth with my fingers. I judged I'd emptied at least five feet of dead leaves and debris and bet myself if I excavated the entire area, I would unearth a deep bowl with remnants of a fire at the bottom. It either had to be a fire pit, or I'd found something else.

I sat down, my hands caked with black rotting leaves and mud. "Oh great, no water! Now what?" I asked the air. A manzanita bush rustled nearby, catching my attention. Spring green grasses, about a foot high, stood beneath it and glistened with moisture. After climbing out of the hollow, I wiped my hands on the moist grass then crawled under the manzanita's canopy. It was cooler here, and I sat at peace.

From my resting place, I eyed the pit and the hole I'd dug in its center. All was bathed in brilliant sunlight. Perspiration surfaced on my skin, even in the shade. Wearing jeans under my long skirt might have been a good idea to protect my private parts and legs from biting critters, but I was getting hot!

I thought about taking off some clothes, staying right where I was, and setting up camp next to this place where an ancient quester might have prayed for guidance. Maybe I would benefit from connecting with the essence of those who had been in the pit, however many years ago. I relaxed. Maybe this questing process wasn't meant to be quite so hard. *'Maybe?'* I thought hopefully. Maybe Estelle's warning about rattlesnakes living on her special rock, the spot I'd claimed as my intended destination, was messing with my resolve?

I grinned, wishing I'd brought one of Estelle's resource books on Vision Questing. Having some kind of instruction would be helpful right now. I listed aloud what I remembered of the instructions we'd read in three of her books. "Go to the highest point you can find"; "Feel the energy and be where you sense it the most"; "Stick to your original plan."; "Everything keeping you from your goal is a challenge to be overcome and is a lesson." It was the final instruction that resonated.

'Which book said which?' I thought. *'That's not the point,'* I answered myself. *'It's not the name of the book that matters, or the author. It's the message! And that one fits.'* My mind wandered over the past few years. I'd been dealing with failures and low self-esteem after reading about everyone else's 'enlightenment' experiences, particularly Lynn Andrews in *The Medicine Woman*.

What I wouldn't give for an old one, or even a 'young' wise woman, to tap me on the shoulder and tell me I was the chosen one. Then, this same elder would commit herself to teaching me her secrets. I guessed it was some form of the 'Cinderella Syndrome' wishing I was secretly someone special. Every human being who walked the Earth had some desire to be unique underneath the mediocrity of their lives. I was no exception.

"Well, no such luck," I said, exposing my neck to any cool breeze.

No written instructions. No wise woman or man volunteering themselves. *'What to do now?'*

As I hunkered under the manzanita bush, I felt boxed in. It was cooler here, that was true, but I was cramped and couldn't see beyond what was in front of me. I had no room to stretch. I felt impatient with myself and couldn't understand why, until I realized I was enacting a metaphor for my life. I was quite literally hiding myself, my light, my being, under a bush. I laughed at the irony, until I sobered. *'Why?'* I asked myself,

I didn't like my answer: *'Because it's comfortable . . . and safe.'* I shifted my position. *'Because I don't have a whole lot of faith in my being able to go the distance.'*

"OK . . . and what else are you doing by staying stooped under this bush?" I asked aloud. I didn't like this answer either. *'Taking the easy way?'* *'Falling short of my goal?'* By not facing my fear of snakes, I was settling for second best and not going where I really wanted to go.

I inspected my resting place. I could only see 25% of my surroundings and nothing beyond the shaded space. I had no overview, no way to gain a perspective of where I was and where a path might lead me. *'Isn't that what a vision quest's about? Getting an overview of my life, seeing my potential future?'*

None of the books I'd read on Vision Questing had offered that definition, but this was the goal I was seeking.

'OK then! I need to do this. Set down parameters,

challenge myself to meet my goals, and watch everything that happens.' That felt right.

I'd left my family for four days. I'd said I wanted some quiet time to prepare myself with Estelle and some time afterwards to process whatever happened. They'd whined at first, then moaned, but Shawna and Sam were both capable teenagers; David knew the ropes of step-fatherhood. He'd survived without me for a long time before we were married. They'd be fine. Everyone knew where I'd be if I didn't come back in two days. I had corn meal and natural tobacco for offerings, colored cloth for prayer tie making, my cigarettes, matches, my hands, and my voice. I was poised on the very edge of my existence, or at least I thought I was. *'Why not do my life differently and go for the gold?'* I asked myself.

I decided to climb to the top of the hill where Estelle had shown me a view of the entire valley. We'd been there one afternoon for a hike. I'd made it then. I could make it now. I had nothing to lose and a good chance of gaining, something.

I thought about making two trips to ease my load but doubted my sense of direction could take me up and back to this same place. I couldn't see a specific path, so I decided to rearrange my pack and bags to free my hands by tying my duffel bag to my front while I carried the pack on my back. Now, I could walk in balance while struggling through tangles of madrone, stickweed, and manzanita, and steering clear of the bright green, triple-leafed plants I knew to be poison oak.

It could've been an hour later, or maybe ten minutes, when I faced a stack of boulders almost two stories high. I heard a rattle. It was faint, then it got louder. To my left, at the foot of the wall, I spied a rattlesnake stretched in the shade. I froze; my heart raced. I wanted to pee and vomit at the same time. It took me more than a moment to find my voice.

"No prob," I whispered. "I see you." Chills enveloped my body. To bolster my courage, I kept talking. "I see you, Brother Snake, or is it, Sister Snake, laying all stretched out.

I'm going around this rock." I took a step to the right and heard it rattle again. I stopped. A thought passed, '*If there's one, there's usually two.*' I wondered where that knowledge originated, then I opened my senses to see if it was true.

UP HERE was another voice filling my head. I looked at the side of the rock wall to another ledge on my left and saw the second rattler staring me in the eye. I didn't just freeze this time, I glaciated. All the better not to pee my pants.

'*Oh! My God! What am I doing here?*' I thought frantically.

YOU'RE TESTING YOURSELF came an answer.

I couldn't move, couldn't feel my body. I was hot and cold at the same time, and my heart pounded in my ears. I wanted to scream, to run. I'd done that before when I'd reached for a rope on the porch at our trailer only to have it wiggle. I'd thrown the snake against the aluminum siding of our trailer, screeched, and run backwards until I'd fallen on my butt. I hadn't been able to keep my eyes on the snake after it hit the wall, but Sam, my son, had tried to reassure me it had slithered around the edge of the wooden rocking couch. I'd been so frightened, I'd avoided sitting there for a year, until David had torn it apart to prove to me the snake had gone.

Here I was, face to face with another one. '*No, correction, I'm face to face with two of the damned things.*'

I couldn't scream and run backwards here, if for no other reason than my feet felt like clods of cement. I couldn't breathe, so I closed my eyes, trying to regain a bit of composure.

'*This isn't the way to handle this.*' I had to keep my wits about me, and my eyes open. Sam wasn't here to watch out for me, and David wasn't here to save me. I gulped. To make sure I wasn't climbing into a rattler nest, I needed to take my time and watch where I was going.

Without moving, I checked around my feet and saw only rocks and small pebbles in the sparse grass. Widening my visual search, a narrow depression of dried grasses wound to my right. I assumed either Estelle had broken that path, or a deer. I moved slowly, keeping track of my feet, my hands, the snakes. I climbed layers of boulders laying helter-skelter and saw fresh animal droppings that could have been from a fox or coyote. It encouraged me.

Would a four-footed critter have climbed here if there had been a nest of rattlers? I didn't think so. With resolve, I climbed the remainder of the stones onto a rock ledge overlooking a spring green valley quilted with patterns of turned earth, green fields, and yellowing grains. It was awesome. Now my chills were from the thrill of accomplishment. I'd made it. I was here, alone, past the snakes and the self-doubt. I'd pushed through my fears to the place of my choice.

As I stood on my stony mountain, I felt heat pound on me from the sun overhead, its unrelenting power descending upon me. I hunched under its extreme glare and felt my skin wither. My tongue was stuck to the roof of my mouth when I tried to lick my lips. My heart sank. I'd chosen a Vision Quest location without shade, cool earth, or a place to hide. *'Now I know I'm out of my mind.'*

"First things first" as my mother would say. I had to get cooler. After checking all cracks, crevices, and ledges around me, I removed my shoes, then my jeans from under my skirt. One of Estelle's books had reported how a woman could benefit from allowing earth's energy to flow into her womb. Wearing pants stopped that process, so I also removed my underpants, since one of my other reasons for being on this ledge was to pray for the healing of my uterine fibroids. Perhaps Earth's energy would flow upward and dissolve them. I offered a prayer for healing as I also prayed for a cool breeze.

Organizing my belongings didn't take long. I had only to build my altar as a focus for my prayers. My tin box held squares of primary-colored material and red string. I placed my pouch of organic tobacco and corn meal, my abalone shell, some dried mugwort and a braid of sweet grass on a folded green bandanna, then, sat and lit a Salem. The menthol was cool on my sticky tongue and dry throat, at least for the first few puffs. Then I watched the smoke rise from my cigarette, straight into the sky.

No wonder the indigenous peoples used smoke for all kinds for prayer. *'It always ascends.'* I crushed out the cigarette before wiggling my body into a more comfortable position on the stone. I didn't feel the need to bring my journal up to date, do ritualized breathing, or create a six-pointed mandala in my mind. I didn't want to force anything at this moment.

After taking a few deep breaths, I trusted my lungs would breathe when they wanted air, and my heart would keep beating without my awareness, as would every other bodily function. I let my muscles relax and tried to sense the world around me. I heard the 'moo' of a cow from somewhere down the valley. A horn tooted. Otherwise, the day was silent and hot. Sweat trickled from my scalp to behind my ears; water seeped between my breasts and legs.

'Why am I here?' I asked myself. I sighed my answer. *'I want time alone so I can review my life and look into my future.'*

In the quiet, my heart began to hammer faster than normal. I tried to believe it was because I'd just climbed a hill, faced down two rattlesnakes, and hadn't had food or water since midnight. And, I'd just had a cigarette.

The hammering in my chest grew loud in my ears. I tried to break my growing tension by breathing deeply, but feelings of confusion and despair pushed up from my chest. What to my wondering eyes should appear? Tears! Leaking from the edges of my eyes, over my lower lids, and down my cheeks. My stomach clenched, and I sobbed from the bottom of what felt like my soul.

I wasn't sure why I was crying, but I didn't try to placate myself. I let the tears and the feelings flow until I felt calmer, which took a long time. After blowing my nose in my skirt because I'd forgotten tissue, I chided myself for this sadness. *'Why did I cry so hard? I have so much.'*

David was a loving husband and a responsible father to Shawna and Sam. My life was safer than when I'd been married to Red. I'd left my first husband in Colorado in 1974 after he'd disciplined our one-year-old son with a spanking so hard that Sam had bitten his tongue. I'd been furious. Red could hit me, but not my son and never my daughter, but he'd managed to leave bruises on all three of us before I'd found my way out of that house. Yes, I was safe now.

'But why such tears?' I had thought I'd released all the sadness I'd carried from the heart-breaking results of my choices in life. *'Some things haven't turned out too well.'* But, did I want forgiveness for the wrong turns I'd made? Did I want to make some kind of atonement?

I shuddered a sob and placed my right hand over my heart. Sometimes my chest felt like an open wound being licked by fiery winds. My mind drifted over the last few weeks, and I got stuck in several places. My constant arguments with Shawna about clothes, friends, and wearing makeup had resulted in her running away one night because she hadn't felt loved. I winced at the memory. I wanted to cut back my hours at the hospital and supplement our funds with massage, which I loved, but was mired in self-doubt and procrastination. David's disapproval of my plan made my throat choke. He worked 50 hours a week so we could build his dream house and move out of his 20year-old, dilapidated trailer. He was a good man with so much energy for me and for my, his, family. *'Why can't I be satisfied with the way things are? Why do I feel there's something more I need to do, to accomplish, to provide?'*

I sucked another cigarette; I didn't need to rush.

Besides, I figured I needed time to be clear about my prayers before I made my tobacco ties. I exhaled. The smoke bent sideways. *'Does that mean I'm thinking laterally?'* I laughed at how I took such an ordinary occurrence seriously. *'It could mean I'm not being direct.'*

My ascent from Estelle's house to this ledge had been hampered by all manner of diversions, until I'd made up my mind about what I'd wanted to do. *'Was this a lesson for my life too?'* I thought, *'Was I supposed to make up my mind about what I wanted and then decide how to go for it?'*

"OK," I addressed the sun. "I want roots!" I answered simply and out loud. "I want a home with enough space for each of us, where I can have my own room with a door. I want to plant flowers and know they'll be there until I or God decide to pull them up." Pictures of all the gardens I'd planted and left behind every time I'd moved over the past 30 years blossomed in the back of my mind. A shadow of frustration at David clouded my heart. He had stopped me from planting flowers every season we'd been together because he hadn't wanted to waste the water on plants that weren't edible. My blossoms had to be of tomatoes, eggplant, squash, and cucumbers. I shrugged.

'What else?' I thought.

"I want to feel that whatever I do counts for something." It wasn't that I needed notoriety, just respect, both at home and at work. Having finished the weekend massage courses at Heartwood College, I wanted to learn more about helping others. If I could know I'd helped someone become fully themselves, then I knew I'd feel good about myself. My mind drifted to Estelle, a very new friend. How would we work together in the future? Whenever we'd traded massages in class, I'd felt shy and unskilled; she seemed much more experienced than I was. Why would she want to buddy up with me? I felt so inept. Yet, she'd helped me do this quest, and she'd always chosen me as her partner during massage school.

I shrugged again.

'What else?' I asked, a stillness settling in my head. No birds twittered. I wondered if birds were silent in the middle of the day. Then I discovered that nothing moved. No breeze. No bugs. No twirl of my hair. I pulled my knees toward my breasts, covered them with my skirt, then embraced them with my arms. My chin rested on my knees. Sun rays soaked into my scorching clothes, past my hot skin, into my core which I hadn't realized was so cold. Memories swam: me as a child looking for approval from my father who was away in his green uniform, searching for approval from my mother who only had eyes for him, hoping for attention from one grandmother who only had time for herself, and the other who lived in an abused stupor. Tears threatened to fall again so I fast-forwarded through my confused adolescence, failed college attempt, and disastrous first marriage.

I swiped the water from my cheeks, enraged at myself. All those experiences were behind me, part of my history, and I didn't have to keep going over them. They were done, finished. I crushed the dead cigarette butt into my hand. No fire remained in the ashes. I relegated my past with the dead stub into the small metal can I carried. "No more!" I chastised myself. I was not going to hack my way through all that crap. I knew I was a different person from the child who'd been left on her own. I had to be better than that needy little girl, but who was I?

I snapped the travel ash tray shut. As I reached to put it with my other things, my hand brushed against the dried mugwort. I'd thought it only an obnoxious weed until Tina had taught me how it was used by the local Indians as a smudge. I lit it. While it smoldered in the green-tinged center of the abalone shell I'd found last spring, I offered my past into the rising smoke and allowed my mind to clear.

"No more memories today," I promised. "Let me form questions that will lead me to my future and how best to be in the world!"

I grew tired of sitting hunched, so I faced the sky and stretched my legs. The rocky ledge fit behind the small of my back and behind my knees, even beneath my neck. She wasn't soft, but she supported me. '*She,*' I thought, interested in my choice of gender. I would have thought a Vision Quest rock to be a 'he'.

Silence continued. My muscles loosened. I was no longer 'me' on top of the rock, but with the rock . . . then of the rock . . .among it . . . within it.

Relax, she said.

'*I am,*' I said with my mind.

Breathe with me and let me hold you.

'*I will.*'

We are one.

'*We are,*' I agreed.

I hear your heart. Can you feel mine?

My body pounded in time with my heart's rhythm. Around me, beneath me, I felt a slower, softer thud. '*I can.*' I answered.

I am your grandmother, your mother, your hope, your grounding cord. I am, here, a stone, but I am more. I am wherever and whenever you touch me.

'*I am thankful.*'

Whatever you do, do your work to honor me as well as yourself, and I will help.

'*Thank you,*' I offered, but felt my words were too shallow. How could I say more to show my gratitude for such a wondrous gift?

Commit yourself to me and to the intent and purpose of bringing health and help to anyone who asks. As I give myself away to you, give yourself to others.

'*I commit myself to helping others so they can be all they can be in health and happiness wherever and whenever they ask.*' I felt her loving embrace and could do no less than offer myself to her.

Speak those words to the four winds. Remember this as a beginning.

There was nothing further. Only my heart beat pulsing with the rhythm around me. I felt complete and never wanted to move. The instant this thought emerged, my shoulders and butt ached. The back of my head felt as if it had grown flat.

I groaned. Pulling away from the Grandmother rock, my body felt as if it were on fire. My eyelids hurt when I opened them. I was scorched on every inch of exposed skin. How long had I been stretched on the ledge? It had seemed like such a short conversation, but the sun was now several hours into its fall to the west. It was so late. My prayer ties weren't done. I panicked. I hadn't done my Vision Quest according to the book.

A laugh rippled across my chest. "Which one?" I croaked aloud.

If I'd planned every detail of this experience, I wouldn't have known to include a conversation with this Grandmother, an unforgettable communion with the Earth.

"I know what I'm praying for now," I said aloud. My smudge bowl was empty so I crushed more leaves between my palms and created a cigar-shaped length of mugwort which I then lit. Smoke wafted from side to side. I smudged each pinch of tobacco and each colored square of cloth, saying my prayer while I folded them together then tied them with red cotton string.

With the red material, I prayed for healing for myself and my family. Into the blue cloth, I placed prayers for the building of a good home. My foremost prayers into the yellow squares were for help in meeting my commitment to assist others in their healing. Three major prayers seemed like enough. *'What an awesome way to be guided to the best words for my prayers!'* As the sky darkened and evening turned into night, I faced each direction with my ties in hand and spoke these prayers aloud.

With each repetition, I grew stronger in my desire for these requests. All thoughts or memories remained in the far recesses of my mind. In the cool darkness, I stumbled and fell to my knees, losing skin across a rough stone. *'An offering,'* I thought, curling to rest, thinking I would arise again in a moment. Sleep drifted across my body as driftwood slips through the waves toward shore, becoming caught in eddies of back-surging waters.

Warmth seeped into my pores from the Earth's crust as heat pulsed from the sunburn on my skin; it was as if we were exchanging energy. I shifted my weight; my body was heavy. Arms and legs felt contained, as if I was swimming through solidifying jello. *'What flavor would I be?'* I wondered, then contemplated what it would feel like to be embalmed. *'Morbid, Sellie! Lighten up!'* I ordered myself. I floated, dreamed I rested on the futon David and I opened each night into a bed.

'No, wait! This isn't right! Aren't I on a rocky ledge?' Confusion skips into panic, makes my heart . . but, I have no heart beat . . . my eyes won't open. I'm scrunched between the edges of a known and an unknown. 'What is this?' I ask then am lifted from the couch, the ledge, the earth, and fly. My eyes feel closed, but I see with a different set of eyes. I hover in a holding pattern, wondering, waiting, for what?

Colored bubbles waltz toward me, each one with a body in residence. Shawna dances in a rose-colored bubble, changing from a girl to a woman with short auburn hair and children of her own. Sam stumbles in a blue bubble, growing from boy to an old man while holding a bat in his hand as small children throw him a ball. David, sweet David, looks at me from his green bubble, a question in his eyes. His bubble bursts, transforming him into a light that waivers near my lips, then disappears. From behind me, a bright yellow bubble throws itself in front of my face, bounces off my head, my chest, my abdomen, then spins near my heart with the shadow of a man inside. In her red bubble, growing smaller and smaller, my mother rocks, crocheting, until she is bumped by a deep blue sphere holding my father, who is standing at attention. His bubble bumps hers askew and bursts. Her bubble twirls in the air, then spins and fades into nothing.

The rapid rat-tat-tat of a drum jerked me awake.

"Estelle!!" Sure Estelle's playing one of her jokes on me, I called again. "That was mean! You scared the shit out of me!"

Still no answer. *'Must be working her way down the hill,'* I decided. But, I didn't hear crashing through the bushes and trees. *'Could the drum beat have been part of my dream?'* I recreated the sound of the drumstick hitting hide; the thumping sounded so close to my head. What else could have gotten so near my perch? I held my breath and stared at the star-speckled sky. My mind twirled with questions until the patterns of darkness and the spread of the Milky Way awed my mind into silence.

Standing to stretch, I saw each star glowing with such a strong light, their numbers were so abundant, I could see shadows in the valley below. I opened my arms and heart to the world of the night, admiring tiny flecks of light dancing in front of me. They shimmered around my ankles, over my shoulders. They were like lightening bugs, but when I reached for one, instead of dashing away, the speck of light settled in my right palm. I reached for another with my left hand. The lights remained still. Both my hands were radiating, and, without my intention, my hands were drawn together into a position of prayer. Light streamed from their edges, then slowly disappeared.

For the rest of the night, my hands were unexpectedly warm whenever I touched myself. I no longer stood to pray, but sat and remained watchful, wondering what it all meant. I was too tired to track a logical sequence of thought. Instead my brain was quiet and bathed in the magic of the rising sun.

I revered the 'tween' time, especially when day turns into night, because I'd never been awake to feel the energy when night changed into day. Today, I saw the gradual brightening of the sky behind the hills and forests to the east, making the stars fade as the dark sky lightened.

'*What a jerk I am,*' I thought when I realized these stars were in the sky all the time. The sun was just brighter than they were. Like when the moon shines so full it dulls the sky and dims the nearest stars so they seem to disappear. As the night faded, I focused on the brightest star in the heavens. '*The Morning Star,*' I thought, raising my arms over my head.

"Maker of All Things, My Grandmother, upon whom I stand, thank you for this way to pray. I've seen so much about myself. Please, be with me as I open to healing myself and anybody who asks me to help them. Help me do what you would have me do, go where you would have me go, say what you would have me say. To all my relations."

I pulled six hairs from my head and twined them around a jutting stone on the ledge. I didn't want them to blow away. I left my ties to decorate the stack of stones behind me, the ones housing my rattlesnake friends on the other side. I thanked those critters for staying put.

When I finally gathered my stuff into its bags and packs, I'd no idea what time it was. It could have been early afternoon, but when I entered Estelle's kitchen, I found it was 6 pm. Smells of potato soup and garlic bread greeted my nose. My stomach rumbled.

"How was it?" Estelle asked, coming to greet me with a spoon in her hand.

"Amazing," I hugged her quick, then headed for the sink to get a drink of water. I found a tumbler and turned on the faucet, relishing the sound of the flowing water as I filled the glass.

"You didn't stay long."

I brought the glass to my lips, then stopped. "Was I supposed to stay longer?"

"Well," she said as she tapped the spoon into her palm. "Some traditions require a four day commitment."

"But you said . . . "

She chuckled. "Don't worry, Sellie. I'm sure it's fine. Other traditions say you only have to stay until you get a sign that you're done." She stopped herself long enough to stare at my face. "My God . . . Sellie, you're as red as a beet!"

"Ah, well . . . quite a lot happened, actually . . . I didn't realize I was frying."

"What'd you do, pass out up there?"

"Well . . . er . . . in a way . . . but not really." I started to gulp the water, but stopped myself to walk to her back porch. I raised the glass to each of the four directions, to the sky, then spilled half its contents onto the petunias blooming in the flower bed. "Thank you all," I whispered, then sipped the precious water. Nothing had ever tasted so fine.

"Are you going to tell me what happened before or after you eat?"

"I . . . er . . ." Unable to decide, I got another glass of water. "I think I'll wait to eat . . . but . . . wait a minute! First you better explain to me what you were doing!"

Estelle had been stirring the soup. She looked startled. "What are you talking about?"

"The drumming you did. You scared me to death!"

A strange look came over her face. "What drumming?"

"Oh, come on, Estelle. Don't play dumb with me. You put Roger up to sneaking there late last night and had him pound on a drum to scare me."

She was shaking her head. "Sellie, I swear, we were gone most of the night to a Grateful Dead concert out at the Ranch. We weren't here."

My skin rippled with heat and chills, and my gut twisted with a remembered pang from childhood that announced my feeling of abandonment. "You mean you didn't even stay tuned to me in case I needed you?"

She shrugged. "I didn't think . . . Selena . . . I'm sorry. I was sure you'd be alright. In fact, I bet Roger you'd be on that ledge for at least two days. I didn't think you'd . . ."

I sank into a chair.

"What's wrong?"

"I . . . I'm . . . the pit . . . two snakes . . . I could've died . . . I saw my future in bubbles . . . you didn't . . . drum?"

"Easy! Stop babbling. Take a breath." Estelle knelt in front of me and rested her hands on my knees.

Stars clouded my vision. When I bent forward to drop my head between my legs, I conked my head on hers.

"Jesus, Sellie!" Estelle fell onto the floor and was holding the top of her head with both hands. "You'd better tell me what's going on before we both start having visions."

I breathed as deeply as I could in my curled position then slowly sat up. When the dizziness passed, I opened my eyes and laughed at her sprawled on the floor. "Well, if it wasn't you or Roger who beat that drum, I don't have any explanation but that some spirit visited me."

"Really?"

I shook my head up and down. "And there were these bubbles and lightening bugs twirling around my ankles and sitting in the palms of my hands.

"Really?"

I nodded again.

"But," Estelle said slowly, "there aren't any lightening bugs around here."

"Sure there are. I saw them."

"They don't live in this kind of environment. They mostly live in places where there's more humidity in the summer."

"But I saw little lights floating around me."

"Well, they were something else."

"What?" I demanded.

She held her hands in front of her. "How should I know? Maybe you were seeing things from lack of food, or maybe . . ." Her eyes grew round. She whispered, "Maybe they were spirit lights."

Thinking of how my hands felt after the lights had settled on their palms, I raised them and turned them over and back. "Do something for me?"

"Uh, OK."

"Turn your back to me."

She slid herself around on the floor and sat in front of me. I placed my hands across the top of her shoulders and waited.

"What am I supposed to . . . wait a minute! They're getting hot!"

"I thought they might." I removed them from her shoulders and tried to see if they were any different as I turned them palms up then down, again and again.

She scrambled away from me. "What does that mean?"

"They seemed to be warmer to me whenever I put them on my skin."

Abruptly she stood, rubbed her hands on her thighs, then walked to the sink. She started washing dishes. I could tell by her quick movements she wasn't thinking about what she was doing. Her body was rigid. I came to stand behind her and touched her shoulder. She jumped.

"I just don't get it," she grimaced, tears filling her eyes. "I've spent thousands of dollars, gone to every retreat and class I can find about connecting with spirits. You . . . you climb a rock in my back yard, spend one night and come back with a wild tale that sounds like you just experienced some kind of initiation, with fortune-telling bubbles, and what sounds like spirit lights. And . . . and your hands get hot with some kind of energy." She busied herself with rinsing dishes. I saw her shaking her head.

She turned abruptly. "I'm really happy for you," she said, struggling for more words. "I'm just jealous, Sellie. I never would've thought, I mean, all you did was read a book. I don't get it," she sobbed. I tried to take her into my arms, but she waved me away. I heard her last words. "It's not fair."

I pulled my shoulders closer to my ears. I didn't know what to say or do. I knew, however,I wasn't going to apologize for what'd happened to me. I didn't know her very well so I didn't know what would comfort her. "I don't understand it either, Estelle."

When I looked into her eyes, I saw a deep hurt. I hadn't been trying to connect with any spirits or to get somewhere or do something differently or be better than this new friend. I'd just been myself, and I'd been as open as I could be about it. Her reaction made me decide to leave out the part where I'd sunk into the Grandmother Rock. Somehow I felt it would have put her over the top of her personal acceptance of my experience. I also didn't want to share the special nature of my new connection with Mother Earth, nor the promises I'd made. Not yet, anyway.

Suddenly she hugged me, let me go, then returned to her dishes. "Want more water?" She handed me a full glass then ladled soup into a bowl. I sat at the table and moaned with pleasure. I felt her looking at me as she finished the dishes, then she left me, and I heard her talking to Roger in the other room. I grew uncomfortable when I heard her giggle. Their voices came to the door.

Estelle was talking. "You just have to hear her story about her time on the hill."

Even though I didn't want to return to my life as a mother and a wife, I suddenly made a decision. "Uh, not now, Estelle."

She raised her eyebrows.

"I . . . think I'd better get home. Kids have school tomorrow. Lunches, you know . . . and who knows if they can find their clean clothes. I've been gone three days."

"But you planned four."

"I know, but Roger's here, and you'll want your time together." Irritation scattered across my back. I'd thought Estelle and I were to have the evening to ourselves. I didn't want to relate my experiences to both of them. I didn't want to feel like a side show. I wanted my experiences all to myself until I was ready to tell my story, ready to share as much or as little as I wanted.

"Thanks for the water and the soup." I rinsed my dish. "Let me tell you, I never knew how good water could taste until I hadn't had any for a while."

"Beer's better," Roger said.

I laughed and thought, "Not anymore!" A cold wind breezed through my middle. I was glad to be going home.

We hugged, and I thought I detected a frown on Estelle's face. I hoped my experience wouldn't come between us. I wanted someone with whom to share my awareness about the presence of spirit and the possibilities of offering more than physical healing to clients. Estelle and I seemed to think along the same themes. I hoped I'd found a comrade, and we'd be important parts of each other's lives.

Chapter XII - April, 2004
How to tell the story?

"So why now?" Flyn asked, plopping a last bite of ham sandwich into his mouth. It was a logical question, only I didn't have an answer for him. During the last two hours of our drive toward Oakland, I'd told him about my Saturday afternoon with Estelle and her request, including the strange sensations and visions I'd had. I'd recounted our history with the ancient Ouija Board, but had deleted that one little personal detail of what had happened during our first meeting. Not that I thought Flyn couldn't handle my conversation with my first unborn child; I just wasn't ready to share the overwhelming loss that surfaced whenever I thought of my miscarriage. Even if he had secrets from his past, a list of former loves or events he'd endured, I had faith there was plenty of time for us to share any details when we were ready. A lifetime, I hoped, for both of us.

Before getting gas and stopping for lunch in Santa Rosa, I'd described my early relationship with Amach and some of the teachings she'd channeled through me. While hearing this, Flyn's eye brows had curled or, at least, had risen and fallen several times. I'd tried to explain how I was now in her life, and how our relationship, this time, was definitely different than when we split up many ago. All my talking had brought us to sandwiches at Subway.

"Why now?" I reflected on his question. "Are you asking me why Amach is coming through at this particular time in my life, or, why she's showing me these particular scenes."

He nodded, rustling through the debris on the table in search of more food. I took his lack of response to mean he had both questions in mind.

"The only reason I can see for her coming through at this time in my life is because of the similarities between what she's done and Estelle's request. It's *what* she's showing me that's mysterious, and how she's showing it to me." I picked through the empty wrappers, thinking every question he'd asked me over the past two hours were the same ones I'd been asking myself. Either he was reading my thoughts, or he was destined to know all of it; every crazy, unhinging detail. I hoped between the two of us, we could figure out what Amach wanted. I scored his unfinished potato chips. He grabbed for them, emptying the bag onto the table where we raced to see who could stuff the most into their mouth first.

"What's . . . so . . . mysterious?" he talked around the chips.

"Uh, well, so . . . as it turns out, the reason Potty called me wasn't because she needed me for healing, but because she'd gotten a message from Amach to call me."

"Now how does *that* work?" he said slowly, scouring the table for more food. He lifted his hand as if to tell me to hold that thought. When he returned, he pushed a bag of Doritos and another drink at me.

"I don't know!" I must have snapped at him, because his movements slowed to a crawl as he opened his package of sun chips. He dropped them, refocused onto my face, and raised his hands above his shoulders as if in surrender. I was instantly sorry and tried again, "I told you, it's mysterious."

Returning his hands to the table, he quietly folded our lunch wrappings. "OK, I'll quit with the questions." He returned my gaze. "Just tell me the way you need to tell me." He said this quietly and made sure I nodded in agreement before he continued. "But, Sellie, it's more than mysterious; it's a mystery. Your visions, as you call them, are guiding you somewhere. We just don't know where, and we won't know until this criss-crossing between yours and Amach's worlds are done." We glugged our drinks and gobbled our chips until he huffed a satisfied sigh, and I moaned in satisfaction.

I had the notion this hunger Flyn and I shared had to do with keeping ourselves grounded while we dealt with the 'other-worldly' aspects of my story. Whenever I worked beyond the earth plane, I found chocolate was my best anchor; it kept me able to return to my life. Sometimes food became a way to keep in touch with my body and stay in it after I'd been in long trances or had done too many massages in a row. Now we were sitting in silence. He brought his hands over mine. "Remind me to tell you about one of my . . ." He was suddenly alarmed, "Don't you have a client tonight?"

"Oh shit . . . shoot . . . yes, at 6pm in Oakland." Startled out of my reverie, I scanned the room for a clock. Neither of us could wear watches because they just stopped, never to tell time again. I spied one over the Subway counter; it was a little after three o'clock. Even in heavy traffic I figured we could get to my office in time, but we had to start driving. "Let's go straight there so I can get the room warm enough. You'll have to shop for dinner."

He somberly pushed his lips forward and considered my suggestion. "I think I can help you out." With twinkling eyes, he added, "'Course there's a fee."

My belly tightened. "And I bet I know exactly what you'll charge."

He nodded wisely. "Let's be gone." We refilled our drinks before we left, and Flyn bought two huge chocolate chip cookies.

As we left, I tucked my arm through the crook of his elbow. "I'm glad you're with me, Flyn. I'm glad I've got someone to talk to about all this. Thank you for trying to understand the things I'm telling you. There's so much." We stopped beside the car and turned to each other.

"And we've got all the time you need," he assured me, pressing his lips to my forehead while my insides flip-flopped.

"I hope so," I answered and pulled back to admire his eyes. "I'm not sure we've as much time as I'd want, what with Potty predicting danger and Amach seeming so insistent."

"What about danger?" He walked around the car and had to holler at me over the traffic noise.

I waited until we were in our car and on the freeway. "Amach gave Potty a message alluding I was in some kind of danger. Potty didn't have any more information, but . . ."

"Hold on! You haven't said anything about danger before. And . . . how does this Potty, who's someone you've never met, know this Amach, who's supposed to be a spirit who's inhabited your body?"

"Uh, I guess I've left something out." I wasn't sure I could explain what I'd never put into words for myself." "It could be completely understandable . . . if . . . you have all the information and . . . uh . . . if you . . . don't get too logical about it."

He sighed. "Like I'm supposed to suspend my logical mind and use my what?"

"Use your other senses. Unscrew your head, like you learned in that Chaotic Meditation class."

After he'd nodded he understood what I wanted him to do, I continued. "Amach is not just a spirit residing inside me. She's a 'free spirit' kind of spirit and has other duties. Potty, who's real name is Delveena, and, by the way, I have met her before, is a psychic. In fact, we met at a psychic reading class way before I met Estelle. We shared a group meditation to the Akashic records." I ignored his double-take, raising my hand to stop him from asking questions, then plunged forward with my story.

"Bonnie, our instructor, guided us to the roof of her house and had us select a mode of transportation. She instructed us to pay attention to the kind of vehicle others were imagining, then we were to meet at the marble steps to the great library in the sky."

I peeked at him. He forehead was creased in concentration. "You can stop me if this gets too weird for you."

"Ah . . . well, that would've been about two and a half hours ago," he answered with a shake of his head. "We're in it now . . . don't stop. It's too fantastic. And yet . . . it fits. Your story can't be any more crazy than when I met Red Buffalo at the wedding this weekend and discovered we're distant cousins."

"What?"

He smiled smugly. "When you're done, I might have a few 'out of this world' tales of my own to tell."

"Why not now?" I remembered my 'hit' regarding Flyn and Red Buffalo.

"Cause you're the one in danger."

Using the only tool I had, I took a deep breath and cleared the increasing tension under my sternum. "OK! But I want to know . . . Promise me you'll tell me later?"

He patted my knee in between shifting between fourth and fifth gears.

"So . . . Delveena and I . . . we took this field trip where we retrieved messages about how to improve our methods of intuition. When we came out of trance, we shared our experiences." I slowed to remember the excitement that whirled through me when we'd done this exercise. "It was uncanny, Flyn. Each of us knew what kind of vehicle the others had traveled in and whether or not we'd changed vehicles for our return trip. We actually saw each other in this group trance."

His forehead creased more deeply then smoothed. I was encouraged he was hearing me and was accepting the details. "Now here's another kinky part!"

"Stop that," he said sternly. His chin lifted in command.

"Stop what?"

"Stop undermining yourself, your skills, and what you've experienced. It's time to believe in them, or you'll never accept who you are and what you can do. I won't berate you. I believe in spirits and higher guidance and alternate realities." He tried to look at me while he drove in the clotting traffic. "You're not weird or crazy. This is real, and I believe you."

He'd stopped me in my tracks. I'd been depreciating these experiences for years, because, not only did they unnerved me, but very few people believed me. I hadn't been able to share with anyone except Estelle who, over time, had grown increasingly jealous. We'd had to split our partnership many years ago. Estelle began advertising herself as a Medicine Woman and teaching classes in mysticism, shamanism, and crystal healing.

I'd opted to practice one-on-one with individuals who were referred to me by word of mouth. Each successful breakthrough of a client brought another personal referral, even from doctors. I was careful to reassure clients the healing power came through me; I was merely God's hands. In that light, I realized if I could accept I was a vehicle for healing, then I could accept I wasn't weird. These experiences were a part of who I was. I wasn't doing anything on my own. I was doing it with guidance and a blessing from the spirits who had promised to help me. I did what I did because of each contact I'd experienced with Amach.

"Thanks."

I could tell by the way he cocked his head he wasn't sure why I was thanking him.

"For believing in me," I said simply.

He encouraged me to continue, "So you and Potty, or Delveena, met at this class."

"We connected so well we sat together through lunch. I haven't seen or heard from her until she called last Friday. In fact, I didn't recognize her until just before I left her apartment.

She's dying, Flyn. And I can't do a thing about it."

"What's she dying of?"

I shuddered. If I hadn't read her yellow binder last night, I wouldn't have had a clue as to why she was fading from this world. The writings in the binder included her personal journal, as well as automatic writings, a kind of psychic autobiography.

"She's dying of her own psychic-ness. She couldn't maintain set boundaries between herself and her clients. Instead of remaining as a channel, she tried to take on her client's personal wounds to bring healing. She pulled symptoms out of others' bodies and took them into herself, without a clear method of releasing the diseases and imbalances from her etheric and auric layers. I'm glad I took the warnings of my teachers seriously. Delveena thought she was different and that's why she started gaining weight, to defend herself against those who took advantage of her physically, psychically, mentally, and energetically. By putting on weight, she was trying to thicken her protective barrier, rather than set limits and work to keep herself clear of others' karma."

"Like you bathe in candle light, sand, and water after your work day . . ."

"And make session notes rather than try to remember every client and their symptoms."

"And like setting limits with that psychic group and Estelle."

"And like the negotiations I made with Amach. I demanded I be able to feel my body when I did my work. I also created a connection with Earth Energy to flow through me so I didn't use my own energy during a massage. I didn't want to get caught off balance by diseases which could draw more energy than I had or were more explosive than I could handle."

We lunged forward as Flyn jammed on the brakes,

narrowly missing a BMW that had crossed lanes in front of us at breakneck speed to make a quick exit off the freeway. Traffic was thickening between Petaluma and San Rafael, and we were caught among cars and trucks moving well above the posted speed limit. Trying to stay at 65 miles per hour made other drivers mad. Some kind of insanity overtook even the most conservative citizens when they got behind the wheels of their car. Maybe, they identified themselves with their powerful V6 and V8 engines. Maybe, they disconnected from their everyday existence. When they became anonymous and grabbed the reigns of power, some became more than aggressive. Driving was more like a play station game, more challenging than pleasurable.

"This traffic's crazy!" Flyn said. "Every trip's a race., but it's not just the driving, Sellie. It's the attitudes of the people, fighting to get more and keep it. I've got to get out of the city."

"I do understand, Flyn. It's this common attitude of people needing to get ahead, of wanting what everyone else has. Amach told me once, 'Greed breeds fear'."

"That's wise."

"She is."

"How often do you connect with her?"

Color burned my cheeks.

"You still meet with her, don't you?"

I shook my head and watched my hands in my lap. "I haven't met with her for a long time. I . . well, we . . ."

"OK, so when was the last time you connected with her? And how?"

I knew the event. I could remember being drawn to sit with pen and paper. "We did automatic writing." I couldn't remember the exact date, but I knew it was some time in the third year of David's battle with cancer. "I went to her when the doctors started making excuses about why David was getting worse. I didn't like what she said, and she wouldn't change her message." Tears pooled just as they had on that day. I hadn't wanted to believe her when she told me I would lose him, or I would survive our marriage alone but know love again. I'd accused her of patting me on the head so I would have hope and leave her alone.

"I wanted to keep pretending he was going to live, but she wouldn't let me hold onto my denial." I gulped, "So I punished her for telling me the truth and banished her from my life! We haven't been in contact for years."

Scenes of the last year of David's illness flashed. Prostate cancer is an insidious disease, creeping to settle in a man's center, his identity as a male, then taking from him his ability to stand and pee on his own. And there wasn't a thing I could do for him but give him pills; blue ones for pain, yellow ones for the hallucinations Morphine brings, red ones to soften his stool. All the skills I'd gained over years of working with energy and with people were useless. I couldn't even divert his attention long enough to get him comfortable.

I'd convinced myself Amach had let me down; I'd wanted her to tell me how I could cure him. She wouldn't be drawn into that kind of talk, so I'd refused to call on her anymore.

"Where are you?" Flyn asked quietly.

"I'm remembering when I threw the pen and paper across the room, and made Shawna carry them to the burn barrel." The noise of commuter traffic was dense and enveloped us in our little car. I didn't feel like talking anymore, about anything, but I owed Flyn more. I tried again. "Look, I got mad and turned into a bitch. I don't know if she has feelings, but I never tried to make contact with her again. That's why she's come back the only way she can, through visions and dreams and other people."

"She sure wants your attention now! What about this automatic writing? Trying it again, I mean?"

"Maybe," I shrugged. I had to admit I'd missed our

direct communication. I'd banished her but she'd remained with me in subtle ways, by pulling my hands toward certain parts of client's bodies or by showing me places where energy was clumped or absent. I felt her presence by the way she superimposed pictures in my mind when I looked at a photo of the person I was counseling over the phone. I hadn't felt the total loss of her presence in my work, just her personal guidance in my life. The mental barrier I'd erected years ago, however, was thinning.

I reclined the seat and tried to relax. "First thing is for me to follow the instructions Amach gave me through . . . Delveena."

Flyn muttered at the driver of a red truck that cut him off.

Knowing he needed to concentrate, I sighed and began a power nap. My breathing and visualization would help me rest before this evening's client.

I settled into the car seat, aware of the cushions supporting my back and neck and floated into a dimension without time or space. I made myself into a cloud drifting under a gently warming sun, with no idea where I ended and where the sky began. Then I traveled as a beam of light, a pinpoint as thin as a laser beam, knowing and perceiving a myriad of sensations and emotions.

I sense a center in myself . . . flow into it with all my perceptions. I open my awareness and find I'm between two dream worlds fast-forwarding on either side of me. I look left into one, then right into the other. One glimpse into either world fills me with complete comprehension. I'm perched on the boundary line between them. Events of both worlds stream along both sides of my awareness at the same time.

One seems more familiar than the other, so I pull into it, leaving that middle space, hoping I can find it again.

Estelle. I recognize Estelle. She's taken her hair out of their braids. It's wavy and caresses her breasts and her shoulders. She's sitting naked in the center of her Medicine Wheel. The sky is darkening, moving toward what we called the 'tween' time, a favorite moment to make our prayers. The trees around her are still. But this darkness becomes more than eventide as turbulent clouds roll across the sky. Crashing winds toss the tree tops while not a hair on Estelle's head is mussed.

She holds a large deer skin roll in her arms, as if ready to make an offering to the Gods.

An electric bolt zigzags brightly overhead at the same time thunder claps and shudders the landscape.

I reach for her, afraid of her plan. I see her tears falling over her cheeks. She raises her arms and the bundle to the sky. A green mist frames her body then tightens around her, coalescing until she is blurred within it. A cone of dark wind snatches her from the Earth. I am alone.

I move toward the space where I last saw her. I'm caught in the sticky threads of a spider's web from a familiar nightmare where my arms are pinned to my sides. I struggle to breathe . . . to open my eyes . . . to move. A pressure falls on my leg. I scream.

"Sellie! Wake up!" I heard Flyn say. "You've got to wake up on your own."

I broke free of what I thought was a dream to see tail lights in front of us and headlights flashing past the car. We'd crossed the San Rafael bridge and were close to our Oakland exit.

"She's going to do it," I announced.

"Who's going to do what?"

I cringed. "It's Estelle. I think she's going to do it, alone."

He nodded to let me know he was listening. I couldn't shake a feeling of dread. "I need to call her tonight. I . . . I think she's decided to make her own marriage bundle, but . . . something's going to go very, very wrong."

I told Flyn the details of what I'd just seen, then realized I'd not told him about the bundles Amach had constructed. I hadn't told him of the overlay of events and visions I'd experienced at the wedding either. There was just too much. *'Would I ever have enough time to tell him all of it?'* I could only hope my dreams and visions would slow down so I could.

As we careened around corners and traffic, I had a fluttery feeling in my chest, as if I had three hearts there and they were all working overtime. I knew part of the feeling came from knowing we were late, but it felt as if we were late for more than my appointment. Anxiety flashed through me as if we might be late for a very different moment in time, that we needed to hold on tight to each other right now, or we'd begin to drift apart. After what I'd told him, I was suddenly uncertain. He was faced forward, concentrating on traffic. I couldn't tell if he was frowning at my secrets or at the jungle of cars. *'Maybe I've misread his reactions?'* I couldn't relax, but consoled myself with the belief we'd have time later tonight, later in the week, or in our lives, to sort through our secrets.

As we neared our apartment, I covered the anxiety in my chest with gratitude at having Flyn with me. I was in no mood to face the challenge of finding parking near my office and our rented studio apartment. It was always a nightmare because Oakland Kaiser's hospital and ER were a block away. Parking spots in front of our home were taken by families and friends of the sick and traumatized. We drove around the block twice, searching for a space. He finally let me out of the car so I could meet my client. I hoped he'd find something close. Lugging our suitcases and food for more than a couple of blocks then plodding up three flights of stairs was a drag. One good thing had resulted from this parking problem: I'd learned to have fewer clothes and better organize our food purchases. That way we never had gobs to carry from the laundromat or store at one time. We used the small dumb waiter for little bags but had to balance bigger items in our arms or on our backs. I daydreamed for a real elevator and envied those in apartment complexes with parking garages underneath.

I'd learned my neighbors envied my unique living space. Its U-shape covered the entire third floor of a refurbished home. Large plate glass windows looked east and west with panels of operable windows on either side for ventilation. Thick rose drapes covered them for privacy and offered shade over the west window in summer. The lined drapes also provided insulation against the damp chill when fog crept into the Bay and up the Oakland hills.

An over-sized bathroom formed one leg of the U and a large walk-in closet the other. The bathroom was so spacious, I had room for an apartment-sized refrigerator and a counter to hold a convection oven/microwave, an automatic coffee maker, and a two burner hot plate, with room to spare. The cupboard space underneath and extra book cases in the closet served as kitchen storage.

I'd found the "For Rent" sign during my appointment to see one of the small offices the owners had created in the basement. The Myers were an older couple who were thrilled to lease the studio to a single adult woman without pets and hadn't raised my rent on either space since I'd moved in. Flyn had ingratiated himself with the old couple by helping with some minor repairs when the water heater broke and when the carpet had worn thin on the two flights of stairs to our floor. Our front door was to the right, just past the front entrance. In the small hall, the Myers had their own door, and we had ours opening onto a small landing at the base of our stairs. There was just enough room for one person to close the door and fill the dumb waiter while the other person climbed the stairs or remained outside. The trek to where the stairs entered our apartment was steep and poorly lit with nothing to prevent cool air from drafting up the squared opening between the closet and the bathroom. During the winter months, I hung a thick drape across the opening between the walls.

My office was below the ground floor. Because the house was built on a hill, the basement area was much smaller than the main and top floors but was large enough for two offices to be created when the house was refurbished. My space was large enough to allow me the ability to walk around my massage table and accommodate a desk and two chairs. I shared a bathroom with Roxanne, a Family Counselor and long-time friend, who rented the larger office. We each had our own entrances under a narrow wooden awning that protected us from winter downpours.

I entered my office and turned the heater on, glad I'd left the massage table in place. All I needed to do was warm the clean sheets by hanging them over the back of my desk chair in front of the heater.

With five minutes to spare, I reviewed Ethel's notes on a 5 X 8 lined card. Many clients returned after a few years or months with what they thought were a new set of problems. Reviewing their session notes gave me hints as to whether their symptoms were the same, or if there might be some connection between them.   I made notes on my phone consults and readings as well.

'Should I open a card on Potty?'

'No,' I decided. I hadn't treated her for any specific ailment. She'd actually helped me. *'Well, that remains to be seen,'* I thought, not feeling I was in danger. *'Or am I?'* Had I been attacked last Saturday with Estelle? Was this afternoon's dream of being caught in a web another kind of attack? I grimaced; all of this must have something to do with Estelle's damn request.

That reminded me. I dialed her cell phone and was sent to her voice mail. I hung up. I didn't want to leave a message without first hearing her voice. I promised myself I'd call later.

Chapter XIII - Fall 1985
Negotiating with Amach

After hustling Sam and Shawna out of bed and delivering them to their school bus stop, I sighed, watching them shift their personas from my goofy kids to nonchalant teenagers. Their antics had driven me crazy this morning. Perhaps because I'd promised myself to confront Amach today, I let the empty car skewer my heart.

I drove slowly through slanted light shining between oak branches shedding their leaves. Pretty soon they'd all be naked with red, orange, and yellow blankets at their feet. I parked my VW bug in the driveway and leaned my arms on the steering wheel. Staring at our trailer, I wondered how to bring this strange spirit being into a place of my awareness where I could see her or converse with her. I had so many questions.

Uneasiness gripped my stomach. The coffee I'd drunk this morning was a volcano of acid juices. Walking between the car and the trailer, I took a shaky breath, rubbed my hands on my jeans, then tucked them under my arm pits. I'd known this day was coming. I couldn't continue being the center of attention at Estelle's psychic group. Or was it that I didn't want to be the center of their 'inattention'?

Even though I felt like running, I wasn't going to put this off any longer. I'd had enough of being invaded. Yesterday, Estelle had refused to relate my messages to Amach while I was channeling. I was angry she was ignoring my feelings. I kicked at the Earth, sighed, and hunched my shoulders. "But how am I going to connect with this . . . Amach . . . this spirit being . . . for a heart-to-heart? I can't use the Ouija Board by myself."

Inside, I stoked the wood stove and watched smoke mixed with the morning fog hover around our house trailer. Moving to the sink, I focused on the dishes, but a shadow crossed my mind, one that seemed to call my name. The hair stood up on the back of my neck, and I opened my eyes wide, giving my full concentration to the cool water splashing over my hands, swirling into the steel sink, glugging down the drain. When I turned the faucet off, I stared into the dark hole in the center of the sink.

'*That's what I feel like,*' I admitted, like I was being pulled down a hole, not sucked into a garbage disposal or a whirlpool of water, but pulled by a source greater than myself. Some kind of heavy-duty gravity, so natural and so inevitable that, even though I tried to keep my channeling of Amach in the realm of unreality, I was losing the battle. The whole of the experience was becoming too natural, too easy. I was losing my sense of self and that scared me. In the cushioned silence of my home, I needed to talk aloud as a defense against the war I'd been waging in my head.

"Listen now!" I begged. "I don't know who you are or what you want. There's no audience here. No tape recorder collecting your words for posterity. So if you've just been showing off for the group, then you're shit out of luck." Nothing stirred. I sighed. What had I expected? A booming voice through the stove pipe? Handwriting on the wall?

I shook myself, and, reaching into the hall closet, pulled out the broom. Everyone in the family knew when I was struggling with my thoughts, I went for the broom. Sweeping clockwise around the postage stamp-sized living room calmed me, helped me collect the cobwebs from the corners of my brain. I stretched my body and mind while I swept the hidden places of the back bedroom and bathroom, under the kitchen table and my treadle sewing machine. The cleaning process had a beginning, a middle, and an end. I pretended I was in control. With dried fir needles, clumps of dust bunnies, and mud clods gathered into a lump on the floor, I felt I'd accomplished something.

"There," I announced.

In the back of my mind, a wizened face smiled.

"OK, I see you! But, how can I hear you?"

The smile continued; her mouth moved as if talking to me.

"I'm not a lip reader," I said flatly.

The face nodded in understanding. As I reached for the dustpan, I realized how strange it was to see Amach outside my body. Every other time she'd been inside me, crushing my soul to a space behind my heart, relegating my psyche to a huddled mass in the back of my mind. I had so many questions for her, but no one was interested in asking them. I wanted to know was she from the past, the future, or the now? When had she lived? How many life times had she experienced? I didn't think spirits traveled around that much, so I had this feeling she was a local entity. Had she taken human form only once, died, then become a spirit? Was she happy doing the spirit thing and not walking around in a body? I wanted to know how it all worked.

When I bent to sweep the pile into the dustpan, my hip caught the stack of mail on the cabinet next to the front door. Everything fell to the floor.

"Damn!"

Her face disappeared. I entertained a fleeting idea: maybe if I cursed more, Amach'd leave me alone. Her face returned within a second, shooting me an angry look.

I squatted to retrieve the fallen mess. The mail stacked easily but a blank pad and several pens, which had been living underneath the pile, fell out of my hands three times before I got a message. Breathlessness clawed at my chest.

"You want me to write your words?"

The face nodded.

"But, if I'm in trance, how will I know what I'm

writing when I'm writing it?"

The entire stack of mail fell to the floor again.

"Alright, already!" I said after sitting with paper and pen at the refinished picnic table along the length of the kitchen. "Talk to me!" I sat on the matching bench, my hand hovering over the blank paper.

I waited. "Or through me."

Nothing happened. My hand lay unmoved on the page.

I was nervous. I dropped the pen to pace the length of the trailer. I returned to sit again. "OK, so what's the problem? You can pop into me whenever you feel like it. Make my hand move!"

I slammed down the pen in frustration, grabbed my sweater, and headed for the hills.

Picking up my pace, I strode west from our trailer past an oak grove, muttering to myself. "Maybe this current set up is best. Amach takes over when she wants to, and I stay out of the way. She gets all the hoopla; I take a back seat to the whole affair. Why should I stop her from taking over?"

Gunther, Crystal and Estelle were quite happy with the status quo. So what if they stare at me every time we're in group. Waiting for Amach to re-appear through me was stressful, not terrible. I'd almost gotten used to them not wanting to converse with ME, my persona. Estelle didn't want to do the Ouija with me anymore. She'd tap her fingers on the recorder, waiting until I got out of the way. Waiting until I became a conduit for this little bundle of spirit I had roaming around inside my . . . my what? My psyche? My brain? My energy body?

Squirrels bounded from branch to branch, chattering and squawking at me, trying to warn me away from their caches. A stellar jay kept me in its sights by fluttering from one tree to the next, its raucous cry trying to get my attention. I strode across our property to my favorite place of solace in a large swamp-like area where a forest of pepperwood trees lived. The densely intertwined branches of these trees blocked the sun from touching the ground, black from pepperwood droppings. Poison oak was the only stubborn bush able to survive at the southern edge. In the center of this grove was a tree I called, "The Matriarch", a massive four-pronged cluster of thick trunks. I curled inside these stanchions of protection and listened to the wind caressing her top-most boughs. Ever since my Vision Quest, whenever I was at my wit's end, I could recline against one of the four trunks and feel supported. Today, I hugged her trunk growing toward the East and asked for insight and strength to survive what was happening to me.

I placed my forehead on her bark, wrapped my arms around her trunk, and held on. I breathed deeply of her crisp, biting odor. Slowly I relaxed with her slight sway as she responded to a wind. A gentle rocking motion soothed my jangled nerves, and my heart slowed. I reflected on the past year and Amach's entrance into my life.

Estelle and I had learned a lot in our sessions. I'd been hesitant to join the psychic group, almost laughing at them in their zeal. Then Amach had entered, and our relationship had changed. I flushed, remembering an old feeling from when I was a young girl, standing alone on the playground as my best friend was invited to play with another child, and I'd been left alone. Those feelings and these were the same and came under the heading of abandonment, threading itself through my heart with the green tint of jealousy. The psychic group didn't want ME anymore. They wanted Amach, and I was jealous of this entity because she was the reason I was being ignored. I wasn't getting any recognition for being willing to set myself aside and surrender to her presence.

I tasted the bitterness of jealousy, the heat of anger. While I wished I could be cherished, I couldn't stop the group from wanting guidance from a source who seemed authentic, and Amach was helpful. I'd listened to every tape and read every transcript and had learned more about energy work and healing methods than in any class I'd taken. I hung my head and chastised myself for being caught in the pitiful place of only thinking of myself, of whining about being shoved aside.

'If I can find a way to gain access to her by myself...' I chilled with the thought. *'I could find out who she really is.'* My mind raced. How would I know unless I let myself speak or write her words? How could she help me if I didn't try to communicate with her? And ... what might she have to tell me ... that's for me alone? Suddenly, I couldn't wait any longer.

I pulled a strand of my hair and wound it around a loosened piece of bark, thanking the Matriarch for her healing center, then hurried home to pick up my pen for a talk with Amach.

I started to sit down, then hesitated. This connection needed as much care and protection as Estelle and I used when we worked the Ouija Board. I stoked the fire and brought my abalone shell to the table where I lit a dry, gray sage leaf gathered in southern California.

I wiggled my toes and settled into a pillow I'd placed on the hard bench. I exhaled, took another breath, and spoke aloud.

"Thaddeus, Helena, Matthew, my guides and whatever other angels, spirits, and guardians I have, guide me as I talk to Amach with my mind and my hand. If this is good for me, let the communication be clear. If this is dangerous for me and my spiritual growth, block our ability to speak in this way."

I smudged my hands and, with the pen in my fingers, wondered how this was going to work. A word came into my mind. I saw it spelled there. Because it wasn't "Welcome" or "Hello" or some other kind of greeting, I discounted it.

Then something, or someone, nudged at me from the inside of my brain, as if it were shifting its weight. I decided to write the word implanted in the forefront of my mind.

Time, I wrote.

The word disappeared and another appeared in its place.

descends

As each word disappeared in my mind, another would appear, and I began writing them as fast as they tumbled forward, one after the other:

and ascends in its own manner. We are not a part of this thing called time, you and I. We are beyond it. Until now you've held me as much as I've held you.

'Who are you? Are you Amach?' I asked with my mind.

I am she.

'Have you ever lived?'

I live now.

'But I mean, have you walked around like I am now in this creation on this earth plane?'

I walked as a woman and as a man, but I am free of the limitations of my body. You see me in a way that has meaning for you. I have walked many lifetimes, in many different cultures at many different times. I am with you as you need me to be at this moment.

'Why are you with me?'

I asked and you asked and we have paired.

'When did I ask?'

You have asked many times for help to do your work and to be all of who you are. You have never stopped asking.

I remembered Estelle telling me to list all the things I'd done or been able to do since I'd first asked for help. My constant question had been, "OK, what do I do now?"

'*Ok,*' I admitted, and took a deep breath. '*So, Amach, tell me how you chose me as a channel?*'

I waited. No words formed in my mind. Instead, I felt a sigh. '*Did I just feel a sigh? Can a spirit sigh?*' Again, no answer, then words began, and I wrote.

When you are ready, the answer, it will come.

'*But what will make me ready?*'

Experience, understanding, readiness to accept.

I felt myself bristle. '*You're manipulating me? If this is how it's going to go, I don't want you in my thoughts.*'

Silence.

'*Are you there?*' I thought.

I felt as if I was standing at the edge of a great void, empty and at a loss.

Nothing is simple.

My body was full again. I was grateful, but cautious. '*Can this work so I can know what you're saying before you say it? I don't want to give myself over to you anymore. I'm feeling like a freak.*'

I am here to help you bring health to others in their bodies, minds, and spirits. I am here to help you understand the need of your Earth. I am here to give you guidance for your future.

'*What about . . . can you guide me when I'm working with clients?*'

To help them heal? Yes.

'*Can you make your words be thoughts in my head without having to speak through me?*'

I can give you the guidance you seek and can

*let you teach with my words at your will. BUT,
you MUST pass on the wisdom when you are ready.
I will also help you see beyond your time.*

I shivered, wondering if I would ever be ready.

You must become ready.

After I asked, *'Why?'* in my mind, my hand wrote these words with a firmer, quicker pressure than the rest of the messages.

Your earth time is threatened.

'Mine or the Earth's time?'

***To gain the knowledge you need, I will bring
you teachers. I will teach you as well.***

'Thank you.'   Gratitude blossomed warm in my chest.

***Keep true to your intents and your
commitments.***

'I can only try,' I thought, and wondered if I could get a list of what she thought my intentions and commitments were.

Do it yourself.

'But, I only . . .' I realized I'd lost the fullness of her presence within me. "I only wanted to compare lists," I defended myself.

Chapter XIV - April, 2004
Healing Past and Present

I was exhausted from our extensive weekend traveling and felt emotionally wrecked from all I'd dealt with: the quandary around Flyn's request and the meeting with Potty, being sucked into Amach's world and trying to stay out of Estelle's. I wanted nothing more than to close the drapes of our studio apartment, get into my comfy sweats, and hang out with Flyn. I didn't want to face a client, even Ethel. I closed my eyes and stretched my arms to the ceiling, trying to relieve the tension I felt between my shoulder blades. I accomplished one yoga pose Flyn had shown me to bring my mind, body, and spirit into alignment, then forced myself to connect to the Earth and Universe opening an energy flow I knew would help me. It began trickling into my body from my crown chakra toward my feet. Warmth filled my cells and a premonition that whatever was going to happen with Ethel tonight was as important for her as it was for me.

I opened my eyes to see Ethel staring at me. One look at her pinched forehead and the circles under her eyes told me she was in pain. "Your back and kidneys?"

She nodded. "I felt better after our last session but . . . " Her eyes moistened with unshed tears. Ethel was 45ish, shorter than I, and built like a pear. I was an apple, wishing I was a banana, but, for the entire time I'd known her, Ethel had never wanted to be anything but exactly what she was. She had two children, was married to a fellow named Henry, and had been suffering from back and kidney pain since before her grown children were born. I watched her walk past me and leave her purse on my desk. Her shoulders were cupped forward as if she was expecting to be beaten, and her shallow breathing told me she hurt whenever she took deep breaths. I left the bathroom door ajar so we could talk while she undressed.

"When did the pain begin again?" I asked while quickly making the bed on the massage table with the warmed sheets.

"There was not one moment when it wasn't there and, then, it was. It's been a gradual increase over the past two weeks, and I'm just beside myself with aching all the time." I heard her fumble with her clothes.

As with other clients, Ethel had come to me as a last resort. Her doctor, Dr. Blakemore, had referred her to me. He was one of the Kaiser doctors I'd converted into a holistic therapy advocate, after I'd helped to set aside his asthma. He admitted he'd tried every medical intervention in the book, yet no pain medication had brought long-term relief. Not one test ever showed the cause for her pain. Her spine wasn't pinched, and there were no tumors. Her kidneys were clear of stones or growths. Her MRIs and IVPs were all negative.

Over the past two years, Ethel had seen me only when she experienced acute periods of bloody urine and bouts of back pain which extended from her left kidney to her right shoulder. Getting her husband to pay for sessions when she wasn't hurting had kept us from working on any of her issues. Because we worked so infrequently, I hadn't been able to get her to delve into the underlying cause for her life-long pain. My multi-focal approach worked on all aspects of healing, not just the physical, but the emotional, mental, and spiritual layers as well. Ethel had never seemed ready to let me guide her past the pain and symptoms. Tonight, perhaps she was ready for something out of the ordinary.

"What's happening?" I asked as I helped Ethel onto the table. Her legs were short so she used a step stool. She was modest, always wrapping herself in one of my larger towels , struggling to keep herself covered.

"Oh well, now, I can't say it's been easy," she sighed. "I keep trying to make Henry see I want to work part-time. He doesn't think I need to do that, but I'm not in the mood to stay home any more, now the children are on their own. He's still struggling with two jobs. I'm beginning to think he likes keeping me in the dark about our finances. At least he's not had an 'episode' recently." Henry had an itch that was scratched by placing a bet or two on whatever sport was in season. "Course, football's done. It's too early for baseball, but basketball's playing."

"He'll stay good for a little while," she said as she lay on the table on her back. Ethel was the only patient I had who needed me to start work on her front before I could approach her back. I arranged her knees on a pillow to ease any lower back strain, placed a thin pillow under her neck, and covered her with a flannel sheet and a fuzzy blanket.

Ethel sighed as she snuggled into the warm sheets and slowly relaxed. "One thing's been odd," she offered.

"I'm listening," I said as I placed my fingertips on her brow to feel the quality of her energy. I was urged to stroke the creases in her forehead.

"I've been having this dream."

I waited.

"Well . . . it's weird . . . because I'm running through a forest and someone's chasing me. They're, or rather, he's on horseback . . . and . . . he overtakes me." Her breath caught. "When I wake up from the dream . . ." She groaned as I massaged her scalp then moved to the back of her neck. "I always have a sharp pain across my back." She took a deep breath as I stimulated the pressure-sensitive area along her occipital ridge that released tension. Her eyelids fluttered as she searched for more of the dream. "I always wake up in a sweat, so when I go back to sleep . . . I'm chilled." She shuddered.

Moving my hands underneath the top sheet, I stroked

along her midline down to her belly, then up along her sides.

"I'm in this cold, dark, damp place . . . and . . . alone . . . scared. It's this part where . . . I struggle to wake up. I have to pass through some kind of liquid barrier until I turn into a ball of light." She moaned as I worked the muscles of her right arm.

I paused to ask quietly, "How often do you have this dream?" I massaged her left shoulder and arm.

"It used to be only once in a while," she answered groggily. "This week it's been four nights in a row," she sighed again as I loosened her shoulders with supported stretches of her arms.

"Remember to breathe when I press a point that brings tension." She barely nodded. Returning to her face, I massaged her temples and jaw muscles. Her jaw loosened.

As I did my work, my body expanded with what I called universal energy, filling me up. Overflowing my hands. I surrendered to the sensation of my body lightening in weight and color. Pictures formed. There were times I had to close my eyes to make images appear. Most often I just had to open a special door in my mind. Tonight, I saw a possibility take shape. I asked for guidance as to how to proceed with Ethel; I'd learned the hard way to keep out of my client's process. Ethel's healing had to be accomplished by her hard work. I was just the facilitator. If I gave her the details of what I guessed was wrong with her before she was ready, her understanding would be jeopardized, and the puzzle of her pain would go unsolved.

This evening I received the impression an imaginative trip into Ethel's past might help her discover the source of her pain.

As I massaged her abdominal muscles then her legs, I talked in monotone, hoping to ease her into an altered state of mind. After I had her roll onto her stomach, I continued with my familiar pattern of healing talk.

"We know your body holds all the information it needs to heal itself," I said. "Some times the body wants to hold onto a problem so it can remain as it is. We humans can become resistant to changing what's familiar. Even though your pain causes you problems in getting around, it is a known entity, and you know how to deal with it. I'd like to suggest to you this pain is here to tell you something, to reveal information meant to help you. It could be linked to some event that's happened over and over again in your life and you might need to change. Or it could be an emotion you need to release. Sometimes disease or pain can be linked to an event which occurred before you were born." Her body stiffened then relaxed.

"For the moment, focus your attention on the area underneath my hands. I'm offering energy to your left kidney through my palms. I'm not going to massage your muscles because this kind of movement might distract you. Can you feel my hands?"

"Uh huh."

"Good. With your inside eyes, do you see a color here? Under my hands?"

Without hesitation, she answered, "A dingy, reddish, purple."

"Good for you. How do you feel about that color?"

"I think I'm going to be sick."

"OK . . . now . . . step back from that color . . . take a deep breath. Good. Let it out. On your next breath, as I know you can do, bring in the color you would rather have under my hands."

I waited until she'd taken at least two breaths. "Can you tell me what color came to you?'

"A beautiful blue," she murmured.

"Good." I was seeing a very light blue under my hands. "Take another breath, and bring more of this color under my hands."

She did as I asked. I sensed the energy shift in that area. Then I formed my hands into a circle on her back and pressed into her skin.

"I've formed a window over your left kidney now. Can you feel it?"

"Uh huh."

"Now, I'm asking you to look through that window. Tell me, can you see a movie playing there?" When she gave a start, I hoped I had guessed correctly. "Let the movie play out. You're just the observer, Ethel. You're just watching the action." When I felt her relax, I asked, "Can you tell me what you see?"

"Someone . . . in armor . . . is riding . . . on a horse . . . chasing me. I can't run . . . faster . . . trying to hide . . . the forest . . . too thick. I can't . . . save myself." She tensed.

"Breathe into this area now, Ethel. Let your breath take you away from any fear you're feeling. Nothing can hurt you because you're only watching this happen. You're safe. I'm with you. Are you better now?" I felt another shift in her tension.

"Yes . . . better . . . but . . . I need to tell you . . . as you were talking . . . I saw a sword hit me across my back."

I'd been watching her torso. As she described this, the shadow of a wide sword blade had swung flat through my hands and across her back. I was staring at a red welt extending from her left side, upward across her right scapula.

"Oh . . . God . . . my back!" She squirmed on the table. "It hurts so bad!"

"A breath, Ethel. Please keep breathing. Remember you're only the watcher. Take a breath and step back from the movie playing in your head." Her breathing eased and, I hoped, her stress was lessening. "What's happening now?" I asked as calmly as I could, even though my heart was pumping so fast with anxiety I thought I might faint.

"He's taking me somewhere. I can't move. I'm like a

rag doll . . over his horse . . . we're riding to a . . . " She gasped. "A town with a draw bridge and a wall around it. It could be a castle. It looks so ugly against the sky. I don't want to go inside. I want to stay and run through my woods."

She was silent, breathing faintly.

I opened my inner sight to a greater degree. "Ethel, I'm here with you. You're not alone. Take a breath and step back to see what's happening. Tell me what you're seeing. "

She was quiet for a long time, then she sobbed, "I'm alone and cold, and the pain . . ."

"Ethel, another breath," I urged as I pressed my circled hands harder into her back. She breathed. "You're only looking. What you're seeing is only a picture for your information. Take another breath and describe what you see."

Again she calmed under my hands. "I'm glad you're with me," she said. "This place . . . familiar, like I've been . . . before, not just my dreams . . . haunted by . . . cold and the damp . . . oh . . . God," she gasped.

"I'm here, Ethel," I said, pressing my hands against her back. "Whenever you're ready, I'm here to listen."

Her voice was strangled. "I was raised Catholic." She tried to keep from sobbing. "My dad . . . strict . . . church every Wednesday, Saturday, and Sunday. I was eleven." She took deep breaths. "I told a lie . . . so I could . . . be with my school friends on Wednesday . . . instead of church." Her voice grew stronger, yet was edged with tears. "I was seen." Her body shuddered. "He locked me . . . in the cellar . . . with the . . . rats!" Her voice ended in a scream.

I didn't want to lose the focus of my hands on her kidney, but I wanted to offer comfort. Using the edges of my hands, I massaged her back.

"I was the only girl," she said finally. "The boys all got whippings when they were bad. I always got locked in the cellar."

"This place in your dream . . . it feels like that?"

"This vision feels older, but it feels the same."

"Are you still there?"

"It's lighter now."

"Why do you think?"

"There's light coming in the bars on the window. I can see squares of stone fitted together and a wooden door with a little barred window in the middle."

"Is this like your cellar?"

"Nothing like it."

My consciousness sank into another dimension. I saw the room as she described it. "Ethel, I can see you. You're in a dungeon, and I'm outside that wooden door, and I'm going to open it and come get you."

Her muffled voice asked, "Could this be some kind of past life?"

"Could be," I answered while still pressing against her back.

"Catholics don't believe in reincarnation, but I do. I'm not so Catholic anymore."

My lips twitched in a smile. "Can you feel me by your side?" I asked, feeling a familiar push inside me as if I were being guided again by Amach.

"There's more light and . . . why . . . I feel . . . as if I'm slipping out of my body."

"Perhaps you are . . . leaving your physical shell from that lifetime. You and I are going through the doorway now. We're traveling in the light. Here we are, moving our awareness through the opening I've formed with my hands . . . where you are on the table. Where I am standing beside you with my hands on the skin of your back. Take another breath, Ethel. Feel the sheet on your legs. Hear the siren on the street. Tell me when you're ready to finish for tonight."

I flattened my hands on her bare back. The red welt was fading.

In a short time, she said, "I'm here, on the table."

"Rest a minute. You've worked hard. When you're ready, ask your body what you'd like to drink or eat this evening. What would be the most healing thing you could do for yourself?"

She answered without any hesitation, "Sleep in the spare room by myself and eat chicken soup."

As I placed one hand on her sacrum, the other at the base of her spine, I wondered at her choices and hoped Henry would understand. I held this position until I felt her energy balance. When I lifted my hands, I flashed on her quote from Henry about 'keeping me in the dark' regarding their finances. Was he afraid of losing her if she went to work and made her own money? What role had Henry played in this life similar enough to this past one and bring on her recurring symptoms? I hoped he wouldn't be too grumpy about her leaving his bed. He was grumpy enough about her using their money for these sessions.

"I don't have any more pain, you know." She sat up slowly and fumbled with the towel as she tried to keep her breasts covered. "You're a miracle worker."

"No, Ethel, you're the miracle worker. You went into your dream and made the connections between a past life experience and something that traumatized you as a child. All I did was open the space so you could do it. Many people don't have the desire or strength to do what you did tonight." I could tell she was thinking over my words as she had closed her eyes.

"I have to believe it was some kind of past life," she said slowly. "Maybe I was a slave, and I ran away from the castle. Someone was sent to get me, and they swatted me with their sword. That's how my back and kidney were injured, then they threw me into the dungeon. Just like when I ran away from my father and the church and got put in the cellar."

I shrugged. "Could be." From my experience, she had a better idea of the details of this scenario than I. What I felt was important was the fact she'd been able to release her body in that past life and come to reside in this one. "The more I witness . . . I mean . . . I'm beginning to suspect that we carry cellular memories from other lives. If something similar happens in this one, a bridge is built, and they potentiate each other. If the event in the past life was traumatic or unresolved, then the emotions can bleed through and intensify an experience in this lifetime."

My developing understanding of the infinite connections between past lives, karma and genetic memories and spirit connection was still very new to me. I was not at a stage in my interpretation where I could explain my thoughts coherently; I just knew they were all connected.

My body jolted, and prickles of ice raised the hairs on my arms. *'Does this have anything to do with my current experience with Amach? Is she showing me one of my past lives to warn me about making a bundle for Estelle?'* Or does this mean I've been a part of her life in the past?

"But what could I possibly be rebelling against in my present life that makes the pain come?" Ethel asked as she stood at the side of the table.

I had to shake my head firmly to bring myself back to my office and my client. "I've no answer to that one, but you did say you're trying to change something and that Henry has been keeping you in the dark about your finances."

"Not just recently! All our married life!" Ethel puffed out her cheeks then blew through pursed lips. She sat as still as if she'd been turned to stone, then suddenly came out of it, jumped from the table and scurried into the bathroom.

I sighed, "You'll have to search for the relationships and check out how your body feels about what you find. If the pain comes back at a certain point, it might mean there's a similarity."

Ethel called from the bathroom, "Do people share lifetimes over and over again?"

"That's seems to be the case, at least from what I've read about reincarnation," I answered. "We can change gender, roles, and relationships every time we come back so we can experience all kinds of lessons and challenges for our spiritual benefit."

"I wonder who Henry was in that lifetime? Do you think we could go back again, and I could find out?"

I chuckled. "Anything's possible. I've not really done that with a client. You might do better with a hypnotherapist. My friend, Roxanne, in the next office does that kind of work. I could give you her number." I finished stuffing the used sheets into a pillow case and covering the massage table.

"I'd rather work with you," she said as she entered the office from the bathroom.

I shook my head in the affirmative. "OK, we can work together, but I can't promise we'll find the answers to those particular questions. I'm more about helping you help yourself. Which is exactly what you did over the past three hours."

"Is that how long we've been here?"

I finished changing the sheets on the table. "Just about. How's your back now?"

"Feels great," Ethel beamed. The change from when she'd arrived, to how she stood now, was astonishing.

"I'm glad. You know, I saw a welt grow across your back when you felt the sword slap you. It faded when you came back through time with me. I truly believe you're going to have less of a problem with it now."

I walked her to her car and enjoyed the feel of the darkening evening, then sat at my desk to log in her check and make my notes. My eyes widened and my mouth 'Ooed' for a good sixty seconds as I stared at what she'd written. Her check was for $250, and it was the most I'd ever made for any session. The amount was unnerving but made the ache in my hands and the strain across my shoulders and lower back seem worth the effort.

As I grabbed my backpack and jacket, I delved into my understanding of reincarnation. I wondered what my premonition had meant? Did the intertwining of partners or husbands and wives through many past and present lives mean anything to Flyn and I, or David and I, or Red and I? Was there some past life connection between me and Estelle? Or between Amach and myself? Or my daughter and son? My mother? I'd never put the reincarnation question to the test in my own life.

'Enough ,' I sighed. I loved this work, but every inch of my almost 60-year-old body wasn't liking it much tonight.

I locked the office and smiled with the anticipation of being with Flyn in this lifetime, tonight, tomorrow, the next day, and the next. How could a girl get so lucky?

Chapter XV - April, 2004
When the world changes

Annoyed with myself that I hadn't thought of it before I locked the office, I used my cell phone to call both Estelle's cell phone and land-line, leaving urgent messages on both of them. While I walked along the sidewalk, I argued with myself. On one hand I believed Estelle could perform any ceremony she wanted. Her life was the result of her decisions, and her consequences were hers, not mine. She was a grown woman. I had no right to interfere. On the other hand, because she'd asked me to help her, I was involved. I felt obliged to make sure she knew I didn't like what she wanted to do, and since my dream in the car, I liked it even less. The repercussions of her actions were without limit. Like Ethel being plagued by an event that seemed to have occurred in a past life, Estelle might be setting up difficulties for herself in her future.

My thoughts followed this new trail. How do we recognize patterns that might have been embedded in our past, not from our childhood, but from other lifetimes? I was fascinated by how earlier incarnations might impact our current lives.

I climbed the stairs to our apartment in a pensive mood.

We were quiet as we settled into our city routine. My dirty clothes were already in a plastic bag ready to be dumped into the hamper for wash day, but I had to dig through Flyn's travel bag to sort his clean clothes from his dirty things. *'Why did he never separate his clean and dirty clothes as he used them?'* I thought.

"Old habit," replied Flyn, startling me by answering my

thought. "Never knew when I'd get the chance to wash 'em. Didn't want to carry two bags." He unwrapped three plastic dishes of store-bought enchilada dinners.

"Makes sense," I answered, "I guess." I didn't think I'd ever get used to his ability to read my thoughts. I repacked my back-pack, wondering which crisis we might be heading to next. I straightened the table where we ate and went through the mail. "Thanks for coming with me," I called to him. "The session went well."

"Uh, huh." He grunted as he punched the start button for the microwave.

I wandered around our studio, trailing my finger through the dust on our dressers and wondered at Estelle's current drama. I pressed my lips together and replayed the scenario on Saturday. How was she going to create an energetic bond between herself and this Eduardo? What was this negative energy around her? Did it make any difference in my life? In my mind, I recreated the color of the turbulent sky and the tornado that had whisked her out of sight and felt my breath sucked out of my body. Chicken skin raised on my arms. I gushed cold water over my hands then splashed it on my face to bring me into the present moment of my life. I stomped my foot on the tiles of the floor of this bathroom-turned-kitchen to make me feel more solid. "Between you and me, there are times when I truly feel I'm close to madness."

"Uh, huh," Flyn said in a distracted voice.

"I AM mad over your cooking," I teased. When I turned, expecting to see his usual smile at my joke, his face was blank. He wasn't listening but staring at the timer on the microwave where our dinner was warming. I made our individual salads.

"Uh, huh," he finally said, as I retrieved salad dressing from a shopping bag and quartered the lime I found there. He popped the tops off two bottles of O'Douls, doctoring our non-alcoholic beers with a squeeze of lime and salt, then divided the enchiladas onto our plates before we walked with our hands full to the table set with place mats and candles.

I sighed. "I wish I could figure out what Estelle might be concocting for herself with this marriage bundle of hers." He looked confused.

"Didn't I tell you about the dream I had in the car while we were in traffic? At least I think this was a dream. It didn't feel like I'd left my body. More like I'd dipped into some kind of dream state."

He stared at me blankly, then answered slowly. "I only remember you started mewing like a kitten and getting agitated, and I couldn't help you."

I wanted to reach for his face across the table. "I'm sorry, Flyn. There's so much happening to me right now . . ." I slowed my speech. Something in his eyes had changed. "You look tired."

When he didn't respond, I bent my head to my meal, worrying about whether I'd told him too much. *'Dear Powers that Be, don't let him turn from me now that I've started trusting him.'* My nervousness soared. "I can be confusing, at least . . . I was as a kid. I seemed to talk from the middle of my thoughts . . . rather than in a linear fashion . . . that's when people . . . used to close down on me. I mean . . . I could tell . . . because I could see a glaze come over their eyes . . . and . . . then . . . I'd know . . . "

I was desperate to reach him, to bridge the distance I felt growing between us. I closed my mouth and reached for his hand resting on the table beside his plate. My touch made him look at me. It was true. I could see it. A window in his eyes had closed. The slender thread that bound us billowed as a draft slipped up the stairs and blew across our faces.

"Be patient with me, Sellie," he said, then he focused on his plate, preoccupied.

I asked, "Has something happened while I was with my client?"

"What do you mean?" He quickly lifted a bite.

"My antenna's picking up some kind of change in you. Are you all right?"

His deep brown eyes met mine, but he wasn't seeing me. Some other picture was playing on the back of his eyes. He struggled to pull away from it. "Never love a psychic," he said with a grim squint to his eyes. "Let's eat before it gets cold . . . then tell me what happened for you at Magenta and Talon's wedding."

"And will you tell me about you and Red Buffalo?"

"In time," he said, busy with his meal.

My nerves stretched, and suddenly I was starved. I dove into my meal and ate without tasting until he pulled out a chocolate cheesecake. I groaned. My mouth delighted in the smooth, rich taste. I was fully sated by the time we were finished, and happy again as we sat in comfortable silence sharing the view.

Having eaten by candlelight, we were sitting without back lighting from the ceiling lamp. Because the fog hadn't crept in from the Bay, we had a clear view through our western window of the lights of downtown Oakland as well as those of the Bay Bridge. The span connecting the two cities was outlined with pin points of orange sparkles. The lights of cars, twinkling back and forth like a slow procession of red and white candles, mesmerized me while the water reflected the movement of the bright colors. Our world felt private, as if we were the only living people in the world. Almost. There was still the rush of traffic, the horns of impatient drivers, an occasional squeal of brakes, and the irregularly modulated tones of ambulances as they raced toward the hospital a block away. If I had my druthers, I would stay in this spot for forever. I had no urge to shatter this comfort zone, dwell on my worries about Estelle, or visions about Amach's experiences. Enough was enough. I just wanted to sit with Flyn and watch the world go by.

"What about the wedding did you like?" I finally asked.

At first I thought he hadn't heard me, then realized he was disconnecting his thoughts from some past moment far from this room. His search for words brought me to an edge of worry, until he spoke. "Never thought about marriage the way Standing Feather described it." He squirmed in his chair. "I mean, I had one of those weddings where I promised to love and cherish my wife, and where she said she'd honor and obey me." More time lapsed. He shifted his position, stretched his back. "Marriage as a sanctuary? Now that's a mouthful." He popped his neck from side to side. "I paid the bills and went to work. She did the housework." His voice dropped so low I could barely hear him. "You and me are closer to what that ceremony described. I'd say we try every day to make life better for each other." He pushed back from the table to straighten his legs.

As I named a few things I'd liked about the wedding, he nodded. "I liked the six direction blessing Red Buffalo did at the end and the concept of Magenta and Talon standing in the middle of their friends."

"And the description of a marriage as a covenant between two people." I thought of my own previous marriages. "Red was a strict Catholic. He was 'man,' and I was 'woman'. There was some kind of pre-marital counseling where the priest said if we'd do it that way, we'd live happily ever after." I scrunched my face. "'Course I discovered the dogma translated into meaning I was to do everything the way he wanted it done, and, of course, I never did it correctly." I paused to think about my time with David. Our marriage had been along those same lines but with less intensity. At least, I think it wasn't as intense.

"That why you left?"

"At the beginning of my marriage with Red, I was more afraid of being on my own than I was of him." I rubbed my hands over my face. "I'd been so programmed to do what he wanted when he wanted it, I'd no idea what I could do on my own. After I left him, it was rough. All through the divorce, I was depressed and working three part-time jobs. But after four years, when he was permanently out of our lives, and I was able to pay the bills and keep a roof over me and kids' heads, I realized I could do anything I set my mind to." I rolled my shoulders forward then back, trying to ease the strain from our drive and working on Ethel.

"You tired?" he asked.

"Hmm, yeah. What about you?" His face was in shadow, making him seem farther away from me than across the table. Something was different, and I didn't feel I could ask him about it. I had to trust he would tell me when he was ready.

"Thinking about taking a walk," he said quietly, then asked, "Is it too late for you?"

"Mmm, yeah. I've got clients all day tomorrow and a meeting in the afternoon. All I want is a hot shower and to get horizontal. Does that entice you?"

He stood, then turned with his plate in his hand toward the bathroom. "I need some fresh air."

I was disappointed he didn't want to settle into bed. I liked everyone I loved safely tucked into their dreams when I closed my eyes. Of course, if I stayed up late while they slept, that was a different matter. "Go out and stretch your legs. You're the one who drove all the way here."

When he turned to look at me, his smile softened the dark brooding in his eyes "I enjoy doing things for you." He watched me closely, then twitched a smile at the corner of his lips. "And you're always so grateful."

I searched his eyes. "Flyn, you've no idea how glad I am you changed your mind. It was such a treat to have dinner almost ready when I was done with Ethel." I stepped toward him with open arms, and he let me hold him. We washed and rinsed plates in the bathroom sink. Empty bottles were tucked into the recycling box, and not one scrap of food was left to dump into the toilet. The remaining half of the cheese cake fit into the fridge.

"Might be back before you're asleep," he said as he found his jacket in the closet. Stopping at the top of the stairs, he turned and hesitated. "Do you think you'd ever want to marry me?"

His question stopped me in my tracks. I stared at him. "I . . . I guess . . .I'd not thought about it until Magenta said something about us having a wedding ceremony. Somehow, I suppose . . . I thought we were already married, but . . . we're not . . . are we?"

Closing the gap between us, he whispered, "We're as married as we can be right now. I don't ever want to lose you." His voice was husky with emotion. He held me so close, I had trouble catching my breath. Just as quickly as he'd gathered me into his arms, he released me, then hurried down the stairs.

Chapter XVI - May, 2004
A Brief Respite

Changing our lives was easier said than done. One simple phone call had stopped Flyn's classes, but shifting our focus from full-time city living with occasional weekends at the cabin to country living with daily drives either to Ukiah or Oakland was demanding more time, money, and energy than I had. Adding to our pressure was the ailing health of Flyn's grandfather and my mother. Pop Pop was over 90 and had fallen, breaking his hip. My mother was pushing 83 and had been hospitalized three times for dizzy spells with no diagnosis, despite any number of tests performed on her blood and brain.

Luckily, we weren't responsible for their direct care. Pop Pop lived with Flyn's mother in Salinas, and my mother, Margaret, lived in a retirement hotel in Pacific Grove. Every day brought phone calls either about their care or financial stresses. Annie was constantly worrying if she was doing the right thing for Pop Pop. I was challenged to decipher what result matched which test and why for my mom. Visiting either or both of them every Friday for the past month had multiplied our traveling and stress.

On top of all this, I was faced with the reality Ukiah had more than enough body workers and counselors for its population. Getting clients and referrals had been easier five years ago when I'd made my escape to the 'cities by the bay'. Ukiah's semi-rural status made its population wary of a Personal Growth Facilitator. In fact, no one knew what it meant. It was too different, even for its broad-minded residents. I needed more time and exposure for clients to know and trust me. I felt I was getting no where with all the effort to change our lives.

I needed a break. Flyn agreed. His attitude had slipped into a withdrawn silence since we'd begun these changes, and I was worried. I missed his positive influence. In the two years we'd been together, he'd never been moody, until now. He'd always kissed me when we left each other and when we met again, until now. Where he'd planned Sunday afternoon or early evening love trysts, our lovemaking had trickled to a stop over the past months. He left the apartment or cabin for walks during my evening showers. I never knew when he returned. No matter how many lamps I left on or how many cups of high-test coffee I drank for supper, I fell asleep alone.

I was afraid I'd gone too far in telling him about my life. Had I scared him with my stories? *'Does he have second thoughts about being with me?'* Should he have stayed in the mountains while I dealt with my schedule and practice in the cities? What had I done? He'd seemed interested in the puzzle unfolding around Amach and Estelle.

He never mentioned the "M" word again. I hadn't needed a public pledge of his love at the time of Magenta and Talon's marriage, and I'd no desire for one now with our world stretched and strained. Our relationship was ballooning with some kind of pressure, as if we'd contained the heat between us with a seal of saran wrap, and steam was amassing inside. There was substance and nourishment to our union, but we were unable to partake of it, and the facade of calm was about to explode.

My heart felt raw from being betrayed. He wouldn't talk to me when I asked him if anything was wrong, and he chronically changed the subject.

Our drive to the cabin was uncomfortably silent. He didn't ask about my practice, and I didn't offer any news or insights about my inner life. We arrived late Friday evening and sat in our patio chairs on the porch. The stars' brilliance with the soft sounds of the night helped me sense the expansiveness of the world so I felt in touch with all things seen and unseen. With darkness surrounding me like a comfortable quilt, I gave myself to the sky and thoughts of other worlds. I loosened my brain, let it float among the molecules of air while I drank in the peace of the night. When I turned to share this with Flyn, I found his chair empty. He was in bed, snoring; I undressed in the shadows.

We slept well, or at least I did. I awoke alone to watch the sun bounce above the eastern ridge. Breakfast was 'do-it-yourself'. We concentrated on our individual concerns: he worked on the wood pile, and I cleaned cob webs from around windows.

In the middle of the morning, Flyn and I followed the local habit of walking our property, making sure no marijuana patches were invading our land and hijacking our water. I'd been warned to patrol regularly since the practice of guerrilla gardening had increased over the past few years. By planting on someone else's land, renegade growers protected their identities from CAMP, The Campaign Against Marijuana Production, or some such thing. Our property was vulnerable, since we didn't live here full time. I sighed; another reason to live here year round.

Climbing the hill toward our biggest water tank, I huffed and puffed more than I liked. Flyn strode to the top without a problem. His late night walking was making him more fit, and I was irritated. *'Should have let him do this alone,'* I thought. I was watching my feet, so I didn't know when I'd made it to the crest of the hill. I bumped so hard into him I nearly fell backwards.

He reached to steady me, but continued to stand like a statue. I looked where he was staring and felt hot flashes cross my skin. Under camouflaged netting stood three rows of ten inch plants with their distinctive palmate leaves, a mild skunk odor hanging around the six by eight foot area. Flyn had his hands on his hips while he scanned between the patch and the water tank.

"What do we do?" I asked, having no idea which neighbor would venture up here and steal our water, plus put my land in jeopardy with the authorities.

"We pull every last one of the God-damned things out of the ground and throw them over the edge of the far cliff! That's what we do!"

"But what about reporting?"

He shook his head. "It'd make more problems, I think. Better to send the message we found them and destroyed them."

I looked over the far edge of the hill to see if I could see any more patches, but no distinctive plastic-leafed netting was viewable. "I don't like this, Flyn." No house was in sight, and I couldn't detect any paths in the dried wheat grasses. "It's like someone came in on a helicopter and planted their crop."

"Not likely. We're just not seeing their footprints. They might've climbed up the rocks over there." He pointed toward the avalanche of stones from here to a ridge lower than this one. He smacked his fist into his hand, and his chin elevated. "Pisses me off that someone thinks they can take advantage of this water." He stooped to grab the closest plant and yanked off its top, then tossed it over the side. "If I ever get my hands on these bastards, I'll rip them apart."

I wanted to get a shovel and dig the marijuana up by its roots, but Flyn was well on his way to destroying the garden we'd found. With my fingers, I raked plant parts that had fallen from his hands as he pitched them over the side. I decided to keep a low profile. Flyn stayed furious, kicking at the base of the thick stems and toppling the plants where they stood. We gathered the netting into a ball and stashed it on the opposite side of the water tank, disconnected the 'jerry-rigged' hoses used to siphon water, and sliced the irrigation hoses to pieces. Anger steamed off Flyn's body, and I didn't like the look in his eye. I was glad whoever had planted this patch was nowhere in sight. Flyn just might have thrown them over the hillside with their plants.

"Let's go," he said as he tugged my elbow.

By the time we inspected the rest of the ridge and down the eastern side of the land, his temper had improved. I explained the heat of his attitude to myself as being his way of dealing with the feeling of being invaded. Having an illegal garden planted on my property was a threat to our security. Knowing someone had violated our space was scary.

Wordlessly, we ate a quick lunch and met in the garden to improve our water system for our vegetables and fruit trees. As we repaired broken black pipe and spigots, we moved in the rhythm of shared thought and purpose. Our energies blended. I felt his presence when we reached for the same tool. I smelled the sun on his skin after he removed his sweat-soaked shirt. I saw the scars from his back surgeries and others he referred to as his drinking scars. The silver slice down the muscle of his right triceps ending just above his elbow was one I could never get him to explain. He'd withdrawn his arm when I'd traced it with my fingers, but I'd seen him stare into one of his dark places while he fingered it himself with his left hand.

I loved watching the way he worked, careful to brace himself before he lifted a shovel-full of dirt, moving his torso as a cylinder instead of twisting unconsciously. He protected his back by making every move count in a style very definitely his. I longed to reach out to him right here in our garden but what if he rejected my advances?

I returned to my construction of a second fencing barrier across the bottom of the current chicken wire.

"This'll help keep our food alive while we're gone," I said.

He stretched his back. "Yeah, it'll keep the deer out and probably the rabbits. Hope the birds and the damned squirrels don't munch too much."

"We can hang dangly things to keep the birds away," I suggested.

"Only works until the critters get used to it. Maybe black netting . . . to keep them out of the grapes and strawberries."

"Maybe, but I've had em happily caught inside a netted tent, eating the fruit and drinking from the automatic drip system." I sighed. "I don't know what to do," I said, pinching the last piece of wire into place.

"I know what to do about those squirrelly bastards that've already leveled the beans and cucumbers we planted yesterday!" He humphed and disappeared.

I finished turning chicken manure into the fledgling bean and cabbage crops we'd planted in barrels, then saw him return with David's BB gun, building the pressure by pumping the handle against the grip. "I didn't know you knew how to use that thing," I teased, until I saw his face.

The hardness in his eyes made me shudder more than his actions on the hill earlier today. I never thought I'd feel uneasy with this man. He stood tensed in the middle of the garden. His chin rose to its commanding pose. He looked ready to kill anything that moved. I cringed and moved out of his way, shuffling sideways to gain access to the house.

"OK, you gray bastards, 'I'm ready'." His chest was heaving. I walked backwards into the house then turned around not wanting to see what he was going to do. I wanted to ask him what he was thinking, but I was afraid to know what was feeding the darkness in his eyes. I was scared. Was this the danger Amach was warning me about? My knees weakened. My hands shook. I entered the kitchen for a glass of water. Several poofing sounds and a 'ping' came from the garden. I jumped and shattered the water tumbler into the sink. A BB must've hit the metal shed.

"Sellie! I got one!" He called from the garden.

Through the window, I saw a gray fluffy tail hanging from his hand. Tears flowed down my cheeks. *'Who is this man?'* I'd never killed anything in my garden before. I'd rather have all the green things eaten and just buy food at the store than kill a living animal. He knew that. *'What's changed him?'*

I locked myself in the bathroom, but the walls didn't block the sounds of several more shots. I showered, deciding I was done for the day. The mood of our togetherness was gone. I was desperate to leave here tonight, even though it was Saturday, and we had another day before we'd planned to return to the city.

He knocked on the door. When I didn't answer, he hammered on it. "Sellie, what in the hell's wrong with you? I thought you wanted to save the garden?"

I opened the door with tears still streaming down my cheeks. "Not at the cost of life. I can't reconcile growing things if I have to kill animals to do it."

He reached for me. I backed away. "What is it?" he asked.

I blew my nose, and squared my shoulders. "I saw a look on your face I've never seen before. Like you wanted to kill something and the squirrel was an excuse. You're scaring me with the way you've changed over the last weeks, Flyn. I don't know who you are right now."

"I'm who I've always been." His eyes hardened.

"I repeat. You're scaring me, Flyn!" I said hotly. "There's something you're not telling me! I don't know why, because I've been as candid with you as I can. Our life's changed in more ways than one." I wrapped my arms around myself so I'd have the strength to continue. "We . . . we haven't even . . . made love for over three weeks . . . and you've been the one always teasing me about dragging my feet. What is it? Have you finally gotten enough of me? Have you changed your mind?"

"It's . . . not . . . that." His body stiffened, warning me to stop pushing him, but I couldn't stop.

"I knew I couldn't tell you everything. I just knew it. That's it, isn't it? You think I'm crazy now, over the edge, a 'nutso'."

He pinned me with his strong fingers and pulled me into the hall. "That's not it," he said in a voice so low, I could barely hear.

"Then what is it?" I demanded.

"Don't do this to me, now, Sellie!" His voice commanded me as he shook me by the shoulders. "I don't need your hysterics. My God, you act as if I'm going to hurt you."

I broke free from him. "I don't know what you're going to do or not do anymore," I said, backing into the bathroom and closing the door.

Sitting on the edge of the tub, I was defeated. He hadn't told me a thing. *If he can't tell me what's going on, how can I trust him?   How can I support him? Or let him . . .'*

"Sellie?"

I jumped. "What?"

"I answered your cell. It's Estelle."

I wanted him to tell her I'd call her later, but I'd been trying to connect with her for weeks. As he started down the stairs, I heard him say "She's in the . . . "

"Here, give it to me," I said as I came out of the upper bathroom. "I'll take it."

We met in the middle of the stairs, careful our fingers didn't touch as he passed me my cell phone. We didn't look into each other's eyes.

"Estelle, are you alright?" I asked.

"Well, hi there stranger," came a sing song voice. "Of course, I'm alright. I'm the happy Grandma to a bouncing baby boy named Seth. Why wouldn't I be?"

"I've been trying to connect with you for almost a month now. You've never returned my calls."

"Sorry, I . . . well, I had to work some things out."

"As long as you're alright. I've been worried since we were together at your medicine wheel and since . . ." *'Did I want to tell her about my dream of her?'* I hadn't shared any extra-sensory details with her for a long time.

"Since, you got sick in my yard? That was something, wasn't it? You must've connected with a powerful spirit that day. Things haven't settled down here since. I swear someone's watching me whenever I go out there."

"Then don't, I mean, don't go out there without someone with you. You may need some kind of exorcism of the area."

"Oh, Sellie, I would rather make contact and find out what they want than just shoo them away."

"I know . . . that's like you. But Estelle . . . something's not right. I don't know if I'm sensing danger around the idea of making the bundle but I *am* sensing evil, maybe as an elemental, maybe another kind of energy. It makes my skin crawl."

The quiet air between us was charged with stabbing energy. Then, Estelle attacked, "First, you tell me it's dangerous, and you won't help me. Now you think there's an evil spirit. Sellie, admit it. You're jealous I'm having this super connection with someone cosmic."

"That's not it!" I yelled at her. "I'm truly scared for you, Estelle." I knew I wasn't going to be able to change her mind, but I hadn't expected this degree of animosity. Chills laddered my spine. Prickles of pain danced on my head. "Don't bind yourself to this man this way. There's something you've not considered."

"I don't believe you! And I will make this commitment to him so he's closer to me than just in my thoughts. I need him by my side, all the time. This is the only way I can think to do it. What else would work?"

I hesitated, but knew I had to speak my truth. "Live

with the situation and do the best you can, Estelle. That's what most of us do."

"I don't like that answer. I'm not going to accept it. You just don't want me to be happy." She hung up.

"Damn," I said, redialing her number. She didn't answer so I left a message. "Please, Estelle, don't shut me out. You could be harmed if you go ahead with this. In fact, I've a feeling you'll harm other people as well. You don't know . . ." The voice mail clicked off.

'Damn!' I wondered where she was: At home? In town? At her daughter's in Stockton? If Estelle was here locally, I could get to her this afternoon, before we returned to the bay area. If she was out of town, I'd no idea where to find her. I had to depend on electronic messaging to connect with her again. In all likelihood, she wasn't going to return my call. Sending thoughts with loving energy and leaving messages on her cell was all I could do.

I descended the stairs. Flyn stood at the bottom. "Estelle being her sweet, non-demanding, non-dramatic self?"

"I suppose you could say that," I answered. Noticing my cell phone batteries were low, I plugged the unit into the charger by the kitchen sink. My stomach growled and reminded me of dinner. I felt strong arms reach around my shoulders from behind.

"I'm not myself," he offered.

I nodded, wondering if I was going to hear the reason.

"All I can say is I'm sorry if I've disturbed you. It doesn't have anything to do with how I feel about you or about what you've told me. It's about things in my life from before us."

I turned to him, wanting to see something other than the hardness he'd had in his eyes when we'd found the garden. He looked downcast but determined. "You're not going to tell me, are you?"

"Not today."

"Then when?"

"When I can?" He kissed me on my forehead, then retreated from me. "How about some Brunswick stew for Sunday's dinner?" he asked.

"What's that?"

"A way to make use of these five squirrels I just sacrificed." He suddenly turned to me, his eyes pleading. "I don't like taking a life either, unless there's good reason. The best one I can muster right now is protecting the garden and providing food. I'll skin these, then soak them for the next 12 hours before we slow-cook them tomorrow."

I nodded and watched him take the dead animals out the door then faced the refrigerator to plan tonight's dinner. Fried potatoes and eggs would have to fill the bill, as the larder was thin.

I tried to locate Estelle with calls to her daughter, her mother, even her grandmother. In the wee small hours of the night, I realized I was focusing on Estelle and my fear for her because focusing on Flyn wasn't doing me any good. In fact, both situations were hopeless and out of my control. The growing glow of morning brightened our bedroom; I stared at Flyn's chiseled features beside me. This was the first time in weeks he'd slept past dawn. I missed him beside me when I went to sleep. I missed our morning wake-ups with soft words and gentle kisses. He lazily opened his eyes.

"Hi," he said, but, before I could answer him, the hardness made his eyes blank. He jumped out of bed. My heart sank to think we were no longer partners. What was I going to do without him? I stifled a crying jag until he was out of the room, then sobbed into my pillow.

Working in opposite corners of the garden and house, I tortured myself with self-denigration. He must need something from me I can't provide. *What am I not seeing? What am I not providing?* When I found him staring into the sky or the surrounding hills, it wasn't as if he was admiring them, but as if he were traveling beyond where we lived together.

In the early evening, we ate his Brunswick stew and a luscious strawberry shortcake. Flyn had outdone himself in the kitchen tonight. Since he'd cooked, I washed the dishes. When tea pot screamed, I wiped my hands to prepare two drip filters with espresso coffee. We needed fortification if we were to drive successfully to Oakland this evening. I poured the water and watched the grounds float, then settle.

"Penny," he said from his seat at the table.

"Funny," I smiled as I brought his mug of coffee. "I was thinking of offering you $10." I brought my cup and settled into the chair opposite him.

He returned my gaze, then dropped his eyes to my mouth. "I could be bought."

As I stared at him over my own cup, I worked on presenting a carefree grin. "I know I can buy your body, or I used to be able to." I said huskily. "I want to buy your thoughts tonight." A shadow flitted behind his eyes, but he never wavered on his attention to my lips. "What's up with you, Flyn?"

Time seemed endless as I watched for an answer. With his eyes focused on me, he sighed and lifted his coffee cup for a sip. He blew at the steam, his eyes never wavering from my face. I was pulled into the depth of his brown eyes, spinning, turning, floating, weightless. I wanted nothing but to hold on to him so tightly our skins would melt.

He lowered his mug to the table. My heart stilled its chattering rhythm. We stood and moved from our chairs to cling to each other. I couldn't, no, I didn't want to pull my lips away from his. Our hands were frenzied. Our clothes couldn't disappear fast enough. We couldn't touch enough skin, and barely made it to the rug next to the table before he entered me, and we joined our bodies in rampaging thrusts. It was over too quickly.

Even as we tried to catch our breaths, the urge to close

around his manhood rose up in me again. He saw it in my eyes.

I uttered one word, "Bed." We stumbled, arm and arm, kissing a shoulder, an ear, a chest, a nipple. In the bedroom, he gathered me into his arms, dropped me onto the coverlet and covered me with his torso. He caressed my face with his hands and eyes, and I took his tongue into my mouth and felt more desire build inside my heart. I ached for his closeness. In silence, we made love again with attention to every nuance of movement and breath. We fell asleep, wrapped in each other's arms amid the scrambled sheets.

I slept until 2 am, then slipped from his embrace to turn off the kitchen light. I had a client at 10am which meant we had to leave no later than 6. We had three more hours of sleep. I groaned, smiling to myself. Whatever he'd put in that strawberry shortcake was a winner.

Chapter XVII - May, 2004
Living Between Two Worlds

Traveling the 101 Highway south at 5am on a May morning was glorious. The awakening sun was beginning to dry the tall spring grasses and turn them golden. The morning smelled fresh with the clinging fog drifting between crevices in the mountains. Fully leafed trees shaded areas of light green grasses. Oak trees spread their branches into the sky while multi-colored leaves drifted from the madrones on gusts of wind. I loved sitting under one of these native trees with its bright red trunk during the dry, mid-day heat, listening to its skin split and crinkle, then drop to the earth.

The water level in the Russian River was low, because last winter had less than its usual 100 inches of rain. Where last summer we saw kayaks and canoes navigating courses of water across chert boulders, this year a person could walk across the narrow stream. It was too dry, too early. Every resident of northern California would be on alert until the autumn rain fell, holding our breaths until then, not knowing when a lightening strike or carelessly tossed cigarette butt would start a fire.

Tourists and long haulers never appreciated the tinder dryness of summer after a below average winter season; they didn't live with one eye on the sky and another on the vegetation around their houses. They didn't have to haul water to their cattle or irrigate crops from their deepest springs and wells. They didn't have to haul their washing south to another town to save the city supply of water. Nor did they watch their lawns and flowers die. The myth northern California had enough water for the entire state was just that. The idea was based on what once had been true, when the vast redwood forests along the coastal hills had collected thick ocean fog and funneled inches of rain into the watersheds, but timber harvesting had stripped the coastal range and changed the weather patterns. Wine-makers fostered the explosion of grapes growing on once forested land, but their acres and acres of regimented rows required poisons that eradicated all vegetation other than the grapes. Erosion sullied the Eel and Russian Rivers and silted their flow, often with toxic chemicals from the pesticides. September to December became a nightmare, if the winter season was delayed.

We lived with the fear of fire the best way we could.

And the dope growers? Well, I'd no idea what the dope growers did when the water supply was so 'diminished.' I supposed if someone had been able to devise a strain of marijuana that grew a great number of oozing buds, then someone could make a strain that was drought-resistant. *'Too bad,'* I thought. Even though marijuana growing had begun as a mainstay of financial support for poor families who needed help during the down times of the mill, too many others had come to the valley to grow and harvest the 'weed' as a multi-million dollar enterprise. From the size of the garden we'd found, I figured it had to be the crop of one individual rather than that of a large operation.

A cloud hanging high in the sky turned pink as the sun crested the hill and blinded us. Flyn was more than silent this morning. I caught him stealing glances at me when he thought I wouldn't notice. I wanted to read his energy field, but I knew I chanced misinterpreting what I saw. I had to wait for him to tell me what was bothering him. Fear curled in my belly. I prayed.

After we returned to Oakland, I worked one-on-one with four clients in my office and did seven telephone consultations from my desk in the apartment. I was exhausted by 10 pm. I ate Flyn's concocted dinner of smoked salmon, crackers, slices of cheddar cheese, and apples. It was enough for me. All I wanted was a shower and bed.

"I'm going out," he said briskly.

"But where?" I asked surprised.

His stilled face told me I'd asked the wrong question. I adjusted. "How long?"

When he shrugged his answer, the curl in my mid-section awakened. He reached for his jacket as he walked away from me. I wanted to call him back, to shake him, remind him of how we were in each other's arms last night but was halted by the quality of the air around him. I didn't know if I'd be able to reach into his heart as we had reached toward each other last night.

Confusion and mixed emotions chased across my mind. Flyn left me with a nagging thought he was running away from something. Was it from me? *'What else could it be?'* I thought. I dropped my clothes in the dark closet and walked to the shower.

The apartment phone rang. "Thank God," I said to myself, thinking it was Estelle returning my calls. I reached back into the closet to grab Flyn's robe then picked up the walk-around phone, vaguely remembering I'd left my cell attached to the electrical outlet at the cabin. "Hi there!" I said.

Deadness met my ear.

"Hello," I said, disappointed that it was a telephone marketer and not my friend. "OK, I don't know how you got this number, but I don't take solicitor calls. I'm hanging up right now." Instead I dropped the phone while grappling with Flyn's robe. Ready to push the disconnect button, I heard a strangled sound.

"No!" Came a moist breath.

"Potty?"

A muffled word sounded like, "Yes."

"Can you . . . ?" A thought jiggled my brain. "Uh . . . do you want me to ask questions, and you answer with yes or no?" I thought of my time on the Ouija Board waiting for the planchette to swing between individual letters. "Perhaps you could spell your words," I suggested.

"No," came the weak reply, then simply, "Ask."

"OK, are you calling to have me send you energy?"

"No."

I could feel my next question forming, "Are you calling about Amach?"

"Have you . . . ?"

"Have I . . . what? Have I connected with Amach to discover more about her warning?"

"Yes," came a clear answer.

"My mind . . . well, I've been able to watch something about her and two other people, but I haven't had time to follow the other instructions in your notebook. I promise I'll do it soon."

"Now," was even clearer.

"But I'm about to . . . "

"Now," boomed over the phone, then I heard heavy breathing, almost gasping.

"After my shower," I negotiated.

"In it," she urged. "No time . . . to lose . . . danger."

A chill crossed my bare shoulders. I stood away from the artificial spotlight caused by the beaming glow from the bathroom, but the windows were uncovered. I felt exposed and vulnerable. "How am I in danger?" I asked. "Is there something around Estelle? Does that name mean anything to you?"

"More."

"Something or someone more?"

"Yes," she was weakening again.

"What about Red?" I asked. My ex-husband had a habit of threatening me, even after all this time.

"No . . . spirits."

The tornado around Estelle shot through my mind. "I

see."

"More."

"Who could be more?"

"Known and unknown," she was able to whisper.

"All I know is Flyn," and I heard her grunt. "Is it Flyn? Is he a danger to me?"

"Not sure . . . something . . . though."

"But I love him," I said in my defense. "How can that be bad or dangerous?"

"Time . . . will . . . tell."

"Oh, Potty, that doesn't help me one damned bit. I need more."

"Be . . . watchful."

"OK, OK, I'll . . ."

"Connect . . . Amach!"

"Alright, I'll do that but if you could write . . . "

The line disconnected. I'd gotten all I could get. But I wanted more. I tightened Flyn's robe around me to ward against the room's chill and my nervous shaking. In my purse, I found her phone number on a slip of paper in a corner of my wallet, then realized all I had to do was hit the last call button.

"Hello," came a male voice.

"Uh . . . Hi. I'm Selena Howells, and I think I was cut off from a conversation I was having with Po . . . I mean, Delveena."

"Just now?"

"Yes, the line just disconnected."

"I'm afraid that's impossible."

"Impossible?"

"This's Dean, her son. Mom passed away on Sunday."

"I . . . but . . ." I stuttered. I was going to say impossible again, but the word wouldn't pass my lips. I finished instead with, "I'm so sorry."

"Thanks," he took a deep breath. "I don't know who called you but it had to be a hoax. We've been here all evening trying to clear things up, but it's . . . "

"I know . . . I was there a few months' ago. It was a mess. She must've been sick a long time."

The line felt empty between us.

"Who are you?" he asked quietly.

Giving my name again, I wondered how much I could tell a grieving son. "We took a class together several years ago, and she'd called me recently to reconnect. She had some information for me, and I'd a feeling she was close to crossing over."

"Well, whatever my mother told you or suggested you do, my advice is to follow it to the letter. She was uncanny in her insights and predictions." His voice caught. "I'm not sure what I'm going to do without her."

His candor gave me courage. "If you believe in spirits, I don't think you'll have any trouble keeping in touch. I'll bet all you have to do is ask, and she'll answer."

"I don't . . . I mean . . . I do. Thanks. I never thought . . . I . . . maybe . . . I could hear her."

"Well, if my last phone call is any indication, I don't think she'll have any problem getting through to you. I swear. She called me." I shivered.

"Well . . . thanks for the call."

He was trying to find a polite way to hang up. I held tighter onto the phone handle, not knowing, but feeling there was something more I needed to say to him. Then it came me. "Say," I rushed to add. "Could I ask a favor? I know it's a tough time, and you don't know me."

"I'll . . . try," he said in a hesitant manner.

"If you run across any information on Amach or under my name, Selena Howells, could you send it on to me?"

"I guess. I mean, she has so much stuff here. I . . . wasn't going to go through every scrap of paper."

"I understand, but if something should turn up?" I had no idea what it might be. As we exchanged names and address,

I was given the sense if there was something I should see, Potty or Amach would bring it to the surface.

I walked to the tub and surrendered to the circled blessing of the water from the shower head. I practiced what I preached and released my worries of Flyn, my mother, Estelle, my children and grandchildren, allowing them to wash down my body and into the drain. Potty's phone call hovered at the edges of my mind. *'How had she . . . ?'* I switched my thoughts as I switched off the water while I soaped my hair and body.

"The important part," I told myself, " is that Amach wants me to see her life."

I reviewed what I remembered of her instructions. "Clear my chakras. Bring in light." I accomplished this easily enough. "OK . . . now what?" Covered in body wash gel, I scanned my memory banks for the next step and was grateful to see the words 'Akashic Records' drop into place.

I sighed as water pounded on my head. Goose pimples cascaded with each drop down my body. When I faced the spray, water stabbed my eyelids, until, on their backs, a pinprick of light appeared, like it was at the end of a long tunnel. My consciousness was drawn toward this golden light.

As I drew closer, I could see a minute picture suddenly expanding into a panoramic view of a waterfall and a rock face glistening in its spray. I felt my bare feet standing on moss-covered stones and smelled fresh air. I wanted to turn 360 degrees to survey the entire scene, but neither my body nor my head would budge. I wasn't in control, nor was I who I perceived myself to be.

I was Amach.

We shudder.

Chapter XVIII - Past and Future?
Amach's Cosmos

Waterfalls gush over the edge of the mountain to splash across shining granite slabs. Three down spouts collect into a pool then overflow as a single foaming stream into the river below. Amach balances on the rim of a hollowed shelf embedded into the vertical rock while crashing waters billow into a heavy mist beading on the ends of her cropped hair, her eye-lashes, her nose. These clusters of moisture join to form larger drops to slip over her face and shoulders, underneath her deer skin dress, over her breasts.

"Dear Grandmothers, what now?" she says, wishing the watery waves of mist would flush her pain, her regret, and her disappointment into the Earth.

"All my hopes . . . " she mourns. Her mind asks over and over, "How could I . . . not see . . . into her heart?"

Dacona had asked for everything and had promised nothing. This woman child had wanted more from her bonding with Marweth than Amach could have imagined. "How foolish am I . . . to hope Dacona would be satisfied to have her lying- in with this stranger?" Amach had wanted only for Dacona to be completed as a woman, before learning the teachings.

"Why didn't I see?" Amach strikes her forehead. "Dacona wanted Marweth as a partner for life to protect her from the other men of the tribe?" Amach groans and hammers her head with her fists. "Now, I have no one."

Amach opens her arms in surrender to the waters and the sky. "All Powers that Be!" she cries with tears joining the misty beads of water. "Forgive me! I was blinded by my desires." A cold wind gusts so strong she feels struck from behind and stumbles to the edge of the crashing waters. "Jeetung!" Amach curses, reaching back her hand to the rock wall to steady herself. She shivers with remorse then steps onto moss-covered steps chipped into the side of the granite to sit enclosed by the brush of the forest.

Wrapping her arms around her knees, she thinks, 'I could not have refused Dacona's wish, even if I had known.' This girl child has been her beloved one every since she saw her head pushed into this world from the other side. 'Was it not the spirits who gave me the sign before she was born?'

Amach lowers her knees and curls her arms around her chest while she talks to herself. "I was sure she was to learn the ways of my mothers." She moans with frustration. "Did I force the meeting of Dacona and Marweth?"

It had seemed a simple plan to help Dacona have her lying-in with a man from over the mountain. The bond was to have Marweth enjoy his time with Dacona, then leave. Perhaps even bring new seed into the tribe. Dacona would have had stature above all others and never have to be with any other man again, unless she wished it.

Amach washes her hands over her face. Her spell had been too strong. Marweth had not only desired Dacona but had promised to stay at Dacona's side, to take her family as his own, and to stay with her as part of this tribe.

'He was meant to leave us,' she thinks, 'but only after the lying in.'

Amach stands to climb toward the high plateau of their winter camp. She shakes her fist at the sky. "Why did you not show me all?"

Her vision had not shown her Radan and Yorot hiding to watch Dacona cleanse herself of her dream time. Searching for the place where the women spent their time of separation, these two had found the secret bathing pool. They and Marweth with his companions had been drawn to watch the glancing light off Dacona's body. All had become entranced.

Their minds had been confused. She scowls. She had not known to protect the meeting of Dacona and Marweth with a dark wall. Radan and Yorot had been too close, had grabbed the lusting Marweth without a struggle while his companions had escaped. It was because of her skill he had been so weak with desire he could not defend himself.

She heaves her chest in a sob. 'My spell. It worked. But what did it bring me? Or Dacona?' She drags herself to the top of the ridge.

Sadness tears her heart. Her mind drifts to the council of last night.

"Something has happened to him," Dacona had screamed. "He would not have left me before the lying in!" With a furious glare, Dacona had stabbed at Amach's heart with outstretched fingers, "And you caused it, old woman. I will never face your eyes again."

Brogan had kept his head lowered to the ground. Tobar and his son, Radan, with his son's friend, Yorot, had stared at the ceiling of the meeting cave.

One half of the sun's travel across the sky has passed, and those accusations hurled into last night's air repeat themselves at every hearth in the canyon. Amach knows she is accused of sullying the bundles, of changing the patterns of the young couple's promises to suit her own purposes. 'What can they know?' Amach thinks. These words, moving so fast between each person, reminds Amach of a summer fire jumping across tree tops. 'It will burn out, but the damage . . . it will take time to grow dim in their minds.' She shifts a hide bag on her hip to reach for a cape to ward off the afternoon chill. Squatting on the path, she sees only her foot falls going and returning from the waterfall.

She looks ahead and studies the differences between the kinds of trees growing at the edge of the mountain meadow and those climbing the rocks near the opening to the canyon of her home. This path from the waterfall meets the path from the valley of their summer homes and leads to the wintering lands. 'What makes the trees grow tall near the valley but stunted here?' she wonders. 'Why do no trees grow in the tall grasses?'

'There is cause for the way this is,' she thinks and sighs. 'Just as there is cause for Marweth's absence.' She rubs her hands to warm them.

From the ridge, she looks back in the direction of the power of the falling water and opens her skin to its chilling shower. She turns to face that direction. "Blessed waters of our Mother, bring me your soothing touch. Help me see what I can see to lighten my promised daughter's sorrow." She sighs, shaking the last of the water out of her chopped hair. Her scalp stings where the flint scraped against it. If it would have made any difference, Amach would have cut her hair to the skin to show Dacona her regret. She covers her head with her hands and falls to her knees. Sickness rises from her stomach. She has failed her instructions to pass on the teachings from the old ones. What little food she swallowed at the break of dawn turns sour in the back of her throat. She gags onto the path in front of her.

"Why couldn't I have born my own daughter?" she moans. The suffering she endured beneath Gandfur at her own lying-in remains fresh in her mind, even though it was many seasons ago. Another spasm of sickness grips her stomach as pain stabs in her woman parts.

"I am greater than you," he had roared at her. "You will never lead this clan."

"I don't want to lead," Amach had repeated, her throat raw from screaming. "I am not meant to lead, but to advise."

"Don't lie to me! You and your kind always have your way. You, with your visions and small poisons."

"How can you believe this?" She faced him naked on her knees, backing against the earth wall of the cave. She had slipped from his grasp as he tore her hide dress from her body.

He lunged. She scrambled to the side, but he grabbed her hair and dragged her closer to the fire. She fought him until he brought his fist into her jaw.

"Your mother used her poisons on my father's brother," he proclaimed, as he slammed her shoulders to the earth. He spat on her bare breasts, his root strengthened between his legs. "You will bear my seed this night, and you will never forget it. Just as my family has never forgotten your mother's deed."

He spread her and lifted one leg over his shoulder so she would open to him. Spiraling pain pierced into her being again and again until she thought the night would never end.

He was gone at dawn. She had lain alone until Morah, her mother, had found her and wept over her bloodied body. Amach had been unable to walk. She could only drink the warm teas and broths her mother brewed for her while they remained apart from the others for the full time between the swollen moons. Both had been grateful when Amach had bled for her woman's time. Gandfur's seed had not taken.

"I fear for you," Morah had said before they returned to their own cave. "You have been deeply injured. You may never bear a child."

"I don't think I will want to try," Amach had said, with great tears falling.

Today the tears are falling for all the years lost since then, for the death of her mother, for Dacona, and for Amach's loss of a future for the teachings. "I must find someone to teach," she whispers. "Perhaps I can still grow a daughter. But who will lie with me now?"

Amach straightens her shoulders and her skins to walk toward her tribe's compound. Rubbing her hands over her face and her fingers through her hair, she calms her breath and clears her mind of dark thoughts. A craggy, stone wall rises to the sky along one side of their canyon and forms a protected corral along the back. Opposite the stone wall, a

dense forest protects them from winter winds. Its wood gives
them material for their homes and fuel for their fires. Two
large thatched huts are built in its center, one as a
meetinghouse and one for Brogan, their leader. Like she and
Labara, other families live in caves nearby, where stone ledges
extend from the cliff-side and large stones have been rolled to
protect the openings from sight and from wind. At the edge of
the forest, others have gathered wood and clay to build walls
for smaller, circular homes and have layered thatch for roof
coverings with smoke holes in the center. After the snows and
rains are stopped, they will return to their meadows and
gardens. For now, they remain on this higher ground, above
the fear of floods. Their cattle are penned at the far end of the
wide canyon. She hears their gentle calls for their evening
food grown and harvested in the marshy valley below.

Murmurings are heard in the shadowy forest, even
when the wind is still. Winter rain makes the ground boggy
with deep holes of thick, black mud. Men have left to hunt and
never returned. Some have been discovered sunk into these
tarry holes.

No one will go alone into the woods now. It is
forbidden to step past the edge into the thick underbrush since
one young child ran from the clearing and disappeared. Even
when his mother had tried to follow his screams and laid a
trail of tied animal thong as she searched, he was never found.

Long ago, when Amach had been but a child herself,
she had been drawn to the whispers of the forest. Morah had
said it was the spirits of the trees talking, and Amach had
wanted to be closer to them. She and her mother had planned
for her to test herself and while she was gone, a winter storm
had tossed the trees as if they were angry at her intrusion.
Trees trunks and bushes had quickly closed behind her, leaving
her no clue as to how far she was from her mother's home.
Darkness surrounded her and the winds erased the familiar
odors of camp. No familiar sounds met her ears. Nothing but

the wind roaring through the leaves of the trees and the crash of falling limbs sounded around her. Panic had filled her chest until she forced her mind to enter into a space of seeing without seeing, of knowing without thought, of sensing beyond scent and sound.

When she had returned to camp, her hands had carried new herbs for her mother to test and use. She was told she had been within the moonless woods for four days and four nights; she was surprised. While she had walked within the world of the trees, she had not known morning from night but had grown in understanding far beyond her years.

Settling in the shadow near the trunk of a pitchy pine tree, so as to remain hidden, Amach hugs her knees and watches Lebara, once a helper to her mother, stoop under the weight of a pack of wood. Amach sees her keep her balance, as she enters their sleeping cave, with the sharp wooden staff that never leaves her hand.

This staff, or one like it, has crashed a thieving hand or a stubborn head whenever Lebara needs to remind a disrespectful one she is watching. Amach smiles as Lebara sits near the opening of their cave and scrapes its pointed end on a special section of rock. When done, the wooden stick measuring from Lebara's shoulder to her knees, will be pointed and as sharp as a piece of worked flint. This staff is a simple piece of wood, but Amach remembers the speed with which Labara can wrap the cord from her waist beneath the carved notch at its end, then fling the rod into a tree. The rope then pulls the dead creature it has skewered to the ground.

When she's finished, Lebara sits alone in a patch of waning sunlight, rocking to her own rhythm, rubbing her matted hair with the hand of her crippled arm. The stronger arm rests with her spear.

Amach has never known why this woman who has cared for her since her mother's death has no tip to her tongue and will not speak, communicating with signings and pointing while she spits and whistles. Perhaps it happened when the scar formed across her shoulder and under her arm, rendering it useless for lifting. Amach traces the body of her mother's friend with thoughtful eyes. Lebara's flattened breasts beneath her work shift of thick hide make the older woman seem more like an old man. Lebara's family remains unknown, as she was brought to Amach's mother after a battle with another clan. Since Morah is beyond the space of seeing, Lebara is all that remains to Amach as a friend and as an elder. Now this ancient woman seems to be fading from view.

In the graying day, Amach comes alert. She feels a nudge inside her mind and opens her senses to her mother's shadowy appearance beside her. Amach's sadness eases; it is this connection that will guide her, will whisper into her mind, tell her which blossoms to pick, which berries to leave on the bush, which words to use for a healing. When Lebara leaves this world, Amach will have a link between here and the beyond where her mother dreams.

Out of the corner of her eye, a quick motion brings Amach's attention toward Amanna with her only daughter, Dacona, who stumbles with her wood load. Amach grieves at the sight of the young woman's slumped form. Neither mother nor daughter have spoken to Amach since Marweth disappeared.

'How can I regain their trust? Will we ever laugh together again?' Amach ponders. Her being is filled with the question, 'Where did Marweth go?' A sense of despair fills her mind until it is split in two, as if a dark cloud has been sliced by a jagged line of bright light; her head swims with stunning pain. She fights to clear her sight and shakes her head then palms her eyes. When she removes her hands, she sees Tobar, with his sons Radan and Rielke, and their friend, Yorot, sitting beneath the farthest ledge of the cliff, near a fire. Tobar's youngest son, Sweth, tries to sit close to his father but is waved away with an impatient hand. Brogan sits with them,

sharpening his arrowed spear. A softness grows around her heart for this man, for his sadness, and his aloneness. She feels no such feeling for Tobar, even though both men are graying and neither have a partner. How could two men of the same number of summers be so different?

Brogan's woman, Edena, left this life after wasting into the shell of her body. Their daughter, Enit, was too young to know her mother except through the stories of her father and brothers, Dearg and Bradach. When he became chief, he sent the three to their mother's family. Amach misses their laughter shared during the time of their second growing. 'Does Dearg remember our summer lives camped near our special stream?' Amach shakes herself, wondering at the gathering of light in her lower stomach while emptiness fills her heart.

She focuses on Tobar. His first woman ran away after bearing him two sons, Radan and Rielke, and has never been found. His second, Nuala, was never strong after the birth of Sweth and died in the birth of Veliz, a daughter, who now lives with the family of Hulack. Amach remembers the birth. Amach remembers how Nuala walked the women's cave for hours without a sound, even though Amach tried to have the woman use her voice to lessen the tightening pain in her middle. When the baby eased into Amach's hands, Nuala's face showed a welcoming sigh across her lips. Her eyes had widened then crinkled with a smile as she passed into the other world.

Amach regards the men. While Brogan strokes his spear edge with a sharpening stone, Tobar sits with his hands idle, his back straight, his eyes intent on the fire. The shift of his shoulders and the turn of his head tells Amach he is hopeful someone might be looking at him. He constantly puffs out his chest and raises his chin. He tilts his head and closes his eyes, as if in some kind of private 'thought talk' with the unseen.

She is thankful Brogan is their leader. Brogan is the best hunter, the best one to figure their movements from one place to the next. Brogan is the male who was chosen to be with her mother for the lying-in but became sickened. Morah learned later Tobar had fed Brogan old meat so he, himself, could take his place. Morah wore scars from Tobar's handling, and Amach bears the shame of having been born from his seed planted in her mother's belly that night.

Amach wrinkles her nose at the sight of Radan and Rielke because they share the same father, and she is suspicious this cruel man may have forced his seed into Amanna, even though her friend was bonded to Ruschk. Amanna never saw who mounted her, but remembers his smell and sickens when she is near Tobar.

Secrets. Amach shakes her head. Too many secrets. She watches Dacona pound leeched oak nuts for tomorrow's gruel. Her heart is sore for what she may have created in this girl's life. 'If only I'd been patient,' she thinks. 'Not brought them together with the sparkle of illusion to manipulate Dacona's destiny.'

An edge to the stone she clutches in her hand brings pain. She winces, then stands to toss it to the ground. Breathing the scent of the evening fires, the roasting meat, and the fumes of bear oil burned for light in the circle houses, she sets her shoulders. There is nothing to do now but pray she will be shown Marweth's place on this Earth. "Help me return him to Dacona," she pleads.

As she steps from the tree line toward Lebara, she considers her life and how she will keep her promises to her mother, her mother's mother, and beyond. Nothing is left for her to do but plant a seed within her own womb, if she dares. She walks deep in thought and releases my essence to float above her head.

I am free to view the scene of her tribe on my own, and I notice Tobar flinch when he sees her; his face souring. His hands clench, then his mouth smiles without his eyes.

I stood in the shower surrounded by Amach's universe

until I came into myself and turned off the freezing water. As I stepped over the side of the tub, I felt I was straddling two worlds: her life in the past and mine in the present. At this moment, Amach's was on the right and mine was on the left. I was stuck in a space again where two worlds crashed past me, and I had only to tilt my attention to one side or the other to be drawn into events of either. Here in the middle, I was separate from them both. Did I want to return to Amach's or did I want to walk around in my own body and life? In Estelle's world and now in Amach's, I had been an observer. *'Would I be able to be more than an observer, or a gatherer of information some time in the future?'*

I sighed as I donned my cotton nightdress, part of me glad I had only been looking through Amach's eyes and observing from the sidelines. Yet, another part of me had questions. Where was Marweth? What had Morah done to Gandfur's family to make him want to hurt Amach so terribly? Why was Lebara without the tip of her tongue and maimed with such horrible scarring? Would Amach find a partner? What happens if she can't pass on the teachings? And how in this world did any of this affect my life?

I pouted at myself in the bathroom mirror as I greased my face. If Amach wanted me to see something from this viewing of her world, she hadn't given me a clue as to what I was to learn.

I fluffed my wet hair with a towel then used the hair dryer. Closing the drapes to Oakland and its lights, I felt loneliness seep into my bones. No one nudged me from beyond. No one had called or left a message, and Flyn hadn't come home. Would I ever know why Flyn was being so . . . weird? Was this that edge he had mentioned? Why wouldn't he answer my questions about it? The look on his face tonight made me think last night at the cabin was our final night of lovemaking, and I shivered in the cold sheets while tears fell on my pillow.

Chapter XIX - June, 2004
Estelle's Bundle

I tossed. I turned. I listened to every creak of the stairs ascending to our apartment, waiting, hoping tonight Flyn would return before I fell asleep. It had been one week since our last trip to the cabin, and nothing had changed but the date. We ate dinner. He left. I went to bed. He crawled in sometime in the middle of the night, and when I awoke, he was showering. I was tired of beating myself up about it, of worrying about him. I redirected my thoughts toward Estelle and our last conversation and let my mind wander through the events I'd shared with her over the years and my current question: *'What's she going to do?'*

I squirmed into a new position, then considered thinking of something else. Perhaps I'd be better off picturing myself walking along a beach on a warm summer day or dreaming of a deep muscle massage in Hawaii. Anything would be better than these questions cluttering my brain.

I took deep breaths to make my body relax. I visualized pine trees and tried to access the fresh smell of daybreak. The early morning was a delight in summer with the birds twittering and tweeting. Fog hovered in the tree tops after it traveled from the sea through the canyons, settling in the wide branches of the evergreens and oaks, cooling the atmosphere from the day before. Sometimes the temperature could be 50 degrees at 6am and reach 100 or more by noon. I enjoyed sleeping in the cool and warming to the day.

I loved to walk through the thinning mist of a morning, so I constructed a vision, making the fog thick enough that water dripped like rain from the branches over my head. I wondered at this world I'd created with my mind. Was it like the ancient forest of the redwoods? Had I traveled back in time, or forward into a world regenerating after human kind had died and left nature to its own devices?

With no more than a sigh, I grew less aware of my body lying cuddled in my bed and more aware of my dream time. I wandered in a state of mind so unclear I had to ask myself if I was dreaming or entering another dimension. Was I returning to Amach's world? Was I walking through her woods? They were so familiar.

Maybe I was walking near our cabin. I'd no idea where my thoughts had taken me until I came to the edge of a clearing. My breath caught in my chest. I was behind Estelle's house and facing her Medicine Wheel. There she was, kneeling in its center. In front of her . . .

I see two bundles of tanned skin. They are the same ones she'd held in her lap on the day she requested my help. She empties their contents into separate wooden bowls with hands trembling. She's crying.

Am I hearing her words? Or am I only dreaming? Are these her thoughts?

"I don't know how!" She lifts her hands and drops them into her lap in despair. A large white candle is lit beside her. Smoke rises from an abalone shell. I am close to her now, hovering above the bowls to see what's within them. Each holds a small package wrapped tightly with strands of hair. Objects are hidden within their centers. I delve into the core of one of these small packets and see a picture in my mind's eye of toenails and fingernails being clipped, of drops of blood being placed on a small fluff of some kind of moss, then the picture fades from my viewing.

I know without seeing that Eduardo's bowl contains hair from the mane of his favorite horse, rattles from a dessert rattler, and what appears to be one-half of a butterfly wing.

Estelle's contains the bear claw she's worn since she

was a child, a hummingbird feather, and a rose quartz crystal.

I am clear of all feeling. No anger. No anxiety. No fear. No judgment.

She lights more smudge, using her hand to focus the smoke over the items in the bowls and across a larger square of tanned deer hide, tissue thin. Beside it are several items I can't see until I bring myself over her shoulder. I struggle to view her hands as she places a quartz crystal in the center of the skin and a handful of uva usnea, a local moss greener than I remember. I watch as she places a small claw on top of the crystal. I gasp. This is the eagle claw I wore for many years on my medicine pouch. I gave it to her as a token of friendship; it has no place in this bundle. What's she doing? I don't want to be bonded with her and this Eduardo for eternity. I try to stop her arm, but my being passes through her body. I am incapable of stopping her plan.

Estelle layers each item from both bowls into this virgin hide and wraps it tightly. I see her melt the pitch over the candle then hold the bundle so the seams are sealed. My heart sinks in my chest as she places the bundle inside a furry rabbit pouch and begins to tie it.

She fumbles with the thong, drops it, begins again, then drops the bag. Sickness enters my body. I work to bring in a golden light so as to prevent the nausea from over-taking me. She struggles to sit up.

Colors around her change from clear to opaque yellow to a yellow green that looks more like pus from a suppurating wound. I pull away from the color and observe her from outside the Wheel. There should be light emanating from the edge of the Wheel, from the protective energy of the four direction stones. though no such bubble of light surrounds it or her. Dread assails my senses. I can only guess she was so intent on her project she forgot to reinforce her protective walls meant to defend against harmful spirits.

Around her now is a web of purple-green strands of

hair, like a cocoon. I am caught in its outer filaments, like a fly trapped in a spider's web. I fight to free myself while she struggles to finish wrapping the rabbit pouch.

I see a cord connecting my solar plexus to the bundle, and I blast it with my will, intending to pull away.

A raging, red force releases me from my connection with Estelle. I am relieved to float away from her until I see a darkened shadow hovering near her. Another energy is present, placing itself between us. I sense the spirit wants me to leave Estelle alone. To test my theory, I rush in and hit a wall of billowing smoke. I am deflected away. She lights sage and cedar and a thick smudge pours around her body and her newly-made bundle. It is tainted green.

My being works to move toward her, but I'm caught again in the sticky threads of a spider's web. My arms are pinned to my sides, as if I'm being wrapped as tightly as the bundle Estelle holds to her chest. I struggle to breathe, to open my eyes. Rattles dance on top of my head . . . I feel pressure on my leg.

I awoke instantly, sweat seeping from every pore. I couldn't catch my breath or feel my skin. The ticking of the alarm clock at the head of my bed told me where I was, but it took all my concentration to slowly regained the feeling of my leg twisted in the sheets, a pillow bulging under my hips.

I jumped out of bed, so thirsty I put my mouth under the sink faucet. I couldn't wait to find a cup. *'What in hell just happened? What's she done now?'*

Shaking in the cool darkness, I fumbled my way back into bed. This was wrong. She had no right to include my eagle claw in her bundle. What would make her do such a thing? Now I thought I understood Amach's warning. But how could something I hadn't worn in over 6, maybe 9, years have anything to do with Estelle and Eduardo? *'Was the fact I'd worn it for 10 years against my chest a factor?'* I thought. I slumped in the dark room, sickened by the thought of the weird green smoke. I didn't know why it made my skin crawl. Being alone, I had to reduce my anxiety by searching for a smidgen of hope. Perhaps, the claw wasn't meant to represent me. But what else could have drawn me to view the ceremony?

"Well, Estelle's just going to have to take her bundle apart and remove it," I announced to the walls. I didn't want that claw in there.

I huddled under my blankets to reflect on the differences between Estelle's bundle and those from Amach's ritual. My memory caught on the flickering light of the fire and the sight of Dacona and Marweth, standing before Amach. In her hands were their small bundles, then I flashed on Estelle's creation. Amach had included something of the other in each of their bags, but had also given them pieces of themselves, as if she were reinforcing their free will.

Estelle had jumbled everything together before she had sealed it. Red streaked across my vision, and I was dizzy. I was tumbling in my mind. The bed was spinning, and I was at the mercy of a force pushing me into the mattress. My body was stretched full, as if someone was inside me, was part of me, and it was no one I had ever felt in there before. My heart hammered in my chest, sweat breaking the surface of my skin. I gathered as much strength as I could from my legs and arms and jumped from the bed. I landed on the hard wood floor and almost toppled but managed to catch my balance. I stomped one foot as hard as I could, then the other, growling in my throat like a woman pushing out a child. I jumped up and down on both feet, shouting, "OUT! OUT! OUT!"

Standing my ground, I turned clockwise, checking all the corners of the room. I fumbled while I lit smudge, then remembered to open a window as the room filled with smoke. Whatever had been inside me was invited to leave my world, to relocate outside my space.

Finally, as the smoke cleared, my vision was my own. I

made sure I could see the furniture silhouetted in the room before I crawled into bed and fell asleep.

Chapter XX - June, 2004
The Beginning of our Nightmare

The aroma of coffee and toast tempted my nose to emerge from the cover, then chilled air settled on my shoulders. Gray light seeped between my eyelids. I noticed my body ached, and wondered if I was coming down with the flu, until I remembered my dream and the battle I'd waged against some kind of intruder. Then I wondered if my imagination had gotten the best of me. Or had it all been a dream? I had to call Estelle. If she had truly constructed her bundle, me included, we were both in trouble.

I ran my hand over the sheets; no leftover warmth remained. '*Had he ever come to bed?*' I thought. Had this been one of his sleepless nights? Breakfast smells taunted my nose. I huffed at him wherever he was because I'd no idea what was making him helpful one minute, then a brooding mass of male the next. I wanted to read his aura, but I held firm to my code. He hadn't asked me to look, and I hadn't been guided by any urging from my spirit guides to peek. All I could sense at this moment was he was hunched at the dining table by the window that overlooked the Bay. The drapes were closed.

Not 'looking', when I knew I could, was a strange rule for those of us who had the gift of sight, but, after seeing Potty and reading her journal, I didn't want to budge from this practice. I had to keep my distance, or I'd take on more issues than my own. I had to be asked before I did any energy reading. If I tried to read Flyn, for example, I knew there was a chance I'd see only what I wanted to see, not what was truly there. That was why having been drawn into Estelle's world last night was so unnerving. She hadn't asked me to view it, and I'd refused her request to be part of the ceremony. It could only mean there was some kind of bonding between her project and me. My stomach tightened. I wanted to believe the entire experience had been a dream.

'Maybe?' I hoped. *'That has to be it!'* I wanted it to be a dream, otherwise I'd read my friend's energy field without her permission. I wouldn't . . . I couldn't . . . I didn't break my rule with Estelle. The colors had to be those of someone else's energy field. I'd kept my rules, and I wouldn't break them with Flyn. I could wait for him to talk to me as long as he didn't take much longer.

Every day, I watched him struggle with his face, trying to place a smile on his lips when his eyes held no such emotion. I had hoped stepping back from questioning him when he went 'out for a walk' would help him know I trusted him and his process, but I was worried. *'Why was he such a sober sides these days?'* Why did I see moisture in his eyes when I caught him looking at me? What had I done? Or not done? Where did he go when he walked the streets of Oakland? Was there someone else? Doubts and questions had to end soon, or I'd make myself crazy.

I stopped my circle of thoughts and sighed so deeply I heard him rustle papers at the table in response.

"Sellie?" he quietly called.

I stirred and turned in bed so I could face him, mustering as much of a nonchalant greeting as I could. "Morning," I called. From my own need to be reassured, I reached my arms to him and wiggled my fingers in invitation. "I miss you," I whispered.

He might have groaned, but I couldn't be sure. All I knew was he made no move toward our bed. I lifted myself onto one elbow to see his silhouette more clearly; he was dressed, his duffel bag sitting by his chair.

Shock swept through my body. "What? What's this?" I asked as I clambered out of bed, grabbing my robe to protect my nakedness. I kneeled by the side of his chair.

He opened his hands helplessly. "I don't know what else to do." His voice caught. "I have to . . . leave." He ran his hands through his thick hair.

"How bad is whatever's going on?"

"Can't you see how bad it is?"

"Not unless you ask me to see."

"Auh!" He groaned. His shoulders shook. I lay my head on his knees, wrapping my arms around his leg, smelling unfamiliar odors on his pants. Was that diesel fumes? Paint remover? Why were his clothes cold? Had he already been out, or had he just come in?

"Flyn, you've got to tell me what's wrong. With all we've shared, you can't just leave without saying why." I hugged his leg and tried not to beg. The duffel bag loomed next to me. "I need you with me. I need you to tell me what's wrong. I could understand if you didn't love me any more, but I know that's not true. You're keeping something from me."

Anger seeped into my center. I looked up at him. "Look, I've tried telling you what my life's like. I've never had anyone listen to me like you do. You understand things no one else has ever been able to understand. You have to give me a chance. I know you love me. I don't care what it is. Not knowing is driving me crazy."

He took me by my arms and lifted me so I could see into his eyes. "You will care," he said in a voice filled with desperation and menace. "You can't help but care! I could kill you."

The power of his grasp and his words shocked me. "What do you mean, you could kill me?" All of Amach's warnings clanged in my head. "What are you talking about?" I tried to pull away, falling backwards when he released my arms. Then he stood and paced the floor.

"My God, Sellie! I can't! It's too much," he whispered.

I stood, feeling a steel rod straightening my back. "Tell me NOW, Flyn," I commanded in a tone more than my voice. I could barely see his eyes across the draped room.

"No more moping about without lights, either!" I stated,walking to the drapes so I could open them to the morning light, then to the lamps so I could light them, then to the table to sit. I pointed my finger at the chair across from me, and he slumped into it. I held my hands in my lap and continued with my commands. "Tell me! There's nothing we can't handle together in the light of day and truth. What could it be? I know it's not murder or robbery."

"I didn't," Flyn admitted, while he hung his head. He was quiet for so long I thought he might have gone to sleep. His breathing became even and shallow. A curl of dread slithered around my shoulders as a shiver started at the base of my spine. His slow intake of a full breath alerted me to his readiness to talk.

"I'm sorry," he said, his deep voice softly settling on my ears.

I reached for him across the table. "I can feel you're sorry, Flyn. Whatever this is, I believe you had no intention of wrong-doing."

His eyes held moisture. "I don't know where to begin."

"If anyone understands that, it's me." I tried to smile but he was too distressed to respond. "Try with the most recent thing, then," I suggested. "We'll untangle the knot."

His eyes caressed my face. He gathered my one hand in both of his. "Remember when we got home from your place a little over two months ago? When I was going to stay at the cabin, and you finally told me what was going on with you?" He didn't wait for me to nod. "I dropped you at your office so you could see a client while I shopped for dinner and ferried our things up here?"

I nodded. I knew that evening intimately; it had marked the beginning of his sleeplessness, of his distancing himself from me, of our lack of love making. I had dissected every moment of that evening, every day since. My heart pounded. He saw me try to ease the pressure in my chest with a deep breath; he took a breath too, while gripping my hand.

"There was a message from my mom on our answering machine." I saw him lift his eyes to touch that place where memories reside in our minds. "She had a message for me to call another phone number. I didn't know what it was about." He swallowed hard. I couldn't believe what he said next. "I didn't recognize the number either. Sellie, I'm sorry . . . it was my wife's. Somehow she found me. I . . . I never . . . wanted that to happen."

His words circled my head like a rocket circles a planet, until I could finally slow the swirl into particles of thought I could understand. "You're married?" I tried to withdraw my hand, but he wouldn't loosen his grip. "But you're always with me," I said, trying to figure how he could have time for another woman, another life.

"It's not what you think," he said, pulling me toward him across the table. "Believe me, I left Yin Sun over ten years ago. I couldn't stay with her. I was clean, and she was using anything she could find. I'm just not divorced from her." He must've realized his grip was hurting me because he looked at his hands and laid them on either side of mine. "At first I didn't get a divorce because I didn't want to leave her daughter, Michele, without a father. After our boy died, I did everything I could to keep the family together, but I couldn't take care of all of us. I was losing my resolve to stay off booze and pills. I needed out. I thought I could go back and get Michele, but I was just the adoptive parent. When I left, Yin Sun refused to let me see her."

He cradled my hand in both of his as if I were the daughter he'd lost. "I made sure they had health insurance through my severance agreement from the construction union and struggled through two more back surgeries. Then there was more rehab." He faced me as if he were facing himself. "They say in NA to put our recovery first. I did, but . . . "

He closed his eyes, reliving his decisions and his regret, I supposed. "I kept track of Michele, especially when Yin Sun was arrested and lost her to the State." He took a quick breath. "Michele turned 18 last year, and I've no hope of finding her."

I held myself as still as possible so as not to cause him to slam shut. "I don't understand, Flyn. Why didn't Yin Sun want a divorce if you weren't . . . if she didn't . . . if you didn't?"

"Doesn't make sense, does it? What makes sense to an addict? I was digging out from under the pain pills. She was digging her own hole trying to keep high."

"OK," I still didn't understand.

"The court? A judge? The paperwork? All a big hassle." He shrugged. "I was as free from her as I wanted; I'd no reason to be legally free. We had no property together, no car, no bank accounts, no charge cards. I was busy with my rehab, with NA, then I learned Yoga. I tried college for a while, started teaching Yoga, then, you came into my life."

He stroked my hand with one finger. "Standing Feather's words keep going around and around in my head. Marriage's a covenant, a sanctuary we create for each other." He dipped his head and hunched his shoulders. When he looked at me, his eyes were filled with tears. "I've tried to keep our lives in that sanctuary, away from the bad."

"But, not being divorced isn't so bad. We can do the paperwork, file before the judge. No problem."

"She's dying of AIDS."

My heart stopped. "But . . . what . . . how . . . how can that have anything to do with you?"

He gripped my hand again. "She says I gave it to her before I left. She says that's how long she's had it, and that now I owe her."

Numbness chilled my mind. I couldn't think. All of

the details of HIV and AIDS disappeared from my brain. I couldn't track a single piece of information about the disease, how it was passed, what the incubation period was. Thunder rumbled between my ears. My vision dimmed then cleared. Was I going insane? My first clear thought was, *'HIV's for other people, not my Flyn.'* I gasped, *'Not ME!'* And then I whispered, "Something's not right here."

He hung his head again.

"Flyn, look at me."

He struggled to raise his eyes. They held a mournful plea for forgiveness.

"You can't have given it to her. I would've had a hint, some kind of feeling about you if you'd been sick. This HIV would've been in your vibrational field. I would've felt it before we became a couple. I firmly believe I would've been warned if your blood were tainted. She's lying." I pounded the table. "This isn't true." He stared at me dumbly, and I saw the etchings of exhaustion across his face. I asked, "When did she tell you this?"

"I knew she was dying from her first phone call, but she didn't tell she had AIDS and she believed I'd given it to her until yesterday afternoon, when I saw her." He scraped his fingers through his hair. "We've been talking on the phone for the past two months. She's been demanding to see me. Said she had some news for me. Couldn't tell me but face to face. I thought it was about Michele, so I went yesterday. I wanted her to agree to a divorce but she laughed. Then she spit out this . . . accusation."

Part of me melted, "You silly man." Then I laughed. "After all these years, you just file your papers and let the court tell her. You haven't been co-joined for so long, it's a slam dunk."

"But, she's still dying."

"How do you know that?"

"I went to see her at this place in San Francisco. She's

at the AIDS Hospice on Castro. Doctor says it's not going too be long."

"And she's still accusing you of giving this to her?"

He nodded.

"But if you just heard her accusation yesterday, why haven't you wanted to touch me for the past two months?"

"Because I didn't feel worthy of you . . . and now . . . it's even worse. If I do have it . . ." He rested his forehead on his tightened fist. "She says I must've gotten it from dirty needles and gave it to her when I was drugging it." He suddenly stood to pace the room again. "Can't you see, that's why I have to leave? We've never used protection. I would never forgive myself if I had infected you. I love you too much." He stopped pacing and knelt before me. "My God, Sellie, this is a nightmare. It's bad enough I'm not divorced. That's been preying on me since she found me; I've felt like a cheat and a liar. I'd decided when she first called I didn't want to make love with you unless I was free. I've felt unclean with this thing hanging over my head. I tried keeping away from you, but then . . . Saturday night happened." He buried his head in my lap then lifted his eyes to mine. "If there's the possibility . . . I can't . . . let it . . . happen again."

After he'd lowered his head into my lap, I stroked my fingers through his thick hair. There was no way this man had been sick with a debilitating disease like HIV for the past ten years. I'd heard no alarm bells. I'd had no feelings of alarm when we'd made love. What I did feel was the heartache and worry he'd been carrying for the past few months. I held him and reassured him with my body it would be alright.

"Flyn, when are you going to take the test?"

"I haven't planned that yet. I knew I . . . had to leave . . . first." His answer was muffled.

"No you don't! You just have to take the test! And today's the day," I announced. "I even think you can have the results in an hour, and I'll be there with you." I lifted his head and steadied it with my hands on either side of his jaw. "We can't go on without knowing. I'm perfectly willing to use condoms for the rest of our lives, but I'd rather not. I'm ready to fight this demon back to hell. I'm not giving you up." His stare penetrated my brain. In one movement, he stood, lifted me into his arms, then turned so he could sit and cradle me on his lap. We sat together, filling in the spaces of doubt with the warmth of our bodies.

I understood it all now. It was like the months of fear had been whisked away by a magic wand. If only the rest of his worry could be made to disappear as easily. I wished I could play the genie in the charmed lamp and blink my eyes, or play a pirate and make Yin Sun walk the plank out of our lives. But day dreams weren't going to give us our life back. What we needed here was truth, and in all sincerity, I knew our answers wouldn't be real if they came through a magic wand. The test results and the divorce had to be on pieces of paper, with special insignias, so we could hold them in our hands.

'He isn't sick, ' I proclaimed, trying to keep fear from running across my arms. *'Unless . . . I'm seeing what I want to see.'*

I needed action. "I'll find a testing place." I started listing, "Maybe the public health department is the first place to call? Or maybe we can get it done down the street at Kaiser's?"

He rearranged me on his lap. "Sellie, I'll do the test as soon as I can."

I didn't register his words. "I'm sure we can; I'll just make some phone . . ."

"Selena, I said I would handle it." His voice was firm, his chin raised.

Slowly I realized what he was saying. "But, I want to go with you. I want to . . . you need me."

"I'll handle it. I'm relieved you'll stand by me, but I've got to do this on my own."

"I don't understand," I said, trying to see through the fog in my brain. He started to hug me, but I pushed against him, then stood. "This is for us to do together. For all we know, I have it too. "

He shook his head.

I decided, "You're being stubborn!"

His jaw clenched harder.

I left him to face the water of the Bay. My heart hurt. "Why?" I cried at the glass. I knew his worst secret, his heaviest fear. Now was the time for us to share our strength and love. We needed to be together. He needed me to help him make his next steps.

"I need to handle this alone," he said quietly and slowly. "I got myself into it. I'll get myself out of it." He turned me around to face him. His eyes steady. "It means a lot to me to know you want to help, but, I know you. You'll make the arrangements and the appointments around your clients. Pester me if I seem to lag behind your schedule." He laid his thumb on my chin. "This isn't yours to do. It's mine to finish." He kissed my nose. "I want to come to you free and clean."

I didn't want him to do it his way. I wanted to be beside him, show my support. I knew how to set things in motion, to get things done, to take care of this. We just needed to find out if he was infected and then we could deal with the rest of it. It was so clear to me. How could the first step not be clear to him? I knew what he needed! How dare he not want my . . . oh, God!

The reality of what he was saying hit me square in the stomach. He was right. This wasn't my fight. In fact, it wasn't even my doing. He was telling me he needed to correct this portion of his life on his own. I had to let him have his space so he could come to grips with what he'd left undone.

I had to have faith in him and hope he'd return to me soon.

His voice had been quiet but firm; there was no arguing with him. A bit of heaviness lifted from my shoulders, but not from my chest. I didn't deal well when I wasn't in control. I tried to stare him down and argue he was wrong, but I could tell by his face, there was no further argument. I had to trust he'd know where to go, how to get there, and when to come back.

"You'll need the car," I said flatly.

"I'll use BART and the bus." His voice whispered. "You'll need to be available for your mother, if she calls."

"Take the cell phone," I groped in my purse for it then realized it was being recharged at the cabin.

"I'll call with my card from pay phones or the hospital."

"But . . ."

"Sellie, I'll do fine."

I wanted to kick him in the shin. I opened my palms in front of me; I felt helpless. My throat tightened as if I were choking; I didn't want to be without him.

I wondered when the tears would fall, but none filled my eyes. I was dry to the bone. I wrapped my arms around myself, and began rocking back and forth, as if I were a baby in my own arms. "I'm sure you're right, but . . . Flyn . . . I won't be able to be without you . . . I'll need to have . . . just a word . . . that you're doing OK." I held myself as tightly as if holding together pieces of a fragile vase that had broken but had not yet fallen apart. "Please, give me a call or leave a message once in a while." I wanted my words to penetrate into the center of his brain.

He opened to me, and I filled his arms. "I love you, Selena," he said. "I've got nothing on my mind but clearing this up and living with you for the rest of my life."

His words danced in my head, and I thought, *'Please! How had Amach worded her prayer? All the Powers That Be! Let his life be for a very, very long time.'*

The cold room enveloped me when he unwrapped his

arms. I heard him walk toward, then down, the stairs. He took my heart with him.

Chapter XXI - Summer and Fall, 2004
The Waiting

I knew I was falling because I could hear the updraft whispering past my ears. It was as if I'd stepped out of an airplane onto a cloud only to discover the thickened air had no substance. At first, I panicked, trying to grab on to anything that might prove substantial, but everything slipped through my hands. Then, I surrendered to gravity, and my falling slowed as I was supported by the wind resistance against my body.

On my back, I chided myself, *'This isn't how sky divers fall.'* They go 'belly first' so they can admire the earth below, then head first, so they can thrill into the rushing wind. I tried to twist so I could enjoy the dive, but only succeeded in making myself spin until my stomach lurched. Nausea enfolded me.

'Not good,' I thought. *'This dream isn't working.'* I knew I only had to open my eyes to stop these sensations, but my lids felt pushed into my head. I managed to lift them and saw blackness. I smelled the bitter aroma of long dead fires, like I was in an ancient chimney coated with creosote, or under the roof of a cave caked with years of collected smoke.

That's where I am. Rock walls form the room. Skulls no longer stare from inset shelves as they had when I'd joined Amach to work with Dacona and Marweth. There is no fire, only a torch plunged into the center of the stone-rimmed circle. Its tightly wrapped grasses flare unevenly. I wonder how long it will provide light and if another is ready to take its place. Another scent comes; sweet but spicy. I see yellow smoke as it spirals from a deep depression in the cavern's floor.

Amach huddles, staring through the smoke toward the

cave's far wall. Her legs are pulled before her, arms wrapped around them. She rocks, her brown eyes glazed. I follow her line of sight to see figures forming in the upward smoke-stream.

Her head nods with each rock of her body, as if she is agreeing with someone, but no one is standing near. I hover, wondering what she's seeing. Then, as if invited, I sink into her being and see with her inside eyes, think her thoughts, and understand what we are doing.

We are concerned for Dacona, who is in bed, laying in a blank stupor, with bone-racking chills. "When?" I ask. "Why?" Panic fills my heart.

I feel our fingers twitch. The movement reminds me: We are Amach. I settle and align into her thoughts.

A cadence of words catches my attention. I rock with their rhythm. "Where is Marweth? Show us where! Trace his footfalls. Show us, now!" These words pound in our head and tell me the theme of our trance. I fuse with her chant and her intention, straining to recognize figures in the smoke-stream. I am gently reminded to release my need to focus, to soften my eyesight, and to relax my shoulders, my neck. I am rocking in her rhythm, chanting her words, feeling a spaciousness grow in the cave. The wall of the cave flickers in the torchlight; shadows fall across its surface as an outline of a form comes clear.

Muscled arms and a sweat-covered body enter our vision. There is no doubt; we are witnessing Marweth. His long hair is twisted on top of his head in a knot and fixed in place with a bone. His skin glistens in the morning sun; the muscles of his buttocks and back rippling with each step. He is naked save for a thong around his waist and between his legs holding a leather pouch over his manhood. He walks with confidence; his head turns side to side with each footstep on the dried grasses of a field. His nose tests the scent of the wind as a gust pushes across his face. He raises his head to feel its direction and the strength of its force. His spear is held casually at his side. Balancing on the balls of his sandaled feet, he loosens his knees. He breathes slowly through his mouth to preserve his ability to smell. He is hunting. We guess to bring meat to Dacona's mother, to prove his prowess as a provider. And he wants to do this alone, to prove his manhood before he beds Dacona. But why has he not returned?

A sound in the dense undergrowth draws him to the edge of thickly standing trees. He steps into the bushes, sniffing to determine what manner of animal he is hearing. He settles his shoulders. We see his lips move as if he is praying. Could he be asking his prey to sacrifice itself to him? Does he promise to use every portion of the meat and the bone and the skin? Does he honor his quarry by pledging the choicest pieces to the leader of his new clan?

His attention is pulled from his prayers by a crashing in the underbrush. He strides on quiet feet toward it. His chest rises and falls in excitement, and he moves quickly toward the place where he last heard the sound. It crashes again. He is being led around the edge of the clearing, and we see his face; his brows are puzzled with a question. Again, he sniffs the air, trying to determine what kind of animal he's pursuing. He halts, waiting in the silence where no birds sing and no wind speaks through the trees. He closes his eyes to concentrate and misses the sight of a shadow arising from the bush behind him. Too late he hears the whistle of the club as it swings toward the back of his head. With no time to defend himself, we watch helplessly as he falls forward onto his face. We shudder with tearful understanding as three more figures move out of shadow and join the first. They waste no time in thrusting their spears with full force into his fine body.

I want to pull away, to scream, but am forced to watch as he is dragged into an opening in the meadow, then lashed, like an animal, to a long pole. His hands and feet are tied so they can be harnessed across the beam, his body drooping heavily between them. He is trussed like dead meat. They carry him through the forest, to a ledge overseeing the falls and toss him to the waters. They say no prayers for his safe return to the Spirit world, and no offering follows his body. The three men turn in full view of our sight, Tobar, Radan, Rielke, and Yorot face us with grim expressions. Tobar struts along the ledge; Radan seems wary. Yorot is the first to smile as he lifts his left hand to show his find. The leather pouch from around Marweth's neck has been captured. All the hairs on our body are standing in fear. It is the bundle made to bind him with Dacona.

"NO" I hear us say. "NO! NO!" I shout myself awake.

As the meaning of our vision became clear, I began to cry. Marweth was dead by the hands of the tribesmen he had wanted to impress. What I didn't understand was the reason for the brutality of their attack. There had to be more to their anger and hatred.

The alarm clock ticked on Flyn's bedside table with maddening consistency. As each second passed, I quieted my racing heart. A siren wailed in the night, and traffic noise filtered through the drapes. I longed for Flyn's body heat to define the edge of my skin with his warmth.

Dacona's sickness was no mystery to me. I understood her lack of will to feed herself, to dress herself, to want to feel sunshine on her body. I didn't want to feel anything either, not the breath of the wind, nor the pressure of clothes. I wanted only to feel his body beside me, on me, in me. I wished I didn't have people who needed me. I wished I didn't feel obliged to worry about Estelle or my mother. I wanted nothing more than to sink into this bed and never surface.

The bitter taste of 'bleak' filled my mouth, making it unusable for food; my lack of hope weighed heavily on my shoulders. I had to admit if Flyn were to receive a death notice from his test, I was sure I wouldn't want to live either.

I screamed to him in my heart, *'Where are you, Flyn?'* It'd been more that a month since his last call, and more than two months since he'd left.

My recent vision of Marweth being clubbed and speared to death overlaid my pictures of Flyn walking streets, dark with thugs and muggers. I gagged with grief. *'It couldn't be true.'* The murder of Marweth was real, but it wasn't true for Flyn. I fought the integration of the images of these two worlds. I had to move, had to do something, anything, so I forced myself from our bed to sit on the floor with my back against the foot of the mattress. I lit a sage leaf and a candle, then pulled my mind into focus so I could picture protection around Flyn wherever he was.

"I love you. I miss you." I whispered this to him, over and over again. "Please call." The chilly floor crept through my bottom. My knees shivered.

A quick trip to the bathroom and I was back in bed, struggling to see the time on our alarm clock. It read, "4am", the witching hour. I had three hours to worry before I started my day.

* * * * * * *

I sat at the dining table, looking at his empty space, wondering what to do with my thoughts. *'What can he be doing? Has he taken his test?'* Another month without Flyn. Another set of 30 days gone without a word from him. The memory of his face shifted to the memory of him sitting in his chair, and I couldn't dislodge them from my mind.

I was like a moon-struck teenager. *'Surely I've more to do with my time than stare at nothing.'* After three months, my resourcefulness still hadn't returned. I wasn't doing my best work for either my massage or phone clients; Flyn's retreat had more than distracted me. It wasn't just the fact he wasn't here, it was the fact he didn't want my help; that he wanted to do it himself.

'*He wanted to be alone with his wife.*' This sentence poked its head into my mind and made me straighten in the chair. '*Now where did that come from?*' I thought. I knew better than to go down that jealousy-laden path, but there I was, on the verge of collapsing into green-eyed martyrdom. In an effort to avoid the trap, I forced myself to remember his parting words. '*I have to remember them exactly,*' I told myself.

Slowly, painfully, I brought to mind our last moments before he left. I pretended to feel his arms around me. "I love you, Sellie," he'd said. "I want to live with you for the rest of my life."

A flicker of warmth licked my heart. That was it. '*I must not cloud his words with my fears,*' I told myself. '*He's doing what he needs to do.*'

'*I have to do my life,*' I instructed myself sternly, then took a deep breath. Being Sunday afternoon, I determined a quick shower and a walk along Piedmont Avenue were in order. No sense moping. I needed out of this place and into the world. With a firm grip on my resolve, I made my plans, chose clothes, and stepped into the shower curtain circle surrounding the spray of water within our old fashioned, claw-footed bathtub.

The water pounded the top of my head, rushed over my shoulders, the rise of my breasts and belly, and down my hips and legs. No vision of Amach's world was invited to enter my mind. In fact, I shut the door to her life. No worries about Estelle's shenanigans or my mother's constant complaints drifted into my protected circle. I stopped time and my thoughts by concentrating on the sensation of the water over my body, of my breathing, and of my heartbeat.

As I closed the faucet, the answering machine bleeped to announce a caller was leaving a message.

"Just calling to say, I'm alright," it said. "I'm either at Yin Sun's bedside or her place, trying to sort through her mess.

She's . . . failing . . . fast now." His voice changed from a dull report to one with some excitement. "I found a note from Michele and an address. I hope . . . I hope I can find her." Then he dulled again. "I . . . uh . . . I'm mired in legal stuff too. I miss you, Sellie."

Mesmerized by the sound of his voice, I drank in every syllable. Concentrating on every word, I stood frozen in place then shook myself alert. *'What am I doing standing here?'*

I hopped over the edge of the tub and slipped on the linoleum. Falling forward, I tried to catch myself before I landed on the floor, but only managed to hit the wall with my shoulder. I scrambled around the door frame and heard him say, "I love you, you know!"

I grabbed the phone and punched the button to connect me with his voice. The closing beep announced he'd hung up. I punched *69, but the numbers on the screen were a jumble. It must have been his calling card number.

I mutely listened to the dial tone while I dripped on the floor. There was so much I wanted to know, to ask him. Had he taken the test? Where was he staying? How was he living?

I wanted to tell him I missed him rattling around in the bathroom/kitchen, interrupting me every few minutes as he talked to himself. I wanted to tell him I even missed his farting or whistling in his breathless, unconscious way. I wanted to tell him I craved his warmth in our bed, especially in the mornings when we used to plan our day and nestle in each other's arms. I returned the phone to its cradle, realizing I probably wanted to tell him more than he wanted to hear.

After his call, I forced myself to dress and wander Piedmont Avenue. I sat in the late afternoon sun and watched people live their lives, trying not to torture myself with the idea of others having more fun than I was. I held onto my purpose of staying 'in the moment', breathing just one more breath and having my heart do its beating thing, one more time. I could do this. He had said he loved me. I hadn't done anything wrong. I was OK. Coming home with a deli sandwich and a container of potato salad from the Market, I turned slowly to survey my studio apartment. I checked my messages and listened to Flyn's voice three times. Like the pool of water by the phone, I turned into a puddle of tears. I cried until I was dry then I hung my purse in the closet. One of his shirts was hanging on a hook and drew me close.

I recognized the scent of his body after he'd finished working in the sun. Pulling the sleeves of his red and white plaid flannel shirt over my shoulders so its back covered my breasts, I sank to the floor. Closing my eyes, I pretended his arms were around me and that he was home. I drank him in, his shirt giving me a sense of closeness his phone call hadn't. I followed the connection of his voice and smell and received a picture of him sitting quietly with a cup of coffee by a hospital bed. He seemed intent on the person there, but my mind toyed with the possibility he was thinking of me, not her. When the connection to the picture exploded into thin air, I was left with his shirt and decided to wear it.

Finally hungry, I prepared my food, formally sitting at his place at the table. I'd been eating a lot of my meals while standing in the bathroom or lying on the bed, but with his shirt around me, I felt more like doing our normal routine. I cleared the old newspapers and throw-away mail into the waste basket and found his yellow pad of lined paper. Flyn doodled when he wrestled with a problem. This page must have been from the morning he decided to take care of his business without me. The triangles and angular arches showed he must have been deep in thought. I smiled at his rendition of my name in fancy calligraphy, embellished with flowers and twirls at the ends of each letter.

I doodled below his work. *'What now?'* I could call Haley again and bore her to tears with how much I was feeling alone and abandoned; she was a good friend and a counselor, but enough was enough. She deserved a night off.

What about calling Roxanne or Berta? I sighed remembering both were out of town for the weekend. Did I want to watch a movie? I certainly could go out again and rent one from Blockbuster down the street. Did I want to channel surf on the cable? I'd been doing that for many evenings now, finding comfort in having a bit of control over my life, even if it was only the damned channel changer. Something else tugged at me.

My hand circled and spiraled patterns across the lined page. My mind paused as if shifting gears. *'I do have my own puzzles,'* I thought and began to scan the moving pictures I'd seen through Amach's eyes. First, I glimpsed her work with Marweth and Dacona, then watched as the overview of her life filled the screen behind my eyes. What had she been trying to show me? What was the connection? And these bundles. *'What is it about these bundles?'* Have I only dreamed Estelle created her own bundle? Where in the long-term scheme of things does Amach come from? Was she Native American or were her origins more Irish or Celtic? Had she lived other lives? Was I only to see this one?

A voice boomed in my head, too rapidly, at first, for me to understand, then it slowed, repeating itself, and I began to write each word as it appeared.

I have lived many lifetimes. Each one has been a lesson. Let me show you what I have learned so that I might help you.

I nodded as my hand finished.

We are never alone. We are here for each other. We are part of a cycle, a spiral, a DNA patterning that is healing into the next millennium.

I was grateful she took a breath and slowed her speech even further.

We are a bridge between worlds and will

continue to do this even when you step from your human overcoat.

A chill spiraled down my back.

Each life we have lived has its individual and community purpose and relationship. Nothing will ever be clear until you sit outside your life and review it. This is my current vantage point.

I kept my hand writing as smoothly as possible as I asked out loud, "Have you been known as Amach in all your lifetimes?" Another sentence formed in my head.

This is how I am presenting myself to you and constructing the information for your understanding.

'Kind of like *Oversoul Seven* in the Jane Robert's novel?' I thought to myself.

You may want to understand me that way. I am only here to help.

I tried to remember the details of that Seth-inspired book by Jane Roberts: how lives were intertwined and how they affected each other over millennia. If I remembered it correctly, it seemed as if the characters' thoughts and actions bled through each other's lives and caused rifts in the fabric of time. I loved the idea that reality might not be linear, that we could flash into the future as well as the past. However, I'd struggled to understand the possibility that something was happening in every moment, that all activity was occurring parallel to itself. The concepts of the book were mind twisters. I'd never really understood it all, even after reading the book three times. I wondered if I should read it again, but realized I didn't have time. Besides, I was living part of it, right now.

I had to admit moving into and observing through someone else's life form wasn't much different from living one's life vicariously by watching adventures on film or reality

TV. It was just deeper and richer, though my presence could be a factor in changing the scenario. *'Life is dynamic,'* I thought, and, in an instant, I realized I might have responsibilities when I moved through lives in this way. If each of us was responsible for our own paths, then it seemed logical I could be accountable when I dwelt in another's. I had to be more aware as a participant in the lives I was viewing. I wondered if I'd already, unconsciously, created changes or challenges in those very lives.

Or your own, came a gentle thought.

'Can that be positive as well as negative?' I asked in my head.

How can you tell which is which?

'Oh, you mean what I might think of as positive, might not be?'

Or may detract from a necessary learning experience.

"But how could I know?" I challenged out loud.

Only from the overview of the entire lifetimes of all involved.

My mind was stilled. *'That seems beyond me.'*

It is not within your current power or situation.

'What about when I moved between Dacona and Marweth as you were making their bundles? I could see and feel their experiences and thoughts.'

Only for the instance of seeing and feeling what they saw and felt.

"That's for sure," I answered, remembering vividly what it had been like with a passionately erect penis and a throbbing vulva. "Their desire for each other was amazing," I said, still in awe of the sensations.

They truly lusted for each other. I made a

judgment that was not good for either of them. Be careful, Selena, of trying to move events and people into a pattern beyond what they can be.

"Have I done that?" I asked aloud.

You have been more aware of the pitfalls of the manipulation of power than I.

"I believe you taught me that years ago, when I was developing my private practice. It had to be you who sent me into paroxysms of vertigo, every time I tried to do something for a client they didn't want or I hadn't asked them about. Who else would have had such a firm grip on my senses?"

You have been a good student.

"Thanks," I said. "I still don't understand how we got hooked up."

In time.

The sense of fullness I felt when she inhabited me was gone.

I was empty. I was alone. In the twilight of the evening, I dropped onto the bed and fell asleep.

*   *   *   *   *   *   *

Ringing. Ringing. Not the dancing tune Flyn programmed into my cell phone, but the harsh ringing of the land line next to my side of our bed. I didn't want to move; I'd finally reached a dreamless sleep. An edge of anger flushed over me. *'Who wants me in the middle of the night? Surely not a client.'* And then I gasped awake. *'Flyn?'*

"Is everything OK?" I asked into the receiver.

"Everything's just perfect!" It was Estelle. "I've been calling and calling your cell phone but you haven't answered, so I finally looked up your apartment number. I just had to call and tell you how wonderful everything is. I mean, when I'm not doing my work, or babysitting with the new grand kiddo,

I've been painting; not my house, but pictures, and big ones too."

"I'm glad for you, Estelle? Isn't it . . . in the middle of the night?"

"Is it? Oh, Sellie, I'm so sorry! I . . . uh . . . well, I . . . uh . . . I did the ceremony."

Cold crept across my back and head. I had so wanted my vision to have been a dream. Now I was in a quandary about whether or not to tell her I'd seen what she'd done. My anger at her placing my eagle claw in the bundle pushed me to be honest. "I know, and you included something from me in there too."

"How? When? I . . . well. Oh, Sellie, I thought it would help make the bundle stronger."

I took a deep breath.

She rushed to talk. "Now, Sellie, don't be mad. It turned out perfectly. I feel so connected to Eduardo. He's with me. I know it. I can feel him beside me as I do my work with clients. I've had so many wonderful things happen, I just can't count them any more."

"That's wonderful," I answered, feeling reassured she was doing alright, but still concerned about being a part of it. Perhaps the green energy I saw around her was really around me. Maybe I'd developed a green layer of jealousy in my aura, especially where her Eduardo and the marriage of spirits idea was concerned. Maybe I'd wanted Estelle to depend only on me? Had I been viewing Eduardo as an intruder between us? Had I been that shallow?

"I wish you could see the changes in my work, Selena. I've never felt so full of spirit and purpose. The only thing is . . . I'm so tired all the time." Her voice trailed into silence. My chest tightened.

"Well, that's too bad," I said. "You've been grounding before each session? And clearing any connections to your clients afterwards?"

"I'm as careful as ever, but, I feel connected to a different source, and somehow I'm not getting the same kind of energy as I used to."

A small worry nibbled at the back of my mind.

"Sellie? Could you send me some energy and maybe do a viewing for me? You know, like we used to do for each other? Maybe you could see if there's some kind of . . ."

A haze filtered over my eyes. The phone disconnected, and my heart lurched into my throat. I hit the automatic dial button I'd programmed for her phone number only to be greeted by a busy signal.

What had just happened? I punched the button a second time and, while I waited, pulled up a mental picture of her and prepared to send her energy after I read her aura.

Her face disappeared.

I tried again, setting the phone down so I could concentrate.

She materialized then faded behind a green, hazy wall.

I was sure now. This barrier was not being caused by my jealousy or by my wanting to isolate Estelle. This was different. The effect of her tiredness and my seeing a green haze reminded me of someone I'd worked with many years ago: a Viet Nam medic who was possessed by spirits. They'd created a psychic wall so I couldn't reach them.

Estelle may have asked me to send her energy, but something didn't want me near her. Now all I had to do was decide who or what it was, and then, what to do about it.

Chapter XXII – Late August, 2004
When Pieces Begin to Fit

Standing to stretch my back then touch my toes, I looked at my phone schedule. Thankfully, I was at the end of my day, with only one more person on the list: Barbara Crandell. Her envelope with her picture and her payment had risen from the bottom of the pile and was now the last one on the desk. I stamped her $50 check, propped her picture behind the smoldering sage bowl sitting between two candlesticks, then headed for the bathroom.

With an empty bladder, freshly-washed hands, and a face spritzed with cool water, I combed my hair and tried to be excited about almost being done for the day. I stretched my neck side to side in an attempt to ease my tightening muscles and sighed.

Today's contacts had been more than tedious. *'Oh, come on, Sellie, that's not it.'* If the truth were known, I'd lost my fervor for getting involved in other people's problems. In fact, I'd much rather have kept the line open for either Flyn or Estelle. With my cell phone hanging forgotten at the cabin, the land line was my only connection to either of them. I would've been happier waiting for their calls rather than for those who were paying me. I shrugged and reminded myself, *'I earned just as much money this afternoon sitting in my apartment on the phone as I'd have made, standing next to the massage table for five hours. These calls are my financial lifeline, right now.'* I instantly regretted how my mind was working, shrinking from the concept of counting clients as dollars and cents earned. That had never been my style, since I'd learned by relegating people to a monetary value, the number who came to me dwindle to nothing. When I stood in a place of service, my opportunity to help people grew, and I was always well reimbursed for my time.

"OK! OK! OK!" I said to no one in particular, while I waited for the water to boil, so I could make myself a cup of Earl Grey tea. I don't do this to make money. I mean, I do, but, it's not my first concern. "Keep your head on straight, Sellie." Reviewing the afternoon, I hoped I'd helped somebody.

Amelia was the first client who came to mind. Over time, we'd been working to make a change in the quantity and quality of her obsessions about weird physical symptoms. Since she'd gone through chemotherapy and radiation after her mastectomy, she'd worried over every strange ache and pain. I'd reassured her time and again I saw no signs of cancer. Today I'd reinforced her inner focus by helping her learn a breathing technique to ease her joint pain and a visualization to reduce her anxiety. Thankfully, she'd reported feeling better by the end of our session. Just as we were saying our goodbyes though, I sensed an energy hovering nearby. I asked one of my favorite questions: "Have you been having any recurrent dreams, recently?"

After a long pause, she'd admitted to one about her older brother. "I figured it was because he died last month," she admitted quietly.

The energy took form, as it does when it's named, and I heard the words, "I'm sorry I hurt you."

I gambled and said, "I don't know what your relationship was with your brother, but he seems to have a message for you."

I heard her gasp. "You can see him?"

"Not exactly, but I see an energy with a long face and hunched shoulders."

"That's him," she whispered.

I waited then offered. "Do you want to find out what he

has to say?"

"Does he look pitiful?"

"No, he seems distressed." I said, perceiving him pace in measured steps behind her photograph.

"He should be!" Angela's voice became firm. "He terrorized me all my life. He should be in hell."

The energy stilled. Again, I heard the words, "I'm sorry I hurt you." I repeated these words to her.

"What good does that do me now?" she asked. "He's dead!"

"I know," I said gently. "But sometimes it helps to know whoever hurt us recognizes their wrong doing. Then we can release ourselves from the dance created when our emotions fused our lives together." A cold wind blew across my neck, and my words flickered like neon lights so I was forced to read them for myself. Whenever this happened, I knew the words would be important at a later date.

"If he's really sorry," she said, "he'll take the pain away in my left leg where it broke after he tripped me."

I hesitated on this one. I'd never requested healing from a deceased spirit, but who knew what could happen across the divide between worlds? I watched to see this formed energy become more defined, disappear, then reappear. *'What do I say?'* I thought. I didn't know what this reaction of his spirit form meant. Then I noticed the energy that was her brother change his location to the front of her picture and turn his back on me. There was no doubt about this message; I was to let the situation go.

Relieved to be out of the middle, I said, "All you can do is request he help your leg to heal and hope," I said. His form nodded but remained focused on her photo. "Another important thing is to have no expectations of the outcome of your request."

"What do you mean?"

"Healing can come in many forms."

"You mean, what . . . the pain doesn't go away, but I learn how to live with it better?"

"Could be or a new therapy becomes available, or, I don't know. You'll have to wait and see."

"I guess."

"Do ask him," I urged. "And let me know what happens?"

"I guess," she answered, then added, "Didn't know you could connect with spirits too."

"Ah, it comes and goes," I'd answered, glad to have followed my hunch, but self-conscious about admitting to seeing spirits. It was a skill developing over time. I'd been aware of presences around me but hadn't realized they were taking form until recently, and I didn't know how much further I wanted this gift to develop because work of this kind could be demanding from both the human and the spirit side of things. "Be sure to call me if you need help with the visualization we did today. I'm available at this number until my cell phone's back."

"Thanks."

The whistling tea pot brought my mind into the small kitchen, and I poured the boiling water over the tea bag. After a dollop of vanilla-flavored soy milk from the refrigerator, I waited for the Earl Grey to steep.

Her session had been the most unusual of the day; the others routine. I'd helped one of my regulars, Arthur, scan his situation; he was contemplating a career change and had needed information about three job offers. Then there was a new client who had asked if tonight was the night to get pregnant. I'd helped her visualize cordings from her chakras to determine if the one between her and her partner was strong enough for this kind of union and if there was any spirit connection with a being wanting to come through them. A third had requested a body scan to tell if the chemotherapy was working on her lung cancer. We'd had a hard time getting a clear picture as she hadn't had a lot of confidence in reading her own body. Someone named Andrea had wanted me to scout her husband's past lives but I'd told her I didn't scan someone without their permission. When I'd suggested I scan her, she'd refused. I was returning her money.

Dropping the tea bag into the trash, I decided I'd done the best I could for those who'd called. Now I waited for the last one, trying not to think about Flyn or Estelle. I had to admit I was getting comfortable doing phone consults rather than standing by a table. My back, feet, varicose veins, and stiffening finger joints were happier too.

The phone rang just as I sat at my desk. I checked the clock. It was 3:45pm right on time.

"Good afternoon, Barbara," I answered.

"How'd you know it was me?" asked the voice.

"It's easy," I answered. "We've an appointment. Some things aren't all that magical." I tried to make my voice smile.

"Oh," she hesitated. "What do I have to do?"

"Are you comfortable?" I asked.

"I'm on my bed like you suggested."

I nodded and faced her photograph, adding a small leaf of sage to the burning mix. "Take a deep breath. Release it. Tell me how I can help you."

"If I knew that, I'd have told you when I wrote you . . . Oh, I'm sorry. I'm at my wits end."

My ears were burning from the blast of energy she'd pushed through the speaker phone. I stayed quiet as I heard her take a settling breath. "Several years ago my husband and I bought this beautiful piece of property at the junction of two creeks here in Bismark, Montana. It's got a house and several outbuildings, and we were told it'd been a cross roads for warring Native American tribes, way back before the white man came. I don't know what tribes they were, but it's always been a little discomforting at night when we walked the land between the three out buildings. We converted one into a studio and the two others were refurbished into offices for each of us." She stopped to catch her breath, nervousness making her go faster than she was breathing. I waited, sensing a number of energies swirling around her.

"Well, that's an understatement," she admitted. "It's not just uncomfortable, it's getting downright scary around here. I mean, I don't know if I can stay here. Clients won't come anymore. Very few attended the recent workshop I held. My art work has come to a halt. It's like I've lost my creative spirit and, well, I met a friend of yours who thought you might give me answers as to why this is getting worse."

Her voice was edged with tears. I hesitated then asked, "Do you have sense of one disruption or are there several chaotic energies?"

"How am I supposed to know? You're the psychic here!"

Her voice slapped through our connection. I realized this session was not going to be as typical as I'd hoped. Barbara was out of sync with herself. I heard multiple voices when she spoke and a progression of energy patterns formed and broke apart around her photograph to be reformed into another colored design. I shook myself away from the mesmerizing display, regrounded, and decided I had to cross over one of my boundaries and be more directive by handling this reading.

In as calm a voice as possible, despite my pounding heart, I said, "I've a sense this land was not only a crossroads and a battlefield for warring tribes but a cemetery as well. It might have also been a trading post, or, at least, used as trading grounds."

"All true."

"I sense there are more than your home and three out-buildings on the property and there might be one . . . no . . . two . . . ruined stone foundations, overgrown fruit trees, and . . . a garage with storage? No . . . a garage with a work area attached. Is this correct?"

"Why, yes."

"This place has a very long history, Barbara. Lots of souls have made their transitions here. Not all of them were buried in the area of the cemetery."

"Could be." She sounded wary.

"I'm seeing you've tried several things. Did you bring someone or several people to help by doing different rituals?"

She was slow to answer. "My husband and I tried everything. Each ceremony helped, but nothing's changed the feeling of the land."

As she talked I saw a parade of individuals: some with smudge bowls, one tossing corn meal to either side, another levitating in a lotus position radiating white light around him for 360 degrees. One man was dressed much like Red Buffalo and was quietly pounding a large, two sided drum. I saw a group in orange robes creating a sand mandala then blowing it to the four directions.

Suddenly, a shadow crossed her face in the picture, and I felt so much grief, I wanted to cry. Then it passed. Her photographed smile changed from warm to strained. "I have this . . . Bar . . . I hope you'll accept this question, but are you still married?"

"No," she said slowly. "He left me three years ago. I just started dating again."

"Has your divorce been amicable?"

"Not really." She released another slow breath.

"You've some loose ends," I said, as I saw chords of brown energy plunging into her throat, heart, and power chakras.

"Tell me about it!" She huffed. "We can't seem to agree on how to settle our land investment. He wants to sell so we can divide the money. I believe I can make a living here, but I can't buy him out. I don't have anyplace else to go if I leave here." Now her voice whined, and its vibration grated on my eardrums, as if there were more voices than hers speaking.

"Barbara, have you been told you were a sensitive?"

She stalled, "Well . . . yes . . . I used to know what another person was feeling, but now I feel like I'm encased in a rug or something. I can't move fast. It takes everything out of me just to go to the store."

How similar this sounded to Estelle's complaint. For a moment, I stopped breathing. What if Barbara and Estelle were alike, and something or someone was sucking their energies? Worry for Estelle clouded my vision and made me want to hang up and call her. How ironic this woman should want my help now. *'That's the way it works,'* I thought. *'I can't hang up. She's part of the puzzle.'*

I focused on Barbara, wondering how she'd been drawn to this piece of land in the first place. Perhaps her sensitivity, coupled with an innate compassion, had drawn her to where spirits could use her skin as their own, like Amach had used me, but with a different purpose. Sometimes inconsolable spirits walk the Earth because they don't know they can leave; some have unfinished business. Others were killed so unexpectedly they don't know their way 'out of here'.

When such spirits are stuck, they wander near their demises as confused balls of energy, not knowing which way to turn, until a living being, going through an emotional upheaval of their own, comes near. This can allow either an attachment between the walker spirit and the living person, or a possession, where the host doesn't have full control of their body functions, like speech. The case of a Viet Nam medic surfaced again in my mind. He'd acquired 22 discernible spirit personalities during his tour of duty overseas. We'd worked for a year before he was free of their presences. That counseling challenge had required 'hands on' sessions. How could I work with Barbara distantly? I didn't know how extensive her attachments were.

I asked, "Are there times when you don't feel like

yourself, or you find yourself doing things which have nothing to do with your current life?"

"Why are you focusing on me? It's the land that needs clearing!"

I lit more smudge in front of her picture and two new candles. Her defensive attitude led me to suspect one or more spirit attachments didn't want to be removed. "You have to be willing to let the darkness go."

"Well, of course, I do," she sounded miffed.

'This wasn't going to be easy.' I thought, before I plunged into her life. "You need to return every pebble, rock, stone, and unusual artifact you've collected to where you found them on this plot of land. If you can't remember, then bury them at the edge of the property."

"But my studio's filled with stones. I paint them, and I've sold many of them. How can you expect . . . "

I interrupted. "Do you want to let the darkness go?"

"You're serious aren't you?"

"So serious, Barbara, that if you can't agree to do this, I'll return your money. I'll release you from all agreements so I can be released from any responsibility for your future. This is your choice. I can't do it for you. The healers you've brought have helped, however, you need to do more."

Her breathing whistled in my ear, and I knew by its change of rhythm, she was getting agitated.

'OK, here's another tricky part.' I took a deep breath. "I also feel you need to burn down the garage and work shop."

"I can't do that! Why would I do that?"

"Are you using it?"

"No!"

"Why not?"

"I . . . we . . . never used it . . . because . . . because it's just too spooky. Oh, my!"

"Have you ever been in it?"

"Once . . . there's a lot of old boards and rusted metal,

like someone was collecting stuff in there."

"It's up to you, Barbara, but I believe you have to do it to clear your land. Something or someone is caught in there." I shuddered as a vision of black blood dripped onto the floor then splashed on four imaginary walls which began to surround me. I escaped by soaring through the open roof as I heard howls of pain and smelled burning flesh. My vision filled with the sight of someone being hung there and branded then dismembered. I shuddered. "I know this sounds weird." I found myself fumbling for some way to make her understand. "I believe your property value would go up, if you could find a way to have this done."

"I'll think about it. Anything else you'd like me to destroy?" She snapped. "Oh dear, I'm sorry. I didn't mean to sound ungrateful. I don't know where that came from."

I ventured again into complicated territory. "Do you find yourself doing that often? I mean, saying things you might not normally say?"

"I'm just not myself anymore," she admitted.

"I think the stress of all this has made you vulnerable to allowing some of these lost souls to speak their frustration through you."

"Are they of the devil?"

"They're just lost. They need your prayers to send them home to God."

"And if I do all this, how long before everything is healed?"

I hedged. "The situation took decades to develop, and your involvement has solidified over the last four to five years. I can't promise it will be gone by tomorrow, but with prayer and action plus perseverance, it could be less than a year."

"I don't think I can last that long."

"You can do anything you put your mind to," I encouraged her, while turning my attention again to her photo. Her forehead and nose were flat, as if her face was pressed against the other side of the glass. She had bushy eyebrows that she must've thinned regularly so they wouldn't overgrow her pinpoint eyes. I got the impression she was wearing blinders, which only allowed her to see what she wanted. Her hair was thin but teased around her oval face in a 1950's sagging flip style. Her even lips were trying to smile but were pressed shut, which made her look as if she were grimacing in pain or with gas.

I started to speak, "Have you thought about . . . ?"

A fluttering candle to the right of her picture caught my eye. When I shifted my head, her face changed. I looked away, then returned to see her original image staring at me. I could hear Barbara getting restless over the phone. Looking at the photo again from the left then from the right, I stood and sat several times. Her face changed character at every angle. I saw six different faces superimposed on hers and knew, for certain, she was carrying other entities.

"Thought about what?" She huffed, her voice impatient.

I lied, "I was seeing if there were any more messages I could sense from those who have been . . . "

"I don't want to hear any more messages. I want to know how to make it all go away."

"I apologize, Barbara." How could I get her to help herself without scaring her? "Please understand, it may take more time than you want, but I truly believe the 'core of who you are' will be able to shift the energy on your land. It isn't an easy 'fix', because you've taken on some of the qualities of the persons who were killed there."   As I spoke, I concentrated strongly on her features in the picture. "I believe you have the ability to focus and direct the course of what's to happen next; I'm also wondering if you attend a church or synagogue."

"I'm Catholic."

'Wonderful,' I thought. "You can invite your priest to help you set up a sanctuary of peace and healing for you and around you."

Breathing deeply I tried to ease the tension I felt in my neck and shoulders by settling them softly and leaning back against my desk chair. "There's also a ceremony in the Catholic Church to release spirits who are stuck on the earth plane or attached to people. Your priest should be able to help you, so you can become who you truly are. I still hope you'll burn that garage and return the stones."

Suddenly, I had an inspiration. "Get a picture of yourself taken before you moved onto that land. Put it in a place where you can look at it every time you look in the mirror."

"You're scaring me," and I could hear the trembling in her voice.

I realized I needed to change the temper of my message. I was trying too hard to empower a woman who was hundreds of miles away and had no idea what I was telling her. Was there any sense in continuing? I felt a nudge inside my body that seemed to answer 'yes', so I tried to settle my nerves and lighten my voice. "I've no need to scare you, only to urge you to identify your own skills and do the work on your land only you can do."

Another thought blazed a path behind my eyes. "You draw angels."

She gasped. "I . . . I've been drawing all kinds of angels."

"Follow that personal creativity. Paint them in all the mediums in which you work. Put these around your house. Put little lights around the large oak you've got in your yard; this'll bring an enormous amount of energy. Invite your priest to help you remove, one by one, the spirits who're clinging to you. All I can do now is send you prayers and energy, and I promise I'll do that every day."

Silence screamed over the phone at me, then she quietly said, "Thank you" and hung up.

After I disconnected my end of the phone, the nature of

our session hovered near me. I continued to think about her situation as I completed my personal cleansing rituals: first using a flame, then by running my hands through a bowl of sand, then water, followed by doing a series of yoga stretches for 20 minutes. By that time, I was ready for a shower and dinner. The one thing I wasn't ready for was another evening without Flyn.

I supposed I could have filled the night hours with more sessions; anything to pass the time without worrying and wondering if Flyn was going to return to me. However, I was exhausted. I couldn't have gone into another trance if my life depended on it. I'd held myself together pretty well for most of the day. Now I just wanted my own worries. The tension in my stomach squeezed most of its empty growls into oblivion, and I drowned the remaining ones with a pint of bottled water. I lifted the TV remote and channel surfed until returning hunger forced me to unearth the last of the chocolate chip cookies, then hypnotized myself with flickering pictures until I was numb. I didn't dare take a shower; I was afraid the cascading water would wake me, and I'd have to start the numbing process all over again.

I settled into bed where Barbara's plight hounded me. The sense of spirit attachment around her was so similar to what I'd perceived around Estelle, I wanted to call my friend to check on her. I found it hard to believe both women had some kind of spirit attachments draining their energy. Maybe Estelle's lethargy was more like Dacona's and mine. We were grieving the loss of our partners. I tossed onto my stomach to locate a more comfortable position in bed.

'It's just grief!' I twitched onto my right side. *'But that's not true. Estelle just bonded with Eduardo. That's not cause for grief.'* I sighed. *'And how's any of this a danger to me?'*

After all, Amach went to a lot of trouble to warn me I was in danger, or was she warning me about Flyn's predicament? Maybe *he's* struggling with some kind of spirit attachment?

I raised up on one elbow and flopped onto my back.

'Oh hell!' I didn't know what, where, how, or why about anything!

I'd no clue why these events were unfolding as they were. Nothing made sense. It had been a lot easier when my life moved in a rhythm of synchronistic events validating my actions and decisions. Now there were just too many coincidences, and I couldn't sort them by myself. I needed help, but I didn't know from where. If I couldn't figure out what was happening to any of us, could I have taken a wrong turn in my thinking? The hair on my arms rose.

'OK.' That could only mean I'd taken a wrong turn in my thinking.

Nothing further charged the air or disturbed the hairs on my body.

'Damnation!' I pulled Flyn's pillow under my knees. Fretting was one of the things I knew how to do best. *'As a matter of fact, I've been very good at it for a long time!'*

I tossed onto my left side, away from Flyn's half of the bed.

I tried my usual mental exercises of worrying about kids, grandkids, a mother, and my business, plus the cabin and some of the characters on my favorite TV programs. They were totally inadequate subjects tonight for keeping my mind occupied. All were completely disposable in the face of sheer loneliness. I was without diversions, except for my clients, and trying to 'fix' their lives was a useless exercise possibly leading me into a condition resembling Potty's figure and her demise.

I tossed onto my right side and stared into the shadows, wishing I could see a familiar head next to mine; just the back of his head would do. That meant I could cuddle near his solid presence and allow his steady warmth to settle around my heart.

I mentally listed my girlfriends, trying to decide who would welcome a phone call at 3am. Haley was a night owl, but I thought her biorhythms gave out at about 2 in the morning. Roxanne was gone for a month on a self-designed sabbatical to Maine to see the fall leaves, and Roberta had a new flame. That left Estelle, who might or might not be sleeping.

"How are you?" I asked.

"Not sure," came the answer in a small female voice, at once, reminding me of my mother and my daughter when they were in some kind of crisis.

I was on the alert. "What's wrong?" She had been flying high the last time we'd talked.

"Can't seem to get any energy, and I've got so much to do. Sellie, I did the ceremony. I made the bundle."

"I know. Don't you remember? We talked about that when you called me last week."

"We did?" she said in a soft, forlorn voice.

I gentled my voice. "I don't recognize you, tonight. You sound as if you're on the other side of the world. What's happened?"

"Oh, Sellie! I don't know. I can't figure out what's wrong. I've taken my vitamins, tried to exercise . . . nothing . . . seems" her voice trailed off.

"Nothing seems what, Estelle? Come on. Keep talking to me." The memory of my reading of Barbara coalesced with her words, but I grasped at any other reason for her tiredness. "Estelle, answer me. Do you have the flu, maybe?"

Her voice was more than pleading. It was on the verge of hysteria. "Why, can you see something? Please, Sellie, tell me if you see anything!"

As we talked, I detected movement around her, an energy in the form of a filmy gauze encasing her, like a shadowed shroud. The color was tinged with a gangrenous green, and I felt nauseated.

"Estelle, there is something . . . I can't see what . . . or who . . . it is, but, babe, it's the same quality of yucky green energy I sensed when you first talked to me about this bundle making."

I pulled more protection around myself, mixing its texture with my intention. "Estelle, I . . . you have to know . . . I saw you make your bundle. I was there. I don't know how or why . . . but . . . this same energy was there too, and the last time we talked, we were disconnected. I couldn't get you back on the phone."

I stopped to get my breath and heard a quiet sobbing. "Estelle, answer me, now! I have to know. Did you set up all the protections you could when you put this bundle together?"

Silence.

"Do you understand my question?" I heard coughing. I didn't like it. A pressure sat on my chest, and I realized I was holding my breath.

"Estelle," I called. "Get up from wherever you are! Light a white candle, do something to move yourself." I felt helpless, and I was. All I could do was bring her face into my sight and send her healing energy. I roused from my own bed and sat before the candles I use when I'm doing my phone consultations. I formed, in my mind, a picture of my most recent contact with Estelle's face and held it while I lit the candles. I felt the energy come through me and whoosh toward her and breathed a sigh of relief when I heard her voice at the other end of the line.

"I'm moving, Sellie." She was gasping for breath. "I'm at the dresser where I keep the candles and the candle holders. I'm doing what you ask. I can feel a change around me. Something's still here, but it's not clinging to my skin like it was. I never would have recognized it if you hadn't called and made me move. I'm in trouble, aren't I, Sellie?"

"Yes, I think you are, my friend. Answer my question,

damn it! Did you put all the usual protections around you when you made that bundle?"

"I thought I did, but I was so focused on what I was going to do, I can't be sure I did all the usual things. Why?" I noticed her breathlessness easing.

"Because some entity, spirit being, incarnate soul or whatever used that opportunity to move closer to you. Damn it, Estelle. Why did you have to make that bundle?"

Her voice was small. "I needed to be close to Eduardo. It wasn't a big deal. Just a little ceremony."

"I was there, Estelle. And it *was* a big deal! You wanted to make that bundle as powerful as you could. That's why you used the eagle claw I gave you." I heard her gasp. "Don't you remember us talking a couple weeks ago? I saw you put it in the bundle. I asked you to take it out."

"I guess . . . yes . . . you were mad because I included the claw, but I didn't mean to include you. That wasn't my intention." Her voice was stronger.

"You know better than that. A negative intention is just like a negative affirmation. They create the reverse. You can't say, 'I do not want to include Selena', because what your soul and the universe hears is 'I do want to include Selena.'"

I kept my voice as steady as I could, but emotion was squeezing my throat and making my head pound. I was now inextricably bound with Estelle and her paramour in her damned bundle; no wonder I'd been drawn to the event. "I just wish you hadn't included me." A niggling tap-tap-tap inside my brain made a light bulb blaze. "That's why you didn't want to show me the pieces you'd collected, isn't it?"

"I . . . you don't know how important this . . . "

I heard fumbling of the phone.

"Damn," she said as shuffling scraped across the mouthpiece.

"What is it? Are you OK?" I heard the phone hit wood, and I strained my ears to catch further sounds of shuffling and the words, "no . . . no . . . no . . ."

"Estelle," I screamed, trying to send as much brilliant light as I could muster to my friend and her surroundings. I loosened my shoulders with deep breaths and cleared my mind of everything but the image of her. Traveling at warp speed, I was floating above Estelle, seeing her fight to quench flaming sparks in the carpet caused by the fallen candle. Estelle was trying to put it out with her bare hands. I sent the thought, *'Use your robe,'* and watched as Estelle gathered her chenille robe around her buttocks and sat on the flames.

"That-a-girl!" I cheered, pulling myself out of her space as she reached for the phone. I couldn't resist the temptation to say to her, "Well, you certainly got out of that one by the seat of your pants."

"You were watching? How'd you do that?"

"I don't know. Maybe because it was an emergency? Or maybe because we're extra-bonded right now? I just focused on you and 'poof' I was there. I mean, I think I was there. You did just sit on the flames in the carpet, right?"

"I couldn't think of anything else to do." Her words were spoken at a snail's pace. "I'm so tired. What was so urgent about lighting the candles?"

"Because, something or someone's draining you, and I don't think it's Eduardo. I've got this crazy notion there's some kind of weird energy cocooning you, and it's gotten stronger since you did this bundle thing."

"Oh, Sellie, could Eduardo be feeling the same way as I am? Oh, Sellie, help me. I think I may have hurt him." Her voice grew steadily hysterical. I had to be calm for the both of us or we'd never sort this thing out.

"Estelle, what do you mean, you might have hurt him too?"

"He hasn't called," she gulped. "He usually calls me every other day. I thought it was because we'd argued about him coming here . . . but . . . now. . ."

I shook my head. Were we all waiting for the phone to ring? For that certain moment when we'd get the answer to our hearts' questions? Not hearing, not knowing what our partner was doing seemed to be bringing three different lives closer to hell. At least now I knew where Marweth was, but not Flyn, nor Eduardo. When my mind touched Eduardo's name, I felt a pain at the back of my neck that grew in such intensity, I gasped.

"What is it, Sellie?"

"Just a pain," I lied. "Slept sideways and scrunched myself. It's gone now, really."

I cleared my body of all sensation, while I tried to picture her sitting in her cabin with its colorful ceiling, candles flickering on the rosewood dresser. "Is your hair still dark and long enough for braids?"

"Yeah, but I've let my hair fall free tonight. Sometimes the braids are too tight for sleeping."

"What are you going to do next?" I asked, not sure what I was asking. Did I mean what was she going to do about not feeling well? What was she planning to do about the greenish energy I saw around her? Was she going to try to contact Eduardo?

She answered the question of her choice. "I've got to get in touch with him. I'm going to keep calling the only number I've got, until someone answers and tells me where he is. I think . . . no . . . I'm sure . . . he's in danger, but I don't know how, or why. He's such a good man. Oh Sellie, I think you're right. I have this sick feeling in the pit of my stomach. I never meant to hurt him. I wanted us to be together the only way we could."

I wanted to encourage her. "It'll be OK, Estelle. Perhaps you're feeling sick for some other reason." As I talked, I realized I was getting exasperated with the whole affair, with the drama, and the second-guessing. "We can't know if things like this bundle even works." Instead of consoling her, though, the hole in my gut was telling me to warn her, to have her know what Amach had said regarding manipulating events and people.

"Maybe you need to smudge the bundle every day? What do you think?"

"I guess . . . when I don't feel so tired."

My scalp prickled. I wanted to ram my hand through the phone and shake her. "Damn it, Estelle. You need to do it sooner rather than later."

"Oh, OK." Her voice sounded as if she were moving very far away.

"Estelle, are you going to sleep?"

"No . . . day dreaming . . . about Eduardo . . . how much I love him."

"Well, that's fine. Uh, Estelle, do something for me. Remove the claw from the bundle. I don't belong there. You've got to take it out."

"No . . . I don't want to chance . . . of changing. . . you know . . . the bundle somehow. Don't know . . . what I've done . . . to us . . . in the first place!"

What could I say? I didn't want to agree with her, but I didn't see me dashing off to her cabin, grabbing the bundle to take it apart myself. "Well then, I guess we're in this together." I sighed, wishing there was something else I could do. "I love you, Estelle. Please take care of yourself. Keep those candles burning and, please, run the bundle through the smudge every time you think of it. I just wish we knew where this green energy came from."

"Maybe . . . Sellie! I just thought of . . ." Her voice grew stronger. She gasped. "Sellie, wasn't there something . . . when we were doing the Ouija Board? Wasn't there a spirit who described all these life times we'd been together? I don't remember . . . I think . . . it happened . . . just before we stopped using my grandmother's board."

"And I've got all the transcripts here, don't I?" I

mentally started picturing the closet, wondering where I'd stashed that box of papers.

"Could you look it up? Maybe it's not the marriage bundle after all. Maybe I've done nothing wrong, and it's just a wayward spirit."

My heart hoped with her as we disconnected. My ears tingled as a foreign high-pitched tone filled my head, like an alarm clock blaring inside my skull. I was awed by the way everything tied together, but it was more than alarming.

Chapter XXIII - February, 1988 & August, 2004
Then and Now

After a week of searching every nook and cranny of our apartment, my office, and our closet, I finally found the Ouija Board records in the attic where our landlords, the Myers, had cleared a space for our storage needs. After Flyn had moved in with me and had helped them with upkeep and maintenance, they did everything they could to keep us as tenants. I surveyed the dusty-smelling room above our studio, remembering my daydream of Flyn spreading his computer systems along one wall, of his being able to work from home.

"Damn," I said as I grabbed the box and nearly toppled down the pull-down stairs. I steadied myself and descended forward with the heavy box against my chest, muttering, "Even if he comes back," as I released the handle to the stairs, "he doesn't want to live here!" My words and the stairs hit the ceiling like exclamation points.

I settled on the braided rug at the foot of my bed and started pawing through the dated files. After locating the transcript, the details of the session sprang into my mind. How could I have forgotten this day of drama? Holding the musty pages, I closed my eyes and discovered I could smell the chill of the day, feel the color of the clothes I'd worn, and sense the tension of that day hanging in Estelle's living room.

Estelle had been more serious than I'd ever seen her as she'd settled at the small table. She'd sighed briefly before nesting her bottom into the cushion. Her hair was spiked in multi-directions and looked like bleached straw. She had 'morphed' into yet another woman, and, for the umpteenth time, I envied her sassiness and adventurousness. It wasn't as if my internal imaginings didn't go wild, but externally, I didn't dare do anything considered 'out of the ordinary'. I was overwhelmed by the activities of my family, my work, and of the voices calling me. I needed routine and to know what I'd be doing tomorrow, the next day, and the day after that. When I looked into a mirror, I needed the comfort of seeing my same image every morning and evening, so I could be sure I was 'still here'. As I contemplated this issue, pressure built at the sides of my head so rapidly, I thought the top of my head would burst. I squinted and rubbed my temples.

"Headache?" Estelle asked.

"Yeah, and all of a sudden, too."

"Well, could be the freezing weather. We've seen more snow on the ground this winter, for longer periods of time than any other winter I can remember. 1988 will go down in the record books." She sighed with a grunt and didn't smile. "Or, maybe it's something cosmic . . . like . . . a reaction to what you were thinking?"

I didn't want to tell her, but I must've given some kind of message with my body language or maybe a facial twitch.

"Oh, come on!" she said somewhat impatiently. "Tell me what you were thinking."

Estelle was making me squirm with embarrassment and something else I couldn't explain. I sighed and watched her frown. "Well," I answered slowly. "I was envying your chameleon abilities. Seems you change your appearance and your partners about as often as I change my clothes. Then I thought about how I need to keep things the same everyday." My headache lunged toward the front of my skull. "That's when I felt my head about to burst."

She wiggled her eyebrows in a leer. "You too could be a bleached blond."

"Never," I grimaced. "David would never . . ."

"Sellie, you're letting your life be driven by a control freak who lives in the ancient world of 'me man, you woman'!

Just because David 'would never' is no excuse for denying yourself a boost to your female morale once in a while by doing something different like cut your hair."

"It's more than that," I protested, wondering if I looked as dowdy as I sometimes felt.

She arranged her grandmother's Ouija Board box on the table. "Then what is it? You just said you'd like to change your hair color."

"I did not," I said hotly, my headache strengthening.

"It's only hair! What can he say?" She shrugged and set the planchette on the table.

"It's not what he'd say, it's what he wouldn't do, like not talk to me for a day or two, or not look at me, or go to bed turned away from me."

"Just for changing the color of your hair?"

"Or cutting it, or . . . well . . . anything like that, even changing our routine." I blushed with a strange level of agitation I couldn't explain. I'd never lifted the covers from this part of my relationship with David. Not to anyone. Not even to myself. My body felt threatened, almost betrayed, with flashes of hot and cold waving across its surface. I wondered what was wrong with me. It's not like I was divulging state secrets, but a nagging thought crept in. *'Did I refuse change because of my desires or because of David's?'* I was restless; my legs twitched. To calm myself, I went to the bathroom and washed my hands in the blue-tiled sink while she talked.

"Besides," Estelle said, suddenly defensive, when I returned to the table. "I don't change partners all the time. Most of them drop off the face of the earth or suck me dry, emotionally or financially, until I turn them loose. I've been attracting the weirdest men recently. They seem fine in the beginning, but in the end . . . Just look at the last three. Each one had a crazy-assed accident that left them useless. One got electrocuted, and his personality changed. One broke his back and wasn't good for anything for months, then I found him carrying marijuana plants off my property so he could get them trimmed. And now, I've got Don, who came to work around here and fell off my roof into the flower bed. I can't let him stay in his trailer with a broken leg."

"OK, OK," I said as I finished drying my hands on my jeans, grateful we'd veered off the subject of me and 'smack dab' onto her. I left my sweat shirt on, deciding if a hot flash overheated my body, maybe I'd sweat off a few pounds, besides, it was cold in Estelle's unevenly heated cabin.

Snowdrifts piled over a foot deep against her walls, and the wood stove was not keeping the room warm. Her ceiling was insulated, but the walls were built of single slats of weathered redwood. Even with material covering the lower part of the wall, a cold draft seeped through them when the wind blew.

I indicated with a nod I was ready to begin. We needed to finish soon so I could get Shawna and Sam from school. We'd have to hike home, as it was. Another storm was coming, and I wanted them home, not staying overnight with their friends.

"Heelllllllooooo," Estelle called from across the board.

"Oh, I'm here," I answered.

"Well, I thought you were, but then your face went blank before it scrunched up like you were thinking too hard."

My eyes danced across her face, and I chuckled. "You know me too well; just thinking about the kids. Made me realize we need to get going with this." I raised my hand between us. "I know . . . don't say it . . . just start."

I placed my hands on the planchette as Estelle set our protection, calling the spirits with the same words we always used when we met to talk to the Ouija board. Then, she described our purpose for this day. "Here we are again. I'm asking for help with some personal work. I'm trying to discover what's causing these feelings inside me, feelings of being unbalanced. If there's anyone who has some information to share with me, please come through at this time, for my healing."

We paused to relax our hands on the planchette. I could see deep circles under Estelle's eyes which told me she wasn't sleeping well now that Don and his leg cast had ended up on her couch. Estelle yawned, then wrinkled her nose at me. She grinned a 'busy all night grin'. That confirmed it. Now I knew the last 'mishap-ee' was making the best of his situation.

I had to ask myself, *'Why has every male Estelle's invited into her home in the past several years met with some kind of accident?'* Did it have anything to do with her personal karma?

The planchette moved with random arcs across the board. At first, we swayed smoothly with the planchette, then it jerked and hesitated, like a stutter. Today's session did not seem to want to move along smoothly. One leg of the table had fallen off when we moved it into position, and my chair had tipped over. We'd had trouble with the tape recorder, and interference had crackled from the speaker when we'd tested the new batteries. Even after demagnetizing the tape, the crackling hadn't stopped, and neither had the jerking movements across the board. We eyed each other in frustration.

Estelle said, "Is this energy presence here for me?"
YES
"Who are you?"
G L A I H G
"Glaihg?" I asked, pronouncing the name without the h.
YES
"That's not a name familiar to us," I said. Estelle nodded in agreement. Her forehead furrowed in concentration. In this light, her bleached hair looked gray, and she, with her frown, looked old.

"Do you have a message for me?" Estelle asked in a voice that sounded lost.

YES

"What a strange energy," Estelle commented, then asked, "Could you give me the message?"

THE WATER IS HIGH INSIDE YOU TAKE THE TIME TO PURGE

"How is she to purge?" I asked, curious about this message.

TEARS FASTING ENEMA

Estelle then confided in me this was one of the questions she had wanted to ask at our last session. She asked now, "So I'm to let my feelings flow and do a fast from food and have colonic treatments? Is my system *that* clogged?"

YES

"And it's sort of making a difference in my overall balance?"

YES

"Anything else?"

DO NOT TAKE YOUR ENERGY FOR GRANTED WE ARE WAITING FOR YOU TO GO ON WITH MORE ADVANCED TRAINING

"What is your connection with Estelle?" I asked formally. The planchette stopped for a long time. The room was absolutely still. I couldn't hear any sounds of the fire crackling in the wood stove or of the wind rattling the naked trees. I repeated my question. The room chilled, then warmed as the the planchette slowly chose its letters.

THE BACK DOOR TO HER SOUL

Estelle scrunched her face and looked to be on the verge of tears. "The back door to my soul? What the hell does that mean? I've no idea what that means!" She stared at me, "Do *you* know?"

I shook my head and felt our hands drawn across the board, stopping at random letters.

T O   R O Y

Her voice strained to ask, "To Roy? Who is Roy? We're confused here."

I looked at Estelle and asked, "Has something changed?"

My friend's face contorted into what I could only call rage.   Estelle spat her question. "Who is this Roy? We've taken you seriously up to now. But you're saying things that don't make sense. Define the 'back door to my soul'" Tears threatened again. "I need to trust you."

G I V E H E R H E A R T T O R O Y

"Who is Roy?" Estelle demanded.

Y O U R L O V E R

"In this lifetime?"

NO

"Is it a past love in a different lifetime?"

P A S T P R E S E N T F U T U R E

Estelle looked at me helplessly.

I asked, "Can you tell us what lifetime and be more specific?" The planchette remained immobile. I had to ask again.

YES

And then the planchette began to spell out:

F A T H E R S O N B R O T H E R
S I S T E R M O T H E R D A U G H T E R

"Does this mean that these are all the relationships I've had with this spirit? This . . . person?" Estelle asked, confused.

YES

"So you're not giving any specifics, you're just telling me ways we've been together?"

YES

"Does this . . . I don't know how we got here. I'm lost!"

For some reason, Estelle wasn't grasping the full meaning of this spirit's words. I tried to explain, "I'm not sure . . . it seems this spirit's come through with an agenda and has been with you many lifetimes. I don't know if it's telling you about Roy, or if this is Roy from some past life, but here we are. Maybe it has something to do with your feeling of being unbalanced. Do you want to flow with it?"

We'd taken our hands off the planchette. Now we noticed it was moving by itself. Suddenly it flew across the room. We gasped. Estelle said to me, "This really feels out of sorts today. I don't know if I want to go any further."

"I agree . . . but . . . I have to admit I'm curious." I retrieved the planchette and set it on the board. It stayed in place as we brought our fingers onto its edges. The hairs on my arms suddenly stood, and a chill crossed my back at the level of my shoulder blades. I saw Estelle shiver. I said, "I'll stop if you want to."

A steely look took hold in her eyes. She was determined to ride it out, whatever this 'it' was.

We returned to our positions. She continued, "I'm not trusting you at this point. I need someone to come through whom I can believe. It may be my mood, I don't know, but I need a grand teacher, like Amaman, to be here for me, and clear out any negative spirit forms playing around with us. None of what you're saying makes any sense, and I need answers for my life right now!"

The planchette pulled us so far to the side I nearly lost my balance. "I don't like this anymore now," I admitted, and called out, "Amaman, help us!"

H E   S H E I S   N O T   G O I N G   T O   G E T   T H R O U G H   A T   T H I S   T I M E

"That's a threat!" Estelle said. "Are you threatening us?"

I   L O V E   Y O U

"I can't believe this!"

The planchette raced across the board. C O M E
T O M E

"Is this Roy?"

I H A V E B E E N M A N Y
P E O P L E T O Y O U

The planchette stuttered. W E A R E T O B E
T O G E T H E R F O R A L L T I M E

A light went on for both of us, but Estelle asked the question. "Do you have anything to do with the accidents that have happened to every man I've invited to be with me?"

The planchette was still; the room again silent.

"You *are* threatening me, aren't you? You've been trying to make me live alone without anyone for the past few years? When did you decide to do this? What triggered your surge of energy?"

Slowly, our answer was spelled for us.

Y O U A S K E D T O H A V E Y O U R
O W N T R U E L O V E I A M T H A T

I jumped into the questioning. "This means you're in spirit form, not walking around in this lifetime, so you can't come to her. Is this correct?"

YES

Estelle's voice was tense, "Does this mean you want me to join you in spirit form?"

N O T U N T I L Y O U A R E
R E A D Y

"That means you don't want Estelle to be with anyone else until then?" I interpreted.

Estelle threw her hands into the air and hollered at the wooden pointer, "How dare you interfere with my life! How can you be my one true love? If that were true, you'd want me to know love now, not wait 'til I'm with you in spirit. You'd offer me the opportunity to experience love with others. You're selfish, not loving. I reject you."

Her voice rasped with emotion. I'd never seen her this

angry and defensive. I wanted to stop, so I removed my hands from the pointer.

She hissed at me. "Don't you dare leave me with this unfinished."

"But Estelle, you aren't letting this spirit talk about his reasons or karmic connection to you. You're demanding he leave you alone, and I . . ."

"You listen to me!" she interrupted. "You didn't want Amach to take you over and speak through you. Fine. I sat through all of that, even though I still think you cut us off without accessing all the information we needed. Don't you dare sit there and tell me what to do when there's some kind of spirit wanting to control my life, my loves, my feelings, and my capacity to love. This is for me to decide and for you to support me."

I shut my mouth and held on to the planchette.

She returned her fingertips and asked, "How do I know you're being true to me and to our love?"

I WANT TO BE WITH YOU FOR ALL OF ETERNITY

An odd smell circulated around my head, and I thought I might vomit. I closed my eyes. When I opened them, a change of color had surrounded Estelle but I didn't know if she were aware of it. I knew I couldn't ask. It was pale, like a thin layer of spring green trying to embrace her.

"But, what if I don't want to be with you? Tell me who are you and what have we shared?"

The planchette jerked across the board, not touching any letters or numbers, then it slowed. Every molecule in the room began to move as if in another dimension, and we were isolated in a fish bowl. My heart hammered while fear crept along my arms, making them heavy and cold. Estelle sat with her hands perched on the planchette as if glued. Her eyes were closed. I used every bit of my strength to pull my hands away from the planchette. "Estelle! Wake up! This doesn't feel right." I shook her shoulders. She was frozen in her seat.

I ran from the table and searched her kitchen for a bowl to fill with water. I knew where she kept her candles and found both a black one and a white one.

Her abalone shell held gray sage. I lit it and the black candle as well, bringing them in front of me to stare at the top of the flame while I chanted, "Bright flame of fire, charge this room with light. Gather all that brings confusion and would do harm." I repeated these words three times as I circled counter-clockwise around our table, the Board, and Estelle. Then I widened my path to include the room. "Darkness cannot survive light. Come to the flame. Become one with transforming fire."

I repeated these words in the same order three times before stopping and slowing my breath to a whisper. The flame engorged as if drawing energy from the room. When I felt it was as full as it could be, I quickly plunged this blaze into the water in the bowl and left it there.

Immediately, I lit the white candle, and walked clock-wise around the room with it and the smoking sage, chanting three times, "Pure white light, pure white flame, build the wall of protection around this house and around this woman, Estelle. May all who enter here bring cheer and aid. Let no harm enter these walls." I made sure a window was partially opened, as I walked three times sun-wise around the room. Gently I removed Estelle's hands from the planchette and smudged them with the smoke and the light of the flame. I led her to the couch and covered her with a comforter before leaving to bury the black candle with the bowl and water in the garden.

Thirstily I drank two glasses of water and returned with one in my hand for Estelle. Her eyes were open, and she was pale.

I talked as calmly as I could. "I don't know when it began, but I think a stray spirit entered your life. I don't believe it has power to do you any harm at this time, but Estelle, I'm afraid what you might have been doing ceremonially in the past few years may be giving it power. You may not have kept your protection strong enough." I scooted her over so I could sit beside her and hold her hand. "The energy of the spirit you called today was way too scary. Promise me you won't communicate with it again."

She nodded her head. "I thought it would give me a name I'd recognize."

"Maybe it did. Roy, even Toroy, doesn't sound that weird. Most important now is we don't call it by name. You might be able to figure the history you've shared with this thing by yourself. Is there someone you know from your past by these names? Someone in one of your regressive hypnosis sessions by those names?"

"I can't think of anyone right now. I'm just too wrung out." Estelle hadn't looked well at the beginning of our session and now she looked worse with skin ashen and corpse-like. With her arms folded across her chest, she looked as if she was guarding her heart and could easily curl into a ball.

"Want some tea?"

"Hmmm, I'd rather have whiskey," she answered in a voice barely above a whisper. I found a glass and the bourbon bottle. After several sips, she said, "Thanks." She looked at me then glanced at the Ouija Board. "When I couldn't pull myself away, I knew I was in more trouble than I'd even experienced before. When I . . . it was like I was shrouded in some kind of energy or bound with gluey threads as sticky as cotton candy. I never want to feel that way again!" She'd shuddered.

I'd poured more bourbon into her glass and tried to listen between her words.

"Whatever you did, you broke the spell." Then Estelle had heaved a sigh. "I'm feeling better."

"I'm glad." I'd said, watching the color return to her

cheeks and begged, "Please, Estelle, promise me you'll be more careful from now on."

She'd waved her hand at me to dismiss my fretting. "I don't think it'll come back."

"We don't know that," I'd stuttered at her. "You can't wave this thing . . . this spirit away. It sounded dangerous . . . and how it got strong enough to affect other people in your life is not something to sneeze at."

Sitting on my braided rug in my apartment, I closed my eyes and brought Estelle's face forward, remembering how she had given me what I now would call a shifty glance.

I had shouted at her then, "Promise me, you'll never let down your guard, ever again."

"Oh, alright," she had answered, avoiding my gaze. "I promise."

Even now her words sounded as if they had no backbone. I wished I'd made her cross her heart and hope to die, but if I'd managed to get her to do that, I laid odds she would've crossed her fingers or her toes at the same time she'd made the promise. No matter how that spirit had entered her life, I bet she'd tried to re-connect. She liked to dabble without any thought to the consequences, just like she'd created this bond between her and Eduardo and me without any thought about what might happen. I was pissed and sat on the floor at the foot of my bed banging my head against the mattress in frustration. "What a damnable mess you've made this time, Estelle!"

When I opened my eyes and faced the contents of the two file boxes scattered around me, I wasn't sure which mess I was talking about: her life, the papers strewn across the floor, or my involvement in the whole set-up. I realized I'd been trusting someone who hadn't been truthful with me.

I was also upset because the transcript had made me remember issues with my marriage to David.

I didn't want to admit my life had been defined by

David's need for order. What I wanted was to believe I'd control over my life, but when I'd lived with David, I had to admit I mostly complied with his decisions and had never questioned our way of life, most of the time. Now I had to face the question was my being miserable because Flyn *didn't* want me to help him the other side of the same coin? Was I still living my life in reaction to what my partner did or didn't do?

I scrubbed my fingers through my cropped hair then laughed. I scrubbed my scalp again, relishing in the freedom of short hair. Here I was, how many years later? I'd finally gotten my wish: I'd chopped off my long locks, then had frosted and spiked my hair with mousse. I admitted I wasn't sure about the 'look' anymore, but it was mine for the moment; I knew I could change it whenever I wanted. Did David know what I'd done? *'How does that old saying go?'* Had he rolled over in his grave?

The air shifted in the room so rapidly, I got dizzy. On alert, I softened my eyes to scan the corners. "Do I have spirit company?" I asked and sat quietly, feeling the air pat me along my face, then blow through the hairs standing tall on my head. I had the strangest feeling David was with me, watching with amusement while appreciating my happiness. Maybe he'd changed his mind about long hair being more feminine. I certainly felt sexier with this hairstyle. *'What the hell,'* I thought, *'I should've done it before he died.'* He might have enjoyed the new me.

Drifting back to those last years with him, when he was bedridden and in pain, I knew I couldn't have done anything differently. He'd needed me to stay familiar as his life had slipped away. The air teasing my hair squeezed me and disappeared. Chills covered my body then slowly receded as I realized I might just have received approval from David's spirit for my hairdo. I basked in the knowledge until I mentally shook myself and forced myself to return to the piles of typed words on the floor.

After an hour of sorting sessions, remembering other moments detailed in print, I had no more information than was typed in that one transcript. What was left was for me to figure what to do about my findings. I also had to decide what to do with myself this afternoon. *'Not much choice,'* I thought from my lounging position on the floor. *'Take a nap or take a walk.'*

I watched the afternoon sun play on the polished fronts of the two dressers I'd inherited from my grandmother. The split cherry wood swirled in irregular patterns; brass handles gleamed. Both stood against the east side of the room, one under the window and the other against the cream wall. Stacks of books were piled high on the dresser claiming my underwear and sweaters, and, on Flyn's dresser top, an accumulation of feathers he'd found were scattered underneath two rattles from his grandfather's collection. I squinted at them. *'Did one of them just wiggle?'*

I turned my head to look at them sideways. Sure enough, they both rolled toward each other, then away. I was spooked but curious as one rocked slowly from side to side on the dresser top. Flyn and I thought this one was a female rattle, with a white feather tied to its handle in a way resembling a fan. Suddenly both flew upward and crashed against the wall, as if trying to get my attention, then they returned just as quickly into their places.

"What's this all about?" I asked them, feeling strange to be talking to the rattles. However, since I thought I'd just experienced being hugged by the air, I could just as easily believe a gourd with stones in its center could communicate with me. "Are you going to rattle me a message?"

Both lay silent. I thought about how, a month before he'd left me, Flyn had brought them home in a battered suitcase. He'd been visiting his mom and his grandfather. After stowing the suitcase in the closet, he'd walked across the room with the two gourd rattles in either hand, shaking them in time with a mock-Indian, high step dance. We'd laughed together, and I'd hoped his moodiness had come to an end. It hadn't, of course.

He'd asked, "Where do you think I should put them?"

"Where do they need to be?"

He'd given them a shake then sighed. "I've no idea," he'd answered, "Maybe back in the suitcase with all the other stuff the old man said was for me. Mom's saved every bit of it."

"Why?"

He pondered my question. "You mean why'd he give the bag to me, why'd she save it, or why'd I bring it home?"

"All of the above," I answered, watching his body language announce his nervousness. He ran one hand through his hair, keeping the rattles in his other and turned his head from side to side as if searching for an escape route rather than a niche for the rattles.

"She only said these were from Pop Pop and that he wanted me to have the contents of the suitcase. I didn't know what else to do with the stuff," his words felt angry. He shook the rattles and sighed. "I had this feeling when I tucked the suitcase in the corner that the rattles wanted to be out in the air." He shrugged and grinned, knowing I would appreciate this 'woo woo' kind of statement coming from him.

I nodded and decided to become a very wise woman by keeping the rest of my questions to myself. His vacillation between wanting to be at his Pop Pop's bedside but not sure he wanted anything to do with the old man's heritage was making me as crazy as the way he'd make sexual innuendos one minute but keep his distance from me the next. All I could think was if I had someone in the flesh who could have taught me about spirits and such, I would be sitting at their feet and washing their toes. I watched him wander in circles until I couldn't stand it any longer. "So, OK! Do you want to hang them on the wall?"

He shrugged. I'd never seen him so unnerved. "I don't know what's correct." His hands were shaking as he held the rattles. "This is part of the life I turned my back on, and I don't think I can anymore."

His statement had my full attention, and I rearranged my dropped jaw while my heart told me I needed to listen to him very carefully. "Why now?"

He stared long and hard at me before opening his arms to the room in a gesture confusion. "I keep thinking, why am I alive after being buried in a mine shaft, after being bit by that rattler five years ago, after falling from that roof? How'd I survive drinking myself near to death? Why are we together?"

I couldn't move. I had no answers for him or for myself.

He'd lowered his head then had looked past me. "I talked with Red Buffalo last week." He'd shuffled his feet, given the rattles a shake. "Ever since the wedding, I've been thinking about my Lakota blood."

He'd sat on the floor cross-legged with the rattles cradled in his hands and continued. "Mom's dad was, maybe still is, a traditional man, raised by *his* grandparents. At one time my grandfather was a respected elder, with four healing bundles. He used to be a Sundance Intercessor, but he's frail now. Having all that power, being in the middle of all that energy, didn't stop him from getting old and senile. Mom says he called for me all the time when he could talk, and he . . . talked to spirits." He'd looked at me with tears in his eyes. "I never took the training he offered, never sat with him when the voices came. I drank instead, and I think I broke his heart." He'd sagged.

I looked back on that day and remembered being thrilled to hear his words. I'd figured this sadness was the cause of his being in such turmoil and acting so strange. I'd also realized why he could understand me. We were the same. As children, we'd both experienced voices and to stop them echoing in our heads, we'd both drunk ourselves silly as teenagers and young adults. I had just stopped drinking sooner than he had.

I'd asked him then, "Are you going to sit with him now?"

He'd nodded his head, "I'm thinking of bringing Red Buffalo too." His voice had become urgent. "Maybe there's something I can do to give back to the world; to show my gratitude for being able to get clean and sober, for all the good fortune I've had, for having you in my life."

He'd lifted his eyes to me, stood, then placed the rattles carefully on his dresser. He'd kneeled before me and cupped the sides of my face with his hands. I'd no idea why he was so sad back then. Even now, I could only guess at his mixed feelings. Had he been trying to negotiate with the Universe? By surrendering to what his grandfather had seen for him, had he hoped his life would turn around again? Find the daughter he'd left behind? Be divorced and HIV negative? Was he trying to effect some kind of trade? He should have told me everything, right then.

I called to the room, empty of his presence, "You should have let me help you!"

Stones tumbled as the female rattle rocked on the dresser top. The gentle sound encouraged me to stop my angry thoughts.

'If I'd known what was going on then, what would I have done?' From this side of the situation, I wanted to believe I would've encouraged him to spend more time with Pop Pop. And from the vantage point of then, knowing 'zero' about his ex-wife and her disease, only the hurt of his leaving me every evening to walk the streets of Oakland, I might have still pushed him to learn more about his heritage.

No matter what, if Flyn came home and wanted his grandfather's guidance, I would encourage him.

After all, even with the confusion Amach was currently

making in my life, she was a blessing. When she walked with me, my sensations were heightened. When I walked with her, I experienced another world. When she wasn't with me, I missed her. Even this puzzle with Estelle, even with the concern for her life and mine, I welcomed the adventure. My skin shivered in response to my thoughts.

Could Flyn and I be on similar paths then? I felt a jolt of energy in my loins. Is that why we were so compatible? Weren't we, before he left, beginning to share something beyond ourselves? Maybe we'd been brought together for some kind of cosmic karma? I laughed. *'Here I go again!'* Trying to find a kind of universal purpose to my life, our life together.   I'd been warned this creating of a purpose in life grander than anyone else on the planet was the first sign of an enlarging ego.

I took it down a notch to the thought of Flyn and I being two souls who'd been brought together because we had a lot in common. We were just supposed to support each other through our processes. Wasn't that what marriage was about? Just being there to support and love each other, helping each other be the most we each could be? Standing Feather had said marriage was more than taking on the housekeeping tasks of living together, more than a written contract, a piece of paper.

She'd said it was an agreement to share joy and hardships, to stand together through every challenge life would bring, but it was even more.

I looked through my files for the exact words I'd copied from her ceremony booklet.

"Marriage is a covenant that says: I love you, I trust you, I will be here for you when you are hurting, and, when I am hurting, I will not leave."

But Flyn *had* left. *'But only to put things right for himself!'* I defended him in my heart. "Maybe," I answered aloud, feeling the torment of my grieving heart for the moments we'd missed in these past months. The female rattle rocked in such a way it rolled itself into a different direction. Was I supposed to change my perspective? I could swear the rattle shiver.

"OK, then" I said, wondering how I could reframe my perspective about him leaving. It has to start with believing he wasn't trying to hurt me. He was trying to protect me and him being gone had to do only with what he needed to do.

If I believed we were committed to a life together, then being apart wasn't any different than us being at work. If I believed he was learning to become more truly who he was, then I needed to do the same. I could hold this time as if it were a phase of being a working unit. I didn't have to count the days and nights since he'd been gone; I could believe each day brought us closer to living more fully together, like the river and the road following the separate paths of their purpose and crossing intimately at points along the way.

I smiled at myself. I knew what I was doing. I was turning my thoughts around so I could face the loneliness and not go bonkers. I was working on a positive perspective so if he walked through our door right now, it would be as if he'd never left. My shift of mind was helping with my feelings and lifting the darkness from my shoulders. As my mood brightened, I felt lighter.

The female rattle rocked back and forth on his dresser, then suddenly stood on end, facing me like it was looking me in the eye. I swear it nodded as if in some kind of acknowledgment, then banged onto the dresser top.

Cold prickles surprised my skin as they crossed my back and danced up my neck. I jumped to my feet. From my lap, several piles of transcripts tumbled into each other and fell to the floor. I groaned. *'Now look at this mess!'* I started to pick them up until a sound made me straighten.

Goose pimples rushed over me. Flyn climbed the last section of our stairs two at a time and stood motionless at the top, holding a deli bag of food in one hand and our mail in the other.

He grinned. "It's negative."

"Hallelujah!" I hollered. The food and mail was pitched toward the table as he came toward me. We met in the middle of the floor as I threw myself into his arms. Laughing through tears while screaming his name, I wanted to wrap all of me around him.

"God, you feel good." he whispered in my ear. "It's been hell." He held me away from him to look into my eyes. "She's dead . . . Yin Sun. I never . . . so hard . . . but . . . I'm . . . we're . . . it's going to be alright now." His eyes skimmed my hair, my face, then focused on my lips. Before I could answer, he gently tasted the corners of my mouth. I thrilled with every cell of my body to have him home, and we were OK.

Feeling his back muscles under my hands, his chest next to my breasts, I knew my anchor had returned. I was part of something good. We drank in each other's smell and tasted each other's lips. When we looked into each other's eyes, the space between us dissolved. I was floating in his deep brown pools, and I could feel him seeping past my shields, into the core of my being. We both had come home.

Chapter XXIV
Amach solves the puzzle

I stood in front of him, unbuckling his belt. He groaned, "No . . . not . . . yet." He struggled to push my hand, and my body, away from him. "I . . . want . . . to shower first." His eyes pleaded with mine. "Please, Sellie," he whispered.

Surfacing from the need to have him as close to me as possible, I gasped for air. "Why?"

"Don't tempt me . . . yet." Flyn's eyes reminded me of the desire Dacona had seen in Marweth's across the fire during their binding ceremony.

A deep breath helped me settle, and I fell against his chest, moaning as I exhaled, and wondered out loud, "What's between us, Flyn?" His heart pounded in his chest as loudly as mine was pounding in my ears. "I just got an understanding of who we are when we're separate, and now you're back, and I'm hungrier for you than I've ever been. My God, Flyn." My breathing turned into panting. "I want to eat you up." I grinned.

He raised his hands to stop me from attacking him. "And I've thought of nothing but when I could be here, beside you, inside you." Without touching me, he leaned forward to kiss me. "Give me a little more time, and hold that thought." A smile twitched at the corners of his mouth. "Or, should I say, hold the tension." He walked swiftly to the bathroom, flinging "I'll be back!" over his shoulder,

"OK, Mr. Swartzenegger," I said to the closing door and stood alone, beaming from ear to ear. I rolled my eyes at nothing and thought, *'I know what I'm doing this afternoon.'*

My feet slipped on the papers scattered over the floor.

'Oh, yeah.' My head might be floating in the ethers, but I was standing in the middle of a mess. Having nothing better to do, I squatted and gathered five years of our Ouija Board experiment transcripts. I guess I couldn't call them experiments anymore; they were sessions. Contacts had been made; pearls of wisdom had been extracted. Now, I discovered, one of these sessions held clues about events in present time with Estelle. How many other sessions could reveal information about our lives?

I muttered when I saw what Flyn's entrance had done. Falling into each other's arms had turned some of the papers upside down. I grunted and stopped myself from breaking down the bathroom door by focusing on returning the papers to their original order. I looked for page numbers, glancing at the written words, trying to figure which session belonged where.

I read, upside down, the page describing Estelle's first contact with the spirit who had stalked her. The hairs prickled tall on my arms. Upside down T O R O Y took on a new name that was familiar: YOROT!

"Why?" I gasped. "How?" That was the name of the man in Amach's life, who'd killed Marweth and stolen the bundle he wore around his neck.

I was numb. What kind of cross-over was this? Dread and excitement mixed at tornado speed. My eyes felt as if they were popping out of their sockets. I stacked the transcripts into order quickly so I could reread the page I'd just found. I could hardly breathe. Information about a spirit yearning for Estelle had been buried in our stacks for 15 years. That had been a dramatic enough find, but, now who was who, and what was what? Wow!

For us to not have remembered the session was understandable. For her to not have protected herself was dumb. This strong connection between past and present was more than my mind could wrap around. If the drain on her body and life had started before she created her marriage bundle with Eduardo, then what I'd remembered about the session in 1988 was more than a match with the threats I'd experienced several months ago at her Medicine Wheel. A draft blew across my neck. I gasped.

"Christ, woman!" Flyn said, "for someone who was as hot and bothered 20 minutes ago, you're sure skittish now."

"Oh, my God, Flyn . . . you don't know what's been. . ." He stood next to me with a towel tucked around his waist, his sturdy torso gleaming with stray droplets of water. His hair was tousled from his shower and a quick rub. The scars on his chest and arm glistened. Heat from his body drew me like a moth to a flame, a hummingbird to a flower. I traced the scar on his chest with one finger and watched his nipples harden. I concentrated on my breathing, afraid I'd forget the next one. I did not want to forget Estelle, but my anxiety for her was pushed to the side as my awareness of Flyn washed over my body. Talk about being conflicted. I asked myself the most sensible question I could, *'What can I do for Estelle, right this minute?'* What did I want to do for her, especially with these deep brown eyes twinkling in front of me? The angle of his chin was relaxed. He wasn't commanding me, nor was he pleading. He was just home.

He took my hand. "Come," he said. I did.

Being late in the afternoon, the sun was on the far side of the building. He'd pulled the bathroom drapes over the long, narrow windows, making the room seem like night, but he'd lit votive candles around the ancient, footed bathtub, along the window sill, the sink counter, and the floor. A faint scent of roses filled the room, and I could see petals floating atop the water that half-filled the tub.

"I . . . what's this?" I asked, breathless.

"Our bath," he answered, as he stood behind me.

I flushed. "I've never . . . we've . . ."

"Shhh." He slowly lifted my T-shirt over my head then kissed my neck and shoulders as he undid my bra. I let it puddle on the floor, sighing as he cupped both breasts in his hands, pinching my nipples with tenderness. Electricity charged through my body.

I leaned back, onto his chest, as he nuzzled my ears and neck. I loosened the towel around his waist; it fell. I spanned his upper thighs with my hands, fingering one of the stray scars on his leg he never wanted to explain.

Wrestling with the string to my sweat shorts, he said, "Too many clothes."

"Here," I said, stretching the elastic so they'd pass over my tummy and hips. I wasn't wearing panties.

"Aha," he whispered, and rubbed close to my back. I felt his penis rise to attention, and another charge clutched between my legs. I tried to turn around, but he held me firmly.

"Slowly now," he directed, as we stepped to the side of the tub. His balance helped me dip first one foot, then the other, into the tepid water. I was glad it wasn't hot; I needed cooling, if we were to make love this slowly. When I stood among the rose petals, he joined me. With my large loofah sponge, he rinsed me with cascading rose water. I closed my eyes and thought of Dacona, the glistening water on her body when Marweth first saw her. I felt as if I carried his throbbing member in my lower body and her breathlessness in my chest. I was lost in my remembered moments of their want and need, as well as my own.

A new scent, burning sage, touched my nose. I opened my eyes.

"This is special," Flyn said. "It's our first time together now that I'm totally healthy and free." Tears pooled in both our eyes. "I love you, Selena. I can't tell you how much, or even all the reasons, but I love you with all my heart and body." He kissed me as if he were tasting a fruit for the first time. He brought his hand under my chin, capturing my head to press his lips closer to mine and lick the edges of my mouth. To slow himself, he paused a hair's breath from my skin to nuzzle at the angle of my nose, across my cheek, behind my ear.

I can't say when we submerged into the water. I never thought we could fit, but we did, facing each other at first, reclining on our sides against the sloped back of the tub. We took our time revisiting favorite places on each other's bodies with our hands and our lips, trying not to drown in the cooling water. Then he was above me, and I was wrapping my legs around his hips, opening to him as he gently eased into me. I felt his fullness as well as my joy to have him there, and soon I felt our release.

I answered his smile with my own, "I love you, Flyn, for better or worse, in sickness and in health, until the end of our time."

A shadow flickered across his brow. "There's much to share with you, before we make those commitments in ceremony."

I shook my head. "I've already made it to you, here and now, no matter what you've got to tell me." I said, simply.

"And I to you." His kiss was long and tender, then soft and playful and with purpose. Later, when the candles had flickered out and our bodies were wrinkled from soaking all afternoon, we found towels to dry each other.

While on his knees in front of me, he traced the scar on my abdomen from my hysterectomy and the slash for an appendectomy, then kissed them and my dimpled skin where stretch marks stamp me as a mother. I stroked his hair and took my turn at honoring his body, the multiple scars atop his spine and chest, his left hip and leg, the unexplained ones on his arm and thigh. His skin rippled in response before he gripped me in an embrace that left me weak-kneed.

"Good to be home," he said, loosening me so my head fell against his chest. I wrapped my arms around him for the sheer joy of having my arms full again. Our stomachs growled in unison. We attacked the bag of food he brought and ravaged the deli sandwiches; ham and swiss cheese for me, roast beef with horseradish for him. Each was piled with lettuce, sprouts, tomatoes, olives, red onion slices, and our favorite mustard and pickles. The extra-sourdough rolls had dried, but the potato salad was moist with mayonnaise. The cold baked beans were steeped in barbecue sauce; cherry turnovers were for dessert. I sighed as I rewrapped my sagging towel around my boobs. "You know the way to a girl's heart."

His eyes twinkled. "And other places?"

We'd finished, and I was licking my fingers. "How about the bed?" I suggested. When his left eyebrow went up, I added, "I could use a nap."

He nodded. We stood, dropped our towels and sprinted under the covers, where we spooned our bodies into each other.

My last thoughts were a mixture of gratitude for my life, a twinge of guilt about the messy apartment, worry about Estelle, and surrender to the comfort of Flyn's protecting arms.

*　*　*　*　*　*　*

I am walking with Amach; I do not recognize our path. We might be in a forest, but the sounds aren't right. It's dark, like her cave, but I don't smell the mustiness of earth packed around me, or the sweet scent of burnt wood. We might be in a tunnel, but I perceive there are no walls. We are surrounded by air cushioning and supporting us. Each footstep floats into a place of 'nowhere', and I realize I am inside Amach while she is dreaming.

Swirls of color flow past. I sense pictures being held in her mind. I perceive Marweth's death, as we saw it; the faces of the men are clear as they raise their clubs. I . . . we . . . shudder. Our sight dims, and we move through a dense atmosphere to . . . Yorot's face, where he huddles at the base of a tree, fondling the leather pouch he pulled from Marweth's neck. He smiles, as he lifts the bag to see it better. He sniffs at it, wrinkles his nose. He puzzles over the lacing. The more he pulls one end, the tighter the knot. I feel us smile. He can't see the seams in the leather. Out of the shadow of the tree, he moves into the sunlight and sees one side is folded into itself. When he pulls at it, he sees the hidden stitching. He grunts and nods.

I wonder how it is we are watching him? Perhaps this isn't dream time, but a visioning trance. 'How can I be here?' I wonder and am squeezed by an imperceptible tightness around me. I have my thoughts but get a message I am to control them. Yorot's image flickers. I refocus; I don't want us to lose our connection. The tension lessens around me.

From a distance, now, we watch. I note his muscular arms and legs. Split at the sides, a tanned hide drapes his body from his waist to his knees. He has tied his unkempt long, flaxen hair at the nape of his neck with a thong. It billows to below his shoulders. His skin is bronze and edged in a fine layer of curling blond hair. A reddish-yellow beard covers his lower face. His eyebrows are bushy, and his nose long. When he opens his mouth, I am disappointed to see worn and yellowed teeth. How old could he be? He has to be in his mid-20s by the looks of his development and facial hair. I realize if I stood next to him, he would tower over me. Living in survival mode has given all these men muscular bodies. All except Tobar, who has idle hands and reaps the benefits of having many sons. I remember his distended belly.

Another tightening around my body reminds me to focus.

Urgency fills us as we watch Tobar sneak behind Yorot and snatch the bundle from the younger man's hands. Yorot grabs for it, but Tobar puts his foot out. Yorot stumbles.

"So this is it?" Tobar demands.

Yorot shakes his head and fists his hands.

Tobar works the seams in the leather, attempting to open the pouch. He finds the double knots that stopped Yorot,

*then removes a sharpened stone from his hip bundle and begins
to cut at the small pouch.*

*Yorot grabs at his prize. "It's mine to open." He
stands tall, but with watchful eyes. "Dacona wears one like it
around her neck. I want to see what it has to do with her." He
puffs his chest in determination. "Give it to me," he demands.*

*The men face each other and move into defensive
crouches. Both are ready to fight, until Tobar grins then
straightens. Yorot is unsure and remains on defense. The
older man tosses the leather pouch to him.*

*"It's yours. If it brings you the woman, tell me how she
screams when you enter her. I am sure he did not lay with her.
She's yours to claim, if you wish." Tobar smirks then walks
away, turning once to sneer at Yorot. "Remember who helped
you." With his smile, he shows broken teeth and swollen gums.*

*As Tobar passes through the trees and disappears,
Yorot is visibly relieved. He holds the soft leather in his hand,
reties the broken thong that was around Marweth's neck and
hangs it around his own then pats it on his chest. A scowl
crosses his face. Removing it, he lifts his apron-like tunic to
expose a belt he wears there. He shortens the pouch's tie so
when it hangs, it falls against his manhood. Patting it as if it
were a talisman, he ambles onto a different path than Tobar's.*

*Roaring fills my ears. The forest blackens. Acid bile
rises in the back of my throat. We vomit into a bowl sitting
beside the skins I am . . . well, we . . . are laying on. Our head
spins, and we close our eyes until the pounding inside our skull
lessens.*

*I am not able to read her thoughts, but, as we lay, I feel
she is forming a scheme. A sense of purpose grows within us.
The set of our shoulders brings me a feeling of resolve. I know,
beyond a doubt, Amach has a plan.*

*We sleep, but for how long? I have no clue. I am
surprised I haven't returned to my real form. Anxiety builds in
my chest, our chest. I think, 'Am I stuck here?'*

NO, comes the reply into my head.

'That's a good thing,' I think.

Be still.

'OK,' I think and pass the time, trying to figure how this experience might be happening. This is more than dipping into Amach's past; it is not a dream now, or a vision. I am sharing . . . perhaps visiting is a better word . . . her body, not privy to her thought processes. I have nothing to do but wonder what's going to happen next. 'So what's the point?' I ask. My answer is a void.

'Why am I here? For what?' I feel a sigh. 'Am I just here for moral support?'

We move our hands across the top of our head. We are bent over a hole in the earth, water cascading over our hair. With a thickly folded handful of moss, we briskly rub our scalp, then finger-comb our hair from our face. Opening our eyes, I see sleeping skins on a ledge carved into a wall. A fire warms our back. I am not recognizing this room.

Our sleeping cave

I settle into her words, and ask 'Lebara?'

Gone to focus the women's dream time

A picture forms for me to see. Lebara, resting near a fire where another woman pokes in the ashes, retrieves a stone, and drops it into a stretched skin bag.

The women's cave

Amach moves, and we turn toward a wall where pouches and drying branches of leaves are hung. Small clay bawls are gathered and baskets full of crackling herbs are stacked. After she rummages among the baskets, I cannot image what she places in her palm. We smell a pungent grease as she mixes selected pinches of herbs in her hand until she grunts with what I can only sense is satisfaction. The consistency must now be correct because we turn toward the fire and begin to massage the mixture into our face and hands. The dry ache of our skin softens.

'What are you doing, old woman?' I ask with my mind.
Watch and be silent.
She waves her hands through the air. The muscles of
her arms are taut from the labor she accomplishes every day.
My arms wobble with stretched skin I think of as my wings. I
am old, I think, 'Isn't she?' I can only guess at what she is
doing.

We duck through the cave's tunnel to the outside. Night
hovers at the edges of the tribe's gathering place. I wonder
where we are again. It's as if Amach has purposely erased all
clues as to who and where she is and lives. As we step quietly
under the starlight, all my questions become side issues. I am
a guest in her body, here to serve her purpose.

We stay in the shadow of the ledge above the opening to
our cave and watch for movement across the sparsely-lit
clearing. We take in shallow breaths; our heartbeat flutters
then steadies as she treads with purpose along the edge of the
forest toward the lodge of Dacona's family. We duck past the
hide door, entering the large room with care. We view the
round hut with its wispy fire in its center; no one is here except
a sleeping form on hides placed near the fire pit. We hear deep
breathing and step toward the place where Dacona is pale on
dark furs. Amach scans the air hanging around the young
woman, as well as the walls. I know when her eyes have found
her target because she reaches carefully for the dress Dacona
wore when I last saw her with Marweth at their binding.
Sadness crosses our being. We retreat with our breath held
tightly in our chest, as the young woman stirs. Standing inside
the door, we listen for any sounds outside before we slip into
the night.

I have no sense of what Amach has planned. Tension
strengthens our muscles.

We do not return to her cave, but dip ourselves into the
deeper shadows of the trees. We remove our stained skin dress
and cover ourselves quickly with Dacona's shift. I smell the

change in the odor, from sweaty to sweet, from musty to fresh. I taste an herb Amach places in our mouth and feel a shift in how our eyes are seeing the landscape before us. I feel our shoulders settle with resolve, despite the pounding in our heart and wonder again at the power of this woman in whom I am living.

Our legs are not trembling. Our heart is not racing. Our steps are directed toward another hut, farther from the rest; we sit, watching.

A dim light flickers from the inside fire when this hide door is lifted. In the growing darkness, I see a man's form coming near our post, fumbling under his skin covering. We watch him urinate. I feel us rise and step from shadow into starlight.

The man is startled, starts to move away from us, then stops. He turns. Surprise is on his face, as if he can't believe who is before him. His hand moves to pat between his legs. Then he offers a small grin.

"It worked," he says. "I knew if I . . . " But he stops when we offer our hand.

He takes it. The moment our hands touch, a picture dashes across our mind. Fear stops our breath. We see what he has done to the tiny bundle. He has spewed his seed over the pouch, and, from a cut on his finger, he has dripped his blood into the knotted opening. He has defiled the contents. We share the wish to drop to our knees, wailing our despair, but there is nothing to do but accept what he has done. We shake off the picture with our anger and sorrow, move with him past the edge of the forest. He takes us beneath the drooping bows of a cedar tree where grasses are bent as if an animal has made their bed here. Grabbing us by our shoulders, he forces us to kneel with him.

In the darkness, I now understand all of Amach's preparations. She has made us to resemble Dacona so Yorot will misunderstand who we are. He thinks his defilement of the bundle has brought him his desire. His eyes glaze in the ecstasy of his fantasy and lays us onto the grasses where small pebbles poke and bite into the thin leather on our back. Grabbing at one breast with one hand, he fumbles at our leather shift with the other to give him better access to our body. He thrusts his hand between our legs. We bite our lips so as not to scream and taste the salt of our blood. Horror builds in Amach's mind as she travels to another time when this groping led to pain. I offer her my memories of loving Flyn and allow pictures of our joining with love and tenderness, so this will not be harder. I can feel something ease within us.

We are glad he has not noticed we are reaching toward the cord around his waist, searching for the pouch. He does not guess that we clutch a sharp stone in our other hand so as to cut the thong. He only sees his dream. He kneels first with one knee, then with the other between our legs, so as to open us to his need. He grunts as he fumbles with his skirt, ripping at it until there is nothing between us. We shout and are smothered by his hand across our mouth as he falls upon us. Our fears build as Yorot's thickened penis strikes against our leg. As he works his way into the dryness of our being, his tainted breath makes us gag. The entry to her womb has been closed for so long the tissue rips as he plunges into her. We scream again into his hand as the pain batters into us again and again. He spills his seed. We hear his groan of disgust, as if what he has done has not matched his dream. While I was lost in the revulsion of his body, his scent, I am amazed to find Amach has kept her mind on our mission; she has her hand on Marweth's bundle.

Now Amach makes use of Yorot's discontent. She taunts him with her moves of lingering desire, making as if to lie on top of him. He rolls us to our sides, freeing our hands to cut the pouch from his waist cord. He holds us, his chest heaving, unaware his treasure has been taken. We are quiet.

"You are mine," he says.

We lift our self from him, pushing him to the ground. He is on his back as we sit across his hips and stare into his eyes. We spit at him, "I will never be yours."

His eyes open in horror as he realizes the truth. We lift our self and race from him, along the boundary between the forest and the camp, staying in shadow, watching our footing.

I wonder what he will say to the others? He can't tell anyone he has done the lying-in with Dacona as she is under the watchful eyes of her family. Will he announce to everyone he was seduced by the seer woman, or will he protect his place in the tribe and say nothing?

I feel Amach hesitate. What next? Breathing hard from the running, we enter her cave and remove Dacona's dress, realizing too late we have left Amach's own tattered, work-shift at the edge of the forest. Sitting beside the bowl of water, we wash our body with our hands. We rub continuously between our legs, but then she stops. Amach wraps us in a fur and lays us upon her bed with her hands on our abdomen. She wonders at the dull ache within. I am allowed to know of her wish for some part of Yorot's seed to have entered the place of child-making so Amach's greatest need can be fulfilled: a child of her own, a daughter to take up the thread of knowledge she holds from her own mother and grandmother, and beyond.

We rest until urgency awakens us. We fumble in the back of the cave to find another shift and shiver as we dress. There is little time to retrieve Amach's work shift before it's discovered. And there is another duty on Amach's mind. I wonder again, why am I still here? What more is there for me to see, feel, hear, taste . . . smell?

Shhhh, stay with me. You will see .

With several containers of herbs and Dacona's shift rolled and tucked under our arm, we walk across the encampment to Dacona's family home. We announce our presence outside by pounding a rock on the door frame. Amanna's face greets us without a smile.

"I've come to bring her back to you," Amach says to her old friend.

"You've done enough!" Amanna whispers in a strangled voice.

"I can bring her back to you,"

"But not to you. She will never be with you."

"I know." We shrug to show we understand the time of teaching has passed. "I will bring her back to be your daughter, not my student."

Amanna hands Amach a flint knife. "Pledge this!"

With heavy heart, we use the knapped stone to lash across our palm. Our hand falls so blood will drip, then we place an imprint of our hand on the door frame. "I pledge to bring your daughter back to you, and that is all."

Amanna allows us in the door, dropping it behind us.

We bow to the spirits of Amanna's home: the fire, the water, the earth, and the roof. With a straw match flaming from the fire, we light an herb roll from one of her many bags and lay it near the central hearth; an acrid odor fills the room. She circles the sleeping form of Dacona and brings a bowl from her pack to set on the earth beside the grieving, young woman. In it, she places a flaming coal from the fire and, atop this, as she sings a wordless chant, she unlaces the double knot of Marweth's bundle neither Yorot nor Tobar could undo. A few items spill onto the burning wood; one item flames, another smolders.

Smoke spirals into the ceiling; Amach fans the fumes across Dacona's head and body, continuing her toning. Now she prays aloud, "Return that which is she to her and let that which is he be burned." Amach continues to shake the pouch, slowly dropping the contents of the bag into the burning embers.

A moan comes from Dacona and her eyes open wide as Amach moves to shake the last of the items from the bundle onto the hot coal. Dacona comes alive. She strikes a blow to

Amach's hand. The leather pouch flips from Amach's grip. As if this world in which I am living was a movie, it slows to show the frame of each action; I watch as the partially emptied bundle spins in the air, crossing over the threshold of the fire to drop into its flames. Smoke issues from the burning leather. Hissing crisply, it suddenly flares, congealing the added fluids dried on its outside with what remains inside.

We are screaming inside our head, "NOOOOOO!"

Dacona cries from her bed, "What . . . where?" She is sitting straight, her eyes wide, her mouth open to shriek. She is struggling to stand, but falls from weakness. Amanna runs to soothe her daughter, stroking Dacona's shoulders and hair, and looks gratefully at Amach while rocking her child.

Dacona shoves her mother away and screams, "What have you done, old woman?"

"I have undone what was done," we say sadly. "Marweth is gone, child. He was killed, and his spirit was pulling you, with him, into the other world. The connection had to be broken for you to survive."

"But I only want to be with him," she cries.

We hang our head in defeat. We know we have lost her forever. There is nothing left to do, so we turn to the fire. The leather saturated with Yorot's seed and blood is simmering in the flames, a darkened spot of nothing in the hearth. We pour the remnants of hot coals and herbs at the edge of the pit.

Amach's words fill my head, as she is only speaking to me.   "All may not have spilled from the pouch before the seed of Yorot was burned. Whatever met the flames together may have caused another bonding." I feel her fear and helplessness. She may have succeeded in returning Dacona to her mother, but she may have failed in freeing her from bondage.

The smoking herbs in the bowl flare; fumes sting our eyes. I feel as if I am smothered in the haze, smothered in smoke . . .

I cough from smudge billowing into my face.

"Thank God," Flyn called, crushing me to his chest. I cringed and tried to pull away, but he held me firmly.

"I didn't know what to do, Sellie," he said as he rocked me. "You've been moaning and crying and tossing. You wouldn't wake up for anything. What in hell just happened?" For someone who was usually able to take control of any situation, Flyn sounded scared and desperate. I pushed against him and opened my eyes.

"How long?" was my first question.

"You've been at this for almost an hour," he said searching my face.

"Water," was all I could say.

He lowered me onto my pillows and jumped over me to bring some from the bathroom. I waved away the smoking smudge rising from the abalone shell and grabbed at the glass. The water tasted so fresh I greedily drank the entire glass. I avoided his stare by slipping out of bed and getting more water.

"Are you going to tell me?" he demanded.

I felt helpless. I had to tell him everything that happened while he was away, and it was going to take forever to bring him up to date. Then the pieces that had been floating out of the reach of my consciousness fell together like the items Amach had released from the leather bundle. "Oh, my God! Flyn! You're not going to believe this! Oh, my God!"

I pulled at the boxes I'd left at the foot of the bed. Turning to him with a degree of despair in my heart, I watched concern wash over his face. As I fumbled to find the page, I said, "You've got to look at this. You won't understand until you read it, and I tell you everything that's happened." I suddenly looked at him. "Oh Flyn! Estelle's really done it this time!"

He was trying to understand, but I knew I needed to start at the beginning. Where was that going to be? I looked at the clock. It read 6pm. I sighed. He looked so good sitting on the side of our bed, his tanned body contrasting with the white, lace-trimmed sheets. I scrambled into his lap, wrapped my arms around his shoulders and kissed him on his lips. When he responded with a cock of his head, I said, "Looks like I'm going to be busy tonight."

He smiled, but I put my finger to his lips, "I've got to catch you up on a whole lot of stuff, lover." He started to hug me, but I pulled away and handed him the transcript instead. "Read this while I put on some coffee, and then I'll tell you all about what I've been dreaming of, other than you."

"Will we break for supper?" he asked.

I looked shyly at him over my shoulder. "We can take breaks whenever we want, but I've got a whole bunch to tell you before we head north tomorrow."

"Can't we hang out here for the next few days?" He pouted, his eyes twinkling. "I can think of lots of things to do."

I called from the bathroom as I filled the coffee maker with water and grounds. "Not sure we've got that kind of time. Read the transcript, then I'll tell you why I'm so concerned about Estelle. She's got herself a problem, and I'm in the middle of it. I've got to make sure she's alright; I've got a feeling she's not . . . and that I'm the only one who can help her out of her mess."

I quickly brushed my teeth and looked at myself in the mirror. I was fully expecting my 21-year-old face to look back at me, but there I was, skin bagging under my eyes, spiky hair looking as if it had been stirred by an egg beater. I saw full-fledged wrinkles winging away from my eyes and around my lips where lipstick drooled whenever I put it on too thick; I was beginning to get jowls and facial hair, for goodness sake! Everything was succumbing to gravity. *How in the hell can that man out there love this?*' I asked.

Then I registered my twinkling eyes. *If nothing else,*' I answered myself. *I'm enthusiastic!*'

Chapter XXV – Late August, 2004
The Walls Come Down

The room was dark when Flyn rolled to check the clock. He was sprawled across the bed, a position usually bringing him into close proximity with at least one of Sellie's elbows or a knee, a hip, but he touched nothing! No smooth skin rubbing against his. No soft butt for him to inch against. His anticipation of waking next to her dimmed; reminding him of the void he'd felt every morning, during the months he'd spent away from her. When he didn't hear her breathing next to him, he consoled himself, '*Must be in the bathroom.*' He waited to hear the toilet flush.

The clock read 4am, the 'worrying hour' as she called it, the time when Sellie awoke to concern herself about a family member, a client, a friend, or something. He smiled, remembering when she first told him of her belief that someone, from every corner of the world, was assigned, between 4am to 5am, to awaken and take up the 'worrying for the universe' from wherever the previous worrier had left off. Just for that one hour, all over the world. '*What a concept.*' He wondered when he didn't hear any movement in the bathroom if she was in her worrying chair, and if he should disturb her.

He pictured her as she was last night, sitting cross-legged in the middle of their bed, describing the sensational details of the past three months. Chills shivered up and down his spine; her story was incredible. How could all this happen to one person, let alone his Sellie? It wasn't conceivable she would spontaneously connect with this Amach. How could an entity move into her body, shove her real self aside, and talk through her mouth. Now, he had to wrap his mind around Selena sharing Amach's body while the old woman seduced this Yorot. It freaked him out.

As a kid, his voices had been bad enough, and his grandfather's ceremonies had frightened him even more. Seeing the old man covered and tied in a blanket then set into an altar-like affair, Flyn had been so upset one time his mother had turned him out of the house. He'd tried to talk to his dad about it, but his father had been sitting in the shed, drinking, not wanting to be anywhere near the old man during one of those 'damned savage' ceremonies.

Flyn grunted. Now he had to handle even greater weirdness as a sober adult, and, this was his Sellie. He had to believe her. Watching her struggle while she said she had lived in some other world, in someone else's body, had been like the nightmares he'd suffered over the years, those where he'd been caught in his fears of the dark, where flashing lights wavered across the ceiling, or when stomping feet sounded and no one was there. Earlier, when he'd been unable to help Sellie open her eyes, he'd been plunged into the memory of his desperate helplessness when the tunnel had collapsed and everyone he'd known had died around him. There was no one in the mine shaft to save but himself.

Flyn opened and closed his eyes, making sure he could tell the difference between outside shadows and inside gloom. It had to be true. How could she have described Amach's world if she'd only heard the details? How could she have remembered the descriptions of the old woman's time and place so vividly? Sellie had to have experienced this other world in person because the details of the cave room, the waterfall, and the houses, the people and their clothes were clearly inscribed in her brain. When she'd told him of the time she'd channeled Amach, she hadn't been able to remember them. People had to tell her what she'd said or she'd had to listen to tapes of the sessions.

He shifted in the bed, changing the direction of his thoughts to tackle the problem of understanding all she'd told him. He just couldn't seem to force his logical mind around any of it. *'What'd she say?'*

"Look at the circumstances with your heart, Flyn."

'Well, I'll try . . . for your sake,' he thought.

Then, he remembered his grandfather explaining the way of the spirits by putting a blanket over the both of them. As a little boy, he'd huddled next to the old man's chest, with Pop Pop's breath whispering against his cheek. Under the darkness of the blanket, he'd asked Pop Pop about the voices. Pop Pop had admitted he heard them and asked Flyn if he understood what they were saying.

"No," Flyn remembered answering. "They mumble and scare me."

Pop Pop had lectured Flyn's voices; they were told to go away. He cautioned Flyn there would be a time when their words would return and would make sense. For now, he'd promised, the spirits would stay away until Flyn was able to handle their messages.

His grandfather's intervention had worked for a time until he'd entered his teens; then they'd returned with a vengeance. He'd dreamed they were chasing him, screaming at him. He'd tried to tell his father about them, but Durk Devon, who rejected everything to do with the Native American part of his son's and wife's lives, had given Flyn a beating, and forbidden his mother to talk to him about them. In fact, Durk had chased Pop Pop out of their house with a shotgun, threatening to report the old man for kidnapping, when the old man had come to claim Flyn to teach him the old ways.

Durk vowed never to turn his son over to a heathen, even when Flyn had begged to go. That request had awarded him another beating, so, he'd run away. Flyn grunted. *'That's a whole 'nother story.'* He paused in his memories, sending his hearing out into the room, trying to locate Selena.

She was by the window, just as he'd guessed, in her rocking chair. Her breathing was loud, like she was moaning.

"Sellie, are you alright?" he asked in the night.

When she didn't answer, and all he heard was deeper breathing with little grunts, he unwound himself from the sheets and went to her. After what had happened earlier, he worried the old woman had her again. He lit sage, confident the smudge would bring her out of whatever trance she was in.

This time, in the glow of the smoldering leaves, he saw her face was altered and nearly dropped the abalone shell. He lit the soft light by the bed. *'No doubt about it!'* Her face was fuller, as if she'd gained weight between the time they'd fallen asleep in each other's arms and now. Shock struck him. Her face wasn't just fuller; it wasn't her face. It was a man's face! Her skin was dark. Her arms and hands were larger, her fingertips blunt.

"I HAVE BEEN WAITING," said a deep and accented voice through Selena's lips.

Flyn's heart stopped. He croaked, "Sellie?"

The person in front of him stifled a sob. "YOU MUST HELP HER," it said. "SHE DOES NOT KNOW I AM DEAD."

Flyn desperately cataloged these words and tried to match them to anything Sellie'd told him during their previous afternoon and evening. He'd read the name on the transcript, agreeing the letters were arranged backwards and that it could be the same person as the one in her visioning with Amach. So . . . whose voice was this? Was it Toroy's? Or Yorot's? Or Amach?

Through drying lips, he said, "Who are you?"

"I AM EDUARDO DELGADO HERNANDEZ . . . I CANNOT . . . WALK ON THIS EARTH."

Flyn frantically searched through what information he could remember about Estelle. Bingo! This was the guy

Sellie's friend wanted bound to her, but that couldn't be. That man was alive in Mexico with his family. The words, 'I cannot walk on this earth' hit him between the eyes and a grief like he'd never felt in his body penetrated his chest.

"I don't understand."

The being in front of him, and that was the only way Flyn could describe Selena's form, crumpled in the chair and gave forth another sobbing sigh. "I . . . AM DEAD, AMIGO. I TALK . . . THROUGH THE MOUTH OF YOUR LOVER . . . SHE IS . . . LIKE A WINDOW . . . BETWEEN OUR WORLDS."

Flyn started to say 'no fuckin' way'. He shook his head in disbelief instead, wishing he had a cigarette, or a drink, something stronger than coffee. His hands shook. His stomach knotted. He knew he had to pull himself together, at least for Sellie's sake as much as his own. He gained as much control as he could before he asked, "What can I do for you?"

The voice was breathless now. "GO TO ESTELLE! SHE IS IN DANGER! I DID NOT KILL MYSELF! I WAS PUSHED!"

Flyn didn't know what to say to this, didn't know what to ask. He decided to hold silent until he could form a coherent sentence in his shattering brain. He struggled to ask, "Can you tell me more about how you died?"

The being rearranged Selena's body in the chair. "MY HORSE AND I KNEW EACH OTHER. SHE WAS STRONG . . . BUT ON OUR LAST RIDE, SHE WOULD NOT OBEY ME . . . RAN TOO FAST . . . FROM SOMEONE OR SOMETHING . . . TOO CLOSE TO THE EDGE OF THE CLIFF. . . I COULD NOT STOP HER . . . AND THEN . . . THEN WE WERE . . . FALLING . . . AND I KNEW . . ."

"What did you know?" Flyn urged.

"SOMETHING CAUSED MY DEATH . . . WILL CAUSE THE DEATH . . . OF ESTELLE . . . YOU MUST WARN HER."

"We're going to her in the morning," Flyn said to the entity. He really wanted to scream at this 'being', wanted to do anything to release the tension building in his body, but felt caught in a place that was unreal, unearthly. *'For Christ's sake,'* he was conversing with the spirit of a dead man, and all he could think to say was, "She's worried about you."

Memories under the blanket with his grandfather, of being chased by his voices, of standing alone in pitch darkness, surfaced in his mind and tumbled with his worry about Selena's limp body. He thought he might explode with questions about his sanity. How could he accept this weird role of talking to someone he'd never met, in the middle of the night, and who was living in the body of the woman he loved? She was his anchor, what gave meaning to his life. Sellie was his woman, damn it. He had to do something!

"Let her be," Flyn pleaded, wishing he could have controlled his tone or the catch in his voice. He shook himself, becoming impatient. He would not show weakness in front of another man, but, he thought, this isn't another man. He eyed the being in the chair, knowing he needed to deal with this in a way that would help both Selena and Estelle, so he gathered his wits and asked, "Do you know what Estelle's done?"

The being raised its head and stared at him. "WHAT?"

"Estelle did a ceremony to bind the two of you. She did it in a way, so I'm told, that included a spirit being, who's been stalking her for years, perhaps even longer than that. She didn't mean to, I suppose." Flyn tried to remember details. "Seems my woman and this spirit are part of this bundle Estelle created." His voice grew excited. "Now you tell me an entity caused your death? It could be the same one . . . and . . . if you're right, it could cause Estelle and Selena to cross over too?"

"AH . . . MADRE DE DIOS! ESTELLE! WHAT HAVE YOU DONE? FOOLISH . . . WOMAN! WHAT KIND OF LOVE WOULD POSSESS?"

Flyn shrugged his shoulders. "The kind that doesn't believe it's worthy of being loved?"

The being grunted. "YOU ARE WISE . . . WORTHY OF GREAT THINGS . . . LISTEN TO THOSE AROUND YOU."

Prickles stood on Flyn's skin. "What are you talking about?"

"THERE ARE SPIRITS WHO WANT TO HELP YOU . . . IN YOUR LIFE . . . LET THEM."

"I don't know what . . . "

"THEY TELL ME . . . IT IS NOT YET TIME . . . REMEMBER THEM . . . THEY . . . ONLY WANT TO HELP . . . THEY ARE SORRY THEY SCARED YOU WHEN YOU WERE SO SMALL." The being looked as if it was smiling with Selena's lips. Flyn started toward the woman he loved, but her hand raised. It stopped him.

"GO TO ESTELLE, AMIGO. AS SOON AS YOU CAN! I WILL HELP FROM THIS SIDE. TELL HER . . . I WILL ALWAYS LOVE HER. I FORGIVE HER FOR THE WASTE OF MY LIFE. YOUR WOMAN . . . KNOWS WHAT TO DO! HELP HER!"

The being settled into the chair, as if it had been inflated with air and was now deflating. Flyn watched from his perch on the edge of the bed until he was sure the entity, or spirit, or whatever the hell it was, was gone. He wanted nothing more than to grab Selena, hold her, bring her back to him. The sight and sound of an alien voice speaking through her mouth was too much, no matter what news or information it had given him. "Oh, Christ!" he said when he realized he was supposed to have paid close attention to the entity's every word. She said she never remembered one word of what was spoken through her.

What had he been told? That Eduardo had been pushed off the side of a cliff while riding his horse. Where, why, or when hadn't been part of the information.

He relit the sage remaining in the bottom of the abalone shell, raised it to drift over his head and shoulders. He inhaled it and felt tension ease across his chest. Silence dominated the room, inviting him to venture closer to the rocking chair. The glowing smudge bowl was in his hand. Her body stirred, and, when its eyes opened, Flyn knew Selena was back.

* * * * * * *

Smelling smudge, then opening my eyes to see Flyn come toward me with the smoking abalone shell flipped my heart in my chest, and tears filled my eyes. I'd been so far away, floating somewhere beyond this room, as if I'd lost my way and was only a spot of light, twisting and twirling as different eddies of air settled or sailed upward. Now I was back, and chills rippled over my skin. "What . . . where have I . . . been?"

He tried to smile, but I saw it was a strain. He came closer. "That's what I'd like to know. Where were you?"

I tried to remember, but the harder I thought, the farther I pushed away any sense of the last few minutes. I used a deep breath to relax my shoulders and my mind. A bright light clicked and shone onto my head like a spotlight. "I heard someone knocking at the front . . . wha . . .!" My body shook like an earthquake. "What just happened?"

"Tell me what you remember first. Where was the knocking?"

Pin pricks of hysteria urged me to scream, but I brought it under control by speaking slowly. "I started to say the front door . . . but we don't have one. We can't hear knocking on the door at the foot of the stairs. But I was sure . . ." I looked around the room, rubbed my bare arms and huddled deeper into the rocker. "But it *was* a door, Flyn. I *went* to it. I *walked* through it." The quaking began again. "Flyn, I walked across a threshold and flew away. I mean. I had no body. I became a speck of light . . . until I returned . . . and saw you walking toward me."

"Did you come back through the door?"

I was holding onto myself. "I don't think so." I concentrated on his face; the worry line between his eyes was a deep crevice. "Why? Is it important?"

"Do you remember getting into the chair?"

I felt as if I was surrounded by a congealing fog, isolated from the rest of the world as well as any memory of the time between the knocking and Flyn's worried face. I shook my head. "Not really."

"So you don't remember getting out of bed, walking across the floor, and sitting there."

I flung my arms to the ceiling in exasperation. "I said I don't remember anything! You're scaring me. What's this about?" The quaking started inside this time, all my organs shivering with cold.

He reached for me. "Let's go back to bed. You look like you're freezing."

I followed his lead and snuggled under his arm, happy to be near him, smelling him, feeling his naked skin against mine.

He stroked my hair and my ear. "Sellie, I think you need to go back to that door and lock it."

"I don't think . . ." I started to say, but felt his hand tighten around my arm.

"Trust me. Go back in your mind and lock that door."

I heard the mixed feelings in his voice so I closed my eyes. The door stood before me. It was made of a dark, antique wood and framed in an archway formed with irregular sizes of stone. The wall was adobe; the door had a wrought iron handle.

I saw no lock, and I realized the door was ajar. I wanted to peek through the opening to the other side but felt Flyn's hand squeeze my arm, as if in warning. With my mind's eye, I pushed it shut until I heard a click. A thought flashed that I should try to see if it would open, but another squeeze of Flyn's hand helped me decide against that. I wondered why I was doing this until chills spread across my scalp as I heard faint knocking on the door. My heart jumped. I retreated from the door and was stopped when I stumbled over a two-by-four board. Stepping over it, I continued backwards, staring at the door. On either side of it were wrought iron brackets to hold the board, so I lifted the dense plank and inserted it into the holders to prevent the door from opening. I was satisfied until I thought, *'Doesn't stop someone from coming over the wall.'* When I looked up, the adobe wall rose so far into the sky, I couldn't see its top. I shook myself and forced my eyes to open.

When I looked at Flyn's ashen face, I said, "That was weird."

Flyn's strong arms tightened around me. "You dropped into that space so quickly I was afraid you were lost."

My alarm bells were ringing. "What's upset you?"

He steadied himself. "I . . . Sellie . . . uh . . . you . . . you weren't you for a while." He said finally.

I stayed quiet.

"I thought you were doing your 4am thing, but your breathing sounded odd, like you were moaning, and, when I looked at your face, you weren't you."

My loss of time and sensations had made me wary, but now, to be told someone had used my body while I was out of it, scared me to pieces, or rather, scared me shitless. "How could that happen? How could someone invite me out of my body, then, inhabit it while I'm gone? Who would do such a thing?"

He took a deep breath and answered me, "Eduardo."

"I don't believe you," I said, and sat forward on the bed. "How could he do such a thing? He's in Mexico and as far . . ." I looked at Flyn's face and saw his frustration.

My land line rang. Even though it was 5am, I scrambled for it, afraid it was one of the kids while hoping it was Estelle, because I wanted to tell her about the transcription. I read the digital readout. The number was not familiar.

"Hello, Selena here." I answered.

"Oh, thank God, you're there!"

"Who's this?"

"I'm Heather, Estelle's daughter; I couldn't think of another person to call. Please help me. Oh, my, God, Selena, my mom's in such a mess!" The voice was a shadow of Estelle's, with hysteria at its edges.

"What's happening?"

"I knew she hadn't called you! I just knew it! And she'd promised me!" Anger made her voice stronger. "It's Eduardo. He . . . well his family thinks he committed suicide."

A rush of hot energy drenched me. "How?"

She tried to control her voice. "I call my mom every day to make sure she's OK. She's not been feeling well, and yesterday, my mom told me she got this phone call." Heather had to take a deep breath. "It seems it was Eduardo's sister. I guess he's been depressed and moody over the last month so she'd been begging him to visit Estelle, but he'd said if he came, he was afraid he would break his vow of celibacy. He had to stay away, but he was miserable. He fought with his family over, oh, I don't remember what. Three days ago, she said, he'd been so upset he'd galloped away on his horse. She'd told my mom they hadn't seen him since and wanted to prepare her for whatever happened next." Her voice deteriorated into a sob.

She gulped. "My mom just called me from her house. His family, just now, they've . . . oh my God . . . they've found his body and his horse in a ravine." She gasped with a sob. "My mom, she can't . . . she's pulling her hair out, Selena. She's raving. I can't get to her because I'm in Arizona. She's uncontrollable, saying it's all her fault. What am I going to do?

Please! I don't know who else to call."

I couldn't focus on anything, not the wall, the phone, the ceiling. I clung to Flyn. I told her, "We're coming, but later today. Is there anyone else who's near who could sit with her?" I heard her sobbing on the end of the line. Through my tears, I stared at Flyn, knowing all he'd told me was more than true, but I was frightened by the way Eduardo's death and his visitation had happened.

Heather voice brought me back to the phone. "There's no one who'll set foot in the house any more. She's a mess, Selena." Tears clogged her voice. "She doesn't know I'm calling you."

"We'll be there as soon as we can," I said, hoping Estelle was not in danger at the moment. *'But then, how can I be sure?'* I needed Flyn to tell me exactly what Eduardo had told him. I also knew we needed to get to her as soon as possible.

When I got off the phone, Flyn was silent as he pulled me into his arms, spooning his body behind mine. "Eduardo's dead?"

I nodded mutely, then said, "Estelle's daughter says he committed suicide."

He slowly shook his head. "He says he got on his horse, and it ran as if something or someone was chasing it, and they were pushed off the edge of the cliff. He believes some spirit did it." I didn't think Flyn could hold me any tighter, but he did. "It's weird. It's bizarre. It's the craziest thing I've heard since I've been sober, but damn, I sure as hell believe there was a fellow sitting in your body telling me all about his murder." He kissed my shoulder between his words. "If I hadn't seen you change . . . with my own eyes . . . and hadn't heard the difference in your voice . . . down to the accent, I wouldn't have believed any of this. But I was here, Sellie. I believe what the guy said. Estelle's in danger . . . and so are you!"

"You'll come with me?"

"Absolutely!" He turned me around in his arms so we were nose to nose, our legs wrapped around and between each other. "We'll sort the rest of the details of our lives later. Right now, I need you out of this thing. I don't know what you're going to do, but whatever it is, you've got a little more than four hours to figure it out."

"I love you, Flyn Devon." I kissed him hard on his mouth and felt myself melt. I was so glad he'd come back to me. I was even glad Eduardo had slipped in for a visit. Flyn had been given a first row seat to some of the strangeness of my life. A giggle bubbled in my chest. *'And he's still here,'* I thought. I didn't care if I was worn out from our night of talking and loving; a sort of happiness burbled inside me I hadn't felt in many months. *'My man's back!'*

We must've decided we needed to be on our way at the same time, because we scrambled out of either side of the bed and straightened the bed covers with a synchronized flip of our hands. "What a team!" he said. "You'd think we'd been practicing that maneuver for years."

"I think we practiced a few new maneuvers last night." He smiled with his eyes.

I felt a tug of desire begin to glow again inside my body. A thought niggled at me. "Am I going to get to know those things you've decided so I can make a decision about whether I want to be with you for the rest of my life? Even though I'm sure I do?"

He lowered his eyes to the floor then raised them. "Might be a good time while we're driving, unless you have to plan what you're going to do when you get to Estelle's," he said quietly.

I cringed at the thought. "Maybe not concentrating on it will help the answers sneak into my brain. I can only hope Eduardo is as good as his word, and he'll be around to help. Between he and Amach, someone will have a plan."

We dumped what edible food there was in our fridge into our travel cooler and grabbed our packed bags. Before we left, I grabbed my appointment book so I could cancel my clients for the next few days.

Heading north, I felt the hot weather of summer and saw it had dried the grasses on the hills to a golden yellow. In some places, the heat had burned them brown. Grapes were being harvested, and the tourists had changed from the summer of families and young people to retirees with white hair. I chafed with irritation as we crawled behind slow moving RVs and campers, especially when we hit Santa Rosa. We were stuck in one traffic jam after another. If it hadn't been for the conversation, I would have been beside myself with anxiety.

Flyn drove with one hand on the steering wheel, settling his other one on my knee. I could tell even though he was watching the road, other pictures were passing across his vision. "I've told you my grandfather wanted me to live with him so he could teach me the old way."

I nodded.

"He knew I could hear the spirits of things. Not only animals and birds, but some of the Old Ones who'd gone before." He looked at me sideways, waiting until I acknowledged him with another nod. "I wanted to be with him but my dad wouldn't let me go, but that's a different story I'll tell you someday." He lifted his hand from my knee, ran it through his hair, then returned it. "Dad's dead now. My mom has wanted me to help her nurse Pop Pop, but I've been with you." He stared through the windshield.

I wanted to tell him he could've gone, but I wasn't sure, in that moment, if it made any difference.

"The voices never went away, even with great quantities of booze and marijuana, some morphine and a bunch of prescription drugs." He cleared his throat as if some feeling was obstructing his words.

I waited.

"I've no idea if I can learn anything from the old man now that he's had his stroke. He's getting weaker. He can barely walk alone and only grunts or motions at my mom with his good hand."

I remained silent. He'd been quiet when I'd told him about my life while he was gone, and I know I rambled, trying to capture as many details as I could so the story I was telling him would be as complete as possible. Now I wanted to offer him as much understanding as he'd given me, even if I did have questions burning my tongue. I was learning he had to tell me his story in his own words and in his own way.

"My mom's got some tapes Pop Pop made. I listened to one of them describing items he wants in something called his Spirit Bundle. I took the tape to Red Buffalo and asked him to go with me to meet my granddad. RB drove me there about three weeks ago. He filled his sacred pipe, and we spent all afternoon in the quiet of Pop Pop's room. I had the feeling more passed between those two in those few hours than ever passed between me and the old man in my entire lifetime."

"You think your grandfather passed . . . information . . . to Red Buffalo?"

"I don't know." He sighed as he stared through the windshield. He didn't look at me as he said, "Maybe things he wanted to teach me himself? Maybe other instructions?" He slapped the steering wheel, then kept both hands there. "RB said when I was ready, he'd help me, but he wouldn't tell me anything else." A red Cruiser cut us off, and Flyn slammed on the brakes, jerking us forward in our seats. He shifted through all five gears before saying, "I'm going to be with my grandpa as soon as our life settles down, Sellie."

I squinted at him, not sure I understood what he meant.

He finally continued. "With all you've told me and with what's happened to us, I've decided I can't be afraid to find out what these voices of mine want me to do."

The hairs on my neck and arms rose. This had to be

another reason why we were together. Tinges of fear and pride covered my skin. "I'm glad, Flyn!" I smiled and patted his knee. "Don't know where it'll take you . . . or us . . . but I'm with you." He squeezed my fingers.

We drove into the late morning, feeling the heat burn into the car. The one drawback to our Tracker was it had no air conditioning, but as we started to climb the hills, cooler air breezed through the open windows. I pushed my worry about Estelle to the back of my mind, and rested my head on the back of the seat, falling into a light sleep.

My body is heavy now. Sinking into the seat and becoming a warm puddle oozing down a tunnel, then lightening until I travel through the air of a brilliant day. I want to stay in the sun, but am forced to keep moving, as if my destination is calling me, pulling me, sucking me.

I enter a hole and turn a corner to see I am in Amach's ceremonial cave, and she is on the floor. There are no skulls sitting in the inserts in the clay wall. She is not on her skins, but crumpled beside a dead fire. A dark stain oozes from her nose. I am not in my body, nor am I in hers, and am frustrated I cannot reach for her, or touch her, or stroke her hair. I try to raise her head, but my mind will not manifest hands. I want to determine why she is laying like a doll tossed aside, but I can only hover above her.

How many hours or days or months have passed since I shared her skin? I have no idea. I hear water dripping from icicles that have formed in one corner of the cave; this is a clue I work in my mind. I last was part of her in late autumn; now it must be late winter or early spring. I drift above her, unable to understand why I am being hampered in my ability to help her. I want to be more than an observer. I gather my thoughts, my sense of myself, and surrender into my breath. Still I hang in the air until I discover I can lay beside her. I am weeping, but I cannot imagine why, until I see the faces of Marweth and Dacona, of Estelle and someone who must be Eduardo, pass across my mind.

I cradle my being beside Amach and feel a deep sense of loss pervade me. I search my heart and mind for a connection to this woman who has become so much a part of my life. I feel a pull and a tug in my solar plexus, and we join. My arms are her arms. My legs are her legs. As her memories become mine, I feel pain over my left eye and in my right shoulder, and, in my lower abdomen, a searing cramp builds.

We are lying on the cavern floor. Our arms and legs are as heavy as rocks. Something trickles under our nose. I slowly find the strength to lift our hand to our face as if to wave a fly away. My finger collects drying blood on its end. The pain in our body sharpens. I gasp as I relive events from Amach's memory.

The fear we had shared of being discovered had become reality. I see him when he had entered her cave, looking her up and down as he spied her growing belly. Yorot had sneered, "What is the whore carrying? Whose seed fills her belly?"

She had covered herself with her hands, begging him to leave her. Everything inside her had quivered with fear, yet, she had remained strong. "This is not your concern. I make no claim. This child is mine. I ask nothing of you."

She had walked away, only to feel her hair jerked in his hand. She had shouted at him, "This is nothing to you. Leave us alone." All the while, she had chanted to herself, 'This is my hope, my promise fulfilled.' She had protected her little one, looking to fight him, but he had twisted her hair tighter and had thrown her to the ground. He had kicked her belly; she had screamed.

"There, that is what I wish I could have heard when I entered you." He had brought her face close to his, spittle falling on her cheek. "I swear, old woman, if you tell anyone I laid with you, I will toss you into the waters." His breath had gagged her before he had dropped her to the ground. Another

pain had stabbed her belly. 'Has he kicked me again?' She had asked herself as she had curled around herself and pretended a faint.

Our belly tightens, and I remember this is what contractions feel like. From deep within our body, we are tearing apart, and we weep. "It is too soon."

We slowly sit and follow the ancient urge to squat. A hard ball pushes from the lips of our womb. When we bring our hand from beneath our leather shift, it is bright red. We sob and struggle to balance over the moss lined depression in the floor. Between our legs, we see the girl child, so small, with such tiny hands and feet; so perfect, lying there, so purple. We lift her to our lips and press our breath into her mouth, but there is no response. She is covered in the wax of childbirth, and her eyes will remain forever closed. We know she is dead. Our struggle to bring her to life has come to nothing. She would have been so beautiful. We hold her close to our breast and keen to the four walls, to the mother of our mother and beyond.

"Sellie, please." I heard Flyn calling. "Not again. What *is* all this?"

I sobbed. "She lost the baby."

"Who . . . what?"

"Amach . . . she lost her little girl."

Chapter XXVI – Late August, 2004
Purgatory

I was exhausted, my heart sore from living with Amach through the death of her little girl. How could life be so cruel to one woman? Grief for her lost hope and for her lost child stiffened my body.

Wanting to stretch my legs and clear my head, I had Flyn leave me at the turnoff on Highway 101 to Estelle's property, while he retrieved my cell phone from the cabin. He protested.

"What could happen?" I asked.

"Anything," he glared.

"You won't be long," I assured him. "It's only a 20 minute drive, and we may need it since you don't own one."

"That makes it over a half hour you'll be out of my sight."

"I'll walk slow," I promised and kissed his ear.

"I'll drive fast," he promised, catching my lips in his. My head swam. I was feeling the effects of having him in our bed, of little or no sleep, and of the mysterious connections between spirit and this life. I was grateful to be out of the car, my feet on the sun-baked earth, and the dusty smell of autumn filling my nose. With the sun warming my back and shoulders, the cramps began to loosen in my heart. I knew I had to clear this feeling of constriction if I wanted to be ready to help Estelle, so, with an in-breath, I brought a visualization of a white puffy cloud into my chest. I let it surround what felt like a dark red, rubber band squeezing my heart muscles. As it lifted out of my lungs, I blew it into the fall air where it could evaporate.

At the same time, I gathered my thoughts. *'What am I to say to Estelle? How can I make her understand the kind of psychic trouble she's in?'* What kind of ritual could I perform to help her return to herself and to her life? *'What will you say when I tell you Eduardo has spoken through me?'*

I let my mind settle then, so I could calm myself by paying attention to how fine the sun felt on my back. If I hadn't been feeling my body as I placed one foot in front of the other, I might have missed the change in the air quality around me. Crossing the cattle guard between two cement monoliths guarding the entrance to Estelle's ranch was like traveling from day into night. On her side of the gate the air felt thick and smelled like a sulfur hot spring. I shook myself, thinking the differences were my imagination but decided to double-check.

I retraced my steps and stood on the outside of her property. Fir trees postured at attention next to the gate and murmured their quiet conversations with the wind. Late afternoon sun dappled the yellowing leaves of a craggy oak struggling to stand as tall as its neighboring firs; dried moss covered its dead boughs, and its live branches sagged under the weight of mistletoe clusters. A slight wind scattered loose leaves across the road. Fall was here. Everything was crisp and dry under coats of dust layering thicker whenever a vehicle drove past. Heated fir needles scented the dusty air as I crushed them underfoot, and acorns, with their funny hats, tumbled along the sun-baked road.

I walked through the gate again toward Estelle's house and felt as if I'd entered a different ecosystem. The firs, pines, and oak trees scattered throughout her front yard were so still, they were invisible with no life force emanating from them. Not a leaf on the ground stirred. No current dog of the month came to greet me or warn me away. No ravens called in the evening light, nor did swallows dip and dive near the barn. The silence was eerie, and my skin crawled.

My legs slowed as I plowed through an atmosphere

thick as cooling tar. My heart hammered. My chest heaved. *'This is ridiculous,'* I thought, still trying to push my way to her house. Slowly the reality . . . no, the unreality . . . of the situation dawned on me. Whatever force was trying to separate Estelle from Eduardo was also cocooning her from the rest of the world. Could the presence I'd seen surrounding her years ago somehow have gained power and now permeated the air around her cabin?

The idea my presence was causing these dark shadows to intensify shot through me like a jolt of electricity. I shook myself, immediately reinforcing the energetic armor I used as psychic protection every day of my life. Within a split second, I could lift my legs and walk faster. I could breath deeper.

'If I'm affected by whatever this is, what must Estelle be feeling?' On high alert, I quickened my pace toward her back porch.

My heart thudded. "Flyn," I cast his name into the ether, picturing his face, trying to connect with him. *'I need you here. It's worse than I thought!'*

My eye caught on a shaft of light refracted through the gelatinous air and the deep shadows around me. A shimmering glow highlighted the geraniums and hanging petunias Estelle had planted under her living room windows; I detected no source for the light, only the flowers being held in some kind of glowing, suspended animation. The window boxes and hanging baskets appeared out of place compared to the disarray in the gardens, where graying weeds choked once thriving flower beds. While I kept my attention on the colorful blossoms, I moved more easily through languid dust sifting over my shoes.

By the time I reached the kitchen door, my breath was again labored. Despite the day's intense heat, chills iced my back. The fear for Estelle I'd kept under control, surfaced, and I grew dizzy. I staggered away from her back porch as despair clutched my heart, and I re-experienced the anguish Amach felt when she had miscarried her child. Memories of loss lay heavy on my chest; my months of loneliness without Flyn and my lost hope of ever having my children approve of my relationship with him. I stumbled in the yard, wanting only to leave these feelings behind.

My eyes lifted to see the brilliant blooms, and the feelings shattered.

I quickly re-grounded and regrouped. Whatever permeated this place wanted me to wallow in the negativity of my regret and fear. *'Stay positive,'* I told myself. *'Stay with the light and in the moment, Sellie.'*

On the back porch, I reached to knock but decided to push open the windowed door without any announcement. Red and white curtains sagged on their rods. The stink of rancid food and cat urine attacked my nose, and I coughed and gagged at the same time. Flies buzzed over a half-eaten meal on a plate at the edge of the red Formica table, once belonging to Estelle's grandmother. That old woman would've had a fit if she could've seen this mess. No wonder Heather couldn't get anyone to help her mother.

Open jars of jam and peanut butter stood on the counter with contents smeared on a knife balanced on a jar rim. Dried bread slices and a half-finished can of tuna fish cluttered the sink. Rotting apples and bananas dissolved in a wicker fruit bowl. I had to breathe through my mouth.

Walking through the stifling heat of the kitchen, I called, "Estelle? Where are you?"

I heard a muffled voice from the main room which she used as her bedroom and living area. Sweat dried on my skin as I neared the pile of blankets and saw her face. I gasped at her pallor, her unkempt hair. Her eyes were smudged sockets, like holes in an empty skull. She looked as if some cancerous growth had invaded her body and sucked all the energy out of her living systems. Trying to reach for her, my arm felt like it was moving through solidified Jello.

"I'm so cold," she murmured between parched lips. I scanned the bedside for a glass of water and saw two empty cups on the floor. Retracing my steps to the kitchen to fill one, I had to fight to keep my balance. Some force didn't want me to approach Estelle, nor did it want me to leave. Every hair on my body stood on end.

As sure as a well-aimed arrow could hit its mark, I knew I was in as much danger as my friend. My heart battered against my ribs; I felt like a caged bird who had just become aware of being watched by a killer cat barely twitching its tail. I couldn't see feline eyes boring into me, but I could feel the pressure of its eyes invading the nooks and crannies of my body and my mind. I felt more than lost. I felt severed from all ties: from Flyn, from my life with my children and my mother, from my clients, from everything. I was in as much a state of suspended animation as the highlighted geranium blossoms I could not quite see out of the corner of my eye through Estelle's windows. It was their eerie brightness that held me and gave me a tiny taste of illumination, but it was too small to ward off the deadness overtaking my soul.

As I shrank deeper into despair, a presence visited inside my skin. It was familiar but faint, as if hiding, but this flash of sanity propelled me into action. I didn't care if this fleeting visitation was Eduardo or Amach, a guardian angel or a spirit guide. I stomped one foot then the other, bringing into my being as much light from the glowing blossoms as I could absorb. My breathing finally eased while my heartbeat slowed.

With no concept of how long I'd stood frozen in the middle of Estelle's living room, I gasped for Flyn. *'Where are you?'* I called to him, wishing we'd brought a feathered fan, or one of the rattles, or a bit of copal to use as smudge. Anything to help to dispel this spirit I feared was attached to Estelle. I was alone with nothing at hand but my mind, body, and whatever tools I could find in Estelle's house.

Moving to get the glass of water, my foot struck an

abalone shell overturned on the floor near her couch. I reached for it and saw a pile of ashes and two leaves of gray sage. Used matches were scattered on the tile floor near her cold wood stove. Their presence caused me to change my course of action. I dropped the glass and began opening cupboard and closet doors, searching for her stash of candles and kerosene lamps. I didn't care if the candle was red, white, blue, or purple. It didn't matter to me how little or how much kerosene was in a lamp. I lit everything I could find and placed them on tables, the dresser, and window sills. A triple-wicked candle lay upside down on her coffee table. I turned it right-side up and lit it as well as a set of votive candles I'd found in her bathroom closet. In their sputtering flames, I started the sage smoking in the abalone shell.

I struck a long, hearth match on the rough metal of the stove; it flared, and I stood with it in my hand while I looked for more ways to add light to the room.

"The sun! It's too bright," her voice whined from the bed.

"Estelle! Wake up! It's Selena. You have to come with me. We need to get out of here!" I held the match higher.

"Leave me alone!"

"No!"

"I want to die!"

"No, you don't!"

"Yes, I do!" she whispered. "I killed him. He's calling."

"No, he's not! "

"You don't know," she sobbed.

"I know he's dead," I said.

She sobbed harder.

"I also know he's *not* the one who's calling you." A fast wind blew out the match in my hand and pushed me to the floor. Dead air sat on my back. I tried to concentrate on the flame of a kerosene lamp I'd set at the foot of her bed, tried to suck in the light and fill my head and body, but I could barely lift my shoulders to turn my head. I fought to stand.

"Estelle, listen to me. Eduardo would never hurt you. Flyn talked with him. Eduardo doesn't need to have you with him. He knows you love him, says he'll help you from the other side." I staggered, nearly falling again. "This is something you've fostered, a presence, trying to take you for itself. It wants you dead, just like it is."

I reached the bed and shook her shoulders. "Listen to me. Eduardo wants you to live! You've got to believe me!" I lifted her from her sweaty bed clothes. As I pulled her to me, the stench of her unwashed hair brushed across my face and made me retch. She pushed her hands against my chest, the sleeves of her nightgown falling to expose oozing cuts and scratches on her arms.

"What have you done to yourself?" I whispered. She fought against my chest, then rotated so her back was to me. I lost my balance and fell on her, crushing her face against the bed. I heard her muffled answer.

"I had . . . to atone." She shifted her head. "Oh, God, Sellie. Eduardo will never forgive me. I'm so . . . sorry," she whimpered. Her breath smelled like dead meat. I wanted to beat my chest with despair. *'Why didn't I come earlier?'*

YOU HAD NO WAY OF KNOWING came an answer. YOU ARE HERE NOW. THAT IS ENOUGH.

'Who's voice? Amach's or Eduardo's?' I groaned;it didn't matter. I had to get us out of here. I pulled at her waist, trying to lift her off the bed.

"NO!" She screeched, clinging to the bedclothes. I lost my balance and fell on top of her again.

"YES!" I said firmly into her ear. "Eduardo forgives you! Listen to me! We've got to get out of here or I'm gonna die with you. If that happens . . . you'll really have some real atoning to do. Flyn'll be pissed!"

She rose onto her knees; her unexpected strength

toppled me from her back, and I grabbed her right arm to pull myself up. She rose above me and struck me with her left fist. Stars whirled behind my eyes. I lost my grip and fell off the bed. She scrambled across the double bed to the other side and dropped to the floor. When I was able to open my eyes, our heads raised on opposite sides of the bed. We faced each other across the no-man's-land of tumbled blankets.

Estelle looked demented, as she glared at me. The whites of her eyes surrounded her dilated irises. Her stare reminded me of a deer's eyes caught in the headlights of an oncoming car. Her mechanical movements resembled those of a robot manipulated by a hidden control box. She rose to her feet like a resurrecting Christ, eyes cast to the ceiling. Her left palm beseeched me. Her right held a fire poker.

When her eyes sought mine, her lips moved, "***Leave us alone***," but her voice was not her gentle lilt. Her speech mimicked a multi-layered, compounded voice, as if scrambled on a computer audio filter, making it rough and scratchy.

I eased toward the bedside table where a kerosene lamp sat. I wanted more light in this corner of the room, so I lifted it and shoved it toward her face. "Look at the flame, Estelle. You don't want to die. I know you don't. Think of your new grandbaby, your daughter, your work. Look at the light, Estelle."

Her eyes were drawn to the flickering light, fluttered upward, then returned to the flame, as if curious about its brilliance.

"Sellie . . ." she whispered. "Help . . . me . . . I . . ." Suddenly she jerked, and her arm raised the poker.

"***Leave us***," she rasped, as she swung at me, hitting my shoulder.

Shock cascaded down my arm. Time slowed as did all action as I turned away from the bed, struggling to keep my balance and to keep the kerosene lamp upright. I saw the tie-dyed ceiling and the dark Persian rug waver in the multiple flames as I twirled in the room. Light glanced off the glass of the windows and the framed pictures of her family members propped on every horizontal surface. Her maroon couch and sky-blue overstuffed chair stood solidly near the wood stove. I turned full circle, hearing the kerosene lamp chimney shatter, feeling my grip loosen around the lamp base as it fell from my hand. I came around to the bed, hitting my knees on the edge of the mattress and saw the depression where her head had lain, a black strand of hair contrasting against the white linen. At the pillow's edge, I spied a tuft of rabbit skin and recognized it for what it was; the marriage bundle she had crafted was hiding there. We both lunged toward the bed and the bundle. As I backed off with the rabbit's fur in my arms, a scorching odor passed my nose.

The bundle felt like dry ice in my hands. I wanted to drop it, but instead clenched it tightly with both hands against my chest. *'What the hell do I do now?'*

RELEASE THE POWER

These words filled my mind as well as the vision of how Amach had saved Dacona. I had to save myself as well as undo the union between her and Eduardo. But where? And how?

Estelle wavered on her side of her bed. I hoped she would flutter into a faint so I would have time to open the bundle and release its contents. I pulled the rabbit skin off the inside bundle and plucked at the hardened, pine-pitched seal, loosening an edge of the tanned hide.

"*Give back!*" I heard the raspy voice, lurching toward me. While Estelle staggered around the bottom of her bed to grab at my hands, I turned my back to her to stop her from grabbing the bundle. A drum pounded in my skull, growing louder. As its intensity increased, I realized it was outside my skull. I tracked the sound to the window. Flyn stood with his grandfather's elk hand drum, beating a steady rhythm. He raised his head to the sky and chanted words I'd never heard him sing. He sounded strong and fearsome. Energy surged through me.

I dropped my eyes to the triple-wicked candle I'd lit, all the while working to open the bundle. I chewed at the leather, finally pulling apart the glued knot and unrolled it, loosening its contents into my hands. I let them fall into the melted center of the candle as smoke billowed around me.

"You can't!" Estelle wailed behind me.

"Yes, I can!" I watched part of a butterfly wing shrivel in the fire. "You included me in this when you included the claw I gave you, and I want out!" The horse hairs singed and smoked. "You will never use me again!"

Estelle screamed. I turned to see flames dancing in her hair. She grabbed her head, spinning like a frenzied top. Her back was ablaze, as was her bed, the wall at its head, the tie-dyed sheets draped across her ceiling. Patches of burning material fell around us, engulfing us in a fiery storm. I gripped the items from the bundle remaining in my hand and felt something prick my finger. My eagle claw. I popped it into my mouth, snugged it between my gum and cheek, then threw the rest toward the candle. I pulled at Estelle's flaming night gown; it fell onto the floor, then I pushed her naked body to the rug and covered her with my own. When the rain of fire stopped, I tried to stand, but she wrapped her arms around me and hung onto my neck.

"I don't want to go, Sellie. I've nothing . . ."

I was choking from the smoke and her arms around my neck. It was as if she wanted us to stay here together, while the house burned around us, swallowing us into oblivion.

The drumbeat sounded closer. Flyn stood at the door between the kitchen and the living room. Its steady rhythm gave me strength to push against the floor and bring Estelle with me. I held onto her, dragging her in Flyn's direction. His arms caught us as we fell from the burning room. We shared Estelle's weight with her arms around our necks and edged sideways through the back door where I grabbed the grimy kitchen curtains, anything to cover my friend. We stumbled down the driveway, as far away from the house as we could, laid her in the shade at the edge of her road, and covered her better with a blanket from the car.

"Call the fire . . ."

"Did that," he nodded, his eyes riveted on my face as if he was drinking in every inch of my skin. "Your cell phone works great."

"What?"

I turned at the sound of the fire's roar. "The tank," I croaked at him. For a moment, I knew he didn't understand me. "Propane!" He handed me his drum and disappeared around the corner of the house. I prayed as flames darted along the roof: *'Let there be time! Let him have time to turn it off.'*

My heart pounded.

Estelle moaned, "Flowers."

I leaned closer and shook her shoulders. "Tell me."

Her hand pointed to the front of her house. "Eduardo's favorite flowers." I tracked the direction of her fingers and saw the geraniums and petunias starting to wilt in the heat.

"I'm sorry. It's too late for them." Seeing them burst spontaneously into flames brought my attention to the trees close to the house. Wind, created by the fire sucking oxygen, was causing a downdraft, bending tree branches toward the house. I spied the irrigation hose attached to her garden well and dashed to turn on the field pump. I sprayed the trees closest to the house, heat searing my face. Even though water surged through the rubber hose, I felt I was holding a dribbling soaker hose. I wanted the water pressure to swell onto the oaks and firs so I could save some part of Estelle's property. While I focused the spray on the summer-dry trees, the fire roared, turning the sky black with smoke. Flyn rounded the corner, stopped, turned, and disappeared again. I wiped my eyes with my shoulder, struggling to train the water on whatever I could reach, while I sobbed. When the roof caved into the house, sparks flew in all directions.

Sirens wailed. I cheered that help was on its way at the same time as I keened for the loss of Estelle's home. I hung on to the hose with desperation, guilt burning in my chest. All I could see was my hand on the kerosene lamp as it slipped from my grasp and flipped onto the bed.

Flyn screamed in my ear. "Let go, Sellie!"

I shook my head. "The trees . . . I can't let it all burn."

"Firemen . . . here now. They know what to do." I fought when he pried my fingers from the hose. "You're only in the way. Sellie . . . come on . . . let go."

I finally understood and let him take the hose, retreating to where Estelle lay.

With Flyn at my side, I watched as flames consumed the redwood siding. At least the barn, other out-buildings, and the trees had not caught fire.

"I turned off the valve for the tank and the main switch for the electricity," he said, putting an arm around my shoulders.

I pointed. Fire hovered in the area of Estelle's living room. A green hue flashed bronze, spewed a ruddy orange into the air then tore the sky apart with a red and yellow flame.

Chapter XXVII - October, 2004
Promises that Bind

Light and shadow from the fire Flyn had started earlier in the afternoon flickered across the eagle claw curled in my open palm. It had been a gift from one of David's Native American teachers, and I'd worn it for years sewn on the flap of my personal medicine bundle. *'Why did I give it to Estelle?'* I shivered then flashed hot with memories of flames falling and Estelle's dead weight in my arms. Memories of the horror of her physical condition, its sight and smell, jolted me at times. The stench of what her life had become revolted me.

Sitting on this side of my experience with Estelle, anger blazed throughout the cells of my body. I couldn't decide if I was angered by her desire to 'bond forever' with Eduardo or the fact that her misguided ceremony had included me.

'No, that's not quite right!' I had to admit I was angry with myself and feeling so sick about burning her house down! *'Oh, Estelle! I'm so sorry!'* I hugged myself and fought against another bout of tears. I needed to stop blaming Estelle or myself for what I'd decided to do. Hadn't I been guided by my experiences with Amach to burn the contents of the bundle? Hadn't the connection between that lifetime and this one been broken by my actions?

I sent a thought out into the ethers, hoping Amach would answer my question. *'Was all this what was supposed to have happened?"*

I waited for a sign from my illustrious spirit guide. I wanted some kind of signal she was going to explain to me why the marriage bundles had melded across lifetimes.   In fact, I'd been waiting with pen in hand for over an hour, but she'd not put one single word into my brain so I could write it down for posterity. I stroked the eagle claw with one finger, wondering if it had been tainted by its inclusion in Estelle's bundle.

WASH IT. The suggestion came into my awareness from a fullness I recognized as Amach.

"In plain old water?" I asked aloud.

FRESH, she said. THEN LET IT SIT IN SMOKE. THEN TURN IT IN THE MOON LIGHT.

"Then there *is* something attached to it?"

ONLY IF YOU BELIEVE IT TO BE SO.

She had me there. I wouldn't be worried if I thought it had been untouched.

ITS ESSENCE HAS NOT BEEN CHANGED, BUT IT HAS BEEN USED WITH A DIFFERENT INTENT. THAT IS WHAT NEEDS REMOVAL.

I understood.

AND WASH YOURSELF FREE OF THE MEMORIES.

"How?"

IN WATER, SMOKE, AND MOON LIGHT.

'Oh!'

IT WILL HELP YOU DISCONNECT.

"Can I do it when I do the claw?" I felt a sigh.

YOU EACH DESERVE YOUR OWN CEREMONY.

I placed the claw in the center of a small rectangle of red cloth so I could give my full attention to the fire, as well as Amach. I scribbled "water" "smoke" and "moonlight" in the spiral notebook opened in front of me.

The fire crackled. Flames extended inches above a pile of oak logs; its red core glimmered where heat vapors danced. Fire fascinated me, as well as scared me. I could watch it controlled in the fireplace or use it contained in the cook stove, but I'd withered with fear when the ravaging flames had spiraled above Estelle's house. What if that fire had jumped into a tree? What if I'd been the cause of the destruction of acres of forest, or someone else's house, or someone's life?

YOU DID WHAT YOU HAD TO DO. DO NOT TORTURE YOURSELF WITH WHAT COULD HAVE BEEN. THINK ONLY OF WHAT MIGHT HAVE DIED IF YOU HAD NOT BROUGHT IN THE LIGHT.

Her voice whispered in my heart. I had to agree. It was better to concentrate on what had been saved than torture myself with all the terrible possibilities I might have caused, but staying positive was proving hard, considering I couldn't talk it out with Estelle.

"Is this rabbit soup for dinner?" Flyn called from the kitchen.

"No, it's a special thing for . . ." I hesitated only a second, then said without apology in my voice, "It's for Amach."

Flyn entered the living room by poking his head around the corner of the fireplace. "OK, so what're we having?"

"Oops!" I crossed my eyes. "Oh, well, you see . . . " I pouted, then tried a sideways grin. "Honestly? I forgot us."

"Maybe, she'd let us join her. There's enough in the pot to feed an army!"

I lifted my shoulders.

"Can't we eat together?" He walked toward me.

"I don't know. You tell me. It was your idea."

He raised his hand to stop me.

"I mean, it's a memory of something your granddad did," I corrected myself.

He nodded, pleased I'd changed my wording.

"So you have to tell me what we can do and what we can't." I waited as he stood thinking, the crevice deepening between his brows.

"All I can remember is once I was told to take a plate of food and put it in the rafters of the back porch and another time to sit a full plate on a stump." He raised his eyebrows. "I don't see why we can't eat the same food, maybe even set a place for her then put her plate outside somewhere."

"OK, just as long as she doesn't get the idea she's invited for the rest of the evening. I don't want her to think she can climb into my body and get familiar with you." I grinned.

"Not likely. I saw you as Eduardo, remember. I'd know if you started turning into an ancient woman." He stood behind me to rub my back and shoulders.

"Nice," I said and meant it. The tensions of the past few months had left my upper back and neck as stiff as icicles. No amount of hot pads or rolling on rubber balls had eased them. "She's not that ancient, you know."

He was quiet as he kneaded the muscles at the base of my neck. "Guess she couldn't be that old, if she got pregnant."

"That's what I was thinking."

"Anything from Estelle?"

"Ahhh," I sighed when a stab of sadness punched into my belly. "Only from her daughter. She helped Estelle convert one end of the stables into a small apartment. I guess Estelle's living there alone. Might not rebuild." I wondered to myself how long she'd survive that way.

He squatted next to me, his face glowing in the firelight. He tried to look into my eyes, but I avoided his gaze by moving around him to stretch across the hearth rug. I felt, rather than saw, his eyebrows scrunch together as he ask, "That's a first, isn't it?"

I smiled, knowing he and I were thinking the same thought. For Estelle to be living on her own without a man in sight was definitely a first. I watched as Flyn stood; we grinned at each other. His giving voice to what I'd been thinking wasn't as uncomfortable for me as it had once been. To be able to communicate without words was smoothing the edges of our relationship. We were confiding in each other; he was understanding certain nuances of my life, my heart, and feeling free to comment on them. I was listening to more of his stories and watching him open to the strangeness of my life as well as his own with less anxiety than I had ever had about the oddness of it all. We were definitely more of a couple now, and, while still living between our apartment in Oakland and this cabin, we were considering the details of our public wedding ceremony.

Several weeks ago, because of Pop Pop's dwindling health, we'd decided to formally ask the man's blessing. Red Buffalo had helped us by preparing and filling his sacred pipe, and he'd accompanied us to Annie's house. She'd dressed her father and had propped him with pillows on his bed. His gray hair was tightly braided and lay over his chest. Flyn had offered the unlit chanupa to the four directions and the up and down then had put it in his grandfather's left hand. Pop Pop had motioned for Flyn to take it up again and for us to stand close together,then he'd waved his good hand from side to side.

Red Buffalo said, "He wants you to make promises to each other."

I knew my eyes widened. Flyn's darkened. "Well now," he said in a quiet voice. We faced each other then. His head bowed until he looked at me over the bowl he held in his left hand and the stem in his right. After a deep breath and fixing his bottomless brown eyes on mine, he said, "I promise you, Selena, to love you and help you be all you can be. I promise to protect you, feed you, clothe you, and maintain our home as a sanctuary for our love and life together." His face cleared as he finished, "And I'll do it cheerfully for the rest of my life." Then he winked.

I smiled through my tears. I had to swallow and sniff before I could talk. Then Flyn passed the sacred pipe to me, and I held it as I'd seen him hold it. "I, Selena, promise you, Flyn, to love you, honor and respect you. I'll care for your physical body as I would nurture my own. I'll bring clear thinking to times when we have trouble communicating. I'll be by your side to support whatever steps you need to take so you can be all of who you can be. I'll share my heart, my insights, my body, and my life with you for as long as my time is on Earth."

Not wanting to break our eye contact but feeling a blush begin to rise from my neck, I'd turned away from Flyn and toward his grandfather, a man we'd learned was known as Eagle Drum Boy. Flyn and I had stood so our hands were together on the sacred pipe; tears dripped down the old man's cheeks. After Red Buffalo lit the tobacco, we pressed the stem to Grandpa Fred's lips. He'd puffed with one cheek then waved toward us to finish. Annie had wiped her eyes with the hem of her shirt sleeve several times before she'd held the pipe to smoke with us.

Red Buffalo had signaled to grandpa when all the tobacco had been smoked by taking the chanupa in his hands, raising it to the sky and lowering it to the earth before disconnecting the bowl from the stem. The old man had nodded with a lopsided grin, then had closed his eyes. We felt he'd approved of us being a couple.

Now it was a matter of telling my mother, my daughter, and my son. I wasn't in a hurry to plan a public ceremony just so I could prove to them I was not longer living in sin or so we could get a marriage certificate. I knew who we were and what kind of relationship we had. Flyn had accused me of dragging my feet and had been showing impatience until he decided he wanted to find his step-daughter, Michele. He said he wasn't looking for approval from her. He just wanted time to find her and show her she had someone who cared about her. It was more a matter of finding a last piece of the puzzle of his life with Yin Sun, even though he realized, we had little hope of locating her. I sighed.

"She still mad at you?" Flyn interrupted my thoughts.

"If you mean Estelle," I tilted my chin toward the ceiling. "Yeah."

"You still not going to channel Eduardo for her?"

I rolled my head back and forth on the rug. "If I did it for her, she'd never let me rest. She needs to find her own way of connecting with him." I struggled to hold back a trickle of tears. "I won't be her medium."

He stood, crossed his arms over his chest, then stretched from side to side to get the kinks out of his back. "Figured out how it all worked?" he asked quietly.

"Meaning?" I murmured.

"Well, was this Yorot, Toroy, and vice versa? Had he been roaming around and pestering Estelle because she was the long lost Decona?"

"I don't know . . . " I sighed.

He looked perplexed. "And if Estelle was Dacona, did that make Eduardo . . . Marweth? And then, what about you? Are you Amach, or were you Amach?"

I wanted to throw a pillow at him. He was asking the same questions I'd been trying to get Amach to answer while sitting with pen and pencil in front of the glowing fire. "Amach's keeping silent on all accounts. I'm not sure I want to create parallels between then and now." I examined the knotty pine ceiling from my vantage point on the floor. "It certainly seems as if the past affected the future, but I'm not sure if the future affected the past." I groaned. "It's possible all our lives are intertwined, and that there's no such thing as a past or a future because it's all happening at the same time." I waved my arms above my head then down to my sides, as if I were making a snow angel. It was more like a dust angel, given the lack of house cleaning I'd been doing for the last few months. I stopped when I sneezed.

"I only know by Amach showing me her life, I was able to figure out how to untangle the problem Estelle created. But even with that insight, it took you and me to resolve it." I sneezed again. "I'm so glad you're with me."

He straddled my waist, one foot on either side, then seemed to change his mind about something. He dropped to the floor, gathering me in his arms. "And what about this thing called a marriage bundle? Wanna make one for us?"

I shuddered. "Not on your life! Putting parts of our hair and skin together in some kind of pouch? Look what happened! One got stolen, and they all got hexed. Love's enough of a bond."

He wrapped his arms tighter around me. "Maybe bundling is the better bundle?"

I tried to hit him, while I laughed. "And maybe it's just as simple as learning to walk together wrapped in a blanket." I nuzzled his chin and reached my lips toward his mouth. His light kiss began a vibration in my body. His tongue traced a pattern around my lips to seek entrance there while electricity charged through my legs and groin until it felt we were melting into each other. He stopped as quickly as he'd started, leaving us breathless and staring into each other's eyes.

"Flyn Devon, you curl my toes," I said.

He snickered. "Funny 'cause you straighten mine."

"And other things?"

"For sure," he answered then became serious, the crease between his eyebrows deepening. "Want Standing Feather and Red Buffalo to do our ceremony?"

"I'd love it."

"Yeah, me too," he said then kissed my nose and rose to a squat beside me. He seemed restless, as if struggling with some kind of problem.

I cocked my head at him. "What's up?"

He shrugged. "Not sure. Nervous is the best word I can find. This thing between me and my grandfather has to resolve soon. I need to know what he wants me to do."

"Maybe it's more about what you want to do," I offered. "Maybe, you can feel the answer for yourself."

His eyes glazed. I could only guess his thoughts were threading between his past and his future. He shrugged again. "I need some exercise. Want to walk the property before dark?"

I stretched, sorting through my feelings. "No, I want to finish what I'm doing here." I sat up for a hug. "And I think I'll take some of the rabbit out of the pot for Amach's offering so I can add some vegetables to the rest of it for us. Then I won't have to create another supper." I laughed, "I don't think she likes veggies much anyway."

"Sounds good to me. I'll take one of those frozen French breads out before I leave, then we can heat it when I get back."

"Thanks, love," I answered, tipping my head back. He kissed my forehead and headed for the kitchen. I heard him open the freezer then something thunked on the kitchen counter. I was glad he'd started the fire; its sunny glow stayed with me as he opened the front door to a brisk, windy day, and the crackling fire kept me company as the warmth of his presence left the room.

I calmed myself and poised my hand and pen over the blank paper, waiting. Nothing happened. Frustrated, I stomped to the kitchen. After adding potatoes, carrots, celery, and seasonings to our stew, I returned to my position in front of the fire. There'd been times in the past month when Amach seemed to be pushing, scratching, almost screaming at me to take up my pen and write her words, but I'd been sitting here with my writing paper for the most of the afternoon, and the only words she'd given me to write were "water", "smoke", and "moonlight".

I sighed and released all my questions about what had happened with Estelle and asked in my mind, "Is there a teaching you want to share?"

A word scrawled in the front of my mind, and I had to rush my hand across the page to keep up with the torrent of words she released:

"Do not stand in front of anyone. Stand to their side. This works better, even when they

come to you for healing or help. Guide each person to his or her point of balance. Let them feel it for themselves. If you try to point it out, the person you are trying to help will not know that place for themselves and will return to the point of their imbalance after your time together is done. They will depend on you too much."

"Is this why you've been showing me your story so I can learn by experiencing it in your life?" I asked out loud.

"I have tried to help you open to the possibilities of seeing the vision for yourself, rather than telling you the details of it. I have tried to help you trust your connection to all that is."

My hand hesitated. I felt a struggle coming from within her, within me. I was grateful we'd agreed for my hand to write her words, rather than for her to take me over and speak through me. I liked being able to read and reread these passages. She brought me so much, and, considering the fact her presence in my life had saved lives, I was no longer unhappy with our roles, even though I still didn't understand why we were together.

"I have come to you to prepare you for our future. There has been much to show you, so you can continue the work. I urge you to grow in your understanding of life and healing. What I have seen in you gives me much to trust about you. I see that you have known your place of balance in the natural world since you were a child. It has only been necessary for me to remind you of it."

As I pondered this idea of my place of balance, I saw

myself when I was small, maybe as young as four-years-old, standing on a little hill in the front yard of our Pacific Beach home, with the ocean wind blowing through my hair. More than a feeling of being in the middle of all creation, I remembered the feeling of everything being just as much a part of me as I was of it. I traced that sense of oneness through my life and saw more places where I'd experienced similar tingles of joy, the same welling of tears I'd had then, and reflected on these similar moments.

Another picture nudged into my mind, of a small tissue-wrapped package held tenderly and offered into a hole under a red rose bush. I remembered my prayer: "Whoever's listening out there. Please, let this little life count for something." Suddenly, my world tilted; I tumbled into a scene of shivering cold.

I watch small flakes of snow fall, cling, then dissolve into Amach's graying hair as she struggles to climb a forgotten path. She stops to catch her breath, hugs a robe of animal skins closer to her thin body then rearranges her burdens strapped to her back and in her arms. I yearn to share her plight, but I am not invited to join her.

In my world, I can feel the warmth of the fire as I sit by the hearth, but I can only see Amach as I come to know her thoughts. I can hear the sounds around her, but I cannot become her because of some kind of barrier between us, a peculiar veil between our worlds, too thick for my person-hood to penetrate. I can only watch and listen to the trees and the words flowing through her mind.

She gulps cold air and tries to fill her heaving chest with energy. She laments her plight to the darkening sky and the stately pines towering around her. "Everything's lost!" She wails, "Why must I climb this path when there is no longer a reason for this?"

Heavy snow blankets the narrow path to the mountain top. Abruptly a warm wind surrounds her. She senses its comfort, its caress. The gale pushes her urgently, and she allows it. With the wind lifting her forward, she takes first one step, then another, until she is climbing more rapidly than before. Unconscious of melted snow dripping from the ends of her hair, but aware of her body's blood saturating the cradle of moss tied between her legs, she brings the doe skin bundle closer to her chest.

On the edge of the meadow, she catches her breath and surveys the clearing. The spring grasses show green through thickening layers of white. A strong wind blows as if from all directions at once, up and down and all around, buffeting the trees, causing them to sound as if cheering her arrival. The wind tugs at her fur robe and pushes her into open space. She turns to judge the center of this natural circle, remembering to be ten paces from the broken blue stone, a remnant from the Day of Fire From the Sky.

While holding her tiny bundle and unwrapping the remaining bundles, she nods her head to an imaginary drum beat. Finding her voice, she sings, haltingly at first, then stronger. At a preordained spot between the base of the blue rock and the entrance to the meadow, she places toward the Path of the Oldest Wind, the brittle skull of her Oldest Relative, her Grandmother's Mother. I see a swatch of hair sitting within this skull. For this time of vision-asking, she places the skull of her Mother's Mother with its tied length of hair in the Path of the Youngest Wind, so that the innocence and playfulness of this warm breath will not create tricks.

Amach places her own mother's skull and its hair in the Path of the Bright Winds, facing the position she will take in the center of the Sacred Circle. To her back, the skull and piece of hide from the She Bear, her Spirit Protector, is placed to guard the Path of the Dark Wind

Once she has arranged the four skulls, the greeting from the trees diminishes to a whisper. Silent snow drifts from a darkening sky. Day is fading as well as the unknown source that fed her strength. She fixes her robes around a hole she cleared of snow and padded with dry moss. She sits over it, settling into the center of the Spirit Circle. On a section of bear skin, she places a single white feather in the way she's been taught. Gathering her precious child-bundle to her chest, she rests, collapsing into a deep, dreamless sleep.

A crashing of trees awakens her to the dark. The wind speaks now with a different voice. Night Light glows behind waving trees. She needs to begin but, instead, bargains, "When you have the strength to fly high into the sky, I will begin." As if in response, the moon answers by breaking free of the trees' grasp; the meadow glimmers with sudden, intense light.

Words stumble from her mouth, "O, Mother of my mothers, I've been too long absent from this place of sacredness. Forgive me for denying the ceremonies you taught me, for neglecting those things that help to renew myself and our people."

Amach raises her head, "I am ashamed of how this child was begot, but I am not ashamed I carried her. Why did you not protect me from the man who caused her death within me? I am ashamed for my neglect and absence from your ways, but how can I pass on the teachings when there is no one to teach?"

"LOOK AT ME," shouts the wind coming from the direction of the skull of her mother, Morah.

Amach stares into the sunken holes growing bright in reflected lights and remembers the deep brown eyes of her mother. She hears a chorus of voices from those who have passed before and who will come after.

"YOU ARE THE CENTER OF THE SACRED CIRCLE, THE CONNECTOR OF THE LINEAGE. YOUR LIFE IS THE LEATHER THONG TYING THE PAST WITH THE FUTURE.

THE LIFE YOU HAVE LIVED WAS NEVER MEANT FOR YOU ALONE. YOU WERE CHOSEN, JUST AS YOU

CHOSE TO LIVE THIS LIFE. IT IS YOUR BODY CARRYING THE MARK. DELAY NO MORE. YOUR PEOPLE NEED YOUR GIFT OF SIGHT.

No sound now. No snow falling or wind breathing.

Lifting her tanned arms to the sky, she demands, "Oh, Great Mysteries of the Day and of the Night! You, who know the possible paths we may step upon, it is I, Amach, daughter of Morah, who is daughter of Lamar, who is daughter of Grild.

"Come to me! Help me see where it is I am to put my feet. Help me focus. Bring me visions of what is to come, where it is I am to go, what it is I am to do."

"O, Silent Giver of the Night Light and of the Dreams of Promise, help me to know who I must train, so this way will not be lost."

Her keening voice is without an echo before the silent wall of the trees. It falls flat across the white snow sitting within the Spirit Circle. Amach moans in despair; her voice must travel upward to the sky and downward to the center of the Earth Mother. Her Spirit Breath has to dance in all directions. It must expand and become like the carrying cord, which every mother creates between herself and her inside children during Birthing Growth, so they can speak with each other. Without this cord, this way for her words to travel beyond her being and back to her, Amach's words will be bound to the earth, and she will never hear her guidance.

'What's wrong?' her mind alone sends out the question. 'I've done this before! What is it, Mothers?'

She opens her senses, thinning the barrier between herself and what cannot be seen, to perceive the source binding her spirit to the earth plane. She must offer her burden as a sacrifice, as penance for her plotting and planning, her desperation and defeat.

Amach holds the tiny bundle of her too-soon dead child to her breast, shakes free from her warm robes, and stands naked in the shimmering Night Light. She steps to the flat altar of the Ancient Blue Stone, barely feeling the freezing air touch her skin. Amach lays her treasured bundle on the cold slab and watches her hand move to loosen the knotted leather tie. The skins fall away, exposing the grayish-white body of her dead girl child.

Her tears begin again, chilling her cheeks. Her hands caress the tiny face and the stiff arms as she whispers, "Spirits of this place and time, I give you this life who was my hope and who is my despair. I have nothing else to sacrifice except my very being."

Like the strange wind that warmed her and enveloped her with strength to climb the mountain, another comes like a whirlwind, creating a circle of fresh snow, surrounding first her naked body, then that of her infant. It leaves the child and the stone dressed in sparkling white, as if they are now parts of each other.

Returning to her robes, Amach raises her arms and begins her prayer. This time her words reach across the Spirit Circle to the trees, and an echo returns to her in a voice full of life and meaning. The sound lifts over her head, swirls and dances to the stars, while descending into the center of the Earth.

All quiets. In her mind's eye, Amach is shown a pair of hands holding a packet wrapped in strange white skins, fragile and shredding. Amach sees these hands make an opening in the Earth, watches the pouch gently buried at the base of a thorny bush, feels awe at red petals falling all around. Within the woman, whose hands tremble as she fills the hole with dirt, Amach senses a sadness matching hers, a shame much like her own, a prayer rising in their minds that share their intent.

"Make this loss into a sacrifice of meaning."

Amach is drawn into the woman's body, knows kinship with the heart making this offering, feels the potential of the prayer . . .

A flash of sweat drenched my body; my mind numbed.

My heart raced.

"I . . . how . . . could we . . . each other . . . at that moment?" I was lost in swirls of energy. *'How could this be?'*

"The Universe, or however you call the Great Energy blanketing our worlds and giving life to our souls, made our connection."

I felt humbled.

"And we have much to do."

Book Order Form

The Marriage Bundle

$19.95 X _______ =_________

Reiki In Everyday Living (Ist Edition)

$12.95 X _______ =_________

Reiki In Everyday Living (2nd Edition)

$13.95 X _______ =_________

Just for Today

$ 5.00 X _______ =_________

Reiki As A Complementary Therapy (Xeroxed copy)

$10.00 X _______ =_________

The Escape (First Book of The Runaways Series)
(Check Web site for this continuing saga.)

$5.00   X _______ =_________

(In California add .0875% tax) =_________

TOTAL =_________

Complementary Shipping for prepaid <u>single</u> orders. Ask for wholesale prices via email: <u>reiki@mcn.org</u>

Name____

Address _____________________________________

State/Zip ____________________________________

Phone _______________________________________

*Mail to: **White Feather Press, POB 667, Laytonville, CA 95454**
or order on line: **<u>www.standinginbalance.com</u>***